The Brushfires of Freedom

Book Six of Blue Dawn

Blaine L. Pardoe

Copyright

The Brushfires of Freedom

Book Six of Blue Dawn

Copyright © 2025 Blaine L. Pardoe

(Defiance Press & Publishing, LLC)

Published by Defiance Press & Publishing, LLC

Bulk orders of this book may be obtained by contacting Defiance Press & Publishing, LLC. www.defiancepress.com.

Defiance Press & Publishing, LLC

281-581-9300

Publishing@defiancepress.com

"It does not take a majority to prevail… but rather an irate, tireless minority, keen on setting brushfires of freedom in the minds of men."

Samuel Adams

Acknowledgements

The start of each chapter in this book has draft material taken from the proposed Newmerican Constitution, short form. A longer version is in the appendix of this book. While my detractors may mock my words, I think many of us know that this is the kind of nation they want.

Dedication

To Donald J. Trump, Elon Musk, Kristi Noem, Karoline Leavitt, Tom Homan, and the rest of the dream team. Mr. President, you averted a disaster by winning a second term. Elon, you are fighting to ensure we have a future as a nation. Kristi, you've secured the border. Karoline, you restored credibility to your office. Tom, you've scared the living shit out of criminals who are here illegally and other political criminals who are offering them shelter in their so-called sanctuary cities.

The Key Characters

Lauren Aguilar. Captain in the California Veterans Corps who defected to America.

Angela Axton. Special Agent, FBI, now NSF.

Alex – Short for Alexandria (no last name given). Former The People's Housewoman from New York; she sits on the Ruling Council and commands the National Security Force (NSF) as its secretary. She removed her opposition and folded the Social Enforcers into the NSF. She is the Newmerica vice president-elect.

Randy Birdsell. Leader of the Sons of Liberty (SOL) in New Hampshire.

Trudy Ford. Member of the Sons of Liberty (SOL) from the Upper Peninsula of Michigan.

Andy Forest. Andy's father was a member of the Sons of Liberty (SOL), and Andy was instrumental in recovering the original copy of the Constitution and the Declaration of Independence.

Arthur Forrest. Andy's father and a persecuted professor at the University of Mary Washington. His actions saved the Constitution and the Declaration of Independence.

Frank Campbell. Private investigator in Virginia.

Rebecca (Becky) Clarke. The Director of the Truth Reconciliation Committee (TRC) and member of the Ruling Council. She was instrumental in seizing control of The People's House during the Liberation.

Travis Cullen. Former Navy SEAL, now a covert operative supporting the American administration.

Jack Desmond. Former Director of the Secret Service and now the American president's chief of staff. Jack was instrumental in bringing the former American vice president to power and for years was the clandestine leader of the Sons of Liberty (SOL).

Lieutenant Duwe. Intelligence officer, New Hampshire National Guard.

Herb Fletcher. The leader of a cell of the Sons of Liberty.

General Hank Griffiths. Commanding general of the New Hampshire National Guard.

Booker Hickox. Self-proclaimed general of the Free Texas movement.

Miley Hines. Supporter of Free Texas and a musician.

Veronica Hinkley. Member of the People's Warden Program.

Gwen Holtz. Leader of the Sons of Liberty unit, the Witches of Wichita.

Braylon Ironsides. Former inmate in Social Quarantine.

Deja Jordan. A Social Enforcer from Minneapolis.

Charli Kazinski. Current Director of the American Secret Service. For years, she lived as an NSF officer named Angel Frisosky to avoid detection. She was with the last president when he died.

Faust Kidder. One-eyed mercenary pilot.

Caylee Leatrom. Former NSF operative who flipped sides and now offers her skills to the Americans. She killed Alex's mother and brother.

Senator Earl Taft Lewis. One of the few surviving senators after the Liberation.

Dr. Weber Liu. A deep-planted Chinese agent operating under the guise of being a professor at the University of Michigan.

Maria Lopez. Sister of Raul Lopez.

Raul Lopez. Former member of the Youth Corps; his murder of a man led to riots in Detroit. As a member of the Sons of Liberty (SOL), he liberated the Social Enforcement Camp at Valley Forge.

Aiguo Lung. Chinese spymaster in North America.

Salem Marshall. Self-proclaimed president of Free Texas.

Major Judy Mercury. Officer in the Texas National Guard and the American Army.

Tate Palmer. New Hampshire patriot.

"Lariat" Paredes. Captain, American helicopter pilot.

Sam Patheal. Leader of a Sons of Liberty cell out of North Carolina, Hell's Tarheels.

Daniel Porter. Former chairman of the Ruling Council and the president-elect of Newmerica. Daniel orchestrated the overthrow of the government during the Liberation/Fall.

John Quang. Chinese agent.

General Trip Reager. Renowned and scorned for his actions in San Antonio several years back, Reager is a Texan who is the commanding general of the American Army.

Thiago "Rumbler" Reese. NSF operative, expert in overthrowing governments. Also known as Luis Fernando.

Kiffin "Kiff" Renner. A government cyber-security specialist and friend of Jack Desmond.

Colonel Dan "The Dancer" Ricketts. Officer in the American Army.

General Hollings Rinehart. Commanding general, Newmerican military forces.

David Steele. Maddie's younger brother.

Grayson Steele. Former conservative member of the Virginia House of Delegates and Maddie and David's father.

Ted (no last name given). Former Texas senator held prisoner by Newmerica.

Pat Templeton. MSNBC reporter whom Trip Reager punched.

Darius Thorne. Veteran and member of the California Veterans Corps.

Valerie Turner. Former New York City police commissioner, leader of a Sons of Liberty (SOL) cell from New York.

Hudson Whitlock. Member of The Patriot Liberation Front.

Rita Zhang. NSF operative.

Hachi Zhou. Wife of Su-Hui and an active member of the Sons of Liberty (SOL).

Su-Hui Zhou. Refugee from Taiwan; he is a leader in the Sons of Liberty (SOL).

Ya-ting Zhou. Daughter of Hachi and Su-Hui.

Acronyms

ADMAX – Administrative Maximum Facility; the Supermax Prison's official designation.

ANG – Air National Guard.

ANTIFA – Acronym for Anti-Fascists. These radicals violently rioted during the summer of 2020 in an effort to influence the presidential election. They evolved into the roles of Social Enforcers in the Newmerican nation.

ATF – Bureau of Alcohol, Tobacco, and Firearms. With the formation of the NSF, this agency is now part of that new organization.

CAB – Combat Aviation Brigade.

BDA – Battle Damage Assessment.

BOQ – Bachelor Officer Quarters.

CHOP – Capitol Hill Occupied Protest. The occupation of Seattle by protesters in 2020.

Fedgov – The Newmerican rebranding of the federal government.

FOIA – Freedom of Information Act.

IWB – The Immigrant Welcoming Bureau, formerly Immigration and Customs Enforcement prior to The Fall.

JCS – The military Joint Chiefs of Staff.

NSF – National Security Force. This is a combination of all federal and local law enforcement agencies.

SAC – Special Agent in Charge.

SE – Social Enforcement. Groups supporting the Newmerican government that operate beyond the law, administering their own "social justice" as they see fit.

SOL – Sons of Liberty. These groups of patriot partisans fight for the restoration of America.

TRC – Truth Reconciliation Committee. Working with Big Tech and the mainstream media, the TRC determines what truth is and what is misinformation. It clears all official stories and either censors or blocks those that would be considered dangerous.

UP – Upper Peninsula of Michigan.

UVA – The University of Virginia.

Second Amendment: The Right to have free government-sanctioned education

It is the responsibility of the state to set education standards and provide approved learning to the population.

Prologue

Second Amendment: The right to have free government sanctioned education

It is the responsibility of the state to set education standards and provide approved education to the population.

Five Years Earlier...

Fort Wayne, Indiana

Braylon Ironsides watched the local TV news images of the so-called Social Enforcers rounding people up and loading them onto buses. His palms became sweaty as one man broke away only to be gunned down in the street. Two of the Social Enforcers jumped up and down, holding their guns in the air, cheering that they had just killed a man.

Braylon turned to his wife, Delores. "We should pack our things and leave."

"Don't you think you're overreacting?" she chided him.

"I wrote a lot of op-ed pieces speaking out about these kinds of people," he countered, running his hand through his salt-and-pepper hair. "These kids are out on the internet, looking for people like me. They will come."

"Where can we go?" Delores asked. "You've seen the news reports. Ever since they burned the White House and shot up The People's House, this has been happening in every city." She looked at him as if he were a child who didn't understand something. "Besides, they have far bigger fish to fry than to come for you. You're an old man."

He winced slightly. "I'm fifty-seven. I'll remind you, I'm six months younger than you."

She's probably right. Why would they waste their time coming after me? People don't even read the websites I posted to. Braylon relaxed a little, deciding to change the channels rather than worry.

They stayed up watching *CSI*, then crawled into bed. Braylon didn't sleep, though. He tossed and turned most of the night. His mind kept going to the images of people being rounded up. It was wrong. He knew that. The problem was that law enforcement didn't have the resources or motivation to get involved. With the new Ruling Council in Washington, D.C., everyone was suddenly unsure if laws were enforceable anymore. They claimed that the president had a heart attack while in custody, but that felt far too convenient. *They would've had people watching him around the clock. The moment he started to feel bad, they would have reacted.*

The death of the president was a symbol of the new normal. The ANTIFA-backed rioters overthrew the government, and no one—not even the DoD—stepped up to stop them. Rumors bounced all over the internet of something called Social Quarantine camps, concentration camps by another name. And there were the televised People's Tribunals, where people were tried, convicted, and in some cases, executed without basic constitutional rights being applied. Nervousness gnawed at him as he tried to sleep. There was a fear he couldn't shake about where the country was headed.

His neighbor, Roy, told him that calmer heads would eventually prevail. There was no sign of that happening. In one online forum, there was talk about armed resistance, but he shied away from such places on the net. *Chances are, it's the FBI prodding those people to take action. It's best not to make any comment or even read those kinds of posts.*

Around four in the morning, he finally drifted off to a restless sleep. When the sun peeked through the crack in the curtains, it slapped him in the face. His joints ached from the lack of rest, but Braylon ignored them as he got out of bed. *I'm glad I retired early. I can catch a nap sometime this afternoon.* He didn't miss going to work one bit. His career had been in IT, and he had worked for a big consulting company. The last few years there had been horrible. The new recruits were lazy. Most put in exactly eight hours of work, even if there was a crisis. They had demands…like working from home, when they barely worked in the office. One even brought his parents in for his performance review so they could defend their son and rebut his manager. He knew they were the same people who were probably rejoicing over the toppling of the government.

Getting up, he shed his pajamas and pulled on sweatpants. It was Wednesday, trash pickup day, one of the few ways he could tell what day of the week it was. *Once I take out the containers and get something to eat, I'll go to the gym.* It was a routine that had replaced his old work pattern, and for that, he was thankful. Going to the mudroom, he slid on his Sketchers and pulled on a windbreaker with his former employer's logo—something given to him years ago as a morale-boosting tool. He only used it now to take out the trash.

Winter was looming, which added to his nervousness. He could feel it on mornings like this. Fighting the cold was easy; battling his nerves was harder. Braylon toyed with getting his gun and stuffing it in his sweatpants pocket, but he held back from doing it. Delores hated the fact that he owned the gun. He was worried that if he went back into the bedroom to get the weapon, he might wake her up. Ultimately, he settled on the simplicity of his action as not being risky, telling himself he was only taking the trash out. *What could possibly go wrong in my driveway?*

As he stepped outside, the sun was blotted out by a long, thick line of purple and gray clouds. *It won't be long before the snow comes.* Opening the garage door from the panel, he pulled out the recycling and garbage containers, tipping them back and starting to wheel them to the street.

Standing at the end of his driveway were three young men. He hadn't seen them when he first stepped out. They simply appeared, probably from the SUV parked in front of Roy's house. Two of the youths wore hoodies. One hoodie was black with a logo he didn't recognize. The second simply had the words "They/Them" on the front. The taller youth wore a lightweight jacket and had a rifle slung across his back. Braylon saw them and froze in place. They saw him, and the two of them grinned.

"Hey, are you Mr. Ironsides?" the shortest of the three asked.

Braylon stood straighter, narrowing his eyes. *This is it. This is what I was afraid of.* His mind darted to the gun he had in the bedroom. Part of his thought process focused on running back through the garage to grab the weapon. Would he be fast enough to get it? Seeing the rifle slung over the shoulder of one of the youths, he doubted it. *Maybe twenty years ago... not now. I can't give them a reason to shoot me.*

"I am," he said. "Is there a problem?"

The one with the They/Them hoodie stepped forward. As he did, he lifted the hoodie to expose a gun shoved into the waistband of his jeans. "We need you to come with us."

"Who is us?"

"Social Enforcement—the Westsiders," he said as if the name was something Braylon should know.

Braylon's body tensed. "I haven't done anything wrong."

The tallest of the group replied, "Then you don't have anything to worry about."

"My wife," he said, gesturing to the garage. "Let me tell her."

"Don't you worry about your wife," They/Them replied. "We'll take care of her." There was something ominous-sounding in their response. "Don't make us pop your ass, old man. We will, and the cops ain't gonna do a thing about it. Either way, your body is getting into the SUV."

Instinct told him to run, to put distance between them and Delores. But they were much younger, and his running days were in the rearview mirror of his memory. In his entire life, Braylon had never felt as helpless as he did in his own driveway. For an instant, he thought about his conversation the night before with Delores. *I've never regretted being right so much in my entire life.*

Surrender was the mental sword he impaled himself on. His head hung low as he walked toward them, leaving the garbage containers. "Smart move, you right-wing asshole," They/Them said, whipping him around, pulling his hands behind him, and zip-tying his wrists tightly to the point where it hurt. Their tone told him that what was to follow was not going to be fair and impartial.

They took him to a formerly abandoned warehouse in the city. He suffered the indignity of being stripped naked in front of a group of young men and women, many of whom made derogatory comments about his physique. They finally let him redress after several cold and embarrassing minutes.

Eventually, Braylon was led into another part of the warehouse, one that had been partitioned off by piles of old pallets stacked up like walls. There was a white plastic folding table at one end with five people seated on folding chairs, watching him as he was led in front of them.

"State your name," the large dark-skinned woman in the center of the table demanded.

"Braylon Jacob Ironsides."

"You stand accused of spreading racist disinformation," she proclaimed. "Do you have anything to say in your defense?"

Racist? What have I done that was racist? "I'm confused. What do you mean, 'spreading racist disinformation?' I'm not racist."

"This op-ed," she said, holding a printout of one of the pieces he wrote. "You said it was wrong to take down Confederate statues, didn't you?"

"Yes. That's not racist. Read the article—I said they were one-of-a-kind pieces of art. I suggested putting up historical markers offering some context about the men."

"Who are you to make that kind of suggestion?" she snapped.

"Well, I just thought—"

"You supported the Confederacy. That makes you racist," a young man in his twenties said from the table's far left end. His face was covered with metal studs and rings to the point where he looked like something from a horror movie.

"I did not support the Confederacy. I simply said that we shouldn't destroy the statues just because people are offended."

"You said that these men should be idolized," a young woman at the far-right end of the table replied. "You are advocating slavery."

"No. You're misrepresenting what I wrote. I said those statues were put up as memorials, not to encourage slavery. They were put up by the men who served under them or by the honorees' families."

The large woman in the center of the table stared at him as if he were a slab of rotting meat. "That makes you the worst kind of racist—you're the kind who denies what you've done. You have a lot of nerve coming in front of this tribunal and flaunting your white privilege!"

Braylon started to grapple with panic. *They've already decided the verdict.* "I would like to contact a lawyer."

The metal-studded youth laughed. "This isn't a court of law, where you can escape justice. This is a tribunal of the people."

"This isn't justice. It's mob rule." He regretted saying the words the moment he uttered them.

"I think we've heard enough," the woman in the center said. She glanced both directions down the table and got nods from the seated members. "You have been found guilty. We sentence you to social quarantine until such a time as you are properly reeducated and fit to atone for your crimes and return to society."

Rough hands grabbed him from behind, jerking him away. Braylon was stunned at the results of this mock trial. He couldn't defend himself. *This was all for show. They were going to send me away no matter what.*

As they loaded him onto a commandeered school bus outside, he saw that there were twenty others already there. Their sullen faces mirrored his own. Humiliation, rage, and fear—each chewed on parts of his mind to the point where he could hear his heart pounding in his chest. *What about Delores? Does she even know I'm here?*

Washington, D.C.

FBI Special Agent Angela Axton felt fairly proud of her decisions that had led to this night. She had infiltrated a group of alt-right veterans prior to The Liberation. It had been tricky work, convincing them of her sincerity to their cause. All of them supported the Traitor President. When she had first slid past their screening process, they had mostly been talk—conversations about how the progressives couldn't be trusted, bragging about what they would do if ANTIFA ever protested nearby. After the Liberation, it took only a few well-placed suggestions to the right members of the nameless group to prod them from talk to action.

They had a bold name, like most domestic terror organizations. It practically screamed that it was full of alt-right crazies—The Patriot Liberation Front, or PFL. One of their members had actually gotten patches made for them, one of which she wore on her urban camouflage. It was a stupid move on their part—the patches made identification of the members easy.

The PFL were clay in her hands, and Angela molded them perfectly.

Angela climbed up onto the rooftop of the Homer Building across the street from Mastro's Steakhouse, the target venue. The smells of D.C., a mix of garbage from the nearby alley and the fumes of vehicles five stories below, were all far too familiar to her. A few minutes later, she was joined by Hudson Whitlock from the cell she had infiltrated. He eyed her suspiciously as he walked over to the parapet and quickly surveyed 13th Street NW below. Whitlock had never fully trusted her. Angela didn't let that bother her. Soon enough, he'd be in jail, along with his comrades.

"We should deploy farther back," he suggested. "It'll give us some distance from the target—a better chance of getting away."

"I think we're good here," she replied, knowing that behind him on the fire escape were three fellow FBI agents, ready to pounce when she gave the word.

Their plan, in which she had an integral part, was to go for the jugular of the Ruling Council: Daniel Porter. She claimed to have a source who knew his daily itinerary and had mapped out where he was having dinner in DC. They would shoot it out with his security and either kill or capture him. The members of the cabal were excited at the prospect. Only a few even dared to question if it was a smart move.

Her biggest detractor was Hudson Whitlock, which was why she wanted to be with him during the pending attack, even though she hated him. She had his background, and he was like many members of the group—former military, highly independent, a gun nut. He was always talking about free speech, regardless of the harm it might cause others. He was one of the few members of the PFL who didn't entirely trust her. He had told the leader of the team, Race Karter, that it smelled like an ambush, which added to her tension.

Was it possible that Whitlock knew she was an FBI agent? Why was he so hesitant? In the end, it didn't matter—Race and the rest of the group voted to make the play. Whitlock came along too, though she could see that he was highly aware of their circumstances. *He senses that this is a setup. After they're apprehended, I'll have to find out why.*

She had alerted the Bureau, and they had set up in the buildings surrounding the restaurant where Porter was allegedly going to come. Of course, that was all a ruse. His limo was filled with agents, and the man posing as Porter was wearing body armor and prepared for the assault. The SAC wanted her to coax them in on their target, moving them into the entrapment zone. Once surrounded, they would be taken down swiftly.

When she had first received the assignment, Angela had reservations that she openly voiced. "These people don't have a plot or a scheme—they just hate what happened."

Her supervisor had told her, "If you don't plant the idea to strike back, they'll eventually get there on their own. The difference is that we can control the situation if we're guiding them along the way. If we simply wait for them to strike at a time and place of their choosing, we run the risk of innocent people being hurt or killed."

That gave her the focus she needed. *I'm not entrapping them. I'm saving lives.* That thought guided Angela's actions every step of the way as she lured the people into her plan. There was a point when they took the scheme on as if it were their own, which seemed to validate what the SAC had told her. *They would have eventually turned to violence—that much is clear. Almost all of them are gun nuts. They actually supported that traitor who sat in the White House.*

Whitlock moved away from her to a far corner of the rooftop. *Once he's arrested, I need to interrogate him and find out why he never fully trusted me.* That was a comforting thought, seeing him in handcuffs. *I'll wipe that arrogant attitude off his face after tonight.*

She waited, playing the role of domestic terrorist, as the faux Daniel Porter's limo arrived. She saw him enter the restaurant, knowing that it was full of FBI and DHS agents. Despite the cold temperature, she was sweating with anticipation. Angela wanted this bust to go perfectly. *If I pull this off, my career will have no limits.*

Then she saw it—the lead car from the PFL rounding the corner, angling into one of the open parking spots up the street from the upscale restaurant. In her earbud, she heard, "Targets pulling up. Snipers, mark your targets." Angela didn't hide her smile, knowing her colleagues were prepared.

The time had come to contact her bureau colleagues. She pressed the tiny stud on her earbud and whispered, "This is Backdraft. Rooftop two is covered."

Then she heard the chambering of a round dangerously close to her head.

Wheeling, she saw Hudson Whitlock standing just a few yards away from her with his Glock aimed. "I knew you were too good to be true." On his belt, she saw a communications device. *That bastard is somehow monitoring our comms.*

With one hand holding the pistol, he pulled out his Baofeng communicator. "Abort! We've been set up!"

Angela ducked and started to draw her weapon on the way down. There was a bang as he discharged the weapon, and she felt as if her right leg was on fire. She collapsed; the agony was so swift and painful. Looking down, she saw that his bullet had hit her in the knee. Blood soaked her camouflage gear as she fumbled with her weapon.

The other agents rose up from the fire escape as Whitlock moved, firing at them. One was hit in the face, flying back and down into the darkness. Angela tried to aim her weapon, but the pain from her now-destroyed knee screamed at her. Whitlock was moving fast as she fired two rounds, both missing him.

As the second agent reached the roof, he fired, as did Whitlock. The PFL member hit him in the arm, forcing him to drop back down behind the parapet. Angela fired again, missing. Whitlock cast her a furious glance, then sprinted, jumping to the adjacent rooftop. *God damn it, he's going to get away!* Shots rang out from the street below, and multiple voices were bellowing through the earpiece.

Her field of vision grew narrower, darker, and she knew she was about to slide into shock. Reaching up, she pressed her earbud. "This is Backdraft. Whitlock has bolted. Two wounded, one dead. Roll EMS. Get eyes on that asshole now!" As she finished, the darkness she saw growing in her field of vision engulfed her.

Chapter 1

Sixth Amendment: The Right of Justice; Legal, Social, and Environmental

Individuals in the nation have a right to equitable justice, weighted to their protected classification. This applies to legal, social, and environmental justice. Only guilty parties will be charged with crimes and will be provided ample opportunity to prove their innocence. Trials will be fair and equitable with balanced juries of varying social, economic, sexual preference, and race as defined by the government.

The District

As the vice president sat across the desk from President Daniel Porter, she did her best to hide her emotions. The president had called for a Constitutional Convention to ratify Newmerica's government and legal system and was basking in his prize project as it crept to fruition.

"Alex, this," he said, thumping his hand down on the three-inch-thick printed document, "is how we will be remembered. When this gets ratified, *we* will be the new Founding Fathers. In one fell swoop, this document will erase the stains of the past and the corruption of men like Jefferson and Adams. Our constitution will usher in a new era and define our future."

It was rare to see Porter so happy, so excited. What was worse was that his glee was all his. He had worked tirelessly on the constitution and was clutching the glory close to his chest. Still, there was room to make her imprint. "I dislike the words 'Founding Fathers.' Too patriarchal. From now on, we need to position this as 'The Founders.' That removes the inherent sexism and still conveys the message," she replied.

He gave a nod to her brief critique of his summary. "I trust that your Truth and Reconciliation Committee will craft that narrative appropriately," he said. "Regardless of how we refer to ourselves, this is something that will resonate for generations, a true change of the legal and social order." Arrogance rang in every word he spoke.

"The real challenge will be getting the delegates to agree to it," she replied.

"I've been working the phones. The governor of California has been stubborn on more than a few points. He named himself as the delegate, if you can believe that."

"Actually, I do. A big part of his problem is that he believes California is the center of the universe. I wonder sometimes if he really supports us or is simply waiting in the wings for us to lose the war and seize power for himself." Alex liked planting the seeds of doubt in the president's mind when it came to possible political rivals.

She had a good suspicion that he did have the votes to pass or was damned close to it. That was also part of her problem. Since Daniel had announced the new constitution and the TRC had promoted it, people were clamoring for it. With the losses on the battlefield, they needed some hope. Internal TRC polling had shown that many in Newmerica were starting to wonder if the war could be won. Her people had turned those worries into fears, with countless news stories about what the Americans might do. Lurid CGI images of concentration camps made people afraid of what might happen. Alex knew it would spur them on to fight even harder.

Daniel was beaming. "This is what will cement our names in history."

From her seat, she saw a problem. Daniel had been the front person on the new constitution. It was his baby. At first, she had encouraged it with the media. If the effort fizzled, his name would be attached to the failure. The problem was that it was gaining traction. Worse yet, if it did get ratified, he would be the one to reap the political capital that came with such a victory.

It was something she could not allow to happen.

"There's still a long way to go to get everyone to agree to it."

Daniel was unshaken. "First, by treating the District and Puerto Rico as voting states, it helps tip things in my favor. Second, that's why it is as thick as it is. I've been working hard to make sure everyone gets something out of this effort. Trust me, it wasn't easy. Every governor is worried that this will erode some of their power."

"That's because it will," she pointed out. *As it should.*

Daniel's grin grew even broader. "True. The thing is, the entire constitution is so big that I doubt any of them have actually bothered to read it all. They are less concerned with what's in there and more focused on getting new things added. The New York governor called this morning, asking that we add an amendment to outline the obligations of a citizen. What she emailed me was four pages long! Some of it is so vague, it really gives us more power than we've ever had before. When I asked her if she had read the rest of the document, she told me she had people looking at it. Can you believe that? Looking at it? It's the basis of our government, and she's treating it like a label on a can of tuna. It's perfect!"

The vice president wasn't surprised at all. It had been that way in the District for some time. Bills and budgets were hefty documents that representatives passed with the promise to look into the details later. For her, it meant she had to know this document just as well as Daniel did. *If it spells out the power we can use, then I need to know every line.* "The governors are dangerous. The old system gave them too much authority. You can't trust them."

"I don't," he assured her. "Once this new constitution is ratified, we will deal with them. Simple divide and conquer.

Most are career politicians. They'll fall in line, if only to preserve what little power they have left. It's in their nature. Even they know it's better to clutch what power you can than risk losing it all."

The president's thinking was sound. Her approach would have been more final. Using the National Security Force, she would simply kill the politicians who refused to follow national policy. It was far more efficient than what Daniel had in mind. *Some threats must be resolved with lethal force. It's the only permanent solution and sends a strong message to others who might think of causing problems.* She was tempted to offer it to Daniel but knew he didn't have the willpower to see it through.

"Where would you like to hold the convention?" she asked.

"I was thinking Philadelphia. It makes a historic statement. As much as we have suppressed history, it's still part of the population's psyche. Holding it there would give it a sense of legitimacy, don't you think?"

It was a good idea, but she didn't want to admit it. There were some issues, though, which she felt compelled to state. "Security will be a challenge. Philly isn't exactly the friendliest territory. Pennsylvania is filled with American supporters once you get outside the cities."

"It's still under our control."

"It is, but it's surrounded by counties that are friendly to the Pretender President. All it takes is a crazed alt-right gunman to disrupt the proceedings."

"The NSF should be more than able to secure a building suitable for The People's House."

Daniel was hinting that she wasn't up to the task, and she loathed that insinuation. "My people will provide your security. On that, you can rely."

"Good."

"That only leaves the question of when."

"I was thinking in the next three weeks. I can have my press secretary make the announcement at the morning briefing."

He said "my," not "our." He's already sensing the shift in power. "That sounds good. Hopefully, we can have a victory on the battlefield by then." The president never noticed her subtle way of changing the topic.

The defeat in New Hampshire had been devastating beyond the battle losses. "Have the Joint Chiefs given us a replacement for General Rinehart?" Porter's contempt for the general who had led his forces to defeat was well known. Even saying his name, he spoke in a lower octave.

"They assure me that they will get us someone by tomorrow."

"Why so long?"

She frowned slightly as she responded. "I think they're nervous about the strategic situation. New Mexico is officially lost. The enemy has driven into Arizona. On the plus side, Boston has declared itself a 'Free City' to prevent the traitor forces from taking it. Frankly, I'm not sure if they're committed to our victory as much as they should be. That's the kind of decision that shouldn't have been made locally. My people are going to identify who made that call, and they will be dealt with."

"The brass at the Pentagon has as much to lose as we do at this point." The military had officially been on the sidelines during the Liberation. They had cast their lot in with the old Ruling Council and now President Porter, but only to a point. The vice president had no doubt that if the Pretender won, they would flip sides again.

"My People's Warden Program is keeping the rank-and-file troops in line. Once we show them the price of failure with Rinehart, that should be enough to convince them to get in line."

"Are we going to air his tribunal?"

She shook her head. "No. We did some internal polling. There's concern at the TRC that if we publicize his tribunal, it will bring too much attention to the defeat in New Hampshire. I will, however, film it and send a file over to the Joint Chiefs. It should provide them with…proper motivation."

"Excellent!" Porter replied. "The sooner we put the ugliness of New Hampshire behind us, the better. The assassination of the Pretender's chief of staff was a boon for us. It almost offsets the problems we're having on campuses lately."

The vice president had been forced to rely on the new accounts of Jack Desmond's shooting. The operative she had assigned to the task had gone silent. Out of the chaos, good news emerged. Reportedly, Caylee Leatrom had been arrested for the crime. *Just as I planned.* In one fell swoop, two of America's assets had been taken off the game board. "Desmond is the brains of the American government. With him neutralized, we've thrown our enemies into disarray." There was no tangible evidence of that happening yet, but she was confident that it would start soon.

She didn't have a retort to the reference to the problems on college campuses. It had started at the University of Virginia, with someone killing campus Social Enforcers. She thought it was a local problem. Then there were murders in Maryland, followed by incidents in Massachusetts and California. Even Yale hadn't been spared. Two fraternity houses burned, resulting in tremendous loss of life. This went beyond copycat killings. People were targeting loyal students at universities everywhere. Alex had assigned a number of top NSF people to investigate, but no one could find the connections. *They're fighting back…that's something we can't tolerate.*

"I've put my best people on this campus issue. And as for the Chief of Staff's shooting, we are going to make sure that gets blamed on in-fighting in the American regime," she assured him. "Any word on securing Canadian military support?"

Daniel shot his eyes upward, a hint of frustration evident. As she had done with the Mexican cartels, Porter had reached out to Canada to ask for troops in the war. The Canadian Prime Minister, an effeminate man at best, had been reluctant to commit any support. "Justy is worried about his army becoming entangled in what he sees as an internal affair."

"He's a weak opportunist. He speaks all the words, but at the end of the day, he's never been a true believer in our cause. If things get worse, he'll side with America just to save his ass."

"You may be right. He's worried about some sort of trucker's strike that he may have to squash, or something stupid like that. To me, it's an excuse to do as little as possible. Justy *has* offered us a brigade of volunteers to come fight here. They're calling themselves the Redblack Brigade. He says they'll be crossing the border at Windsor in the next two weeks."

"It's better than nothing."

"Yes. Hopefully, we can deploy them south into Ohio and take some of the pressure off other fronts."

"We are going to win this war, Daniel. It's just a matter of time," she assured him.

Daniel was pleased with her support. His face told her that. They proceeded to wade through three other topics, all of which were far beneath her. They broke up as usual, and she stepped out into the office hallway at the Capitol, where the president now conducted business.

The Newmerican vice president could not shake the feeling that she was being overshadowed by Porter's work. *If he gets that new constitution pushed through, it will be a big win— for him!* That thought gnawed at her. She had been slowly and carefully amassing power in Newmerica. The TRC, the NSF, the People's Wardens… all of it was under her guiding control. Now Porter had found a way to diminish her despite her successes.

She had always thought that when the time was right, she would soar past him, seizing the Presidency for herself. *If the new constitution goes through, he'll be in office for nine more years!* That tore at her. It nudged her thinking into an alternative way to gain power. If Porter were to die in office, it would all be hers. The more she contemplated that thought, the more appealing it became to her.

I oversaw the execution of The People's House when we came to power. Social Enforcement has killed tens of thousands in the camps. What's one more life? Yes, he was the president, but she controlled his security with the NSF. It was a matter of finding the right asset to commit the deed, someone who wouldn't link the assassination to her but would be more than willing to accept the blame. Of course, such a person would be expendable. There could be no loose ends, like other assassination attempts. Conspiracy theorists would face immediate People's Tribunals, which would prevent the masses from attempting to lay the blame at her doorstep. *Fear keeps people in line. It forces them to think correctly.*

Daniel thinks he's on the brink of his greatest success. In reality, he's on the verge of putting me in the Presidency! For the first time all day, she cracked a broad smile.

Gold Canyon, Arizona

General Trip Reager looked skyward at the contrails that marked the pair of Reaper drones the American forces were employing. Standing in the shade of his command Bradley fighting vehicle was welcome as he stared skyward. The Reapers had been liberated from Cannon Air Force Base under protests from the Department of Defense. The terse message he had received was that the DoD considered itself neutral in the civil war raging across America. Trip pointed out that Cannon AFB had been used against his forces, negating the claims of neutrality. Their response was to threaten him with court martial.

They'll have to catch me first.

After New Mexico's governor had surrendered to his approaching forces, Trip had pressed across the state, heading for Southern California. He bypassed the base at White

Sands, not out of fear of reprisal by the Joint Chiefs, but because the base was remaining neutral and not assisting in the Newmerican war effort.

Arizona was merely a waypoint on his map, a place to resupply. His troops entered Tucson to the south with only a minor skirmish with Social Enforcers, who folded the moment they saw AFVs shredding their positions with machine guns and cannon fire. They were tough against unarmed civilians, but when faced with actual military opponents, most broke and ran the moment the shooting started.

There had been some setbacks. While Fort Huachuca surrendered without a shot being fired, a large number of the personnel had already fled by the time his forces arrived. Trip understood why once his people secured the facility. The vast communications arrays and systems there, which were designed to monitor foreign nations, had been turned by the Newmericans against their own citizens. *Those responsible for spying on our own people are cowards. They know what they did was morally and legally wrong, but did it anyway under the mask of loyalty to the government...a government we are finally crushing.*

The Arizona governor decided to make her stand in Phoenix. She had deployed elements of the Arizona National Guard to block the road into the city. Captain Harnessy's intel reports indicated that the enemy was there as a reinforced battalion, along with several SE units, no doubt pressed into action as militia.

To their credit, the Arizona force had chosen good ground to dig in. Gold Canyon's terrain was rugged, with steep hills flanking the Superstition Highway and lots of boulders—excellent terrain for defense. The town itself was small but well-sheltered by the surrounding hills. Reager's enemy had thrown the 285th Aviation Regiment's helicopters at Reager's forces before they had deployed. The cost had been five vehicles, and they had run his own Bradley off the road to avoid being another casualty due to a temporarily thrown tread. A swarm of Stinger anti-aircraft missiles had taken out half the helicopters. He hated seeing the enemy Apache helicopters crash but knew it was necessary. *Such a damn waste of personnel and material. When the dust settles, it's going to take a while for us to be a military threat to our global enemies.*

"Captain Hill," Reager called over to his Air Force liaison. "When do we start seeing fireworks?"

She was working at her comms station inside the Bradley. "They are tagging targets now."

The Newmericans weren't waiting. He saw the streaks of anti-aircraft missiles racing skyward. *Shit!* "Captain, you've got incoming missiles."

"Firing now," she replied. The Raptors overhead unleashed their AGM-114 Hellfire missiles at the ground targets and banked away, climbing as they tried to put some distance between themselves and the incoming fire. It was hard to spot the Raptors as they attempted evasion. There were two explosions in the sky, but only one set of contrails left the area.

Then came the echoing blasts from Gold Canyon as the Hellfires found their marks. Trip turned and saw only the oily black plumes of smoke rolling skyward from the canyon. There were four of them, each at least two miles away, marking destroyed targets.

Trip watched the black smoke dissipate in the light breeze. He wanted Phoenix, and Gold Canyon was blocking his highway in there. He had been pushing his personnel and equipment hard for some time. Logistics won wars, and his vehicles and weapons needed servicing if they were going to push on into California. Forcing them into another battle right now would be a strain, but he knew it was necessary. Reager also knew that the key to winning was not to get entangled in a battle of attrition.

That left him with two options: swing south, skirt around the Newmerican forces, and hit Phoenix from the south. That would work, but it still left a sizable military force on his flank, able to pinch his supply lines. They needed to be neutralized, but it needed to be done smartly, not with brute force.

"Captain Harnessy," Trip called out, still looking through his binoculars toward the canyon. "Isn't there a Sons of Liberty group operating in Phoenix?"

Harnessy was quick to reply. "Yes, sir. The Maricopa County Mounted Posse."

"See if you can get their leader here."

"Yes, sir."

* * *

Chris Luke, leader of the Maricopa County Mounted Posse, looked more like a character from a John Wayne movie than a rebel cell leader. His barrel chest, thick midsection, weathered skin, Stetson, and dusty boots all screamed cowboy. He eyed Reager from top to bottom. The fact that he didn't leave spoke volumes. "General."

"Mr. Luke."

"I understand you need some of my people's assistance."

"It looks like the state of Arizona is prepared to dig in at Gold Canyon."

"That they have. Some of my people watched them trek in there. They are dug in like a tick on a hound dog."

"If I bypass them, there will be hell to pay on my supply line."

"That's what I figure too, General." He planted his big fists on his hips.

"As tempting as it is to dump artillery on them and whittle them down to the point where they surrender, I don't feel like wasting ammo or time."

Luke nodded. "Before the so-called Liberation, my posse was used to help find missing people. Our folks augmented law enforcement. We were on horseback, knew the lands around Phoenix, and were damned good at what we did. When they rolled all law enforcement into the NSF, we got the boot, since we were never technically official. The reason I tell you this is that we know Gold Canyon really well. We've helped find lost hikers there before. My people have seen every nook and cranny of that canyon."

Trip smiled. "I was hoping that might be the case."

"So, what do you need us to do?"

"The way I see it, they think they're in an impenetrable position. No doubt they think I'll rush in and they'll bleed us. I don't want to play their game. People are pretty confident in their position until they realize that it's tenuous. If you and your people can come in behind them, act as snipers, picking them off, that will shake them. We won't come in heavy, but we'll send in some snipers of our own. A few days of that, along with some artillery that you can help us direct, will make them realize they're surrounded and pinned down."

Luke smiled. "I think we can help in that regard. All of us have experience hunting wild game. Shooting at Newmericans will be a downright pleasure."

"We'll outfit you with radios and some training on how to spot for our artillery. Remember, we don't want an all-out engagement. They think they laid a trap for us. In reality, they've boxed themselves in. All I need you to do is remind them of that."

"Don't you go a'worrying yourself, General. Me and mine, we know how to make people feel miserable."

Two Days Later...

Artillery explosions erupted in the confines of Gold Canyon, throwing dust into the air, followed by smoke. The barrages were intermittent and surgical, thanks to the observation skills of the mounted posse. Reager's own snipers were playing a deadly game of hide-and-seek with their counterparts in the Arizona National Guard.

"Sir," his communications officer called out. "I've got the posse. They say they need to talk to you."

Reager took the headset and held it next to his ear. "This is Reager."

"Chris Luke here," came the voice. "I thought you should know. It looks like they are preparing to break out. We're seeing them pack up their gear and hearing their vehicles starting to fire up."

"Which way are they going?"

"Right toward us. If I were the betting type, I'd say they're going to try to get past us and into Phoenix."

Trip remembered the urban combat in Knoxville and cringed at the thought of a repeat. Even though it was a victory, fighting in a city could be as brutal as trying to pry the Newmericans out of the canyon. Glancing at the map, he immediately formulated a plan. "I'm going to deploy a force on that fire road off to the west. We'll then have them move north, and we should be able to link up with you along Highway 60 west of the Gold Canyon."

"I know that road. Send suitable vehicles. There are bound to be places where it's washed out."

"Noted. Have your people still pepper them. See if you can slow their packing process long enough for us to get a force out that direction."

"I'll have a man waiting for them," Luke assured him.

The conversation ended, and Trip put the headset down. *When they get moving, they'll be the most vulnerable. All we need is a big enough force to block them from fleeing to Phoenix. I can then send the bulk of our forces right up the highway and catch them in the middle.* It was a sound plan of battle, if the Arizona National Guard cooperated.

Federal Correctional Institution, Memphis, Tennessee

Caylee didn't mind solitary confinement. The attorney general thought it was a prudent move, given that she had been an operative. She didn't fear being put in the general population of prisoners, but not having to deal with them made her day go easier. If anything, she enjoyed the solitude, at least for a few days.

After the first week had passed, she found herself missing her small circle of friends. It was a strange concept for her. Her years in the NSF, doing Newmerica's dirty work, precluded her from having relationships. They were a burden. Worse, they put her friends at risk. Things were different now for Caylee. She had actual friends for the first time since high school. They had shared risks together, fought for each other, and had each other's backs. Missing them was something that she struggled with at first but slowly came to embrace. It wasn't the kind of thing she would ever admit out loud, but she did have feelings for her comrades in arms.

Being in prison was a compromise, a show of good faith for the AG that she was not really Jack Desmond's assassin. Desmond had survived but had been in a coma since the shooting. It was an ugly situation, compounded by the fact that the assassin had been disguised as Caylee when he had pulled the trigger. While the shooter had been apprehended and DNA testing was underway, she sat and waited.

Her former employer, the Newmerican NSF, had set her up. She had little doubt that it was payback for the chaos she had caused them. *I did kill the VP's mother and brother. I'm sure that with her, it's quite personal.*

Caylee's days had been dull, which was a strangely welcome break for her. The Newmerican Truth Reconciliation Committee had proclaimed her the assassin, a clear attempt to distance their own government from the act. She ate in her cell. Once a day, they took her out for exercise. Other than that, she had time to sit and think about the civil war and what was looking more like its inevitable conclusion. *Everyone thinks that the Newmericans will surrender. They won't—they can't. The list of their crimes is so long; they have no option other than doubling down. They will fight to the bitter end if only to ensure they never face justice for what they've done.*

Sometime in the afternoon of her fifth day, a pair of guards showed up. "Stand up. Put your hands behind you," the larger of the two men said.

Caylee turned slowly, complying, while at the same time thinking through how she might overpower and kill the guards. She was accomplished in savate, fighting with her feet. As they placed handcuffs on her wrists, she was already running through scenarios she might face if pressed into action. The guards didn't appear to be threatening, but she also knew that such people could be bought for the right price. There were plenty of people who wanted her dead, so such thoughts were the norm for her.

As they led her out of her cell, the large guard held her forearm and broke the silence. "So, you're really her...the Operative?"

"You never can tell," she replied.

"They say operatives know thirty ways to kill a person."

Caylee cast him a sideways glance. "People say a lot of things. I've never counted. The rumor alone makes some surrender. Words and fear are potent weapons." *God knows our enemy has used them to their advantage.*

The other guard spoke up. "You were the one who broke into the Supermax, right?"

"If you must know, yes. Though I didn't do that alone. There was a team."

"That is *so* cool," he replied.

Great, I have fans. I have zero use for fans. "A lot of what you hear about operatives is propaganda. It's designed to generate fear. It enables interrogations to go much faster."

"That makes sense," the larger guard said as they led her through a security door. "Fear is a pretty powerful narcotic." They turned and went through another set of doors that required him to show his ID and get buzzed through. Finally, they stopped at a room. She felt him tug at her handcuffs, then felt them come off. The smaller guard then opened the steel door. On the inside was Charli, who flashed her a smile. Caylee rubbed her right wrist where the handcuff had chafed, then stepped in.

"Pleasure meeting you, ma'am," the large guard said, walking away as the door closed.

"I take it this isn't a visit?"

"You've been sprung," Charli replied with a thin smile.

"We both know I'm innocent."

"Now the AG does too. Your DNA came back as a non-match for the evidence we gathered. That, and Jack woke up yesterday and said he was sure it wasn't you."

"He's awake? I didn't see anything on the news about that."

"We're keeping that quiet for the time being. No point in tipping off the bastards who tried to have him killed."

"Is he doing all right?"

Charli gave her a nod, handing her a folded stack of her civilian clothing. "You'll get a chance to ask him yourself. That's where we are heading after we leave."

Nashville VA Medical Center, Nashville, Tennessee

Security on the floor was heavy, with four checkpoints just to get outside Jack Desmond's room. Caylee appreciated it. *He should have had this kind of security at the cemetery where he was shot.* The last guard outside his room checked her ID and Charli's, then opened the door for them.

Despond had the bed raised and a rolling table across his chest. His face was drawn with more wrinkles than usual. He had some beard stubble, mostly gray and white, making him look older. His eyes, though, were still as penetrating as ever. When he saw the two of them enter, he leaned back from the papers on the table surface and forced a smile. "About time," he said.

"How are you, Jack?" Charli asked.

"I've been better."

"I didn't know you were out of your coma," Caylee said.

Jack sighed and winced slightly as he shifted in the bed, clearly still in pain. "We all thought it best for the Newmericans to think they might have pulled off their hit."

It was a prudent move. "Shouldn't you be resting?" Caylee asked, looking at the files on the table.

"There'll be time for that when this war is over."

"You were shot. More than once." Caylee took a step closer.

"Three times. I knew it wasn't you. The height was off, and the earlobes. Besides, if it had been you, I'd be dead."

Those words brought a small grin from Caylee.

"I got her out as soon as the AG cleared it," Charli said.

"Tulsi is a stickler for detail. Now that I'm awake and you're out of the hoosegow, we can use the Newmericans' ignorance of our status to our advantage." Jack's body had taken three bullets, but his mental focus was as crisp as ever.

"What do you have in mind?" Caylee asked.

"The president is tasking General Reager with resolving St. Louis soon. That will allow us to push out on three fronts. To the west, we need to get a foothold in California, assuming he gets Arizona under his heel. In the east, once we have St. Louis in our pocket, we'll send a force out of Ohio into Pennsylvania. From the north, we'll push south toward New York." He paused and took a sip of water from his white Styrofoam cup.

"This war will not be won on the battlefield alone. There are psychological and political moves that need to be made. That's where you come in, Caylee."

Leatrom shifted her stance and nodded once. "Go on."

"Our opponents are planning a Constitutional Convention. Word is that President Porter wants to do it in Philly. I'm sure he loves the historical significance of doing it there. His intent is simple—erase the past and implement his totalitarian regime with some legitimacy in the law. They want to pass a new constitution. While we haven't seen any of the details, I can only assume it will turn the nation still under their control into the kind of oligarchy that will be harder to eliminate."

Caylee weighed in. "That's a safe assumption. Once they change the laws to justify their crimes, they'll be emboldened to commit more crimes. They'll tell the population that they're giving them freedoms when, in reality, they're taking them away. The weak-minded will simply believe whatever the propagandists put out. Most won't go digging for the truth. It's easier just to accept what the government tells them. Besides, those who do rebel and see the world as it is will be labeled as threats to their form of democracy. Sadly, it's an old game, and one that works."

Jack rallied his resolve—she could see it in the muscles flexing on his face. "We cannot allow them to hold this Constitutional Convention and steal a political victory, not at this stage of the war. That's where you come in."

Caylee felt his eyes piercing her. "What do you want me to do?"

He drew a long breath. "First, the convention needs to be disrupted. General Reager has some ideas for dealing with some of the delegates, but we need those who are attending to be afraid. The sound of our guns in the distance should make them extremely nervous, but this is about breaking their spirit. I also think having some boots on the ground there, stirring up confusion and trouble, will help. Maybe we can prevent them from ratifying this damned thing."

"That's doable. You said 'first,' which implies there is more."

Jack gave her a nod. "I can't get anything by you. For the second thing, I want you to do the thing I can't ask you to do. It's not enough for the convention to fail. All the key players of the Newmerican government will be there. It's a target that we shouldn't pass up."

Her mind danced at the possibilities. *There's a reason he's not telling me what to do specifically.* One course of action kept coming to the forefront. "We're talking about killing the vice president."

"For the record, I never said those words."

"You didn't have to," Caylee replied. "She's the lynchpin of Newmerica. That witch was one of the insiders of the coup to overthrow the government. It was on her word that The People's House and the Senate were executed. She staged the false flag bombing at the Capitol so she could seize control of the TRC and eliminate her opponents. She controls their media, the NSF, and, with her Warden program, the military."

"But President Porter is the brains behind this new constitution of theirs," Charli countered.

Caylee shook her head. "She's letting him believe that. I doubt he'll remain president much longer. There's no way she'll allow him to continue in power with her in the second seat. I understand the woman, as unsavory as that may be. She'll want to steal his thunder out of fear that it will overshadow her. He's a dead man but probably has no idea what's coming or when."

"I came to that conclusion months ago. She was a cancer inside The People's House. She said things people knew were ridiculous only to get her name on everyone's tongue. That whole stupid former bartender routine was a ruse from the start. The VP has control of much of the true power of the Newmerican state. With the war closing in around them, she needs to take her shot at Porter fairly soon or risk never having a chance."

Caylee was impressed with the logic of Jack Desmond's perspective. "Her ego is such that she will see herself as the true savior of their country. Disrupting the convention will only forestall the inevitable. Like all tyrants, she'll simply install herself as the true leader if it collapses."

"Caylee, you're the only person who can do this. Not just from a skills perspective, but from a plausible deniability standpoint."

"It's not going to be easy," she pointed out. "Security in Philadelphia is going to be heavy. And you're talking about troops thrusting into that state. Even if she is taken out, Porter is still there."

Charli spoke up. "We broke Raul out of the Supermax. We'll be able to do this."

Caylee turned to her and shook her head. "No 'we' this time, Charli. I need to start this journey alone. Besides, as Jack said, he needs some deniability on something like this. I need to get on the inside of Newmerica, starting in Philadelphia. If I'm not successful, you'll be left with a military solution."

Jack drew a deep breath and offered his view. "We will win on that front, but it will cost tens of thousands of lives and leave much of the country in ruins."

"But you can't go in there alone," Charli protested. "They know you. She'll surround herself with other operatives. If *we* know she's so important to their cause, so will she. The woman's not a fool—Jack said as much. She'll be expecting some sort of attack."

"I made it personal when I killed her mother and brother," Caylee said. "She won't just have me killed if I'm caught. She'll demand retribution. She'll torture me."

"How can you be so cold and rational about that?" Charli demanded.

"I'm not looking forward to being captured. I need to find a way to turn her hate of me to our advantage in case something goes wrong."

"Caylee," Jack said in a lower tone of voice, "I know I'm asking a lot. You can say no. No one is going to hold that against you. But if it will save lives, it's our best shot."

She took in his words and processed them slowly. *Charli is right—the odds are against me. Andy would tell me not to fight the math and to abort.* Other thoughts tore at her from her past. *I've done a lot of things that were evil. I didn't question them; it was all about following orders. Now I have a chance to clear my slate, to wipe my board clean. If I can take the VP out of the game, this war will collapse.*

"I'm in," she said after a few moments. "I'll make sure that the convention falls apart, and I will take out their leadership."

"Then this conversation never took place," Jack replied. "We are both moving into uncharted territory here."

"There are resources I will need."

"Handle it all through me personally. Our president doesn't need to know about this. I'm expendable. He isn't." In other words, the American president was unaware of Desmond's plans. This wasn't like Jack Desmond. She liked his new attitude. *Being the target of an assassin himself, he realizes how precarious his life and the fate of the country are. This war is as costly as hell. People are dying everywhere. Taking out the VP is the hammer shot. It could end the war quickly.*

"I'd be glad to take on this mission," Caylee said. "But understand this: there are always unintended consequences to such actions. Just as someone trying to kill you set this in motion, there are bound to be some things that happen as a result of this that we can't anticipate."

"I know," Jack replied. "But the opportunity cost of not doing this is thousands dying in a war we never wanted."

Caylee drew a deep breath. *This is going to be much harder than I positioned it. Much harder...*

Chapter 2

Seventeenth Amendment: The right of clean energy

The population has a right to energy that is clean and produced by the government for consumption. Energy will be allocated according to the needs of the state and guidelines that the FedGov will publish.

Minneapolis, Minnesota

Deja Jordan looked at the plain black casket that held her mother as it was lowered into the ground. Her sisters stood on the other side of the casket, giving her icy glances between wipes of their tears. Deja felt their anger toward her, and it only made the inner turmoil she felt boil within her soul even more furiously.

She had been at the top of the world months ago, having arrested the domestic terrorist Raul Lopez. *Time* and *Newsweek* had featured her on their covers. She had been interviewed on *The View* and countless other news programs. The vice president had congratulated her personally for her heroism. Deja's career had tanked. She had gone from being a good Social Enforcer to an iconic symbol for the Newmerican cause. Her family had benefited from her fame. The government had granted her a mansion in the exclusive Lowry Hill neighborhood in Minneapolis, liberated by the local SEs from some undeserving family. Deja had moved her mother, sisters, and their families into the sprawling home. She basked in the glory she had brought to her family and friends.

That all ended with the prison breakout.

Caylee-fucking-Leatrom and a group of her terrorist friends had done the impossible. They had broken into the Supermax prison and released Raul and another high-profile prisoner. Deja had been badly injured in the gun battle that took place. It brought about an immediate fall from grace. She had lost her A-Class government healthcare rating, demoted to D-Class. The doctors didn't do much in the way of corrective surgery for the gunshot wound in her right hand. Two of her fingers were curled inward permanently as a result. Her artificial knee, another remnant of the gunfight with the terrorists, left her with a slight limp, mostly due to the fact that only two weeks of therapy were covered by the FedGov insurance because of her D-Class rating. Even as she watched the coffin being lowered into the ground, she felt a dull ache in her knee, a constant reminder of her failure.

The minister's words were a jumble in her mind as he finished. Her mother's death from cancer had been mercifully swift, but that had done nothing to lessen Deja's anguish. As the group of mourners broke up, her sister, Kammi, came over to her. Kammi's face was angry rather than sad. "You got a big damn pair of low-hangers a'comin' here," Kammi snarled, her angry street jive fully engaged.

"She was my momma too."

"Because of you, we didn't qualify for the good casket! She died because of you, Deja!"

It was an argument that she had heard in the last week; one that she refused to accept. "She died of cancer. You know that."

"She died in a shack, with shit for healthcare. If you'd done your job, we wouldn't have been kicked out of that mansion. Momma had to fend for herself. Eatin' charity food. You saw the place she ended up living in. It was a dump. She got sick living there."

There was truth in what Kammi said, which made her words hurt. After Deja's fall from grace, they had evicted her family from the mansion. Deja had managed to find a SE-liberated home, but it was nothing at all like the posh living they had been enjoying. The little ranch had belonged to a conservative newspaper reporter who had been sent off to Social Quarantine. It was drafty, ill-kept, and despite being small, it was more than her mother could care for. Deja had tried to help her, but her mother insisted that she had everything under control.

"Don't you try to lay the blame on me," Deja said in a snappy tone of voice back at her sister. "I didn't see you doing anything to help out." Deja held her voice in control, not allowing herself to drift into a yelling match. That control was what separated her from her sister.

"We aren't privileged enough to have a job like you had," Kammi snapped. "If it wasn't for reparation points and assistance, we would have been in a worse situation than Momma." Her use of the word "privileged" hurt. *That's the kind of language we use as social enforcers! I'm not privileged. I worked for everything I've gotten.*

"Being in that house had nothing to do with Momma's cancer coming back, and you know it," Deja said louder than she had expected, causing some of the stragglers at the funeral to turn their heads to listen. "And don't you dare lecture me on privilege. I put a roof over your sorry ass when you had nothing."

"If you hadn't let that fuckin' spic go, we'd all still be living together, high on the hong" Kammi retorted.

Deja held out her gnarled right hand. "Take a good look. I didn't *let* anyone go. I got shot—twice. I'm damned lucky they didn't kill me."

"All I know is that we were living the high life until you screwed up. The next thing we knew, our FedGov benefits were all downgraded, and we were told we had to find a new place to live. None of that helped Momma at all."

Deja wanted to tell Kammi she was wrong, but deep down, she knew that being forced out of the mansion had been traumatic for their mother. She had been so proud of Deja when she was on all the news shows and in magazines. The mansion they had been moved into wasn't just a home—it was a symbol of her success. When that had been taken from her family, it had been hard and painful. Everyone blamed her for what had happened, and that was a difficult feeling to shake. "I tried my damnedest to prevent Lopez from getting away. His team poisoned us, every guard in that prison. I was walking down the hall with my own shit oozing out of my pants—that's how hard I was trying. And I paid a price for my failure."

"You didn't. We all did," Kammi replied coldly.

"This is a funeral," Deja said, reining in her loud voice. "Momma wouldn't want us fighting like this."

"What do you know about what she would want and what she wouldn't? You were on the road, all over the country, doing whatever it is you did. We were home with her, taking care of her."

"In a house that I provided."

"For how long? A few months? We all got booted after you got out of the hospital. You were so focused on yourself, you didn't even help with the move."

"I wasn't focused? Screw you. I was recovering." Deja waved her hand between them. "In case you haven't noticed, I'm permanently injured."

"Oh, I know. You bring it up all the time. Rena and I don't have a bit of pity for you. You keep playing up that you're a victim, but you had everything, and we didn't. When you lost it, who did it hurt the most? Us!"

Deja's lip quivered, if only for a few moments, as she faced her past head-on. When Deja had gotten out of the hospital, she had been depressed. The pain was horrible, and still was. Her painkillers were addictive, and she was hooked, but there was no alternative. The injuries in her hand were a constant reminder of her failure. There had been times when she had wished that Leatrom had killed her rather than leaving her maimed the way she was. "I did the best I could."

"Well, it wasn't good enough."

"I'm your sister. We're family. We need to support each other."

"Momma was always so proud of you. You were her favorite."

"That's not true."

"Shit! It was. Don't you go denying it. When you fell in with the SEs, she was so happy. 'Deja is out there sticking it to the people who have held us back!' We all heard her say it. She thought the world of you. Then when you got us all in that mansion, she rubbed our noses in your success every day. It tore her apart to be forced to move out there."

Deja was ashamed, angry, and sad. Each emotion clamored for dominance inside her, but instead they were a blur, churned together in her mind. Kammi was ungrateful, but she was also hurting. Deja felt the need to say something in response, but everything that came to mind only seemed to make things worse. She finally settled on two words that might help. "I'm sorry."

Kammi glared at her. "That doesn't change a thing." She pivoted and walked away, leaving Deja alone at the gravesite.

* * *

Two hours later, Deja found herself sitting at the People's Tribunal, still wearing her black funeral attire. She was markedly overdressed compared to the other members of the tribunal. She had been numb since the confrontation with her sister. The family had gone out for dinner afterward, but she had opted not to go. It would only have rekindled the argument with her sister. *Momma wouldn't want us to fight. I accomplished that by not going.*

The tribunals were now as common as when the Ruling Council took power. The difference was the targets. With the war not going in Newmerica's favor at the moment, many SEs were attempting to flee or go into hiding. From her perspective, they hadn't done anything wrong—rounding up and prosecuting threats to the state, sending them off to Social Quarantine or execution.

In her eyes, they were cowards. They feared an American victory and retribution. She looked out from her elevated seat on the stage down at the five SEs who had been apprehended in Chokio. They averted their gaze from the tribunal members, looking at the floor of the school gym where the proceedings were taking place. *They never really believed in Newmerica.*

Wilson Jacobs, who sat next to her, spoke up. "You were apprehended in a camper, heading for South Dakota without travel papers. It is clear that your intent was to defect."

One of the women spoke up. "We were just looking to go camping. We weren't running."

Deja cut in. "Your SE unit is in Minneapolis. There are a lot of places for you to camp outside the city. You were apprehended by a *loyal* SE team on the road heading for the American lines. Don't compound what you've done by lying."

"This is all a misunderstanding," the skinny man spoke up from the defectors' ranks.

"Indeed it is," the tribunal leader, Jumbie Hart, said. "As Social Enforcers, you were expected to do your duty. Instead, you turned on the cause. You tried to flee like rats on a sinking ship."

The woman on the far end of the accused started to cry. Deja was unmoved. The toxic mix of emotions from her mother's funeral earlier was still bottled up in her mind and was now seeping out in the tribunal. "Stop your crying. You are only confirming what we've already suspected—your guilt."

"We are not traitors," the tall man said. "We've done good work for the cause. From the very start, we rounded up extremists and enemies of the state."

Deja leaned forward. "Yet you ran when you were needed the most."

Jumbie spoke up. "Given what you had in your camper and where you were found, your guilt is apparent." She surveyed the other members of the tribunal. Deja gave her vote in the form of a slow nod. "Very well. This tribunal has found you guilty. You have betrayed your duties and Newmerica. Your execution will be tomorrow and will be publicly shown. You will serve as a lesson for anyone else who might find themselves questioning their loyalties. It will be your final duty to the state."

Before any of them could try to plead, the NSF guard came in and ushered them out. Deja sighed. Killing SEs only left them weaker, but letting such traitors live was something she couldn't stomach either. *There have been too many of these tribunals lately. Every week, we're killing more SEs than the enemy.*

She got up and stepped down from the stage. A fellow SE walked forward and handed her a folded note. "You got a message. I was going to pass it to you earlier, but I knew you wouldn't be long."

Deja unfolded the paper. *Deja, report immediately to the office of the vice president for a special assignment.*

Despite the events of the day, she suddenly felt a surge of excitement. *The vice president! Is my time in purgatory over? Is this a shot at redemption? This time I won't fail!*

Fort Wayne, Indiana

Braylon Ironsides shifted on the inflatable mattress in the tiny flat he now called home. Myriad old aches and pains protested as he did so, reminders of the last few years. The blanket he used was old, and he snugged it up tight against his face, giving him a false sense of security. The Salvation

Army was the source of most of his clothing and bedding. His two roommates were like him, freed from Social Quarantine camps and suddenly dumped back into society.

America was back in control of Indiana, which had probably saved his life. The SEs who ran his camp had begun to kill the inmates systematically. They ran out of bullets in one day, which was one of the reasons he had likely been spared. Hangings took the place of guns, but the SEs were far from efficient, something he was thankful for. When the word came that the state had returned to the American fold, the SEs boogied out, leaving the prisoners half-starved and confused.

Resisting was met with beatings and a cutoff of food—not that the food they were provided was plentiful or nutritious. The prisoners were fed propaganda pumped in via videos and pseudo-classes. It began with each of them being forced to confess their biases and continued into the virtues of supporting the Newmerican government.

Braylon had relied on his faith in God to get through, though it was constantly tested and under threat. Praying was an offense, so it had to be done out of sight of even his fellow prisoners. Inmates in Social Quarantine were regularly rewarded for turning in their peers who might violate any one of the dozens of rules. It didn't matter if the offense was real or not—some simply wanted the extra serving of food or the very rare right to call a loved one.

The six times in four years that he had spoken to Delores became hard for him to bear. She had been evicted from their home by the Social Enforcers, kicked out with only what she could carry. She had gone to their daughter's house, and her health started to fail. The new government-run health care was far from helpful. When she became stricken with lung cancer, they gave her painkillers rather than the surgery she needed. By the time they started chemo, the cancer had spread to her bones and eventually her brain. Braylon's daughter told him it wasn't the cancer that killed her but the chemo. He had asked for permission to leave the camp and attend Delores's funeral, but got laughed at by the camp leader instead.

He resisted their reeducation at first, but that brought him pain from the Enforcers. Then he pretended to play their game. Braylon said the words they wanted him to recite. He read their books, watched their films, and pretended that they were changing his values. Over time, he started to question what he really believed. Slowly, methodically, they were eroding his thinking, blurring the line between the two realities of the country. There were times when he was confused, not sure if what he believed was based on his own values or the ones they were drilling into his senses.

For the most part, the inmates were well-behaved. A few were thugs. Once a week or so, he went without food because they threatened him. Their behavior encouraged some of their targets to squeal to the guards about them. Sometimes the brutes were beaten as a result—sometimes the informants were.

There were escape attempts. The camps had been cobbled together in the first place, built with cheap lumber and materials often assembled by people who lacked carpentry skills. The Social Enforcers were not trained guards; they were more like members of a gang. Despite the abundance of barbed wire and fences, some prisoners tried to get away. When they attempted to escape, the SE's solution was to punish the entire prison population. One midwinter night after an escape, they lined them all up and sprayed them with fire hoses. He was sure he contracted pneumonia. They had isolated him in a building they called a hospital, but it was really just another bunkhouse. How he survived that illness was still beyond him. Maybe it was the prayers or his willpower. It was the last escape attempt at the camp. When someone plotted to leave, the other prisoners would turn them in rather than face cruel punishment themselves.

The reconstituted American government wasn't prepared for the liberation of the prisoners—that much was clear. All had health issues on top of their mental issues. The reeducation process the Newmericans put them through was a mixture of physical abuse and outright indoctrination. Upon Braylon's release, he talked to a counselor who told him he was suffering from PTSD, which was, in his mind, useless information. She offered him a prescription, something he couldn't afford.

His former employer didn't have any job openings. They were on the verge of going out of business themselves. Braylon's retirement account still existed, though it took weeks to convince them that he was who he claimed to be. When he saw the balance, he was stunned. Newmerica had taxed it heavily. They plundered such accounts from those in Social Quarantine, all for the alleged greater good.

Homeless. Jobless. Penniless. Mentally broken. Together, these defined who he was for a long time. Eventually, he was able to secure a job at a small munitions plant. They built bombs for aerial drones. There were a lot of hobby drones that were being pressed into the war effort. The small incendiary and explosive ordnance he helped build could be dropped on the Newmerican forces in the field. While he hadn't worked with his hands throughout his career, he found his job rewarding. He indulged in fantasies that each completed bomb killed the people who had ruined his life, and that was better than any medication the counselor might offer him. He found the work rewarding as well. As a consultant, he had struggled to see the results of his work. In the factory, at the end of the day, he saw his output.

It was Saturday, which meant no work. For someone with no computer, no television, and little money, it was not something he looked forward to. His plans for the day were as Spartan as his flat: go to the library and get on the computer to check the news and email, then visit his wife's grave. He rolled off his mattress, which had a tiny leak that left it half-inflated by the time he woke up. He showered and trimmed his beard. Before Social Quarantine, he had never worn a beard. During his time in the camp, it was not an option. Looking in the mirror, he saw the gray in his facial hair. His hairline was receding too, back nearly four inches from the days before the so-called Liberation.

The walk to the library was invigorating. Breakfast consisted of an apple purchased at Kroger and a small pack of crackers that he nibbled on during his stroll. There were two people ahead of him at the library. He checked his email and got little more than threatening spam sent from Newmerica. It was commonplace for people to receive a steady stream of disinformation from the enemy. Big Tech had crawled into bed with the traitors who had overthrown the government and were persistent, if nothing else.

His check of the news on the net was encouraging. The war seemed to be going America's way. New Mexico had fallen, and the Army was in Arizona. St. Louis was holding out, but a recent cutback on their food supplies held the promise that they might surrender. The victory in New Hampshire was the best news of all. The new temporary governor, Su-Hui Zhou, had convinced Maine to return to America, and a huge swath of New York State capitulated out of fear of invasion. There was a part of Braylon that wanted to be there when they fell. *They've taken so much from me. I'd love to be there when the traitors face justice.* Before his time in the camp, he was not a man given to violence. *They changed me. Now I find myself wanting it constantly.*

It had been the theme of his latest op-ed. *The Journal Gazette* ran his articles. They didn't pay much, but it was a nice addition to his day job. Braylon wrote about what life was really like in Social Quarantine and his desire to see justice befall the architects of the downfall. In some ways, his writing the articles bordered on fantasies he had. The VP, in particular, was the target of his ire. She controlled the TRC, their propaganda machine, the SEs, and the NSF. He had never met her, but Braylon saw her as responsible for what had happened to him, as if she had been there giving the orders herself. It was going to be the theme of his new article, *The Demon.* He planned on writing it Sunday afternoon when the library had fewer people, and he could get more time on the public computers.

When he finished, he walked to Concordia Lutheran Cemetery as dark clouds began to gather. He knew the path to Delores's gravesite from memory. When he reached it, he pulled a weed that had dared to sprout over his wife's remains. Kneeling on the grass, he looked at the plain grave marker that simply bore her name and the years of her birth and death.

"Delores, you deserved better than this. You died alone, all because the government hated me. You always said that those articles were going to excite the wrong people in the wrong ways. You were right. I wish I could have been with you." Tears ran down his cheeks as he spoke to her. "I wish I'd been the kind of husband you deserved."

He stared intently at the grave marker, wishing she could send him some sort of sign. None came. Closing his eyes, he prayed. The only sound he heard was birds chirping and fluttering away in the trees above him. He rose slowly, his knees protesting his movement, and headed back to his flat.

As he reached the street he lived on, Braylon glanced across it and saw a familiar man walking. His gait was distinct: short, fast steps, hands thrust in his pants pockets as he moved. It was a guard from his time in the camp. The man didn't seem to notice him, but Braylon remembered him. He had come at Braylon one night with a broom handle. He had sodomized him that night. No reason was given, nor did anyone come to his aid, despite his cries for help. Everyone knew that to get involved would have resulted in them getting the same treatment, if not worse.

Freckles... we all called him Freckles. His red hair and peppering of freckles had earned the guard his nickname. Braylon thought it was too kind. It made him sound less threatening. He still remembered the night the man forced the broom handle between his buttocks and tore at him. There had been a struggle, but it was one-sided. The broom handle hitting Braylon's jaw had chipped a tooth. Only recently had he gotten it fixed, costing him a full week's pay.

The memories of that night were something he had tried to suppress. Now they came back. His face was hot, and his palms instantly started to sweat as his breathing became faster. That guard had done unspeakable things to him that night, simply because he could. Anger surged in him, a hate that he didn't even realize he still possessed. *I want him dead!Why is he still in town? They told us that the guards all fled the area.Is he stalking me, and I was just lucky enough to get the drop on him?* All of the questions and emotions tore at Braylon at once. Somehow, he managed to maintain his composure and calm.

His jaw set, he followed the man from across the street, matching his pace. When the former guard turned into a small café, Braylon moved outside. As he waited, he saw a police officer walking slowly on patrol. "Hey, officer!" he called out. "Come here!"

The younger man trotted over. "What's the problem, sir?"

"Inside. There's a man with a gray coat and a black ball cap. He was a Newmerican guard at my Social Quarantine camp."

The officer stiffened at those words. "Are you certain?"

Braylon nodded rapidly, his teeth clenching. "I'd know him anywhere."

For a fleeting moment, he feared that the officer might do nothing. The younger man seemed to hesitate. Braylon eyed the officer's pistol at his hip. *Let me have your gun. I'll save you the time and expense of a trial.* Finally, the officer pulled out his radio and called for backup. "Sir, I need you to step around the corner. We'll handle this."

A police SUV pulled up. The NAF logo had been spray-painted over with white paint and replaced with a decal for the Fort Wayne Police Department. Two more officers got out and were briefed by the younger man. One moved past

Braylon, no doubt heading to the rear of the café. Two officers entered from the front at once, moving quickly.

Deep down, Braylon wanted the guard to resist. He was hoping for a confrontation. He wanted the police to shoot the guard. *Give me a gun—I'll do it!*

They forced him out roughly. Braylon stepped out enough to be seen. The guard didn't even seem to notice him as they pushed him into the back of their vehicle. The younger officer came over to him. "We're going to need you to come down with us and give a statement."

"I will. But I won't ride with him… not after what he's done to me."

The officer glanced at the SUV and its prisoner, then back to Braylon. "I understand. I'll stay with you until we get another car here."

"Thank you," he managed as his torrent of emotions waned.

"I'm glad you spotted him," the officer offered. "If he's who you say he is, we can't have people like him wandering around. Former Newmericans cause a lot of trouble."

"I don't know about that. I just know he was a guard at our camp." Braylon hoped that he wouldn't have to tell what the guard had done to him. It was humiliating. He also didn't want the man to go free. His inner rage slowly eroded his shame. *Whatever it takes. Freckles can't be on the streets, not after all the things he's done.*

Gold Canyon, Arizona

Darius Thorne wondered why anyone would want to live in Arizona. It was hot and dusty. The landscape was ugly, at least to him. The wide valley of Gold Canyon did nothing to improve his opinion. From where he stood, behind a Bradley fighting vehicle nestled in the rocks along the road, he could barely make out the shimmers of enemy troops adjusting their positions.

"Look at 'em scurry," Corporal Manchester said at his side. "Your old buddies don't have the testicles for this kind of fight, I guess."

"They ain't my buddies." Darius scowled. *Not anymore.*

"I don't know. I heard that's where some of the Veteran Volunteer Corps are positioned. You going to be okay shooting at them?"

It was a common jab at his loyalties. That didn't make him resent it any less. Darius had been coerced into joining the California Veterans Corps under the threat of losing his benefits. They had been thrown into the fighting in Texas and had been driven out of the state. In his mind, the Corps deserved it. *We had no business going into that state and thinking we could force them to surrender.*

He had seen several of his comrades die. It was the cartels from Mexico that had saved them, only adding to their humiliation. Ultimately, he and a few of his colleagues walked away, heading into America.

Their ordeal had just begun. There were concerns that they might be deliberate plants, infiltrators posing as deserters. They had been separated and then vigorously interrogated. In his case, they polygraphed him. Darius had passed easily. He was a man who had nothing to hide. They had asked if he was willing to fight against Newmerica, and he said he would. The words flew out of his mouth without any hesitation. They had thrown him and the Volunteer Corps into a fight they could not win, and because of them, good people were dead. Darius had surprised himself with his response.

He had come to realize what a corrupt state California had become. Their solution to drug-related crime was to hand out drugs to users so they wouldn't have to rob people. They corralled the homeless in tiny towns, little more than sheds. These became run down in a matter of weeks. The problem was never homelessness—that was a symptom. People with mental illness and drug addiction couldn't take care of themselves, let alone a home.

California had embraced social justice with vigor. It was a way to punish the rich, to take their homes and cars from them. It played well to people who felt that the divide in wealth and status was someone else's fault. The people who were sent to Social Quarantine never seemed to come back. Everyone knew what the implications were, that they were death camps, but no one spoke out about them. To do so ensured that you would join those who had been deemed guilty of some unspoken and undocumented crime. While Californians basked in the belief that they were a progressive utopia, the stark reality was that the cities and their infrastructure were corrupt, run down, and crime ridden. No one complained because, in some way or another, everyone was receiving money from the state or the FedGov, and none were willing to rock that boat. Darius had come to hate the state that had cost him his friends, his business, and people's lives.

Joining the American fighting force brought him the disdain of those who didn't trust him. He had been placed in a militia unit, two combined groups from the Sons of Liberty. Their formal name was the 51st Freedom Militia. His new comrades were unsure where his loyalties lay, despite his polygraph results. It was hard to blame them; a few weeks earlier, he had been shooting at them.

"All right," Sergeant Howell, his NCO, called out. "We're going to advance on them. The Purebloods are on our right. We're going in supporting the fighting vehicles." As if the Bradley in front of Darius heard his words, it fired up its engine, rumbling to life.

He clutched the AR-15 that had been provided to him, pulling it tight against his body armor. The Bradley started to advance, emerging from its cover. Almost immediately, the high-pitched pinging of bullets started echoing off its armor. Darius moved farther to the rear of the vehicle as it returned fire.

"Holy shit!" said a private hunched over next to him.

"First time?" Darius asked, walking slowly behind the Bradley as it fired a trio of rounds from its turret. The explosions in the distance were joined by controlled bursts of machine-gun fire from the Newmericans.

"Yeah. I was in Junior ROTC in high school." ROTC hadn't existed for a few years, courtesy of the government in the District.

It wasn't the biggest endorsement Darius had ever heard. "Stick close to me."

The Bradley moved forward about fifty yards, and the fire picked up, rattling and dinging off it. Darius checked his weapon, eased out around the cover of the vehicle, and looked for flashes to show where the gunfire was coming from. It was everywhere in the canyon, as if every boulder and rock were spitting fire. Aiming quickly, he squeezed off two rounds each at three different targets. It wasn't much, but it was suppression fire. *Why should we be having all the fun?* When he emptied his magazine, he recoiled to cover.

The machine guns weren't from the volunteers—he knew that from experience. *It's got to be the National Guard.* Looking some thirty yards to his right, he saw the Marines, the Purebloods, keeping low, coming up behind another Bradley. Beyond them was a unit of the Kansas National Guard, darting between rocks for cover. It was the Purebloods who had his attention. Their reputation preceded them. The fighting at Cannon Air Force Base had been fairly brutal, but they had prevailed. As he reloaded, Darius wondered if he was about to witness their prowess.

The Bradley in front of him accelerated, the main gun banging out rounds at the enemy lines that were getting closer with each burst of fire. Sergeant Howell edged out alongside the vehicle opposite Darius and provided close support fire. A machine-gun burst pinged off the Bradley, and Darius saw the sergeant crumble. A corporal grabbed him, pulling him back to cover.

"Sergeant!" Darius called over. "You okay?"

He held up his hand, and it was covered in blood. "Do I fucking look okay?"

"Get him to the rear," Darius barked. Two privates responded, grabbing the sergeant by the arms and knees and rushing him back. Darius felt all eyes on him, but only for a moment. *They're looking for someone to lead them. It might as well be me.* An explosion went off as something slammed into the Bradley in front of them. Hot shrapnel flew over his head, and billowing black smoke rolled over them. The support troops pulled back from where they had been providing cover.

Darius moved around the Bradley's rear and saw that the right tread was destroyed. The firing from the turret had not stopped. It banged out, blasting the trench line that was some forty yards ahead. The troops there rose and fled, heading back to their rear.

The crew is still alive, but this Bradley isn't going anywhere. "What do we do?" Corporal Omer asked him. Darius's eyes darted over to where the Purebloods were getting ready to break out and seize the now-abandoned trench line.

"We do our job," he replied. "Toss some smoke out toward the trench. Follow me, and you might still get out of this alive."

Omer nodded, pulling a smoke grenade as explosions echoed off in the distance at the far end of the canyon. Omer's toss was good, and the smoke grenade billowed out a dense gray visual barrier. Darius looked at the rest of the squad huddled behind the crippled Bradley. "Low and fast!" With that, he rushed out, firing a few shots in the direction of the enemy, if only to get them to duck.

As the smoke dissipated, he found himself in front of the trench. He jumped in, surprised to find a uniformed member of his former unit, the Veteran Corps, curled up in a tight ball. Looking at the frightened man, he saw nothing but terror in his eyes. Darius reached down and grabbed his weapon, tossing it off to the side. "You make a move against us, and you're toast. Got it?"

The man nodded.

"Good. Raise your hands and walk toward our lines. If you so much as fart funny, you're dead." The curled-up man slowly rose, trembling and complying.

Darius stood just enough to look in the direction of the rest of the enemy force. What he saw was a number of troops fleeing or dodging behind every bit of cover they could find. Beyond them, in the small roadside town, explosions were going off, belching long, ugly streams of black smoke into the sky.

A few shots rang out in his direction, which he returned, hitting rocks and sand more than anything else. The rest of his squad fired as well. Farther down the line, the Purebloods were advancing beyond the trench, pressing toward the enemy. *Well, I ain't going to stay here while they go off and do that.* "All right, we advance by twos. Everyone else, provide cover fire."

He rose out of the trench, shots peppering the dirt around him. He aimed for a pile of rocks off to the right, moving diagonally and keeping low. Private Tilson was with him, hugging the rocks for dear life as they dove behind them. Shots ricocheted off the stones. Waiting for a moment, he rolled to the left, aimed, and fired. The shot caught his target dead center, dropping him in place. Tilson's shots cracked off to his right as the team slowly moved forward in pairs, almost leapfrog style.

Shots from the Bradley they had left continued to rain down on the Newmerican troops, adding to the carnage downrange. Explosions tore into the ranks, two of which devoured an entire fire team that was attempting to redeploy.

As he rolled back, he saw one of the Purebloods rise with a Carl Gustaf 8.4 cm recoilless rifle. The shot cut through the dust and smoke in the air, destroying one of the boulders. Darius saw an arm spinning skyward from the blast, flopping down on the desert floor. *If I hadn't changed sides, that could have been me!*

Another trio of explosions from the town in the distance echoed around him. He and Tilson rose and darted for a low pile of stones some twenty yards forward and to the left. Sliding on the sand and stones reminded him of diving for third base as a kid, only rougher. Angling around the edge of the pile, he fired several bursts, emptying his magazine. Pulling back, he reloaded as the dust stung the corners of his eyes.

The Bradley had been silent for a few long moments and now rejoined the fight, spraying the positions with its 25 mm M242 Bushmaster. Rocks were devoured in explosions.

Then he saw it—a torn piece of white cloth tied to the end of the rifle barrel, hoisted from behind a rock formation. Gunfire still cracked up and down the line. Then another white flag rose, only to catch a bullet. *They're really surrendering?*

Tilson fired a few rounds, but Darius's voice stopped him from firing more. "Squad, hold your fire."

An officer from the Purebloods gave the same order. The Bradleys must have seen the flags, and they too stopped unleashing death and destruction on the opposing force. Darius summoned his last reserve of courage and slowly stood, exposing himself to potential enemy fire. "All right, you people, toss out your weapons and hold your hands over your heads!"

It started slowly, with two or three people complying, then it grew exponentially with the soldiers who had been in front of him. The Purebloods moved forward and started patting down the prisoners, lining them up, gathering their weapons.

Darius walked forward, and his people joined in, helping with the disarming. The officer in the Purebloods moved over next to him. "Nice work," he said. Darius saw that the captain's name was Dolio, according to his name tag.

"They folded pretty fast," Darius replied.

"Yeah. They got hit in the rear door while we hit the front. You surround an inexperienced enemy, and they'll do just about anything to make the fighting end."

One of the prisoners was from his former unit. "Darius?"

"That's right."

"You fucking traitor!" the man said as he was forced past them.

Captain Dolio cocked an eyebrow as Darius turned to face him. "I was with the Veteran Corps until that shit went down in Texas."

"That guy was pissed."

Darius nodded. "That's his problem."

"Well, I have no doubts about your loyalty. I saw you fight," Dolio said, then stepped away.

As Darius watched the line of surrendering troops walk past, their heads hung low in bitter shame at having fought for a losing cause. *I made the right choice. We were being thrown into fights we weren't prepared for. They used us to do their dirty work. Even our name was a lie. We didn't volunteer—we were forced to fight for them.*

As they passed, one of the Marines of the Purebloods jabbed the butt of his weapon into the stomach of the prisoner. Darius stepped over to him, resting his hand on the Pureblood's weapon. "Don't do that."

"They're turncoats. He fought against the rightful government," the Marine replied. "They're lucky we aren't shooting them."

Darius shook his head. "They chose the wrong side. Now they're our prisoners, and that makes them Americans again."

The Marine shot a glance at his commanding officer, Captain Dolio, who had walked up beside Darius. "The man is right.

Show the prisoners respect." He then turned to Darius. "Good call."

"I know he was your man, but he was wrong. When the war is over, it's going to take a lot to heal all of the bad feelings. No point in making more of them."

"We can finish up here," Dolio said. "See to your people."

Darius gave him a nod, shouldered his rifle, and followed the long train of prisoners to the rear.

Chapter 3

Fourteenth Amendment: The Right to Ethical and Balanced Information

News outlets and posters on the internet must have their stories approved by the Truth Reconciliation Committee to ensure they are free from disinformation.

Arnold, Missouri

Major Judy Mercury looked at the map of St. Louis and felt her stomach tightening with each passing moment. The commandeered classroom in the school the Americans were using as their forward base felt increasingly small to her. With all of the officers in the room, claustrophobia nibbled at her nerves. The décor was still that of an elementary school. The Newmerican flags had been taken down, and the desks and chairs were piled neatly in the corner, but it was still a child's school. *Maybe when the fighting is over, it can be that again.*

St. Louis was a tough nut to crack. Since the start of the Civil War, the Newmericans had been entrenching there. Rumors were that they had stockpiled food to wait out a siege. They had a lot of force, mostly in the form of Social Enforcers and a few National Guard units.

As she eyed the map's details, she tried to ignore the reality that General Reager had given her St. Louis as a target. "I hate to give you this one, but you're the only one for the job," he'd told her. "It's a complex task, given I can't afford to give you more than a couple of regiments to pull it off."

The problem was insurmountable for many. Mercury saw it as a challenge. While she loved a good puzzle, this one was giving her a headache. *I can't even secure the city with two regiments of troops, let alone take it by force.* For three days, she struggled with the problem, then called in help in the form of Lieutenant Colonel Mihalek from the Oklahoma National Guard. He had helped her plan her boldest operations. A fresh set of eyes might be the key to figuring out her dilemma.

"Clearly, a conventional assault is out of the question," Mihalek said as he surveyed the map she had been focused on.

"You've got that right. Urban combat always favors the defenders."

"We could starve them out," he offered. "We did that in Atlanta."

Mercury shook her head. "The president doesn't want that, at least not wholesale. He's already looking down the road to when the war is over and the country needs to pull back together. Apparently, starving rebels into submission doesn't fit into his plans."

"Understandable," Mihalek said, crossing his arms in several moments of silent thought. "Maybe we are looking at this from the wrong perspective."

"What do you mean?"

His hand waved over the map on the table. "We're looking at this from the view of us conquering the city."

"That's the mission."

The lieutenant colonel nodded. "Look at this from the perspective of the citizens of St. Louis."

She paused. "They probably feel trapped. Everywhere around them has returned to American control."

"Do you think they are solidly behind the SEs and officials who are telling them to hold out?"

It was a good question, one that required a moment of thought. "Not really. They are likely in survival mode. As long as they have the basics, they do what they are told. From what I've seen in the intelligence reports, only a minority of people are really Newmerican diehards. Most of the followers are moochers. As long as they get their grift, they play along."

"So, they are hostages," Mihalek said. "They don't know it, but they are."

"How do we use that to our advantage?"

"Do we know who the ringleaders are, the leaders who are calling the shots?"

Mercury nodded. "We have people on the inside who get us information. One Sons of Liberty cell, the Hole in the Wall Gang, has been in there from the start. Yes, we have a list of names."

"Maybe the solution isn't a siege. Maybe if their leaders were to be removed, the citizens would simply invite us in. After all, they just want the necessities. They aren't behind Newmerica—they just want to survive."

Mercury soaked in every word he said, her eyes still locked on the map. "The president didn't want us to cut off all of their food and medicine. There's a lot of ground between a total cutoff and doing nothing. What if we don't cut it all off? Instead, what if we just reduce it?"

"I thought they had food stockpiled for that contingency."

"We blow their food warehouses up. Targeting them should be easy, and these bozos would never see it coming. After that, we allow in enough food for them to survive, but still be hungry. Hungry and angry. That way, we honor what the president wants but cause strife and conflict within their ranks."

"The reaction of those in power will be to hoard it and try to control its distribution. Like most petty dictators, they will siphon off food for themselves first. It's an old game."

She smiled, leaning over the map and holding herself up with her hands planted on it. "That's exactly what they will do. But when people get hungry, they get aggressive. We've seen it all over the world in times of crisis. When the UN food trucks arrive, they get swamped. Even the guys with guns can't fend off hundreds of hungry people. Organizing food distribution is probably way above the heads of these Social Enforcers. Before the Fall, they were gang leaders or college students hooked on protesting. The NSF is augmenting them, but by now, many of them see that this is only going to end one way, and their loyalty can't be relied on. We're military. Logistics is right up there with war-fighting. These folks don't know squat about how to manage it. It will get out of hand quickly."

"That causes strife but doesn't give us the city," Mihalek pointed out. He drew a long breath, then continued, "But we could make it turn against them."

"Go on."

The grin that crossed his face was that of someone who knew the answer to the next question on the test. "Your intel reports from our insiders. Do they have photos of the Newmerican leaders in the city?"

"Most of them. Why?"

"We plaster their pictures on the food packages, like wanted posters. We put it in black and white for the locals. If you want to get food and medicine again, turn these people over to us."

Judy then smiled. "I like it! Get them to turn on each other."

"That's the idea."

It's better than us fighting them—it's them fighting them. Her mind went into challenge mode, trying to find the flaws in the idea. "They'll see the wanted notices and pull them off the food before the citizens can lay eyes on them."

The lieutenant colonel shook his head. "They will eventually. We can get creative on that, though. We don't have to put the notices *on* the food packages. We can put many of them on the inside, especially the dry goods and things in boxes. They don't have to be big, either. We can make them baseball-card sized."

"And as we said earlier, they are not experts at food distribution. The trucks we do allow in will get swamped before they can pull off the notices," she added.

"The key to such an operation is to get the population to turn against the right people. As it is now, we are the baddies. We do this right, and the citizens will see the Newmericans as the bad guys."

"You got it. We can even offer bounties for turning over certain leaders. People love a chance at lining their pockets. It'll be like *The Hunger Games*, with the Newmericans in the roles of forced contestants." Judy rose to stand again. Suddenly, the big map didn't seem as daunting. "For us to execute this, we will need to coordinate with the SOL, who are operating in the city. We need good images of the targets, and we need to pinpoint all their food warehouses. Not to mention, I need to get this strategy cleared with General Reager." She knew Trip would love it. *This saves us from racking up a body count to take St. Louis and should leave most of the city intact.*

Three days later…

Matt McDonald of the Hole in the Wall was a short man, five feet three inches, but every bit of him was muscle. His face was in a constant scowl. Judy knew he wasn't mad at her—it was simply how the man always looked. "Tell me, Mr. McDonald. How are they reacting to the cutoff of food in the city?"

"The leadership is pissed, but they're doling out rations from their stockpiles. So far, the citizens are going along with the party line that this is inhumane treatment, blah, blah, blah," he replied.

"And have your people pinpointed all of their stockpiles?"

McDonald nodded. "We had pretty good ideas of where they were before this change. Now all you have to do is follow the trucks. The locals are doing the same thing. They line up outside of the warehouses now, starting first thing in the morning. With fresh food not coming in, they are nervous they might be cut off entirely. It has made finding these places easy." As he spoke, he unfolded an old map of St. Louis. There were red X's in a dozen locations sprinkled throughout the city.

As he flattened the map, Judy leaned in and looked at it. *We'll have to take them out at night. I'd like to avoid civilian casualties.*

"Are there any that you and your people think you can destroy better than we can?" Lieutenant Colonel Mihalek asked.

"Better? No. You've got big guns and bombs. But this one in Vandeventer—there's a lot of low-income housing right next to it. If one of your boom-booms is off by a few yards, they'll get a lot of press out of you killing civilians. We can take it out. With Molotov cocktails and a few sticks of dynamite, we can make it a fire that the department can't put out, but with minimal risk to the locals." McDonald's finger pointed at the location on the map.

General Reager had approved of her strategy. If it failed, it left her with wiggle room to try something else. She had arranged for a printer in Texas to produce the wanted poster cards that were being inserted into the food supply and had a group of volunteers hiding them in the reduced food shipments she intended to let through the blockade around the city. It was a slow process, but it was working. The irony that the Newmericans would be distributing their own reward notices to the public was something that made even Trip Reager chuckle.

"Can you pull off your attack tomorrow night?" she asked McDonald.

The stout man considered her request for a full second. "I don't see why not. It's not complicated. Security around those warehouses is almost nonexistent. This food crisis really hasn't started to make the population aggressive."

"That will change tomorrow night. Once they're cut off from food, they are bound to get edgy," she replied.

"That's an understatement," McDonald said. "They'll go into full-blown survival mode once they realize they're one hundred percent dependent on food coming in from America."

"Good. That's the first step of what we want. The second step is for them to take matters into their own hands. If they rise up and turn in the goons holding on to the city, their transition to returning to America is one of their choice, not us forcing it on them." *People accept change faster and easier when they convince themselves it was their idea to begin with.*

"Tomorrow night, then," McDonald said.

"We may need you to give us a battle damage assessment the following day," Mihalek said. "To make sure those warehouses are destroyed."

"Sir, it would be my pleasure. Does this operation have a name?"

Mihalek looked at Judy as she considered it. "Thunderbuns," she said, spouting the first name that came to her mind. For an instant, she both loved and regretted it.

"Finally, something I can remember," McDonald said, a thin smile crossing his face as he walked out.

Social Quarantine Camp AZ50, Camp Pelosi, Outside of Morenci, Arizona

Raul Lopez deployed his security team just outside the perimeter of Camp Pelosi. He had been liberating camps since the fall of New Mexico, and he knew that some of the Newmerican camps were well-guarded and that a few had even tried to put up a fight. The Social Enforcers who ran the Social Quarantine camps were generally not the best troops. Most of the time, after a few shots were exchanged, they either tried to flee or surrendered. Where the Americans were willing to die rescuing fellow citizens, the Newmericans were mostly cowards.

The camps were almost always positioned away from the cities. It was clear that the people who ran them didn't want the locals to know what was happening to the people there, beyond the propaganda that the TRC had put out. Raul had seen the ugly truth too many times now. They had started as punishment and reeducation. They had changed into forced labor camps over time. Then they had become death camps. It wasn't enough for the Newmericans to remove conservatives from their communities. Now they wanted them exterminated. Raul had come to the conclusion that it had probably been their goal all along, but with the civil war raging and their losing, they now accelerated their efforts. As he moved into position, Raul could smell the stench of death, of rotting flesh. It did more than make his stomach pitch—it infuriated him.

Pulling up his bullhorn, he turned it on and called out to the camp, "We have you surrounded. Surrender now, and you won't be hurt!" He said those words and hoped he could live up to them.

There was no callback from inside the camp. For Raul, it was simple. Either the guards were gone, or they were waiting in ambush. He had seen it in New Mexico, where the guards of one camp he had liberated had tried to use the prisoners as human shields. Things were no different in Arizona. That had ended in a bloody shootout, with no guards left alive to prosecute. He pulled out his Baofeng radio and switched to the channel of his sniper team. "Any sign of the guards?"

"Negative," came the voice of Tara, his lead sniper. "I think they've boogied. I see a few dead bodies in the yard. No movement otherwise."

The decision was his, and it weighed heavily on him. People could die on both sides. Then again, if he did nothing, prisoners might die. That thought alone made his choice easier. "We go in. Demonstrate at the rear of the camp, get their attention, then the rest of us will breach the front."

The gunfire began a few moments later, shots fired by the team at the rear. Raul moved out from cover and kept low, darting to the gate along with half a dozen of his team.

The gate was held shut by a chain and a Harbor Freight padlock. One of the team hit it with the butt of his rifle, and the lock popped free. As soon as the gate opened, Raul moved alongside the first building on the left, hugging it for cover as the rest of the team deployed inside the camp.

Moving forward, he came around the corner and saw a pair of dead bodies lying in the dirt. Both had been shot, one in the neck and one in the head. Flies buzzed around the dried blood and splattered brains in the dirt. Such an image would have made him throw up six months ago. Now he had sadly come to expect it.

The shots at the rear died down. He received word that they hadn't gotten a response from inside the camp, so he ordered them to cut their way through the barbed wire and inner fence. In a matter of ten minutes, his people were everywhere in the camp, checking buildings.

Raul joined one pair of his people opening a barracks door, sweeping it with their weapons. The stench was not rotting flesh, but human filth. It was so thick in the air that he could taste it. Bile rose in his throat. At first, he thought the barracks was empty. Then he saw movement. Not swift, violent movement. The crude wooden bunk beds shifted, and humans slowly began to emerge.

They looked like zombies. Their clothing was little more than dirty rags. He could count the ribs on them all. Their faces were sunken, their eyes blinded by the daylight from the open door behind him. The survivors ambled forward.

Raul slung his rifle over his shoulder and moved to help the closest survivor. It was a young man whose hair was a matted mess of dirt and oil. The survivor struggled with a limp. Raul slung his arm around his back and helped him out of the barracks. His medical team had entered the camp already, and two of them took the man from him, gently lifting him in their arms and carrying him to a bus that would take him to a hospital. Raul's people understood what to do and how to handle a camp, but that didn't mean that the images he saw didn't rend his soul. *How could other human beings treat people like this?* It was tempting to say that the Newmerican guards weren't human. But he didn't go there, despite the urge. They were human and would face the justice that human beings needed to face.

He went back to get others to the point where he lost count of the number of trips. Tears streaked down his cheeks as he worked. At least they were alive, though he received reports of several dozen shot dead in the camp.

Ted, the former Texas senator who helped with his camp liberation efforts, joined the line helping the survivors. It was the first time he had been with Raul in the field. As Raul watched him assist, he saw that Ted's color had drained from his face; Ted's mouth hung agape.

His sniper, Tara, moved in close. "We talked to a few of them," she reported. "The guards shot some of the prisoners, then took off in a truck three days ago, heading toward Phoenix."

That tore at him. The guards were inhumane criminals to Raul, and the thought that they were skirting justice infuriated him. "Find the office. A lot of times, there are records there of who was on guard duty. Contact whoever had cell service for this area and get a list of who was connecting to the cell towers. One thing's for sure—it wasn't the prisoners." As he spoke, the last of the emaciated prisoners were loaded onto the bus for transportation to the hospital.

Ted was still in a daze from what he had seen. "These people need to face justice for this."

"I agree. We need to identify them first. There's no place they can hide that will be safe," Raul assured him.

The former senator shook his head, almost as if he hoped he could shake the images out of his brain. "I thought it was bad being held in prison. This is far worse than I imagined. When you're here and you see it, smell it, it's horrifying."

Raul understood. "Chances are we will find some graves outside of the camp, too. The camps we liberated in New Mexico had mass burial sites."

Ted gathered himself, rising upright and taking a deep breath. "The TRC is claiming everything we're putting on the net is fake, that we're doctoring footage of these camps."

"They're comfortable with the lies they tell. They have to be. If the people knew the truth, if they were here and saw what we saw, we could defeat the lies."

"Then let's do that," Ted replied.

"What do you mean?"

"Phoenix is about to fall. The word I got is that General Reager is meeting with the mayor today to work out the details of their surrender. Once that's done, let's bus the citizens out here. We can force them to go into the barracks to look at the dead. General Eisenhower did the same thing in World War II. He felt that if people saw what the Nazis had done, they wouldn't be able to deny it years later."

"Did it work?"

Ted hesitated. "Not entirely. In the short term, it did. People forget things over time—sometimes deliberately, sometimes out of their own hate. Facing their crimes is like facing their own complacency. That doesn't mean we shouldn't try. You're right—their propagandists are saying that what we're uncovering is a lie. It's hard to deny what people experience."

"I hate the thought of the dead in the camp remaining out here like this."

"I understand, Raul. We can cover them up. I think they would not want their deaths to be in vain. If that means not burying them right now, so be it. We're talking about a higher justice here."

"Do you think we can convince General Reager to allow it?"

"I doubt that will be a problem. If it is, I'll call the president. This needs to happen."

"Not just this. We need to find those guards. I want them in front of me, explaining why they did what they did." There was more; Raul wanted violence to rain down on them.

NSF Regional Center, Hamden, Connecticut

Newmerican National Security Force Special Agent Angela Axton sat at her desk, glaring at her screen. She hated her job. There was no sense in trying to deny it. Day after day, she scanned material forwarded from the Big Tech companies that were flagged as subversive. Her job was to review the material to see if any of it could be tied to a database of known members of the Sons of Liberty, the Daughters of Liberty, or another one of the hundred or so known domestic terror organizations.

Several times each month, she was able to find a suspected link, which she then forwarded to field agents. They would confront the poster, making the appropriate arrests. The NSF field agents would get to go to court and ensure that convictions were secured, which made her jealous. That was the part of her job that she used to enjoy the most.

And it had been taken away from her by Hudson Whitlock.

The shot she had taken to the knee the night of the assassination attempt had destroyed the joint. She had it replaced, courtesy of the national healthcare, but it had proven defective. Two more surgeries later, she could walk and even jog again but was declared not meeting the standard of field agents. The NSF considered her valuable and kept her in the ranks, just away from the work she loved.

That wasn't the only time Whitlock had hurt her. She had a horizontal scar on her left cheek from when she had almost captured him in Kentucky. Every morning, when she looked in the mirror, she saw it and was reminded of her failure and shame.

As she stared at the three monitors on her desk, she paused the search routine she was running and fired up her inquiry for Whitlock. For over five years now, he had managed to evade her. She would search for him on her own time. Two years ago, she discovered where he was, and in defiance of the agent in charge, she went after him. It was a pursuit that had only managed to taint her career.

Whitlock was known to use several IDs on the few occasions he risked going on the net. Only rarely did he actually go online, and when he did, she wanted to know about it. The NSF considered him a low-priority target, especially after the arrests and convictions of the other members of the Patriot Liberation Front. The cell had been eliminated as a threat, as far as her superiors were concerned. For Angela, however, the matter was far from closed. *He took away my career that night on the rooftop. Worse, he got away...twice...the only member of the PLF we didn't capture.* He was the reason she had been sidelined to a desk and why she wasn't able to advance in rank.

Her sweep for his known IDs came up blank. Accessing the NSA's database of email addresses, she cross-checked his family members to see if he had contacted any of them. After he had first evaded her, she had rigorously interrogated each member of his family to try to find him, but to no avail. Checking their inboxes didn't reveal anything out of the ordinary other than spam.

She felt a presence behind her, closed the windows on her screen, and turned around. Her supervisor, Mike "the Spike" Teel, stood behind her, arms crossed. "We've talked about this before, Angela."

No, you talked. I was forced to listen. "I'm just taking a break and thought I'd see if he had tried to contact his family."

"Whitlock is dead. You saw to that."

"No body, no verification of death. Show me a body and I'll agree with you," she countered. That day was etched into her memory. Months of tracking invested in finding her prey. She had used her last favor to be on the team that took Whitlock down. Then it all went south.

For her, Whitlock wasn't just a domestic terrorist; he was a criminal mastermind. From what she had learned of him, he was brutally intelligent and crafty. *Two times now I have made the same mistake. I underestimated him.* Bringing him in to face justice was not just an obsession—it was the road to her redemption.

"Look, you need to face it. It's not healthy for you or your career to keep looking for him."

She patted her damaged knee. "I owe him."

"And you paid in full. He's gone. Fish food."

"What if he's just lying low? The man is a domestic terrorist who was involved in a plot to kill our president."

"A plot that you helped craft, if I remember correctly."

She felt her jaw clench slightly. "That's what we do, sir. You know it. We infiltrate these groups, plant seeds with them, and see what sprouts. It doesn't matter who suggested what— he was part of a conspiracy to assassinate Daniel Porter."

"It's been, what, two years now? If he was going to surface, he would have."

"You don't know him the way I do," Angela countered. "He's not stupid. It took me three years to track him down as it was.

The guy is not your typical terrorist. He suspected that I was an FBI agent from the start. That was how he got away the first time."

"It's all moot. You put a bullet in him."

She glared up at Teel. *I can't convince him. I've never been able to. He's sure Whitlock is dead just as much as I'm sure he's not.* "It can't hurt to check."

"Don't force me to make this an order."

"What I do on my breaks is my business."

Teel sighed, uncrossing his arms. "Fine. But if I catch you doing this on shift or neglecting your other surveillance work, I will reprimand you."

What are you going to do, not promote me again? "Yes, sir," she replied coolly.

Teel walked away, and she returned to her work. *Whitlock is out there. I know he is. The only way I can repair my reputation in the department is to prove it by bringing him in.*

Chapter 4

Tenth Amendment: The right of equitable government.

The powers and authorities granted in this Bill of Privilege's shall be applied to guidelines established by The People's House. These privileges will be applied according to an aggregate social credit ranking, weighted accordingly.

The Newmerican vice president hit page down again and shook her head. It wasn't a gesture of frustration—it was one of awe. Yes, the proposed Newmerican Constitution was huge. It had to be. The constitution encapsulated all of the ideals and values of their nation. It wasn't the size that stirred her deep veneration—the document was a piece of art. There was a magnificence about the wording and what it stood for. *Daniel has outdone himself. He was right. This is a piece of history.*

Even the title, the Bill of Privileges, was strangely appealing to her. The "rights" in the document were really what the government was willing to grant the population. It was the epitome of what the vice president had always wanted. Gone were the days of people hiding behind their alleged freedoms and rights given to them by God. Going forward, the FedGov would determine what people could and couldn't do. She saw the new constitution as the leash that the Newmerican people needed. *We'll walk in unison, speak as one, vote together.* The document was everything she could have hoped for, and more.

There was no room for dissent in the constitution. She was confident that those who opposed the Newmerican government would be eradicated by the end of the troublesome civil war. At her urging, the president had given her the authority to change the Social Quarantine camps from reeducation and punishment facilities to work and human erasure camps. For too long, the nation had suffered under two-party rule. The Liberation had changed that. Given enough time, the loudest voices of the resistance would be exterminated. *Once we have won the war, the camp system will be in place to address the Americans who started this conflict.*

Daniel had a degree of plausible deniability in the change of camp focus. He never asked about the camps or the news stories out of America about them, and she never shared what she had them doing. She had the TRC running stories constantly to counter the allegations of war crimes that the enemy proffered. They labeled the videos coming from there as "deepfakes," AI-generated lies. The Newmericans consumed the TRC's answer easily. It was far better to call the Americans liars than to admit you backed a government that had extermination camps. *People will accept even the ridiculous to avoid looking guilty, complicit, or criminal. All I'm doing is easing their collective conscience.*

Her subtle amassing of power in the Newmerican regime was something that only historians were likely to give her credit for. The average citizen had little idea of who held what power in the government. As long as their benefits came on time, they didn't care. Most of the time, she didn't mind not getting the credit she deserved. *There will be a time when people realize that I'm not some insipid bartender who stumbled into power. For now, ignorance is a powerful tool.*

She closed the file on her screen and leaned back in her leather chair. *If Daniel is the person who gets this new constitution in, I will have to contend with him for years.* In light of this, she arrived at a very simple solution: Daniel Porter, the president, had to die.

She had arrived at the decision to assassinate him long ago but knew that timing was everything. The key was not to leave a trail back to her. *People love conspiracies and enjoy speculating about grand plots and schemes. Those who try to link me to Daniel's death will be dealt with swiftly.* Whatever she did, she wanted layers between her and the person responsible. Multiple fall guys would insulate her from the crime.

She needed someone to coordinate the entire affair. There were plenty of operatives under her control, but using them would link right back to her. What she needed was an individual people would not associate with her. She had spent hours looking over the files from the NSF for the right person, and then a familiar name came up on her screen.

Deja Jordan.

Interesting... I haven't thought of her in months. The Social Enforcer was disgraced by the vice president herself. No one would expect Deja to be working for her, not given her failures. She had captured, then lost, the terrorist Raul Lopez. She had fought against the VP's sworn enemy, Caylee Leatrom. The vice president had demoted her, kicked her family out of their confiscated house, and then shuffled her off to a meaningless position.

Jordan would be hungry to get herself out of the proverbial doghouse—she was sure of that. And when it came time to clean up, no one would notice if Deja Jordan were to simply disappear.

She was to blame for the breakout at the Supermax. Before that, she was a packaged story for the media, a great tale of someone who rose up to greatness. *People love a comeback story. It's part of our shared culture. We love to see our heroes rise and cheer when they are knocked down. It makes us love them even more when they turn themselves around and rise out of the gutter, regardless of how they got there.* Deja Jordan could be a perfect candidate for that kind of position.

The vice president was sure she could manipulate Deja into accepting the assignment. Deja wouldn't betray her because she knew the nature of the VP. *If she tries to turn on me, she knows the kind of power I wield.* Long-term, it wouldn't matter anyway. This would be Deja's last assignment. She would make sure of that.

That left the picking of the right assassin. It needed to be someone who was loyal to the Americans. Daniel's death must be laid at the Americans' doorstep. It would galvanize the population even more against the Pretender President and his hordes. Even better, it would ensure that his constitution was passed, but under *her* leadership.

She had an operative prepare a list of people in the American states who might have a grudge against Newmerica to the point where they might take up arms. She was surprised at the length of the list. Meticulously reviewing it for candidates took a few hours. Of course, in the states that had flipped over to America, there were bound to be a lot of people who resented what Newmerica had provided them.

Working late nights, she had whittled down the list. She removed women because she didn't want any perceived backlash against females. Having a male assassin would create a great patriarchal narrative in the TRC's hands after Daniel's death. The VP had removed military personnel from the list. *Too many of them are free thinkers. They might see this as the false flag event early on.* Filtering the list further, she focused on people who might have suffered (their word, not hers) under the benevolence of Newmerica.

The list was still long but far more manageable. One night, she cut the list again, looking at people who had come out of the Social Quarantine program. Revenge could be a powerful motivator. Then she looked for people who had gone public with their experiences. It would save considerable time over having to invent false accounts of their time during reeducation. She arrived at a list of thirty or so names of potential assassins.

It was a perfect plan. She would assign an operative to investigate assassination threats. That would give her a shield from the public, should anyone point to her as being the instigator of the plot. A good false flag event needed to protect the guilty from prosecution while having a desired political result from the act itself. *I will be installed as the president, and with Daniel's blood, I will be the one who gets credit for this constitution. No one would dare vote against it once I evoke his name in regard to it.* The VP was practically giddy at what was going to unfold and the results it would bring.

Reaching over to the small panel on her desktop, she called out to her admin. "I need you to contact Deja Jordan. Tell her I want to talk to her in person, here. Make arrangements to have her here tomorrow at the latest."

She didn't wait for the confirmation from her assistant. *I've worked through all the contingencies. Once this is done, Newmerica will have a president it deserves, one who can put an end to this war.*

Apache Junction, Arizona

General Reager let the mayor of Phoenix and the governor swelter in the tent for a few minutes before stepping in himself. He brought with him a small entourage, including the head of the Maricopa County Mounted Posse, Captain Dolio of the Purebloods, the CO of the 51st Militia, and Raul Lopez. Lopez came with a former Texas senator of some renown, filling him in about the camps they had been liberating. When the senator saw the videos they brought, he insisted that Lopez join him.

The desert-tan tent was hot as he entered, but not nearly as hot as his temper. While the American media posted a great deal about the camps, Trip had been able to dodge the images. He had a mission to fulfill, and his time keeping up on the news was limited. When Lopez showed up and outlined his mission and what he had experienced, it infuriated the general. *They have the gall to label us as monsters when they are systematically slaughtering their opposition.*

The middle-aged Hispanic mayor looked pissed off, probably because of the hot wait. Trip didn't care. She had her arms crossed, her glasses slid slightly down her nose, as if she were looking down on him. The governor, an older woman, tried to paint on a face of congeniality. Her forced smile and extended hand were ignored by Reager as he stood before them.

"General," Governor Holcomb said, verbally acknowledging him.

"Governor."

"We would like to discuss the terms and conditions of our standing down," the governor said, dodging the word "surrender."

Trip looked her squarely in the eyes. "This will be short, then. There are no terms. You will surrender the rest of the state of Arizona unconditionally. Your forces, including the NSF and all SEs, will report for disarmament and detention." His tone was casual but firm.

"That is unacceptable," she replied.

"Very well. I will order in the bombers and start the artillery barrage in five minutes. You probably should remain here. That isn't enough time for you to get back and take shelter." He then turned toward the tent flaps.

"You wouldn't!" the governor stammered.

He turned back to her. "Watch me."

At this point, Mayor Alfaro jumped in. "I am declaring Phoenix a free city. That means you can't fire on it!"

Trip walked up close enough to her that he was certain she could smell the coffee on his breath. "I don't recognize your free city bullshit. You can't just make up new things and try to impose them on us. We are here because your defense force surrendered."

"You'll be labeled a war criminal," Alfaro countered. "You'll be firing on innocent, unarmed citizens."

Trip planted his fists on his hips as he narrowed his gaze. "War criminal? You throw around those words as if you understand them. I find that amusing. A little while ago, I saw what your people have been doing in the Social Quarantine camps. Your people are anything but innocent."

Governor Holcomb cut in. "I don't know what you think you saw, but the videos out there are all deepfakes. That's been proven."

"That's a lie," Raul Lopez said. "I liberated a camp in the Apache National Forest just north of Morenci. Prisoners were shot. More were starved to death."

Trip gave him a quick glance and a short nod, as if to say, "I'll handle it from here." He then turned to the Governor. "It seems that the two of you may have to answer to someone regarding war crimes."

"I don't know anything about those camps. That was the FedGov, not us," Alfaro replied.

"Well, our intel says that the guards who ran that camp may have fled into your city. If you are harboring them, you are linked to their crimes."

"The camps were administered out of the District," the governor added.

"People like you make me sick. You had no problem with people being slaughtered. Now that we are here, you want to claim... what? That you didn't know what was going on there?"

"We didn't," Holcomb replied.

"From what I've been told, there are four camps around the city. If the conditions are even half as bad as what I've seen from the one in Morenci, you'll both be facing some pretty severe charges."

"But we—" Alfaro said.

"Save it for your trial. Let me tell you how this is going to play out. You are going to transmit to your people the unconditional surrender of the State of Arizona. We will tell you where your armed forces are to assemble to be disarmed. Then you will be placed under protective custody until the officials in Nashville decide what to do with you."

"We came here under a flag of truce!" the Governor snapped. "You have to honor that."

Trip moved over in front of her. Clearly, he was too close for her comfort, as she took a step back. "Do you really believe there is some sort of protection that a sheet on a stick provides you after the shit I've seen? Please tell me you're not that ignorant."

She was stunned at his words, her mouth hanging open in dismay. Trip continued, "Those are the conditions. So, do you want to signal your surrender, or do I start bombing Phoenix back to the Stone Age?"

Governor Holcomb's head lowered, a sign that she had been beaten.

Camp AZ 22, Camp Bowman, Wintersburg, Arizona

Trip stood inside the camp. He thought he would get used to the stench after a few hours, but he had been proven wrong. When he first arrived, he had embarrassingly thrown up. The shame of that cleared as several other officers vomited as well.

Looking out over the long line of commandeered school buses, he knew he had done the right thing. The locals had been rounded up randomly from nearby Phoenix and driven to the camp to witness it for themselves. He had ordered the governor, the mayor, and their staffs to the burial detail. There had been resistance, but prods with bayonets encouraged those brave enough to resist, curbing their defiance. *They need to see this, experience it.* Trip knew it would scar some of them for years, but he also didn't care.

They allowed this to happen. Many knew what was happening but turned their heads, either out of fear or guilt.

Lopez and his team had liberated the camp the day before. The guards had shot many of the prisoners. They tried to cover their crimes by chaining the doors of the crude barracks and setting them on fire. The guards fled as half of the camp went up in flames. The sun-dried wood barracks were easy kindling.

There were survivors, people who had somehow gotten out of the buildings or those who were in barracks that had not caught on fire. Trip's medical team was overwhelmed with the problem. All the prisoners were malnourished, and some were sick with typhoid, cholera, and a dozen other ailments.

Before he sent the civilians through the camp, he had ordered his own people in. No one emerged untouched. Even the battle-hardened leader of the Purebloods, Captain Dolio, dropped to his knees in tear-streaked prayer after what he had seen. It had been a gamble, making his own people see what the enemy had done, but it was necessary. *They now understand why we're fighting this war. They understand just how depraved the enemy is. Most of them thought we were waging this war for our freedoms. Now they understand that we are fighting evil.*

Captain Harnessy came alongside him. "I've had our forces secure hotels on the edge of the city for the night."

"Good work."

"Sir, this was... horrible."

Reager nodded. "And necessary."

"I brought the local media in. They are filming it all. The burial teams are going through the recovered remains. Unfortunately, the guards torched all of their computers and records. We have no idea who the dead are and have to rely on the survivors to help us figure out who is who. The folks on our perimeter have found—" Harnessy hesitated.

"What is it?"

"It's worse than we thought. They didn't bother to bury the dead they'd been killing. They just piled them up out in the scrub brush. We've found a dozen piles of human bones out there."

Trip wasn't surprised, which was disturbing to him. "Get into the city and find the coroner and some funeral homes. They are to be treated as murder victims. I want this done by the book. Find me the head of the NSF. I want those guards rounded up."

"General, the sheriff killed himself once he found out about the camps. He blew his brains out in his office."

He knew what was happening up here and couldn't face the music. He saved us the expense of a trial. "Then grab his second-in-command and get them out here."

"Yes, sir."

"We need to billet here for a few days and map out the next steps. Our people need some rest, especially after all this. Have the maintenance teams get to work on preventative maintenance and repairs on our vehicles. Have our communications officer tell the people of Phoenix that they are under American control again. She knows the routine."

"Already in motion, sir."

Trip's eyes scanned the camp again from one end to the other. He could hear weeping from the civilians he was forcing through but felt not a bit of pity for them. *The Newmericans paint themselves as benevolent, but they're just like other totalitarians before them—brutal killers.* It saddened him that good people had done nothing to prevent what had happened in the camp. Doing nothing was a crime almost equal to those who had done the killing.

I can't wait for this war to be over. The cleanup and repair to our nation's people are going to take decades. Worse, there will be those who deny that this ever happened, despite my efforts to make them experience what was going on in the camps.. Disgust, rage, and weariness were constantly pulling at Trip, and he was doing his best to hold them all at bay.

Smyrna, Tennessee

Caylee saw the anger in Charli's face and the concern in Andy's. Travis sat leaning back in his chair around the small dining table, as if he were drinking in all the information he could gather. She had waited until they finished eating Andy's enchilada casserole. Caylee knew her friends were going to react poorly to what she was telling them, and there was no point in ruining their dinner.

Caylee had spent several days doing her overall planning for the mission Jack Desmond had suggested. While a team might prove helpful, the timing of everything was tight. She needed to be nimble. Having a group try to infiltrate Newmerica, especially a group of wanted people, would potentially be problematic.

There was something else. The people in the room, along with Raul and Jack, were her friends. It was one thing to put herself at risk, but something else to bring people she cared about into the fray. *There are a lot of ways this can go south. I don't want to see them dragged down with me if something goes wrong.*

"I know what Jack said. I also know that you don't always follow the rules. What do you mean you can't tell us where you're going and what you're doing?" Charli pressed.

"Those are the parameters I was handed," Caylee replied. "I have some discretion, but I think you're better off not knowing. This needs to be a solo run."

"We've been through hell and back together," Andy stated.

"Andy, this is sensitive information. I'd like to have a support team, but the dangers are too great. All of us are wanted by the Newmericans."

"None more than you," Charli jumped in. "And you're going. Let us come with you. We can help."

"I may need it. But not at this stage of the op," Caylee countered.

"I know we're not trained like you are," Andy said. "But we have more than proven that we work well together."

He was right, so arguing that point was not going to get her anywhere. "You're right, Andy. This isn't about that. This mission is ugly on a lot of levels. Trust me, you don't want to be a part of it."

"Why not let us decide that?" Charli pressed.

"Not this time. The limited time to plan this, the complexities involved—it's going to be hairy. A lot is going to be done on the fly. That being the case, it would be too hard to coordinate with you. I need to be light and fast. This is the work of a trained operative."

She could feel the frustration in the room, and with it came a sense of guilt. *They only want to help, and I'm shutting them down.* Caylee wanted to be able to offer them something to hold on to other than a slender thread of hope. "I appreciate your willingness to help. Realistically, if this does go wrong, I may need you to help get me out."

Just saying those words seemed to energize the room. She glanced at Travis, knowing she did have a role for him. "Travis, I was going to engage you for a task tied to this mission, if you're willing. If you are, then should something go wrong, you could engage the others."

"A fallback plan?" Travis asked, leaning forward in his seat.

"Something like that. Let's just say, if this falls apart, I have a good idea of what's going to follow. I was hoping you might be able to be in a position to help."

The former SEAL gave her a lone nod. "Sure. It's not like I have other plans at the moment."

Caylee swept her gaze over the others in the room. "Will that meet with your satisfaction?"

Andy seemed satisfied, but not so much Charli. Caylee knew the look on her face all too well. She was angry and frustrated. Slowly, begrudgingly, Charli nodded in agreement. Caylee masked her relief with a stern expression.

It took a few minutes to get back to a normal conversation. Marie had prepared brownies for dessert, which were delicious. Caylee rarely gave in to sweets. Even while eating the brownie, she knew she'd spend a few more minutes at the gym to work it off. It was never about weight or appearance for her—it was about performance.

As they finished up, Travis moved beside her at the sink, where she was washing dishes. "So," he said in a whisper, "where are we going?"

"I'm going to Philadelphia," she replied in a low tone so her voice wouldn't carry. "You... I'm sending you someplace worse."

"I've been to Philly. If you're going for worse, I assume I'm off to Toledo or Cleveland," he said with a grin.

She turned to him, leaning in. "I'll give you the details in the morning, if you're free. Let's just say there's a good chance I will run into problems. I want to pre-position you so that if that happens, you're already on the inside."

"Gotcha," he replied. "I appreciate your planning ahead."

"I know how the NSF and my former colleagues work. It's both a blessing and a curse. Hopefully, this will go off without a hitch. If not, I'm counting on you."

"Sounds dangerous."

"You're a former SEAL. I'm sure you've faced worse, but I will be asking a lot of you."

"I look forward to our talk," he replied.

You may want to change your mind. I'm asking you to go into the lion's den...

The next day...

After they finished their discussion, Travis left. He'd be going in before her, and the path he would be walking would be as dangerous as hers, if not more. With Travis in play, she turned her attention to her mission.

There were two elements that had to be pulled off. One was to disrupt the upcoming Constitutional Convention. The Newmericans had not named the location beyond the city at this point, which was clearly designed to subvert missions such as hers. Disrupting it would be complicated, but she had some ideas. She understood politicians. For all their bravado and harsh language, they were essentially cowards at heart. Sure, there were exceptions, but they were rare—even rarer in Newmerica. When frightened, they would scurry like cockroaches exposed to bright lights or cower. Either way, it would delay or prevent them from ratifying their constitution.

The TRC will want this to be a production. That meant a lot of participants, and that meant they would need a venue large enough for a big stage show. For her, that limited the places where they might hold the convention. The larger the facility, the harder it would be to secure all the points of access. Caylee used her iPad to pull up possible locations and narrowed it down to four. *I'll need to get in there early and scope out each of them.*

The second part was far harder. The vice president had an NSF/Secret Service detail. She was in charge of the NSF, so she would likely have more than a typical team protecting her. *I won't be able to get to her directly. I need to get her to come to me without knowing that she's doing it.*

The Secret Service had patterns they constantly changed to make assassinations difficult. There were weaknesses. Wherever the vice president was, she had to get from point A to B, which meant a vehicle. *They'll have decoy limos, and no matter what, those vehicles are like tanks. She's most vulnerable when she's getting in or out of her ride.* The tricky part was getting into position and ensuring that the VP would move to her, where Caylee could verify the VP was dead if shot. It was a cold calculation, one she was glad she didn't share with her friends. *There are parts of what I do that might turn them away from me. It's best they don't know the details of how I work.*

Killing the VP was one thing. In some aspects, that was relatively easy. Getting away from an assassination—that was the more difficult part. Most assassins were killed during the act or captured shortly after their act. That was why she had engaged Travis. Still, Caylee had some ideas about escape.

If I do this right, the true power in Newmerica will be dead. Their war will crumble. The country can reunify. All I have to do is put a bullet in that bitch...

Chapter 5

The Twenty-Second Amendment: The Privilege of Travel

The population of Newmerica is free to travel. Travel over three hundred miles requires a travel permit and prior authorization. Travelers are required to carry their FedGov identification ID at all times in order to ensure security. Travel over three hundred miles must be on approved, green modes of travel.

The District

Deja was nervous. The summons to the District to meet with the vice president had come out of the blue. It had forced her to rummage through her Rubbermaid storage bins, looking for a good suit and shoes to wear. When she stood in front of the mirror before leaving for the airport, she reminisced about the last time she had worn this outfit. *It was for the Newsweek article.* Her mother had complimented her when that issue came out, telling her that the suit had made her look so skinny. Thinking of her mother, even for a moment, still tore at her.

Her initial reaction to the summons was to think that it was bad news. The last time she had heard from the vice president, she had been told of her demotion. That call had come while she had been recovering in the hospital after the attack at the Supermax. After that call, she slowly came to the conclusion that it was good news. *She wouldn't call me all the way to the District to chew my ass.*

During the plane flight east, she wondered what could be the impetus for her summons. *Maybe Raul Lopez has been caught again!* She had seen him on an uncensored newsfeed from America, liberating a Social Quarantine camp. Lopez had proven himself tough, both physically and mentally. Deja had tried to break him, but she had failed. *Now he's parading around, accusing us of human rights violations! What a joke! Nobody believes those lies. Those camps are for reeducation —everyone knows that.* It's clear that those supposedly starving people were doctored images and videos.

Perhaps it was news about Caylee Leatrom. The last Deja heard, Caylee had been implicated in the assassination of the Pretender President's chief of staff. A run-in with Leatrom was not something Deja looked forward to. *She could have killed me. Instead, she left me maimed.* For a few moments, Caylee was sure that Deja was dead. Leatrom had spared her, which proved to be far more agonizing than simply killing her. *It would have been more merciful. At least everyone couldn't blame me for her freeing Lopez.* Thinking of the former operative only made her cringe. *I can only hope they have her locked up in prison for killing the chief of staff.*

When she arrived at Clinton National Airport, she noticed some subtle changes to the District's landscape. There was a missile battery poised at the end of the runway. There was a checkpoint on the bridge into the city, and she was forced to show her travel authorization and identification. There were military vehicles patrolling the streets, far more than the last time she had been there. *I wonder if the war isn't going as well as we've been told.* The TRC's newscasts all said there had been minor setbacks, but for the most part, Newmerica was winning the civil war. It was on the news every day. Seeing the troops and defensive measures, Deja found herself questioning the official narrative.

As the car wound through the mall, she mentally corrected herself. It wasn't healthy to have negative thoughts about the nation. One of the TRC's daily messages was that doubt was as much an enemy as the troops in the field. *If I'm meeting with the VP, I can't go in with that frame of mind.*

She was dropped off at the old Executive Office Building, went through three checkpoints, and was patted down. It wasn't this thorough the last time she had been here. She was assigned a guide who took her upstairs. From there, the admin led her in to meet with the vice president.

The woman smiled when she saw Deja. It was a mix of faux pleasure and craftiness. "How nice to see you," she said as her admin closed the door behind her. The sound of the door clicking made Deja nervous, as if she were being boxed in or caged.

"Ma'am," she said.

"Please," the VP said, gesturing to the chair across from her desk. "Let's not assume any pronouns or preferences."

Deja lowered herself into the chair. It was lower than the VP's, making her feel that the smaller woman was actually taller than her. The VP hit a button on a small panel on her desk, and the blinds to her office closed, making the room a little darker. "I suppose you wonder why I reached out to you."

"I was surprised after . . . well, you know."

"I always liked you, Deja. That was why it disappointed me so much when you let Lopez and Leatrom slip through your fingers."

Deja raised her crippled hand, in case the VP hadn't seen it. "It wasn't a matter of letting them go. I took bullets trying to stop them."

"So you did. Yet they still escaped. I imagine that was a blemish on your career you'd like to erase. After such a failure, redemption might do you some good."

The shame was there, no matter how much Deja tried to hide it. "Yes," was all she could say.

Blaine L. Pardoe

"I'd like to give you that opportunity, a chance to do something for the nation—something important. It's not an easy task, and at first, you might not like the sound of it, but it must be done."

"What is it?"

"I need you to help me arrange the assassination of President Porter."

The words hung in the air between them, propped up by a deadly silence. "If this is some sort of test . . ." Deja stammered.

"No," cut in the vice president. "It isn't. You see, I've learned that Porter has been conducting an affair with his underage babysitter." She produced a folder and slid it across the desk.

Deja opened it and saw reports and eight-by-ten photos of the president kissing a very young girl. She was stunned for a few moments. *I should have known. He advocated against prosecuting pedophiles when he came into office, claiming that they were "minor-attracted persons."* People went along with the policy since a parade of scientists claimed it was a legitimate psychological condition that shouldn't be suppressed. It made perfect sense now. He was a pedophile himself. *It was all to legitimize his own crimes.* She pushed the photos away in disgust. "Can't you force him to resign, or just impeach him?"

The VP dipped her head momentarily, then locked her dark brown eyes onto Deja's. "I've tried to reason with him multiple times. He has threatened to strip me of my duties— that's how desperate he is to cover up what he's done. With the war on, I doubt I could get The People's House to step up to try to impeach him. It would send the wrong message to the Americans and would be a blow to our nation's morale."

"But assassination?"

"I know. It seems extreme, but it has to be done. It's for the good of the nation. We can't have a child molester holding the highest office in the country. Imagine what would happen when the Americans found out. You know their intelligence people eventually will. When they do, they'll use this information against us. Our foreign support will wither on the vine. Porter's perversions have put us all at risk."

Deja's mind reeled at the information and what she was being asked to do. There was a certain logic to what the vice president was saying. Still, this was about killing the president! That wasn't something she had ever envisioned. *Is this really how governments work?* "I don't know if I can do that. I'm not a sniper or the assassination type. Wouldn't it be better to use an operative for this kind of mission?"

"The conflict has our operatives spread thin. Besides, I don't need you to be the one pulling the trigger. I need you to be a coordinator of sorts. This is an ugly business, but we both know it has to be done. As such, it would be better if this is not linked to us."

"I understand."

"Good. For this to work, we need to lay the blame at America's doorstep. They already attacked the Capitol. It would be easy for them to be responsible for killing our president."

"How would we find such people?"

"I've already done some legwork on that front," she said, sliding over a flash drive. "The list of candidates isn't long. Most feel they have somehow been mistreated by our nation. Any of them would be believable—that they were out for revenge."

Deja slowly picked up the flash drive. "So, I'd have to go through the lines?"

"Yes. You'll be fine, though. From what I've read about your expertise, you won't have any issues. We'll arrange for security to get you in and out of the country."

"Where is this going to take place? Or is that something you're leaving to me to work through?"

The vice president shook her head. "We want the attempt to take place at the Constitutional Convention before the ratification vote."

"Won't the security there be a bit over the top?"

"The NSF works for me. I will ensure your assassin has an open path."

"Then what happens?"

"You'll kill him. We can't afford him talking to the media, claiming he was some sort of patsy like Lee Harvey Oswald. You'll kill him right after he does the job. Then, once more, you'll be the hero our nation deserves."

Deja held the flash drive between her thumb and forefinger, thinking carefully about what was being asked of her. Being a heroic media star would silence her sisters. They would have to see her for what she really was.

The harder part to process was that she was going to be helping someone kill the president of Newmerica. She despised pedos, but she never took Daniel Porter for one. The photographs didn't lie. One of those showed him with his hand sliding up under the young girl's skirt. Seeing that image not only angered her but made her want to protect the victim. It made the idea of killing Porter easier.

Why me? The vice president had endless resources at her disposal. It struck Deja as strange that she would be the one chosen for this grisly assignment. *There's got to be other people who would be better for this.* "I don't understand why you picked me."

"Deja, I like you. I have from the first time we met. In truth, I felt a little guilty about what happened to you after that ugliness at the Supermax. You always struck me as a good citizen and an even better Social Enforcer."

The VP paused and then continued. "My mother, before she was killed, taught me all about the value of second chances in life. Mistakes happen… twists of fate. She instilled in me that some people simply need the right opportunity to prove themselves. When I started looking for someone for this job, I remembered you and how you impressed me. I hope you can forgive the NSF for how you were treated."

It was hard, if not impossible, for Deja to turn down such an opportunity. She had been hoping and praying for such a chance, and now it was being handed to her by a woman she had admired—a person who would be the next president if Deja was successful. It made sense. The VP had apologized, in a way, for what had happened. *People do make mistakes. It couldn't have been easy for her to apologize.* "The Constitutional Convention is coming up shortly. If I do this, I'm going to need some things." A simple disguise, for one. Deja's face had been highly publicized by the TRC. The last thing she wanted was to be arrested as a spy in enemy territory.

"I will have one of our quartermasters tasked to you. Whatever you need, you'll get," she assured her.

"Okay," Deja said. "I appreciate your trust in me. I won't let you down."

"I'd say I'm counting on you, Deja, but in reality, the fate of our country is counting on you. This is bigger than me, than us. You are going to help us pave the road into the future." She rose from her seat and extended her hand.

Deja shook the woman's hand once, then was gestured to the door. As she stepped out, the VP's admin escorted her to an office on the same floor. It was windowless—just a desk, a PC, and a phone. Sitting down, she realized that the next few weeks of her life were going to be the most challenging she had ever faced.

Camp AZ22, Camp Bowman, Wintersburg, Arizona

Darius threw up for what seemed like the tenth time as he watched the locals drag the body of a dead woman into the grave that had been dug for her. He had become accustomed to the stench, having overseen the digging of graves for days now. What made him reel was that while the corpse was being carried, one of the arms detached, and her body hit the desert floor and seemed to come apart at every joint.

Wiping the residue of vomit from his lips on his sleeve, he called out to the two civilians who had been carrying her. "Don't just stand there! Pick her up—and you'd better do it with some respect!" he barked. The pair looked at him angrily, but he didn't care. General Reager had assigned them to the duty, and by God, they were going to do it.

If the rumors were true, this wasn't even the worst of the camps that had been liberated. There was one north of Phoenix, near the Colorado border, where the guards had machine-gunned most of the prisoners before the American troops showed up. The prisoners had been used to load bullets for the Newmerican war effort. From what he had been witnessing, there was little doubt of that.

When he had been living in California, there were a lot of rumors about prisoners in Social Quarantine camps being used as forced labor—harvesting crops, doing road repair, building demolition, and other such jobs. It was said that if a prisoner didn't work, they would be killed. At the time, he wrote it off as what it was—a rumor. Darius had assumed that the prisoners were forced to work and disregarded the part about them being shot. Now he questioned his logic. *I didn't want to think that my government could do this kind of thing to other people. I was dead wrong.*

The civilians heeded his words and carefully moved the torso and limbs of the dead prisoner to the grave. They were handed shovels and started to fill the hole as a private placed a grave marker with the number on it at the head of the hole. Another civilian wrote down the details of the victim, usually nothing more than something like, *White, female, mid-twenties*. If there were tattoos, those were jotted down as well, but in this case, the body was so badly decomposed that it was impossible to see them. *It will be years or never before the identities of these people are known.*

With that burial, his detail was relieved. He was thankful for it. Watching dead bodies being buried in the desert made him feel filthy, even if he didn't have to do the work. When he got back to his tent, he sat down, took his boots off, and lay back for a few minutes of quiet.

The 51st Militia had treated him as a suspected traitor when he had first been assigned to them. Things had changed after the battle. Darius didn't know it, but he had assumed command and had been in the lead unit rushing into the fighting after the sergeant was wounded. After the fighting, troops who had given him the cold shoulder were now warm and friendly toward him. It made sense to Darius. Actions always spoke louder than words.

"Darius," came a familiar voice from the tent flap. "Is that you?"

Sitting up, he saw Captain Lauren Aguilar, with whom he had fled the Veteran Volunteer Corps. As he stood, he noticed she was no longer wearing captain's bars but instead was a second lieutenant. The patch on her sleeve was from the 196th Maneuver Enhancement Brigade, South Dakota National Guard. When he saw her, he hesitated. A part of him wanted to give her a hug, but another part respected her rank. "I wondered where you ended up... sir," he said, flashing a smile.

"You can shit-can that 'sir' stuff when it's just you and me," she said, stepping forward and giving him a hug. "It took me a while to track you down."

"You're a lieutenant now?"

Aguilar nodded. "They pulled up my old service records and reinstated me at my former rank. There was some grumbling that I was just joining the winning side. I shut that shit down. This isn't about who wins. This war is about what's right and what's wrong."

"That's the truth."

She shrugged. "To be honest, I thought about just remaining a civilian after we turned ourselves in to the Americans. Our experiences with the Veteran Volunteer Corps really left a bad taste in my mouth about sides and the kind of war we were fighting."

"It left a nasty taste in my mouth about California and Newmerica in general." Memories of the cartels coming to their rescue in Texas, bombing the city with fentanyl. To Darius, the cartels were criminals. To the Newmericans, they were allies.

"Yeah. They had my unit march through a camp north of here at some place called Teec Nos Pos. It was as bad as what you have going down here. I had no idea that things were so horrible in the camps."

"I heard rumors."

"We *all* heard rumors. We just lied to ourselves about the people in power over there."

"I hate that I looked the other way," Darius admitted. "I wish I'd questioned things more."

"I understand. My dad used to say that our lives are the culmination of the lies we want to be the truth. I never understood it at the time. Now I do. We all looked the other way, otherwise we were as guilty as those running the camps."

"Smart man, your dad."

"He would have taken a stand against killing people, even if they were from the other political party."

"Have you heard anything from Sergeant Ingersoll?" Darius inquired.

"Not a peep. They took him to a hospital when we turned ourselves in. I lost track of him. It was hard enough for me to locate you."

"He's a good man."

"Are you on leave? Or is your unit deploying here?" Darius asked.

"Deploying. The scuttlebutt is that we're going to be invading California next. I thought we were going to Colorado, but we heard they have their own little civil war going on. Denver is a die-hard Newmerican hot spot, but the rest of the state is rejoining America."

"I assume we're heading west at some point," he said. "I just go where they tell me."

"Spoken like a true soldier," Aguilar replied.

Soldier. That's what I am again. Unconsciously, he reached up and felt his left breast pocket where he still carried a medal he had recovered at the Presidio when the Veteran Volunteer Corps had cleared out a homeless encampment. He had thought he lost it at one point during his desertion and felt immense relief when he found it in his gear. The medal was his anchor point, a reminder of what he had done—just following orders. "I'm not looking forward to going back to California," he said in a low voice, more to himself than to Aguilar.

"It's not going to be easy," she said. "There are a lot of civilians packed in around LA. I imagine many of them are going to put up a hell of a fight when we show up. Newmerica and the state government have propped them up with a lot of welfare and handouts. America isn't likely to be as generous."

What she said was an understatement. The state provided free meth under the guise of cutting down crimes committed by addicts to purchase drugs. There was a hint of logic in the policy, but it was shaky at best. The program was a failure but continued regardless. Results were just one casualty of the state of California's social equity laws. The FedGov provided free medical care and treatment. Housing was subsidized as long as you lived where they told you to—all in the name of diversity. "I don't know about that. I think a lot of them won't fight. They'll demand free shit, but in the end, will they lay down their lives for Newmerica? I'm not sure."

"Well," Aguilar replied with a smile, "we'll find out soon enough, I guess."

Fort Wayne, Indiana

As he listened to the organ music and the singing of the church congregation, Braylon Ironsides took time to reflect on what had happened the week before. He hadn't wanted to do the interview with the local NBC affiliate. The prosecutor's office had pressured him into it, along with the Fort Wayne Police Department's public relations people. "You don't want this man on the streets again, do you?" Braylon knew they were using him, hoping to taint the jury pool ahead of the trial. He had tried to worm his way out of it, but in the end, consented to the TV interview.

The arrest of Jason Ritter, aka Freckles, had been big news locally and had even been picked up nationally. Initially, Ritter had tried to lie his way out of his predicament, but a check of camp records exposed his mistruths. After that, he had lawyered up. Others from the camp came forward as well. His trial was one of many that were taking place across the country as the SEs were starting to face justice for what they had done. It reminded him of the Nuremberg war trials after World War II, except in this case, the war was still raging. *People want to see that justice still works, that evil pays for what it has done. That's something that can't be pounded out of us. It's part of our nature.*

Braylon was hailed as brave...a hero. It was an identity he disliked. He couldn't just walk away and say nothing once he saw the former guard. To let Ritter escape, to roam the streets, after all he had done, would have been wrong. Worse, it might allow him into a position again in life where he held sway over others. *I had no choice. I had to call the police.*

Braylon's interview felt like it was an hour long. He had waited in the lobby of the NBC studio and they showed him the edited cut—it was only two and a half minutes long. To his relief, no one had asked him for details of his time in the camp or his interaction with Ritter/Freckles. The police had his detailed report, as humiliating as it had been to give.

The sermon was one he had heard before, the sacrifice of Abraham. He savored the minister's words, not because they were important to him, but because he could hear them. Religious services had been banned in the camp, deemed subversive. He understood the true reason. Newmerica wanted to set the morals and values of society. Churches and organized religion were obstacles to that, often presenting differing views of morality. In a totalitarian regime, that was something that couldn't be tolerated. While there was nothing fancy or glamorous in this tiny church, it was free from the oppression he had endured.

As the service ended, Braylon could feel the gazes of people homing in on him. He had felt it everywhere he went. When he turned to those looking at him, they averted their eyes, turning their heads away, but he knew they had been watching him. That was what the media had done to him. It had taken his life of solitude, his horrible past, and made it public. *Perhaps I should never have consented to the interview.* He smothered that thought quickly. *No. I had to speak out about Ritter. The world needs to know what happened to those of us who were rounded up.*

After church, he stopped to purchase a cup of coffee. The place where he got his caffeine had been a Starbucks before the Fall. Then it, like so many other businesses, had been crushed under the weight of the regulations and taxes that the Ruling Council had pushed through. Now it was open again under a different name, The Queen of Beans. He ordered a small cup with triple cream and moved to a window seat. Gray clouds had come in while he had been at church. It would rain later in the day. He could feel the change in weather in his knees.

Braylon savored his coffee as customers filtered in and out of the shop. There were two people there working furiously on their laptops, mooching the Wi-Fi. His plans for the day consisted of returning to his tiny flat and reading. Going to church had been the highlight of his day.

"Hi," a voice said from his side, startling him slightly. Turning, he saw a Black woman. She was dressed in jeans with a denim shirt over a T-shirt. In her hands, she cradled a large cup of coffee. "Do you mind if I join you, Mr. Ironsides?"

He wanted to say no but knew it would be rude. "It's a free country," he said, nodding at the chair across from him.

"It is now," she replied, taking the seat and giving him a reassuring smile.

Braylon took a sip of his coffee. It was his intent to get up and leave. Strangers had a way of making him nervous, and this woman knew his name, which added to his edginess. "I saw your piece on the news."

"Oh, that," he said, now convinced that he should leave.

"You are an inspiration to people out there," she said.

"No," he replied. "I'm just someone who did the right thing at the right time."

"You don't give yourself enough credit," she said, taking a tiny sip of her coffee. "This is a precarious time for America. You are a person people look up to; the common man who had been wronged and made a stand."

He had never considered the perspective she had laid before him. "That sounds all nice and good, but I'm no inspiration. I was just a victim."

"You sell yourself short." She extended her hand. "By the way, my name is Tonya."

He shook her hand. "Braylon."

"Like I was saying, you don't realize what one man can do in terms of boosting morale. I'm part of a group of people who are exploring ways to end this war quickly. Like-minded souls, good people. We all saw you and said, 'There's a guy like us, someone who puts himself on the line and calls out criminals.' We've been talking about you since you did that interview."

She must be with a cell from the Sons of Liberty. "I think you may be putting too much stock in what I did. I just reported a crime."

"A war crime. You stood up to an SE who held you prisoner and tortured you and others. That takes a lot of courage. The NSF is still out there. We have no doubt that they might be looking to give you a little payback. That's why I've been shadowing you, just in case things get out of hand."

Braylon had given thought to retribution from Newmerica but thought it was a far-fetched idea. After all, Fort Wayne was a long way from the front lines. He was in America again, and the war was several states away. The fact that she had been shadowing him to make sure he was safe was comforting, despite her being a stranger. "You've been following me?"

"Just to make sure you were kept safe."

"Should I be worried?"

"We all should. As long as the president of Newmerica exists, we are all in danger." As she finished speaking, her eyes swept around The Queen of Beans.

"He won't for much longer," Braylon assured her. "The way the war is going, by this time next year, Newmerica will have fallen."

"At what price?"

Her question was biting. *Lives? Property?* "I don't know."

"The thing is, Mr. Ironsides, that when governments fall, often their leaders get away. Look at the Shah of Iran. He loaded up a plane with gold and came to the United States. His people never got justice. In Ukraine, when the Russian forces took the capital, Zelenskyy fled with a big pile of his treasury. There had been rumors that the Newmericans had helped topple him in exchange for lower oil prices from Russia, but that didn't change the fact that he had gotten away. When you become a supreme evil, there are always ways to escape justice."

He understood what she was saying. He had felt the same thing, a deep fear that Daniel Porter might somehow escape justice. "You may be right. But what can I do about it? I'm just an old guy living in Fort Wayne."

Tonya tilted her head slightly and cast a thin smile. "You don't believe that. I know you served in the Army for four years, which means you are a patriot at heart. You are the kind of person who takes matters into their own hands, just like you did with this Ritter character."

"My stint in the Army was a lifetime ago. Yes, I love my country, and I hate Newmerica. But I'm just one man. I live alone. My family is gone, and so is my career. I sleep on an inflatable bed that leaks. I wasn't even there when my wife died—they took that from me. I've been humiliated in ways you can't imagine. Newmerica took and took and took until there was nothing left. Am I a patriot? Yes. But that's about all I am."

Tonya shook her head. "I don't believe that. Neither do my associates. We see you for what you are and what you can do. We think you're more than what your life is now. We see you as a hero."

"I think you've got the wrong guy."

"What I think is that you don't have a purpose. You don't realize what you can do...what your true potential is."

Braylon looked down at the table, then back into her dark brown eyes. "Like I said, I'm just an old fart in Fort Wayne."

Tonya leaned in across the tiny table they shared. "How would you like a chance to be more? How about a chance to end this war faster, saving lives? Is that something that might interest you?"

"Of course," he replied. "But I don't see how that's possible."

"You just need help. My associates and I think you might be the right person for that chance."

"Sure, I'll play along. What is it you have in mind?"

She leaned a little further over the table, her eyes doing one more fast sweep of the room. "How about a chance to kill Daniel Porter? Take the head off the snake. If he falls, the war ends. You do that, and you'll be remembered in the same breath as Lincoln and Jefferson in our nation's history."

Braylon was stunned. *An assassin? Is she serious?* His mind was a jumble of thoughts. Revenge surfaced in his brain, and he didn't try to shake it off. Newmerica had beaten and broken him. Killing their president was not an evil act—it was a sacrifice on the altar of freedom. Deep down, he found himself embracing the idea. It started small, but that feeling grew exponentially. She was right. Killing Porter could end the war sooner. It would be a blow to the Newmericans, one he hoped they might recover from. Each beat of his heart made him like the idea even more. "I—I don't know what to say."

"Just say that you're interested. We'll help you from there."

He felt warm, his senses more alive than they had been in months, even more than when he had called the police on Freckles. "Okay. Tell me more…"

Chapter 6

The Twenty-First Amendment: The Privilege of Protest

Members of the population are free to protest, boycott, or express their opinion to any non-government entity.

Weldon Spring, Missouri

Major Judy Mercury stood in the Highway Patrol Troop C Headquarters, her gaze off to the east toward St. Louis. The NSF at the post had flipped sides as soon as the American army had shown up. It was a smart move on their part, given she would have been forced to kill them to take the position for her operation.

Judy checked her watch for the tenth time in five minutes in anticipation of what was about to start. *I should relax. This is simple. Hit the warehouses... ratchet up the tension in the city. The plan is going to work.*

Mercury was used to operations where she was fighting for a military objective either directly or indirectly. St. Louis was a different assignment. This wasn't about fighting the enemy in battle. This was a psyop. Pinch off the flow of food to the city and convince the locals to rise up and overthrow their Newmerican occupation force. She preferred a straight-up fight to the mental manipulation of Operation Thunderbuns, even though it was her plan.

The battery of M777A2 155mm howitzers that were positioned in the parking lot was a mile from the NSF checkpoint along I-65 leading into the city. No doubt, once the shooting started, they would panic, which she was completely comfortable with.

Adjusting her ear protection, she looked toward St. Louis. From her vantage point, she couldn't see much, but once the explosions started going off, that would change. She had mortars and artillery positioned strategically, each gun targeting a warehouse. It wouldn't take much to destroy the storage facilities. Judy had toyed with spreading out the attack, making it last most of the night. If her intent had been to rattle the defenders, she would have gone with that approach. Instead, she wanted it done simultaneously from around the city, quick and direct. That would allow her forces to withdraw the artillery before the enemy could unleash counterbattery fire. The population would be awakened to explosions all over, then a return to silence.

As part of the plan, she didn't intend to give an order to open fire. When they hit 0100 hours, the barrage would start. Everyone knew their duties, she assured herself. Some rounds were bound to miss. There would be some civilian casualties—that couldn't be completely avoided. Fortunately, many people didn't live near the warehouses. There would be fires—that too was inevitable. With a number of targets, the St. Louis Fire Department was going to be hard-pressed in a few minutes.

In the skies above, a smattering of clouds concealed three drones equipped with Hellfire missiles. They were a one-night loan she had dug her heels in to secure. They would be taking out a few enemy artillery batteries whose locations were known, as well as hitting two supply hubs controlled by the military. The Newmericans had been sloppy, putting their ammo storage close to the food storage. Tonight, they would pay a hefty price for their arrogance and lack of foresight.

Judy had arranged with the Sons of Liberty and other loyalists in the city to help perform a battle damage assessment after the barrage was over and assist as observers. She had her communications team monitoring and tracking the damage she was about to unleash. In front of her, the gunnery officer was reconfirming the coordinates. His voice was muffled in her ears, but she found a moment of calm watching him do his job well.

The barrage shattered her tension as the battery in front of her erupted. The flash from the muzzles created a jumble of instant shadows. Her body vibrated, throbbing from the blasts. Dust flew around her as the 155s sent their deadly salvo into St. Louis. Even with ear protection, the booms made her head ache, if only for a moment. They were followed by the metallic tinking of shell casings hitting the pavement.

In the distance, she saw orange lights flickering in the low clouds, signs of the explosions beneath them. The distant echoes of other batteries washed over the parking lot as the battery in front of her reloaded and fired again, this time less in unison. Judy held her binoculars up and saw the flickers of light peppering the sky. War had come to St. Louis. Not a vicious salt-the-earth conflict, but a very precise war...the war of a surgeon.

Several more salvos were fired in rapid succession, each one making her body quake. For a millisecond, she wondered if they were dumping too much firepower on the city. *Have we gone too far?* Before she could form words to question it, the shelling stopped.

Mercury walked over to the officer in charge of the battery, who was talking on the radio. More echoes came from all around the targets being hit, a low thunder-like rumble of the guns and mortars firing and the explosions. Slowly, one battery at a time, the outgoing fire stopped.

The officer put down his field radio and turned to her as she took off her ear protection. "We hit dead on according to the SOL," he said loudly.

"Our targets are burning rubble."

As he stopped, she could hear the distant sirens of the city. A few secondary explosions went off as well, crack-booming in the distance. She adjusted her binoculars and saw smoke illuminated by several fires. *At least this battery plastered their target.*

"Captain, break 'em down and roll them out. No doubt the Newmericans are trying to figure out where we are now." She didn't have to tell the artillery officer twice. His troops knew the drill all too well and moved quickly.

Judy walked over to her vehicle and headed back to her HQ. It was going to be a long night of assessing the damage. As if to prove that point, she heard explosions in the distance, no doubt being fired by the enemy in response to her attack. Those sounds seemed to speed up the work of the artillery crews, who understood their implications.

We've slowed their food supply, told them who's responsible, and now we've destroyed their stockpiles. Hopefully, the citizens will do the right thing.

Camp AZ10, Camp Sanders, West of Cameron, Arizona

As his car approached the long line of the walled facility, Raul Lopez looked out at the staggering size of Camp Sanders and felt a sense of dread. This was one of the largest camps he had seen. It had a wall with barbed wire on top, the wood bleached from the heat of the Arizona sun. The barracks were far more crude than those he had seen at other camps. They looked more like homeless shelters, with repurposed plywood, tattered tarps tied down for roofing, and bits of corrugated sheet metal held on more by gravity than nails. As his Army driver pulled up to the gate, Raul showed his ID. With the window down, he caught the stench in the air. It was far too familiar. The guard handed them masks with filters like the one he wore.

The car pulled in near a guard tower along the perimeter, and a staff sergeant stepped out to greet him. "You must be Mr. Lopez," the man said, his voice muffled by his mask. He gestured to the door. "Let's get you inside so we can talk."

They entered the lower portion of the tower, which looked like an office. Once inside, they peeled off their masks. "Can I get you something to drink?" the sergeant offered.

"Water would be fine," Raul said. The sergeant quickly complied with a tall glass of ice-cold water as they sat down around a plywood table in the center of the room. It was painted gray, but done so poorly that Raul could make out the wood grain. The sergeant introduced himself as Sergeant Marks and quickly explained that his platoon had stumbled across the camp on a patrol.

"Is this camp as bad as I've been told?" Raul asked.

"I'm afraid it is," the sergeant said, bowing his head for a moment. "It looks like it started out as a work camp. We found a lot of molds and equipment to make wind turbine blades. They were running a small factory to crank those things out. No safety gear, and those folks were working in scalding-hot conditions with unfiltered fiberglass and carbon fiber dust. Then, a few months ago, that all came to an end. After that, they turned this place into a death camp."

"How bad was it?"

"I can take you on a tour if you like."

I've seen enough dead. Words will do. "If you please, just give me the rundown."

"From the records we have, they had over four hundred and twenty thousand people here at one time or another."

"The camp is big, but not that big, not unless there's more to it than what it looks like."

"No. It's not. They set up gallows in the center of the camp and killed the prisoners by hanging. Their bodies were dropped into wagons under the gallows and taken to the processing building."

"Processing?"

"They ground their bones up in large machines. The rest of the bodies were burned. Apparently, they were using the bones for some sort of fertilizer, shipping a lot of it into California and Utah."

This wasn't the first time Raul had heard this. The camp where his mother and sister had been did something similar with their dead, but not on this scale. "How many were alive when you took the camp?"

The sergeant shook his head. "Five hundred and eighty-three. Since we got here, eighteen of them have died. The docs say the rest have a fighting chance of pulling through. It's going to take time, though. They cut off their food weeks ago, from the looks of things."

The numbers were staggering to Raul, despite all that he had seen in other camps. "They killed the others."

"I'm afraid so. We brought in doctors from Flagstaff and Phoenix and are doing what we can for the survivors. Suffice it to say, it's a mess."

Raul understood the nightmare of logistics that was in play. "Your call indicated you had some things that might be of use to me."

"First, this camp appears to have been the hub for this state and Colorado. Our cyber people were only able to get into one of the computers. We couldn't see the details, but it looks like we have the names and photos of every Social Enforcer assigned to these camps in the two states."

That got Raul's attention. If true, they would have the information to apprehend the SEs and make sure they saw justice. *Caylee and Charli talked about a hacker working in the government, someone they trusted. Maybe he could help.* "You weren't able to get the data?"

"No. It's encrypted, but we know it's there, sitting in a file marked Camp Personnel. Along with it, we got the names and personal data of every prisoner who was here. We're able to see the folder structure, but the data is a hot mess."

The information was priceless. It meant that family members could be informed of the fate of their loved ones. The guard information was priceless to Raul because it meant that it could be used to track down the SEs who ran the camp and bring them to justice. The encryption was beyond him, but there might be resources he could bring to bear. "I know someone who might be able to help."

"We hoped that was the case," Marks replied.

"Where did the guards go?"

"They scattered, from what we've been able to tell. We think a few went to Utah, though I tend to doubt that. Utah is American territory. We think most of them headed for Nevada."

Raul paused for a moment. He wanted to organize a pursuit of the guards, but at the moment, their files were essentially locked and unavailable. Even if he had names, the Army was consolidating in Arizona for the next big push and most likely wouldn't go off looking for some guards. "Let me make a call and see if I can get someone to break that encryption."

"Sure." Marks gestured for him to a small office for some privacy.

Raul had slowly gotten better at asking for help. Before the war that he had been sucked into, he rarely asked for assistance. With everything that he had endured, he had learned not only to ask for help but to rely on it. Pulling out his cell, he dialed one of those resources.

"Raul?" came Charli's voice. "I hadn't expected to hear from you."

"I hope I've caught you at a good time."

"Sure. What's up?"

"There's a camp here that we just liberated. They—they killed thousands of people here. We recovered their servers, and the Army techs are pretty sure we can get the names of the dead off the PC. We also believe the guards' personnel files are there, which would help us track them down. We lack the expertise with systems like this though."

Charli didn't hesitate with her response. "I'm connecting you with my guy, Kiff. I think you've met him before. Let me ring him, and he'll call you back."

"I appreciate it."

"For you, no problem. Take care."

The name Kiff rang a bell, but he couldn't place his face. Within five minutes, his phone rang with a government number from Nashville. "Raul Lopez?"

"You must be Kiff."

"Charli told me you need some help…and that you're a friend of Caylee's."

"She was right on both accounts."

"Any friend of Charli and Caylee's is my friend. I hear you need a server cracked."

Raul walked as he talked, stepping back out to where Sergeant Marks was waiting. "That's right."

"I can't make any promises, but I can give it a shot. You have a computer guy there?"

Lowering the phone, he looked at the sergeant. "Do you have a computer tech available?"

Marks turned and called out for Corporal Shasta. A young Latina emerged. "Yes, Staff Sergeant?"

Raul extended his phone. "This is Kiff. He needs to talk to you."

She took the phone and immediately began responding to Kiff's questions with words Raul didn't understand. She took off with his phone into another adjacent room. "I have no idea how long this is going to take," Raul said. "Perhaps we could do that tour now?"

Sergeant Marks agreed, pulling on his mask and leading Raul out into the camp.

* * *

The tour took two hours, and that was more emotionally grueling than anything else. It was the largest camp found to date and was deplorable in terms of conditions. The gallows were appalling. What stuck with him were the little details, like the worn ropes of the nooses, which were stained a darker color from the oils and dirt on the necks of their victims. In the room with the grinding machines to pulverize the bones of the dead, he saw dust piles around the base of the equipment and realized they were human remains. *The people who ordered this, who ran these places—they are monsters. They have to be dealt with.*

When they returned to headquarters, Corporal Shasta handed his phone to him. "You have friends in high places. You didn't tell me that you were putting me on with the Assistant Director of Cybersecurity for the whole country."

Raul smiled. *Kiff—Kiffen Renner.* Now he remembered the young man's face and role. "Did you have any luck?"

She nodded. "Your friend has access to a lot of tools that were beyond me. He got in a half an hour ago. I'm printing hard copies, and he downloaded a copy of the files just to be safe."

"Then we can track down the butchers who ran this place?"

Shasta nodded. "Oh, yeah. We even have their home addresses."

Raul allowed himself a weak smile. After all that he had seen, the horrors that people could inflict on each other, it was hard to be happy. But this was big. *If there's a chance that we can bring these people to justice, we need to do it.* He knew that his next call was going to need to be to Ted.

NSF Regional Center, Hamden, Connecticut

Angela Axton sat in her cubicle, nibbling at her cheese sandwich and occasionally dunking it in her lukewarm tomato soup as her eyes remained fixed on the screen. The lunch she had prepared was one she remembered from her childhood. Try as she might, she couldn't quite replicate the way her mother made it.

Work was becoming more difficult as the war dragged on. There were more people to investigate, and the field resources were dwindling. When states rejoined America, the NSF melted away, and the resources returned to their original local authorities. Those who were loyal Newmericans either fled or found themselves locked up and under investigation for their conduct during the NSF reign.

Many went to the District, thinking of it as a safe haven. Angela didn't see it that way. *I can read a map, and it's not looking good.* Southern Virginia was in American hands. To the north, New Hampshire was solidly American, along with much of New York State. Ohio and rural Pennsylvania were now American territory as well. *Everything is tightening around the District. Sooner or later, they will be going there in force. They have to. It's the only way to end the war.*

Closer to home, the supply chain had become a nightmare. She could only shop for food on Mondays, Wednesdays, and Fridays. Her days were chosen by her birth month. When she did go to the store, many shelves were empty. Angela purchased whatever was available that day.

Then there were the problems with gasoline. Most of the oil production was in America. President Porter had brokered a deal with the Canadians for gas and oil, but getting it to Newmerica was a challenge. The Americans shut off pipelines. Angela had almost been out of gas for a week now. She had switched to riding a bike the six miles to the office. The first three days had been painful, but now she was getting used to it. Cars with fuel to run them were a luxury. With the power grid disruptions, those who had EVs found their ability to charge hindered as much as gas car owners. *This is good for now, but when winter comes, what are we going to do?*

Lunch was her time. Most of her coworkers migrated to the cafeteria, but she stayed at her workstation and began the part of her job she truly lived for—looking for Hudson Whitlock. Her preset search parameters ran and came back with little but potential hits. One by one, she went through them, each as disappointing as the next. *By now, he probably knows that I am looking for him online. He'll avoid the net, but he might slip up, and if he does, I need to nail him.* Checking the NSF's vast array of photo images took ten minutes. The NSF had cameras everywhere. It was one of the ways they controlled crime and ensured stability in Newmerica. Two images came up as marginal, less than a twenty-percent chance of being him. She zoomed in and ran AI against the images to clear them up, but came back with nothing of use. Avoiding cameras was difficult, if not impossible, but somehow, Whitlock was doing it.

Her checks of his family came back with something new, something different. His mother, Jolene, had an obituary in their hometown paper. Angela scanned *The Cumberland Times-News.* There wasn't much to the woman's life. Angela would have expected more as the mother of a traitor. She graduated from high school, got married, had three children, and was survived by two children. Was this an implication that Hudson was really dead, or was the family simply protecting him? Hudson's mother had died of cardiac arrest while working at the small farmers' market.

Angela saw her death as an opportunity. *If Hudson's alive, he might risk showing up at her funeral!* It was a tantalizing thought. *I need to be there.* Checking the obit, she saw that the service was going to be in four days.

For the first time in a long while, she was excited. This was the best opportunity she had to either capture Hudson or confirm that he was indeed dead. There were some challenges. Far western Maryland, their panhandle, was a hotbed of American supporters. While the state was still in Newmerica's camp, once outside of the urban areas, America held sway.

The other challenge was that her manager was not likely to approve the trip. *I can use my banked vacation days, but purchasing the fuel to get there is going to require some finesse. I can only use enough of my gas ration to afford to get about halfway there.* She cringed at having to secure a black-market ration card. *There are other ways to do it, some less savory than others.*

She finished eating, memorizing every detail about Jolene Whitlock's obituary and service. When done, she closed out her windows and went to her supervisor's office. Teel looked up as he saw her. "What's up?"

"I'd like to take a few days off, maybe five."

Leaning back in his chair, he gave her a nod. "You've got a lot banked up. I don't see that as a problem. What do you have planned?"

"I was hoping to do some light travel—get away from all this."

Teel chuckled. "Good luck with that. With the war on, there aren't a lot of vacation places you can go. I used to take the kids down to Disney for the whole World of Diversity Experience. Can't do that now with Florida solidly being in the American camp. Before the war, we should have secured the good tourist states." It was a joke, but there was a ring of truth to it.

"The big challenge is gas. I just need enough to get somewhere quiet and back again."

Teel leaned forward, eyeing her with an almost fatherly gaze. "Your job performance has been improving in the last few weeks. I've noticed an attitude change, too."

"Thank you."

"There's a way for you to get enough gas rations," he said in a low tone, then nodded his head toward his office door.

Angela stepped in the rest of the way and closed the door behind her. "I'm listening."

"You might want to go see Tony down in the evidence room. Tell him I sent you. Keep it on the QT, if you catch my drift."

She did. Angela knew something unethical when she heard it. "Thanks."

"Shoot me an email with the dates you want off. I'll approve them. Some rest and relaxation will do you good."

"Thank you, sir," she said, turning and leaving his office.

* * *

The evidence room was in the bowels of the NSF center. Angela had only been there a few times since being moved to analysis, usually to review evidence taken in from criminals to help round up their associates. The officers assigned to evidence control were marginal at best. As she swiped her ID to get access, she was greeted by a portly officer. He sat behind the counter, his stomach resting on it, right up to the edge of his keyboard. The buttons on his blue shirt were straining, so great was the strain on them. He was mostly bald, and the hair he did have over his ears was in need of washing. It shimmered with body oil under the white LED lights he sat under.

"What can I do for you?" he asked. She saw that his name badge said *Anthony Livingly*.

"I work for Mike Teel. He told me I should come down here and ask for Tony."

"You got 'im," he replied, shifting slightly on his stool. "What are you looking for?"

This was the dance. She understood it well. "I'm taking some time off. We were talking about gas rations and how hard the cards are to get."

Tony eyed her with a bushy, cocked eyebrow for a moment. "Uh-huh. I think I understand why you're here. Come on back." He hit a button, and the door next to his caged seat buzzed. Angela swung the door open and stepped through. Tony hopped off his seat and led her back through the long racks of evidence. "You understand this conversation never happened."

"Understood."

He turned down one of the aisles, waddling slightly as he walked. She followed him to a rack of boxes secured with red tape. There were six shelves, each at least twenty-five feet long, from ceiling to floor. He gestured to them. "Welcome to dead cases."

"Excuse me?"

"Dead cases," he repeated. "This is evidence we secured, but the cases never came to court. Most of the perps had, you know, *accidents* while in custody."

Accidents. That was the phrase he used. She understood completely. The NSF-run jails often had prisoners who ended up dead. There were no longer any inspectors general to look into the cases. Most NSF agents thought of those deaths as saving the government the cost of a trial. "So, how does this work?"

"I go back to my desk. What you do back here—well, let's just say the cameras have been on the fritz for a year. When you come out, we make arrangements for a nominal fee."

"What is nominal?"

"Two-fifty—non-trackable cash transfer."

She eyed the man and nodded. "Sounds good."

"You've got twenty minutes. After that, I go on break." With that, Tony lumbered back.

Angela pulled a large box and started rifling through the goods, looking for a wallet that might hold a ration card. She struck out on the first box, but on the second, she found one. The wallet was empty of cash—no doubt Tony had pocketed that long ago—but it did have ration cards. *I'll need a few of these to add up to enough for the trip.* It was a flaw in the system. The Department of Transportation that controlled the ration cards was rarely informed when their owners died. So each month, their rations would be added to the cards.

Having a few of them would ensure she had enough for her trip to Maryland.

Angela paused for a moment, looking at the wallet. There were pictures in it: young kids, a family shot taken at Disneyland with Mickey Mouse. For some reason, the images felt old, like they were taken in a different time. *Probably before the Liberation.* She allowed herself a moment to wonder where the people in the images were or if they were even still alive.

Opening another box, she saw a small gun, a Beretta. *If I do run into trouble, it might be good to have a non-NSF weapon.* She took out the 3032 Tomcat FDE and cleared the chamber just in case the arresting officers hadn't. It was an old habit, one she had no intention of breaking. *Thirty-two caliber, not great, but enough punch to kill.* Grabbing the two magazines, she stuffed them all into her suitcoat pocket and looked for another ration card.

After she secured what she had come for, Angela headed back to the cage to make her payment. A wave of irony passed over her. *I was always a good agent. I did everything by the book back in the day. Now I'm committing a crime by stealing evidence, and my boss is complicit. Is this what the NSF is now—a criminal organization?*

She purged that thinking quickly. It wasn't her problem to solve, not at the moment. *Besides, if I bring in Whitlock, it will more than justify how I did it.*

Chapter 7

Twelfth Amendment: The Privilege of Public Safety

Citizens have the right to feel safe in public. Only sanctioned government agents my possess guns or ammunition in order to preserve public safety. The right to feel safe in public shall not be denied to the people.

The District

The vice president walked into the Pentagon with deliberate boldness. Neither she nor Daniel had ever gone to the building across the Potomac before, so her presence was aimed at sending a message: *We are in this together, like it or not.*

Ever since the start of the Great Reformation, the military had kept the Newmericans at arm's length. They had failed to come to the Traitor President's aid the night of the Liberation. They had supplied the commanders for the Newmerican military, but they had refused to commit the regular Army or Marine Corps to the fighting. Many military forces had deserted to America, no doubt guided by a false sense of patriotism.

The military tried to walk a tightrope. They didn't pursue deserters while at the same time "leasing" bases and equipment to Newmerica's fight. She and Daniel saw eye to eye with them. *They knew they committed treason when they didn't come to the aid of the previous president. They also know that if the war ends and we lose, they will be held accountable for their actions and inactions.* No matter how hard she and Daniel pressed, the Joint Chiefs did their best to resist joining the fighting.

A lieutenant led her through the rings of the building, finally taking her to the office of the chairman of the Joint Chiefs. He held the door for her as she and her two NSF/Secret Service agents entered. The VP didn't wait for a further invitation. She walked into the chairman's office and closed the door behind her.

The general was caught a little off guard—she could see it on his face. He probably wasn't used to someone barging in unannounced. He rose to his feet, gesturing to a chair. "Madam Vice President."

She took the seat. "I take it this meeting didn't screw up your schedule."

"Not at all," General Young replied. It was a lie, but he said it with conviction. "I would have been happy to meet at your office. I hope this wasn't an inconvenience."

"Not at all. I love riding in the helicopter. I trust you know why I'm here."

He nodded. "Yes. We've done a fairly exhaustive search for a new ground commander. We wanted to make sure that the person we chose had the correct political perspective and the skills needed to turn the war around."

"Excellent. And who did you settle on?"

He hit the intercom. "Send in General Busse."

A few moments later, the door opened, and in walked Busse. He was in his fifties, pale, shorter than she would have expected, and skinny, too. In her mind, that didn't make him look like a fighter. *If anything, he looked more like a clerk or an accountant.* He saluted them both as she rose to her feet. Despite all of his training, *I think I could beat him up.*

"A pleasure to meet you, Madam Vice President," Busse said, extending his hand.

She eyed it, but she did not return the shake. Turning to General Young, she glared. "Is this some sort of joke?"

"Ma'am?"

"First, you bring in this short little man. I'm sure those ribbons on his chest all stand for things, but I need a war fighter. My dog walker could probably take this guy out."

General Young's face went red as General Busse spoke up. "If I may, I am a Ranger and have spent ten years in Special Forces, Madam Vice President. I've spilled blood on three continents and been shot twice myself. Yes, I have a lot of ribbons. That's because I'm good at killing people."

General Young jumped in. "You'd be making a mistake to think that because he's short, he's not lethal."

Good. I've upset them both. "It's not just that. He's a white male."

"What has that got to do with winning the war?" General Busse asked, slightly more agitated than before.

She turned and faced him. "We've had two men leading our forces so far. Both proved to be abysmal failures. What we need right now is a more balanced, equitable choice. Surely you have a woman general, preferably one of color, you could give us." She slowly turned back to General Young so he knew the question was leveled at him.

"You asked for the best. That's General Busse."

"What I need is someone who represents the people of our great nation. No offense to General Busse, but he's a white man. In the eyes of the population, he represents the losses we've had up to this point. We need someone people can identify with, someone they can look up to. Male and pale isn't going to cut it."

"General," Young said to Busse, "I need to talk to the VP alone."

Busse left the room, and Young waited until the door closed. "We have women we can put in this role. You need to understand that none of them have the background or depth of experience General Busse has."

"I'm surprised you didn't offer one of them first. Are we clear on what the priorities are?"

"We have implemented diversity mandates throughout the DoD for the last five years. You know that. Our commitment to an equitable command structure is well known—the TRC has reported on it many times. We've even flexed hard to incorporate your Warden program into our ranks."

"Yet, here we are, with you pushing another white man on us. I think it's safe to say that the president and I expected more out of you."

Young's face sagged slightly, despite his attempt to reel in his temper. She didn't care that it bothered him. *People like him need to die off before the rest of us can enjoy the diverse and equitable utopia we're building. As much as he says the right words and does the right things, in the end, he's just a white man attempting to uphold his racial patriarchy.*

"There's another candidate who may fit your needs: Colonel July Woodworth. What she lacks in terms of combat experience, she makes up for in logistics experience. She did wonders in the Defense Logistics Agency, straightening out our hodgepodge of inventory systems," Young replied.

"Her race?"

"She's a woman of color. Her father was Black, and her mother was of Eastern Indian descent."

"Perfect, though her rank concerns me. We need a general, not a colonel, leading our forces."

Young nodded. "We will give her a brevet field promotion to general. I can sign off on that without having to go through The People's House."

The vice president raised a smile on her face, knowing she had pummeled the chairman of the Joint Chiefs. "I look forward to meeting her."

"I will make arrangements to get her here ASAP, if you don't mind the short wait."

"Not at all. Perhaps you could give me a tour."

"I would be honored," he said, almost convincingly. She didn't care that she had upset him or derailed his choice to lead the military in the field. *We tried it twice their way, and both times we suffered losses. I was almost killed in that attack in Virginia myself! The military mindset needs to change. Once this war is over, General Young and his kind are going to be sent packing. Then we'll show the whole world what the true strength of diversity is.*

El Mirage, Arizona

General Trip Reager had a plan for the war but kept it close to his chest. Not that he didn't trust the American administration—he didn't trust any politicians. To their credit, the president and the chief of staff had given him free rein in running the war, and so far, it had worked out well. But now, after days of rest and refit, the time had come to launch the next phase of the war, and he had to share his ideas with his command staff and a select few officers.

He had assembled them in a long-closed Dick's Sporting Goods. They had cleared out the shelving and displays that had been left after the chain went bankrupt, and someone had even managed to get the air conditioner running. Trip didn't care about the locale. After all he had seen in the retaking of Arizona, he was looking forward to putting the state in his rearview mirror. *The crimes they committed here are so horrible, it's hard to look at the civilians and not think they were all somehow involved.*

They had erected a screen for his slideshow. Reager hated PowerPoint, so he kept it to four slides and two maps. "Thank you for coming," he said, glancing over at Major

Mercury, who had arrived only a few minutes before the meeting. "We have a lot of balls in the air right now, so I think it's a good time to take in the big picture in terms of our operations."

A map of the East Coast came up with a click of his mouse. "New Hampshire, Vermont, Maine, parts of Delaware, and a significant chunk of New York State, as well as counties in Massachusetts, are now under our control, or more accurately, no longer in control of the enemy. Boston has called itself a free city, and New York is planning on doing the same, no doubt to make sure we don't starve them out." The freed areas showed up in red on the map. "General Griffiths, are you in a position yet to kick off an offensive?"

"With the surrender of a lot of the New York National Guard, we're actually doing quite well with equipment, ammo, and fuel. Our people are rested and ready to fight."

"Good. Keep that thought. Major Mercury, what's the status of Operation Thunderbuns in St. Louis?"

"Sir, there have been food riots for the last three days. One got out of hand, and the NSF got violent with the protesters —fifteen in the hospital, four dead. The mayor issued a demand that we restore the flow of food into the city or else. Initially, people put the blame on us. Now it's on the Newmerican administration. I think in another week or so, they will fold, or the locals will round them up."

"Excellent," Trip said, turning to Gwen Holtz, the leader of the SOL group, the Witches of Wichita. "Ms. Holtz, it sounds like Operation John Brown has been making some headway in Colorado. Can you give us an update?"

Holtz was uncomfortable with the brass. He could see her eyes darting around the room. Chances were she wasn't used to public speaking. "Well, our plan was to go into Colorado and stir things up. A number of the counties were given the chance to side with us and did so. Denver, Boulder, Aspen, and a few other cities are digging in for Newmerica, but the bulk of the state is siding with us. We're getting arms in, doing some training, and running guerrilla operations against the Newmericans. Half of the National Guard has defected to us, and Colorado Springs and the Air Force Academy capitulated yesterday with the promise that we wouldn't occupy their campus or interfere with them, per your orders. The fighting is intense and nasty. A lot of people are just fed up with the Newmerica bullshit—sir."

"Good work. Let's keep the pressure up on the cities there. With all that's happening around the country, they are bound to cave in eventually."

Holtz nodded, red-faced, in response.

"That leaves us with the next two operations. The first, Blind Weasel, is a strike toward Philadelphia. The Newmericans are preparing for a Constitutional Convention there." He paused as several members of the group moaned or shook their heads in disgust. "I know that all of us would like to ruin their little party, and that's our intent. General Ricketts will assemble an assault force in Ohio and drive across the state toward Philly."

"You want me to take the city?" Ricketts asked.

"No. You won't have enough force for that. I just need you to be a disruptor. It's going to be hard for those delegates to look to the future when they can hear your artillery in the distance. We just need to rattle them, as well as cut off Pittsburgh from assisting them. Blind Weasel's intent is to frighten the enemy and leave us in a good position for the ultimate prize, the District." He pointed to the map and let it sink in.

"At the same time, General Griffiths is going to launch Operation Maniac from New Hampshire, swinging to the I-95 corridor. Hank, I want you to make it look like your goal is New York, but then swing around it to the west and continue into New Jersey."

"New Jersey?" Griffiths said. "What did I do to piss you off, sir?" His response brought about a wave of chuckles that were needed to slice through the tension in the room.

"Taking New York would be like trying to eat an elephant. If the Newmericans want to hold it, let them. It's an albatross around their necks. There are over eight million people in New York. Once you swing around and drive south, the Newmerican leadership is going to have to figure out how to feed all of them. Meanwhile, once you get south of the city, drive like hell toward the District. Hold your advance when you cross into Maryland. Just being there will have the politicians wetting their beds in the Capitol."

"Understood, sir. I'm a little surprised we aren't thrusting north through Virginia, though."

"I considered that course of action. I think they would be expecting us to do that and have dug in, hoping we take that route. It's always best to hit your enemy where they don't expect it. Besides, if we were successful, we'd have to slog through the urban nightmare of Northern Virginia, then force our way across the Potomac. Too many possible points of failure."

That seemed to sate Griffiths, who gave a nod of approval. Trip continued, "For the time being, I will remain with General Lessman and launch Operation Black Tarantula." He clicked to the next map, that of the West Coast. "I'd love to leave California until the end of this war, but there are more Social Quarantine camps there than in any other state. And, as you've all seen, they are slaughtering thousands every day. We need to take California and put an end to the mass murders." His words brought nods of agreement.

"The way we see it, the Newmericans know we're here. They probably think we're going to thrust our way right to San Diego, then up the coast. In reality, we're going to fake them out. The drive for San Diego will kick up a lot of dust and make them think that's our primary target. In reality, the bulk of our attack force will head north into Nevada. We've had SOL units operating in Las Vegas for weeks now, opening up negotiations with the, uh, informal owners and operators in the city."

"The mob," General Griffiths said out loud what everyone was thinking.

"They prefer to be thought of as business owners, but yes, the mob. We've been given informal assurances that they will capitulate once we get there rather than risk damage to their investment. They were quite supportive. The regulations and travel restrictions that the Newmericans put on the city have been cutting into their bottom line for years. They see our liberation of Las Vegas as a chance to cash in."

General Reager continued, "The diversionary force will break north along the Salton Sea, up to Highway 10, then toward the west and LA. There are about a dozen SE camps out there in the desert that will need to be liberated. I've asked Raul Lopez to form a team of medics, transportation, and security personnel to save anyone still alive there." He glanced over at Lopez, who smiled broadly.

"Meanwhile, we will come in on I-15, running like a bat out of hell. We'll come up on the city with a two-pronged thrust. Hopefully, that will scare the shit out of the locals, and they will capitulate without a fight. If not, chances are they won't be able to handle a pair of assaults."

"Are you thinking we occupy Los Angeles?" General Ricketts asked.

"Let's hope we don't have to. Occupations are drains on resources. Once LA falls, we'll need to move north. But without LA, the state's economy will fall fairly fast. We have split the country, with a few holdouts like Minnesota. The only way Newmerica will be able to get things to California is by sea. Washington State is going to hoard everything they have once they realize we're on their coast."

"Are we going to drive up the coast into Oregon and Washington?" General Lessman asked.

"The North and South Dakota National Guards are going to feint a thrust into Minnesota. In reality, they are heading west. The goal is to frighten Washington State enough that they won't send their National Guard troops to try to help California. I have a separate operation in the next few days that should cause some chaos in Cali's political structure. Once California has bent the knee, we'll deal with Washington and Oregon with our air assets."

"What about Black Tarantula's supply lines?" General Griffiths asked.

He appreciated the question. Logistics was always the key to successful military operations. "We're going to shift our main hub to Las Vegas. Once we take the city, I've made arrangements for shipping goods through the Panama Canal to the port in L.A. Those ships will start their trip once we get underway with the offensive."

General Lessman spoke up. "I expect that the Newmericans will encourage their cartel allies to hit us from Mexico again."

Reager grinned. "I've already dispatched the Twenty-Fifth Carolina Tortilla Militia to the border, along with the Texas Rangers. If the cartels try to come across, they will be engaged and destroyed."

Griffiths spoke up. "They can still cross into California."

"Not as of three hours ago. Our aircraft and drones destroyed the border crossings in California. If they do try to cross there, it will be in very limited numbers, based on the craters I saw."

As he finished, Reager killed the PowerPoint. The questions came at him like a missile barrage. It didn't bother him. If they hadn't asked questions, he would have been concerned. For the first time, it was clear that the war was over the hump, that the end was not only possible but in sight. Everyone had a part to play in the coming victory. As they finished, Trip offered words of caution. "I see your excitement and encourage it. Don't let it blind you. We could still lose this war. We're dealing with a desperate enemy, one who has everything to lose and is willing to fight to the bitter end to save their own asses. They have committed mass murder and other atrocities, and they know that we know it. Desperation can make even the most seasoned vet do things that are reckless and dangerous. Don't let yourself get cocky."

As his officers filtered out of the room, Trip approached Major Mercury. "You good?"

She nodded. "This was the first time that I started thinking about the war actually being over."

"With that fentanyl attack the cartels unleashed in Texas, we already saw that they are willing to use chemical weapons."

"I'll take care of St. Louis as soon as possible."

"Good. When that's wrapped, you're heading to Ohio to help out there."

"I'll handle it. I'm more worried about you, sir."

Her words caught Trip off guard. "Me?"

Mercury nodded. "Even before the Fall, California was a strange place filled with weird people. They've had a half-decade of progressive socialism, being told none of life's problems are their own, that it's all because of race or religion. I'm going to take a city. You're going into the first level of hell itself."

Trip nodded, understanding fully. *She's right. I'm going to need some help from people who have boots on the ground in California. Otherwise, I'm not going to know what I'm walking into.*

Smyrna, Tennessee

Caylee packed her kit carefully. The prosthetics she carried to mask her from facial recognition software needed to be concealed carefully. If they were discovered, there was no explanation she could give to the authorities that would be convincing enough for them to let her go. Her weapons needed to be packed with equal care, slid into pockets in the bag that would hide them. Guns were banned and confiscated in Newmerica. While that was official policy, the reality was that guns were still everywhere. Confiscation had been vicious and brutal, but in the end, the criminals still had them. Coming across the border with a gun was going to be tricky.

She had a bag dedicated to disguise. There were four wigs inside, a specialized makeup case, a small container with false fingertips, and a number of IDs and documents, along with Newmerican cash, gas ration cards, and other bits of tradecraft. This wasn't her first time going in behind enemy lines, and Caylee wanted to make sure she was prepared.

An NSF border guard searching her gear might very well find the two pistols and ammo, so the key was not to get searched in the first place. She was attractive, which helped. With Newmerica cracking down on travel, she had not only needed to forge good identification, she also needed to have travel papers that would stand up to investigation. A year of tradecraft training early in her career had proven to be a great asset to fall back on.

Maria Lopez, Raul's sister, knocked at her door lightly. "Come in," Caylee said. "I'm just finishing packing." She wrapped her handheld wireless jammer in her underwear and tucked it in her bag.

"So, you're really going to do it—go north?" Maria asked.

"I am."

"I wish you wouldn't." Her voice was almost pleading.

"I have to. The Veep is a bad person, beyond bad. She's the architect of a lot of what has happened in this country. She's tried to have me killed, painting me as a traitor. I thought that going after some of her family members might shake her up enough to stop, but it only made her worse. I always knew it was going to come down to her and me in the end."

"How will you even find her? They haven't announced where the convention is being held."

This was a question that was far less emotional for Caylee, one she liked answering. "That is actually simple when you think about it. Every politico in Newmerica wants to put their fingerprints on this new constitution. That means a large gathering place. A convention center might work, but the one in Philly has been closed for renovations for the last six months. Hotels are too small, not big enough for the show that the TRC is going to want to put on. That leaves you with sports arenas. The football stadium would be perfect, but it's open air, and there's no guarantee of the weather. That leaves you with Fetterman Center, where the Flyers play. It's indoors, large, perfect for the event."

"Won't they have a lot of security there?"

"Yes. I was able to have some of our intelligence assets get me blueprints to the arena. The rule of thumb is that no matter how hard you try, you can't make any location perfectly safe. Once I get there, I'll get my hands on the IDs they're using so I can get in."

"How will you do that?"

Caylee cocked her head as if to say, "Are you serious?"

Maria understood. "Oh."

"Getting in is tricky. Getting out is even trickier. Once I accomplish my mission, they will try to cork the bottle. It will be sticky because things will be fluid, but I should be able to clear a path out on the way in."

"What happens if you fail?"

"I'm either killed or captured." She regretted saying something so flippant to Maria. The young woman looked up to her. They were family in many ways. *Damn! I should have watched my mouth.* "It won't come to that, Maria. I'm unaccustomed to failing."

Maria moved in and hugged her tight. Caylee wasn't a hugger. Close physical contact, other than when training or fighting, was not something she enjoyed. Still, it was impossible for her not to reciprocate and hug Maria back. "I want you to promise you'll come back. Swear it to me," the young woman said as she loosened her arms.

"I'll be back," Caylee said. She didn't regret it. *I have every intention of coming back. If I'm going to die, it's not going to be in Philadelphia.*

"Take this," Maria said, handing her a small silver medallion. "It is St. Jude Thaddeus. It will bring you luck."

Caylee held the cold metal in her palm. "What is he the saint of?"

"He is a patron saint of lost causes. We pray to him in hopeless situations, when all is dark. My mother carried that necklace with her when we came over the border into this country. It kept me alive when all else was lost. Maybe it will do the same for you."

Caylee looked at the silver medallion, rubbing it between her pointer finger and thumb. *Who am I to refuse good luck?* "Thank you," she said, zipping her bag shut. "I need to get on the road. If you have any issues, you've got Charli and Andy's numbers—call them."

Maria paused, wiping away tears from her eyes. Caylee grabbed her bag and walked past the young woman. She had long miles ahead of her and a tricky border crossing to contemplate.

Chapter 8

Third Amendment: The Right to Control Your Own Body

People residing in the country have control over all aspects of their person with the exception of mandated vaccines or treatments. Birthing people control the life of their bodies and anything coming from their bodies up to one hour after birth.

Fort Wayne, Indiana

Deja, who had chosen to go by the name Tonya for this mission, brought the beers over to the table where Braylon Ironsides sat in the Latch String Bar & Grill. The band had stopped playing a few minutes ago, allowing her a chance to continue their conversation.

Manipulating Ironsides was a structured process, but it was going smoother than she had anticipated. The more she talked to him, the more the hate boiled out in his words. He spoke about torture at the camp where he had been held. As an SE, she knew that such things happened in the camps. Sometimes the physical abuse was necessary. Prisoners resisted, fought, or were caught planning escapes. Punishment was necessary for keeping the camps orderly.

Memories of her torture of Raul Lopez surfaced, though she did her best to keep them mentally at bay. *That was different. That was necessary. He is a terrorist. What I was doing was trying to protect innocent lives. I was doing my duty.*

She had seen the American press footage of the alleged crimes in some camps they had "liberated." Deja doubted it all. It smacked of lies. There was no way that the Newmericans were taking part in mass murders. *I know a lot of those people. They are good at heart. We would never do things like that. If that was all going on, someone would have exposed it much earlier.* To her, it felt staged, pure propaganda. *They are putting out these stories to break our spirit. The TRC has got to get better at blocking them.*

This mission was a strange one. Deja knew she was being asked to kill her own president. Strangely, she felt it was a just decision. *He molested a young girl—took advantage of her. I saw the photos. I always knew there was something off about him. Now I know what it is. Doing this will save the country an ugly scandal in the middle of this war.* She had repeated those thoughts in her head so many times that they seemed natural.

Braylon took a long, almost loving sip of his beer, then looked at her. "It's been a while since I could afford real beer. I almost forgot what it tasted like."

The ambient sounds around them ensured their voices wouldn't travel. "We have much to prepare."

"My biggest concern isn't doing it." It, being the assassination of the president. "How will we get out of there? Most assassins end up dead or captured. I won't go back to a camp again, not after all the things that happened to me there."

"I have inside people who will help us. Once you've... performed the act, we'll be able to get away. Trust me."

"I barely know you."

She leaned back. "True. What do you want to know?" Deja knew that the best way to bring him in was to give him what he wanted. *If he wants answers, I can provide those.*

"You seem to have a lot of information about where the president is going to be. You have accomplices. What do you need me for?"

"The people I'm working with are dissatisfied with what Newmerica has devolved into. They were in the NSF and have seen the corruption and rot from within. Like me, they hate what the nation had become under the old Ruling Council. Almost all of them have lost a loved one in this civil war. If Daniel Porter isn't stopped, the war could drag on for years, killing hundreds of thousands more." Her lies flowed naturally from her mouth because she had rehearsed for such a question.

"But why me?"

"My expertise is in planning. Look at me." She held up her deformed hand. "I can't fire a gun anymore. If I could, we wouldn't be talking. Besides, my people have all agreed, this needs to be done by an American. You seemed like the perfect person for the job. People know your story. Newmerica hurt you, but you still had the courage to take a stand against the guard who wronged you. It's important that when the dust settles, we have an American face that can take the credit for ending the war. It will help the country heal."

Braylon nodded as if he understood. "What about you, Tonya? What's your story?"

"Me? I was a cop at one point. I lived in Minneapolis. During all the riots and stuff during the Fall, I was out there, fighting bad guys. I always thought that was what we were supposed to do. You know, holding that blue line. The thing was, once all local law enforcement got rolled up into the NSF, things went wonky. The mission, protecting the citizens, seemed to disappear overnight."

She paused to take a sip of her beer, savoring it as an opportunity to make sure she told the story as she had crafted it. "I lost my little brother to some gang banger. They flipped their street gang into service for the Social Enforcers. That made him untouchable." Deja hesitated, as if struggling with

...

the memories. "I wanted to see that prick go to trial, but he was above reproach. That was the end for me."

"You quit the force?"

Deja nodded. "It seemed like the right thing to do. I had a lot of time after I left the NSF to see what the country had become. It feels like everyone is suckling at the tit of the government. Hell, I was doing it too! I wasn't living—I was just existing. You know what I mean? Well, I met up with some folks who were in the resistance. At first, I was just listening to them. After a while, I wanted to be a part of America again. I saw through the bullshit the TRC was force-feeding us. It's amazing what you can realize if you take the time to do your own digging. I came to see that the war was a waste of human lives, and the people responsible for it, like Porter, had no problem sending people to die for their cause." The talking points came to her quickly. Her research was NeoFox News out of Tennessee. Regurgitating their talking points was simple.

Braylon nodded. "I'm amazed that more people in Newmerica haven't seen the light. I mean, Porter overthrew the government! They killed the president. If the rumors are true, the vice president was the one who gave the order to slaughter most of The People's House and the Senate. They started from corruption and went downhill from there!" He took a much deeper swig of beer.

"If you're up to it, we can put a stop to Porter and the rest of them. My daddy used to tell me that one person with determination can make a difference. I have never forgotten that. When I saw you on TV, I thought you might be the right person, the person who can make that difference."

"I want to," Braylon said. "I'm a little worried. I've gotten old beyond my years, thanks to my time in that damned camp. You may have been better off choosing a younger person for this mission."

Deja reached out and rested her hand on Braylon's. "My momma used to say that age is just a state of mind. Besides, I don't think this calls for a great deal of athletics. Just a steady hand, a good eye, and a sense of purpose."

Braylon finished his beer in two gulps. "Well then, Tonya, I'm your guy."

Deja grinned. Her assignment was proving easier than she had expected.

El Mirage, Arizona

Darius wasn't sure what he'd done wrong, but it had to be something pretty bad to be summoned to meet with General Reager. When he had been in the Veteran Volunteer Corps, the TRC had pumped them with all sorts of stories about Reager. They called him the Butcher. The broadcasts out of Chicago during the election claimed that he had slaughtered women and children. They said in San Antonio that he had killed hundreds during a peaceful protest. They said he had given orders to shoot anyone who dared to surrender. As with everything that came from the Truth Reconciliation Committee, you either took it as gospel or saw it as news tightly wrapped in propaganda. Darius was in the second camp. When he had surrendered, he had no fear at all that they would be lined up and shot. *When your media lies to you enough, it ceases to be a source of information and becomes merely untrustworthy background noise.*

The driver who had brought him stopped in front of an old Dick's Sporting Goods. The windows were boarded up with sun-bleached plywood. In the parking lot was a mobile anti-aircraft missile battery, its weapons pointing into the stark blue Arizona sky. His identification was checked by a pair of guards at the door, and he was ushered inside.

There were several areas where officers were being briefed. A low murmur echoed in the empty store space from the conversations that were happening. Darius was led through a maze of people to the back of the store. There, he saw a man sitting at a folding white plastic table, a single laptop computer in front of him. "General, this is Darius Thorne," his escort said.

Darius stood at attention. "At ease," General Reager said, gesturing to a folding chair. "Have a seat."

"Thank you, sir."

"You came to us from the California Volunteer Corps."

"The Veteran Volunteer Corps. That's correct, sir."

Reager grinned slightly. "You can drop the 'sir' shit. You're not in trouble."

Darius wasn't sure how to respond. "Okay."

"Look, we're planning an operation in California."

He nodded. "I've been hearing rumors about that."

"I'm not surprised. Regardless, I need someone who can tell me what things are like there. More importantly, how the civilian population will react once our forces start pushing into the metropolitan areas."

It was an intriguing question that Darius had not given much thought to. He took a few moments before speaking, trying to process it himself. "Californians are a people who live their own lies. Everyone sees themselves as part of some group that is being oppressed. They believe they deserve more."

"More what?"

"They feel the government owes them everything, and the government is more than willing to give it to them to keep them in line. Personal responsibility doesn't exist. If someone robs a store, it's because their family was denied rights, or they were held back. The people there justify everything based on their feelings, not the facts." Memories of his own trial that had cost him his business surged forward in his mind.

"It feels like a form of slavery."

He had never thought of it that way, but the general's metaphor seemed accurate. "You're pretty close with that. I would say it's more like a drug user and their dealer in terms of the relationship. They feel they deserve things, and the state government gives them just enough to keep them hooked."

"Jesus! That doesn't sound like living life at all."

"It's not. Even when the government does something bad, the people accept it as long as it doesn't interrupt their welfare or services. We were sent into the Presidio in San Francisco to evict a homeless camp. It resulted in people being killed. The media barely covered it. No one cared about what we'd been forced to do or the victims."

"So, what happens if we show up on their doorsteps?"

Darius pondered that for a moment before responding. "I can't say for sure, but I'm willing to bet they will simply turn to you as their masters. They will overwhelm an invading force, demanding that you provide them the same thing the state government does."

The general shook his head. "What about armed resistance?"

Darius chuckled. "It took years for them to do it, but they went door to door, using dogs and whatnot, finding every gun and bullet out there. They didn't get them all, but they got a lot of them. I remember they melted a bunch of them down to make that ugly-ass statue of Kamala Harris in Beverly Hills. The Social Enforcers have guns, and the crooks, but they aren't going to mount up much against this force."

Reager seemed to drink in every detail Darius gave him. "You were in the Veteran Volunteer Corps. Why'd you leave them?"

He sighed, wishing the general hadn't asked that question. "They used us. Pushing into Texas was a mistake. A bunch of us knew it. Then when I saw the Newmericans had the cartels come in to pull our asses out of there, well, that was the straw that broke the camel's back."

"You felt betrayed?"

"Damn right I did—sir," he caught himself, pulling back his rage. "They used fentanyl to bomb that town. My sergeant damn near died from an overdose. I had no problem fighting for California, but they used us as an invasion force and didn't care what happened to us. I lost one of my best friends to drugs, and the damned Newmericans had no issue with siding with the cartels. That was wrong." It felt good to say it, as if he were suddenly unburdened by the bad memories he had been forced to live through. It wasn't a complete purge of his raw emotions, but a good start.

"We may be going up against your old corps," Reager said. "Are you going to be comfortable with that?"

Darius nodded. "That was my past. I'm not the man I was then." He could almost feel the weight of the medal that he carried in his breast pocket.

Reager's eyes narrowed as he looked at him. "You know LA and San Francisco, right?"

"Yes, sir. I lived in both of them."

Reager straightened in his chair. "I'd like to add you to my staff. You'd be reporting to Captain Harnessy. I need someone I can turn to once we're in the state who knows the ground and the people—someone who has been there recently."

Darius shifted in his chair. "I'm not sure what to say."

"Then say yes."

It felt right. His respect for Reager went up. *It takes a lot to admit that you don't know everything.* "Yes," he blurted out.

"Excellent. I'll put in the orders. In the meantime, grab your gear and hustle back here. We have an invasion to pull off."

Fort Wayne, Indiana

Braylon Ironsides hadn't fired an assault weapon since he had been in the Army decades ago. The Palmetto State

Arsenal Nitride M4 Carbine felt good in his hands as he aimed at the target Tonya had set up in the woods. It had taken two magazines to zero in the scope. After that, he had fired from several ranges, making the necessary adjustments as he went. Braylon was surprised at how his old skills were coming back to him.

Tonya stood at his side with binoculars, watching his progress and giving him words of encouragement. When he fired the last round of his current magazine, he paused and looked over at her. She cast him a sideways glance, smiling.

Braylon liked Tonya. Not in a sexual way, but as a person. What she had brought him was something he didn't even know he was lacking—a sense of purpose. Since he had been liberated from the camp, he had felt like he was wandering in a haze. He had merely accepted whatever life had thrown his way. In turning in the former guard, he had risen above his fears. It had been frightening, embarrassing, and exciting all at the same time.

Then Tonya had come along. She brought with her a feeling of control over his life. It was exhilarating to think about what he was about to do. Killing Daniel Porter might just end the war. He would no longer be a former prisoner—he would be a hero. People would look up to him. More importantly, if he was successful, it would save lives.

Thinking about the opportunity Tonya had presented him had dominated his days and nights. At work, it was all he could think about. He had fantasies about it. While he knew he should be afraid, each day that fear diminished. *This is something I can do. I can pull this off. His security detail has to be perfect all the time. I only need a second of opportunity.*

Tonya had assured him that he would be successful and that she would ensure that he got away. She'd secured accomplices, people who felt the same way he did about Newmerica. That gave him even more assurance. *I am not alone in this. I have people backing me.*

He removed the magazine and cleared the weapon, then walked down to the target to see how much he had improved. *Still a tad low, but better.* That could be resolved with a tiny adjustment to the scope. As he put a new target up, he realized something. He was smiling. At first, it was a strange feeling, but he embraced it.

Tonya walked up to him, limping ever so slightly, holding her phone and reading the screen. "Good news," she said, her own smile matching his.

"What is it?"

"Our friends have gotten us President Porter's itinerary." She stopped next to him, scrolling down on her phone.

"What do they think?"

"The Constitutional Convention will be at the Fetterman Center, as expected. His hotel is a mile away. There are no hotels attached to the center, so he'll be arriving in the limo. That's too armored of a target for us. Ever since the Ronald Reagan assassination attempt, the Secret Service has always been highly attuned to transfer points in and out of the vehicle. That part is too risky, or so they say. And trying to shoot him in the arena won't work. There are five rings of security around him. Even if we could get in with a rifle, there's no way to get close enough to be sure that he is taken out."

"There's got to be a way," Braylon replied.

She gave a quick nod. "There is. The way they have the Center staged, they have to use one of the side entrances to get in. They have set up a cordon to escort him in, but the president and the TRC have insisted on letting the media line that walkway. I guess they want a shot of him going in, you know, a photo op."

Tonya paused, lowering her phone. "They can get us in with the media, complete with a van. From the van, you should be able to take the shot, and you'll already be in a vehicle. Before they lock down the area, we'll be on the road."

"But everyone will be looking for that van. We won't get ten blocks."

"We'll use it as a decoy. One of our comrades will drive off, and we'll walk away, as if we don't know what's happening. He'll ditch the vehicle next to another car. By the time the Secret Service finds the van, there won't be anything there to find."

In Braylon's mind, he could see it all unfolding just as Tonya said. *It will work! It's perfect. I only need to open the door to the van a little. Firing from inside, no one will see me or the rifle.*

Overjoyed, he hugged her, and she held him tightly back. *In just a few days, this war will be over, and the world will have me to thank for it.*

Chapter 9

Eighth Amendment: The Right to Meaningful Employment

Individuals have a right to work in a job consummate to their skills, education, and the needs of the nation. They will be provided wages and benefits according to standards outlined by The People's House. Those that are unable to find meaningful employment will be provided an appropriate job within the FedGov.

Mehlville, Missouri

Major Mercury listened intently to the sound of gunfire in the distance to the north from St. Louis. The pops and cracks of guns echoed in her direction as she stood in the bed of the truck she had used to reach Mehlville.

Until yesterday, Mehlville had been patrolled by Newmerican forces. Once the shooting started in the city, they had pulled back. While there was some risk in pushing closer to the enemy, she had to know what was going on. What she heard was a battle. So far, there was no machine-gun fire or explosions, just the banging away of small arms. Her small security detail fanned out around the CVS parking lot, making her feel comfortable.

She had gotten back from General Reager's meeting two days ago. The last three convoys of food they had allowed into the city had been swarmed by the citizens, preventing the authorities from handling the distribution. It was chaos, exactly the kind of pandemonium she had hoped would break out. Some of the locals got a lot, but many walked away with

Blaine L. Pardoe

nothing but their anger. The local TV stations had been broadcasting guidelines for distributing the food, warning people not to approach the convoys, but all that had done was what Judy had hoped for—it spurred people into action. The thought that they might not get anything to eat made them take matters into their own hands. Strangely, TV and radio went off the air in the city hours ago.

A flashlight flickered from across the street, three steady pulses. It was the signal she had been waiting for. "Hold your fire," Mercury called out as a trio of men emerged, their hands held up to show nonbelligerence.

One she knew from experience. Matt McDonald of the Hole in the Wall led the trio over to her truck as she climbed down. She extended her hand, and McDonald shook it. He was wearing a black cowboy hat with a band of checked blues, greens, and reds. *No doubt his McDonald tartan.* "I take it you have an update?" she asked.

"Indeed I do, ma'am," he said. "As you can probably tell, the situation has become fluid. Despite attempts to round up all the guns, the locals are well-armed. A few hours ago, the National Guard convoy escorts found themselves in two nasty little firefights. One they repelled, and the other, they fell back, and the food went into the mob's hands."

"What's all that shooting going on now?"

McDonald grinned. "That's your plan coming to fruition. People are officially pissed off. The mayor ordered SEs to shut down the media. I guess she didn't like the fact they were criticizing her office about the situation. They pulled the plug on the cable system for the city. The TV was the only outlet for the residents, their only form of entertainment. The people got pissed. Of course, this was all fueled by rumors that the mayor and the SE leaders were hoarding food at city hall for their own use."

"Were they?"

"I don't know. My job, per your orders, was to stir the shit, so my people planted the rumor. It took root. As we speak, the

164

National Guard is being forced to form up around city hall. That gunfire is the locals going after the SEs. At least two of the folks on your little wanted cards that were tucked away with the food are dead." There was no joy in his voice, only cold facts, which were something that Judy appreciated.

"How bad is it in there?"

"The people are at a tipping point for greater violence. The city has been surrounded for months. Food and medicine getting in there was the only thing that kept them from popping their corks. Now that's being threatened. The nature of people changes when they don't have the basic necessities. They become different animals. Individuals who might normally be docile become vicious. A lot sit back and wait, but the majority start taking matters into their own hands. When you destroyed the warehouses and cut their food supply to a minimum, it pushed a lot of people over the edge. They're pissed off and want blood."

"Nobody is coming to help you," she said, echoing the old adage.

"That's right," McDonald said. "And those little wanted posters in the food gave the people targets to go after. The Social Enforcers are in a panic. One group, Westside, just walked off their patrol routes and faded into the city rather than trying to protect the mayor and the city hall cronies."

"Sounds like our plan is working."

"It is. That's why I reached out to you. City hall is cut off. The National Guard can break out, but to do it, they have to kill a lot of civilians. Once they start firing back, they know it's going to be bloody, and they're still surrounded by your people. Nobody wants to face trial for shooting innocent people."

"That's good. We want them paralyzed."

McDonald crossed his arms over his chest. "That's happening as we speak." As if to emphasize his point, a burst of automatic gunfire reached Mercury's ears from the city. It was the sound of intensification. "Do you think they will capitulate?"

The SOL leader cocked his head slightly, looking into the black night sky for answers. "I say hold off for a day or so. Now the Newmerican leaders are trapped in a pocket around city hall. The food that is coming in is being mobbed by the locals. When you're trapped, you get desperate. Let them simmer for a bit and see what it's like to feel the noose getting tighter around their necks."

"We will need a way into the city, something that doesn't get us shot."

He smiled. "I can arrange it. With the SEs all going into hiding, you could drive a regiment right in at this time and probably not face resistance. Still, my people will get you a route in that is sure to be safe."

"We'll need a signal as to when the time is right."

"We'll be using 3555 megahertz. When you hear Halo, we'll connect with you here and guide you into the city. But know this: once we get you there, I can't say for sure how all the parties are going to react. We don't have anyone right now inside city hall, so it's hard to tell how they are going to respond. And with the civilians...I think they'll part like the Red Sea, but that's just an educated guess."

Mercury nodded. "Understood." McDonald and his two people turned and walked out into the darkness as the sound of gunfire bounced off the surrounding bricks. *This has to work. They have to see they can't win.*

El Mirage, Arizona

Raul Lopez felt overwhelmed for the first few days. Before General Reager had toured the camp, he had been forced to scrounge for equipment and personnel for his cause. Now he was on the inside, getting more resources than he knew how to manage. At first, he was clumsy, made mistakes, and had people standing around not doing anything. Then he got a staff sergeant named Ellis who showed him how to seize command and ensure everyone had something to do. In less than an hour, Ellis was barking out orders and getting results.

Captain Harnessy provided him with intelligence regarding the network of Social Quarantine camps in California. Many were labeled "work camps," but Raul knew they worked their prisoners to death. Others were labeled extermination camps, and a few simply had a question mark under them. The number was daunting, but now that he had assets that he didn't have to beg, borrow, or steal, things were bound to go better.

Ted, the former senator from Texas, arrived and gave him a hug when he saw him. "I know what you've been going through," he said to Raul. "I've been working the media. I have to tell you, as horrible as what you found in Arizona was, it has really galvanized the American people."

"What is galvanized?"

"Fired up, filled with resolve. The film footage of the dead and the survivors has horrified people. You have no idea what is happening back in Nashville. The president signed an executive order to form an agency for camp relief. He's established a special court to look into the people responsible for these facilities. Literally tons of goods have been donated for the victims. Raul, this is a big deal now."

Ted's words washed over him. For a moment, he felt his face get hot. His fingertips tingled. A tinge of dizziness hit him. Everything was growing so fast, he was worried that he would be letting people down. Pressure momentarily overwhelmed him. *How did I end up here? Everyone is counting on me, and I'm not sure what I'm doing!*

Ted saw the panic he couldn't hide on his face. "Raul, are you okay?"

He drew a breath and gained some composure. "Yes. It's just that this has gotten so big suddenly. General Reager has given me security and medical teams. You've gotten the president on board. I'm not sure I'm the person to be leading this. Maybe you should. You were a senator. People know you—they trust you." To him, it seemed like the perfect idea —handing off the power that had been heaped on him to a reliable friend. Raul hoped in that instant that Ted would accept.

Ted chuckled.

"Why are you laughing? I was serious."

Ted's smile was genuine. "I know you are."

"You are more qualified than I am to do this."

"You may be right, but that doesn't make me the best person for the job."

"I don't understand."

"A long time ago, I learned that the people best qualified to hold power are those who are reluctant to do it. I've held power, and all it did was land me in the Supermax. I trusted that the wild progressives would work within our system of government—that we could compromise. They never wanted compromise. I was a fool to think that—I see that now. As you've uncovered, all they wanted was for us to be gone, murdered. They were all about power and control. They masked it under a dozen different names—DEI, climate change, you name it—but in the end, it was all about keeping the American people under their heels."

"California is going to be difficult. So much territory, so many camps. There's even one in downtown Los Angeles."

Ted nodded. "Back in my day, California was a social wasteland. We all just let it go. It was their problem, not ours. We didn't know that's where the Ruling Council was testing all of its social manipulation programs. It was a hotbed of poorly executed politics, yet the people continued to vote for the progressives, even when it wasn't in their best interest. It was a perfect model of Newmerica to emulate. Don't worry —you'll do fine when you get there. Just know that the people you will encounter have been morally broken for generations."

Raul heard his words but still was afraid. "What if I make a mistake?"

"You will admit it, fix it, and move on. That's what real leaders do."

"But I'm not a leader."

Ted laughed again. "Yes, you are. You have been from the very start. Starting in Detroit, you have been walking down the path that has led you here at this precise point in history."

"But I'm a nobody."

"Our country was founded by nobodies. Nobodies fought to free the slaves. Nobodies saved Europe's ass—twice! Nobodies orchestrated the fall of the Soviet Union. Every hero we have began as a nobody. That was always the best part of our country before they took it over. Every nobody had the same opportunity in life, the same chance to succeed. All you need is to be the best nobody you can be."

Raul had never thought about it in the context that Ted explained. Memories of the liberation of the camp at Valley Forge, of the riots in Detroit, and his time in the Supermax all came back to him. *He's right...everything led me here.* His fear ebbed with each beat of his heart. "Thank you, my friend."

"I'll handle the politics, if you'll allow me to. I have a knack for running interference with politicos. That will be one thing you don't have to worry about. But this is your show. It always was. If you want me to carry equipment, I'll do that. I'm here for you. Use me as you see fit."

Raul wetted his lips and drew himself to standing fully upright. "I know nothing of politics. I am here to save as many people as possible. If you can deal with Nashville, I will deal with the rescue efforts."

"Deal," Ted replied, reaching out and shaking his hand. "So, where do we start?"

"I want to introduce you to Staff Sergeant Ellis, then have you see how we're structuring our teams. If you have ideas about how to make them better, say something."

"You don't have to worry about that, Raul. It's sometimes hard for me to keep my mouth shut."

With that, Raul led him outside to see what he had been assembling.

Cumberland, Maryland

NSF Agent Angela Axton edged her car forward in the long line of vehicles heading into Cumberland, Maryland. The police checkpoint at the border was moving slowly, which was irritating. She wasn't crossing into enemy territory, but Cumberland was a city on the border with West Virginia and America. There had been reports of civilian defectors trying to make their way to American territory. Such checkpoints were necessary to find and arrest such *traitors. Why would anyone think that going there is safe? What do they think will happen if we win the war?*

She idled forward a car length and paused again. The car in front of her was being checked by a German shepherd that sat down near the trunk, clearly getting a hit on something. The NSF officer used gestures to have other officers move in, surrounding the vehicle. Angela tensed up. If this got out of hand, she was a police officer and was armed. Mentally, she was prepared to jump into action if needed.

Orders were given to the driver to pop the trunk. He was pulled from the vehicle and forced to lean on it, arms and legs spread. He was young, in his late twenties, leaving her wondering why he wasn't in the military. *We started the draft. You'd think a young guy like that would enlist.*

Angela relaxed slightly. They had the suspect in their control. Three officers started going through the luggage. Clothing got tossed around in the trunk and on the road as they rooted through it. In her mind, it was unprofessional. She had been in the FBI before it became the NSF. *You always need to treat people's property with respect.*

Then she saw what the dog had detected. An officer pulled out a long gun and a pistol. Another officer extracted three boxes of bullets. *That guy is fucked.* Newmerica had banned ownership of firearms early on. Many people surrendered their weapons, but others had gotten creative in hiding theirs from the authorities. Getting caught with a weapon was an easy felony. *Why do people think they can just do what they want in defiance of the law?*

When the young man saw the rifle, he tried to bolt. The officer standing behind him body-slammed him into the side of the vehicle. The man's arms flailed, but with the help of another officer, they grabbed his wrists and handcuffed him. The look on the young man's face was a mix of rage and fear. *He's got a lot to fear. Judges have no leeway when it comes to gun charges.*

The officers forced the young man off to a waiting vehicle as another officer picked up the clothing on the road and tossed it into the trunk. She could hear the man cursing and yelling, things that were not helping his situation at all. Minutes passed before another officer moved the car off the highway and motioned for her to come forward.

A Maryland NSF officer leaned toward her window, and she rolled it down. Before he could ask, she held up her badge. "Good morning," he said, taking the badge and scribbling notes on his clipboard. "What brings you to Cumberland?"

"Vacation," she lied.

He cocked his left eyebrow at her. "In Cumberland?"

"I've been sitting behind a desk doing analysis for months. I need a place to unwind. My mother once told me that it was a quaint little city."

He handed her badge back. "Quaint isn't the word I would use."

"Any suggestions while I'm there?"

"Yeah, stay away from anything butting up to the river. We've put up walls and wire all along there to keep people from West Virginia out. We've had a few accidental shootings down there. The border folks are pretty jumpy. It's best just to stay clear."

"Understood. I've got a reservation at the Best Western in La Vale at the far end of town."

The officer rolled his eyes. "Look, just past this checkpoint is a Hampton Inn. Stay there. Trust me on this one."

"Thanks."

"You're good to go," he said, motioning her through. *One of the perks of being a cop is that other cops look out for you.* She drove through slowly and then saw the exit for the Hampton Inn. Pulling in, she got out and secured a room, then got on her phone and canceled the one at the Best Western.

After getting her bag to the room, she took a few minutes to freshen up. While not in a rush, a part of her wanted to scope out where the memorial service was going to be. So she got into her car and set out for her destination. Angela pulled up to the Upchurch Funeral Home, where Whitlock's mother was to have her service. Tomorrow would be when they had the public showing. After she parked in the tiny lot, she went in, sizing the facility up.

It looked as if it had been a brick house that had been converted into a funeral home. There wasn't a lot of room. It was the kind of funeral home people used when they didn't expect a big crowd. One of the staff approached and asked if she needed help. Angela told her she was there for Mrs. Whitlock's service, pretending that she had gotten the day wrong. The employee offered condolences and told her it would be tomorrow afternoon.

Angela's eyes drank in every detail. There was a rear door to the facility. The windows had wooden blinds and white lace curtains. As she moved to leave, she checked out one of the two viewing rooms. It held around twenty-five chairs. *It's not going to be easy to blend in with the crowd because there won't be one.*

As she left, she glanced back at the funeral home. *If Hudson is alive, he'll be back. And when he shows, I'm going to prove everyone wrong and bring him into custody—that, or drag his corpse out for them to see.*

Interlude

Three years earlier…

Social Quarantine Camp Jasmin Crockett, Huntertown, Indiana

Braylon Ironsides sat at the tiny bench with his needle-nose pliers, pulling off chips and other components. It was dull, mind-numbing work that left his fingers raw from holding the discarded circuit boards. Calluses on his fingertips helped protect him from the cuts that had been common when he first started, a small thing to be thankful for.

Stripping the boards was easy. In another workroom, they used a chemical dip to melt away the circuit boards to extract the metals used. The rumors were that there was gold in some of the discarded computer parts, though Braylon never saw that. He was merely thankful he didn't work near the chemical baths. Far too many of the people there were seen hauled out on stretchers, never to return.

He tossed the extracted parts in the barrel next to his stool and pulled another board off the pile. No one knew for sure where the old boards came from. The speculation was that there was another Social Quarantine camp tasked with recovering them from garbage dumps. Certainly, a few of his were sticky and had a nasty garbage stink to them. Everyone knew enough to not ask the origins of their work. Questions sometimes came with a beating.

Sitting at the next table was a young woman, Trix. Women slept in separate barracks. The guards wanted to make sure the prisoners couldn't have sex, not that Braylon wanted any with the inmates. He missed his beloved wife. The guards claimed it interfered with their reeducation. The alleged reeducation consisted of an hour of lectures, sometimes "documentaries," and other times straight-up classes. Braylon resented the classes the most. It was rote repetition of slogans cranked out by the Truth Reconciliation Committee. Saying things like "Social justice is the only real justice" didn't change reality. Still, he found himself murmuring the lines in unison with the other prisoners.

As he made fleeting eye contact with Trix, he turned his attention back to his work. If a guard saw him, there would be pain. There was no doubt of that. The guard watching his detail was Freckles. That wasn't his real name—the guards always used slang names. It struck him that they were afraid. *They must be worried that if any of us get out, we might be able to identify them and get revenge for what they've done.* Freckles was a ginger with short, greasy hair and a nasty attitude.

Beatings happened. He'd only endured two since coming into the camp. Now and then, in the night, he would be awakened by women screaming. Deep down, he imagined what was happening to them, and he felt ashamed. *I should be able to do something to help them...but what?* Even opening the door to the barracks at night would result in punishment. Over time, he realized that the rapes were all part of the organized torture of the inmates.

Freckles paced on the wooden flooring behind Braylon and the other prisoners as they worked. It made him nervous, wondering if at any moment, he might be accused of some imagined infraction. Prisoners learned not to turn their heads but to follow the guards with their eyes. He saw as Freckles moved in behind Trix, seeming to pay attention to her work. That thought evaporated when he saw the sick grin on Freckles' face.

The guard reached out and grabbed her by the arm, twisting her around. "You, come with me," he commanded, standing her up.

Braylon couldn't help himself. Pushing the circuit board aside, he slid his stool back, scraping it on the crude wooden plank floors. He started to rise, as if on instinct. *He's going to harm her. I have to do something.* Braylon was halfway to standing when Freckles glared at him. "Whatever you're thinking, shut it down," he growled.

Braylon stopped moving as Freckles dragged Trix to her feet. She was frightened, but he held her skinny arm tight in his grip. He looked at Braylon, his eyes narrowing their gaze. "That's right, old man. You aren't going to do anything."

Words were in his mouth, but he couldn't let them fly. He felt his face redden as he stared back. Freckles twisted Trix's arm again, dragging her to the door. Braylon rose to his full height. The guard looked back at him. "I'll take care of you tonight, you old fuckface," he said, then opened the door to the outside. "You'll get to say hello to Mr. Broom Handle."

Braylon stood trembling, not from fear, but the rush of adrenaline. *I should have done something. Now I've made matters worse...*

Cumberland Falls, Kentucky

Three years earlier...

For the last two years, NSF Special Agent Angela Axton had been tracking Hudson Whitlock, but that journey was at an end. As she slid around a pine tree, approaching the campground where her target was, she held her rifle at the ready. She paused and swatted a mosquito that had tried to feast on her cheek. What she got from the swat was a thin film of sweat. As she looked, there was no hint of the insect, but a little yellow hue in the wetness, no doubt from the pollen.

It had been an arduous duty tracking down Whitlock, but she was highly motivated. She still had a slight limp from his shot to her knee during the foiled assassination attempt. This was not just about justice—it was about revenge. Whitlock had taken a lot from her, and she intended to return the favor.

Her meticulous checking had led her to Kentucky. He had been making a living during the summer months taking people on whitewater rafting trips on the Cumberland River. If it hadn't been for a suspicious email to his mother, Jolene, she never would have found him. Once that had surfaced, she ordered the post office to pull his mother's mail daily. One postcard came from the Cumberland Falls Campground. It bore nothing more on the back than a smiley face. To the casual observer, it might be thought of as junk mail. To Angela, it was Hudson letting his mother know where he was.

She had gotten a surveillance team to the thick woods around the facilities where he worked. Reviewing the footage they had sent her only confirmed what she suspected. It was a perfect place for Hudson to be. He was a hunter, an outdoorsman. The rafting company was a log cabin lodge near the campgrounds where he lived in a little log cabin set aside for staff.

The footage of Whitlock showed that he had lost weight since the last time she had seen him. Now he had a beard, scraggly, probably only trimmed once in a great while. *Time hasn't been kind to him... good!*

When she saw the small cabin where her target had been living, she pulled back behind a hickory tree, using it for cover. Her team was starting to constrict their circle around the cabin. Excitement filled her like an electrical jolt. *Finally, my manhunt is going to be over.*

"This is Backdraft," she whispered into her shoulder microphone. "I'm near the front door. I need a position check."

"Spanner here. Coming up to the rear now. We need another five to be in position."

"Flapjack—we're coming in from the east. His car has been disabled. We will be in position in two."

With the river in the distance, there was nowhere for him to go if he did manage to get out, which she doubted. *In a few minutes, it will all be over.*

Whitlock had been an obsession for her, the only person involved in the assassination attempt on Porter who had evaded justice. It had been a black mark on her career, though none of her supervisors said it out loud. Officially, she had been decorated for her valor that night. She knew there was some doubt if she had done all that she could have. They had pulled her from normal duty due to the knee injury. *That's something else I owe that son of a bitch!* Now her hunt had come to an end. *There's nowhere to hide, Whitlock. You're mine!*

She edged around the hickory tree and heard the crack of gunfire. Blood splattered in her eye, and she felt the violent thrust of her head snapping back. Angela's feet tried in vain to keep under her, but she fell over onto her back.

Her cheek felt like it was on fire. As she sucked in air, she tasted the copper of blood in her mouth and felt a ripple of searing pain tear at her mouth. She reached up with her tactical glove, and it came back soaked in her gore. *My face —he shot me in the face.*

More gunfire broke out, sporadic and dangerous. Multiple voices came in her earbud. Ignoring the wave of agony, she sat up, spitting blood out of her mouth as she struggled to her feet. In the distance, she saw a flannel blur as someone raced toward the river.

Raising her rifle to her wet and bloody cheek hurt, as did the recoil, which seemed to twist her agony to a new level. The running man jerked slightly, which was a moment of satisfaction. *I got him—I know I tagged him!*

The figure staggered a half step, then bolted for the river. She lost her line of sight in the trees as he reached the docks. Whitlock dove into the river. She could hear the splash as she tried to reposition. As she rounded a scrub cedar, there was no sign of him.

No! This can't be happening! Pawing her shoulder mic, she tried to talk, but instead coughed a thick glob of blood. Bumpercar, a fellow agent, called out, "He's in the river!" More gunfire rang out. Angela broke into a jagged run, and with each step, a stream of dizziness turned into a tidal wave. *I can't pass out, not after all of the work I've done.*

When she reached the dock area, she stopped, leaning hard on the handrail to the steps leading up. Her vision tunneled, and darkness overcame her.

Voices, muffled and confused, were all around her. Time became a blur. When a painful light brought her back to consciousness, she was facing an EMT who was taping a gauze pad to her cheek. "Good. You're awake," he said.

"Where is he?" she demanded.

Agent Morrison, Bumpercar, appeared in her field of vision. "We've got a team coming in to comb the river," he told her.

The coagulated blood in her mouth tasted horrible, and she wanted to gag. Her tongue felt a shattered tooth in her top row of teeth, no doubt taken out by the bullet that had torn her cheek. Angela ignored all of that. "Did he get away?" she managed.

"No chance," Backdraft replied. "Waller was sure he wounded him. Even if he was alive, he would have gone through the rapids by now. There's no way he survived, not after all the rain we got earlier in the week. We're putting teams downstream to find his body, if we can."

She wanted to join them, but she knew she couldn't. *Whitlock knows the river. If anyone could survive, it would be him.* Anger, frustration, and shame came over her, mingling with her pain. *That bastard shot me again, and if we're not vigilant, he might just get away.*

Chapter 10

Fourth Amendment: The Empowerment of the Electorate

Anyone in the nation may cast a vote from the age of sixteen on. Individuals who reside in multiple locations may vote in each jurisdiction they reside. The right to fair and safe elections is recognized at approved government voting centers and web sites. The FedGov will maintain the approved voter role for the nation. Those individuals that do not vote who are on the roles, will have their votes allotted as seen fit by the National Board of Elections.

The Fetterman Center, Philadelphia, Pennsylvania

The Newmerican vice president stood outside the Fetterman Center and eyed it with a hint of pride. She'd never liked the man it was named after. The true irony was that she had been the person to order his demise. It had been done by one of her operatives, disguised to look like natural causes, another unfortunate stroke. *In death, he is contributing more to our cause than anything else.*

Her security detail surrounded her as she marched to the doors. Once inside, she was immediately greeted by the rainbow of colors that the arena had been adorned with. The sweeping banners draped from the ceiling were perfect, representing every aspect of diversity. Pausing, she soaked it all in. Then she saw one banner that stood out to her. It had red, white, and blue. Turning to the convention coordinator who followed her by several feet, she pointed to it. "What is *that* doing here?"

"What, ma'am?"

"That banner." She jabbed her manicured finger at it.

"We thought it might be good to have the traditional national colors represented. It gives a hint at our past without making it a focal point."

"Remove that banner. I don't want anything that hints at where we came from. America was a failed experiment. Red, white, and blue—what were you thinking? Anyone clinging to that failure is part of the problem in our country. We're in Philadelphia—that's enough patronage to our past." *Once I am president, even the names of these cities will be changed. Erasing America will finally be completed.*

"I will have it taken care of immediately."

Walking forward, she got a better view of the stage. It was traditional, which made it stand out to her. "We should double the height of the central stage. That way, we can use the stage itself as a prop. We can put some of the national slogans along the stage base so the cameras always pick them up."

"Excellent idea," the coordinator replied. The enthusiasm was weaker than before, no doubt because it meant more work, but the VP didn't care. *We should be higher, not just for everyone to see, but so we can highlight our prominence in the video.*

The seating of the delegates was off to stage right. The seats were black, with white lettering designating each state. She liked how they were arrayed in the stands, flanking the main stage. The vice president didn't cling to any illusions when it came to the delegates. The governors were petty men and women, and their delegates weren't much better. No doubt they would be signing like John Hancock on the final document, wanting to gloat about their contributions. Many were already in working groups at the hotels around the city, bickering over wording and trying desperately to put their fingerprints on the final product. All were vying for power and saw the convention as a springboard for their careers.

The nexus of power would shift with the new constitution. States would be little more than administrative players in a strong centralized government. The delegates thought their participation might give them a leg up in the scramble for seats at the new table of power. In reality, those who would eventually be brought into the fold would be those carefully vetted from the District. *Those who seek power are going to be minimized in the new pecking order. We don't need or want competition from the rank and file of the party.*

As she surveyed the area, her phone beeped. The name that appeared was that of Burke Dorne, the Director of Special Operations, the man in charge of her operatives. She stepped away from her security people and the coordinator and answered, "Yes, Burke."

"I just received intelligence from some of our people in Nashville." Dorne was smart enough not to say that there was a problem because he knew she hated hearing that word.

"Go ahead."

"Rumbler is in their custody. He's been wounded."

Thiago "Rumbler" Reese had been the operative sent to kill Jack Desmond and frame Caylee Leatrom for the crime. "Is he talking?"

"Unknown. He's still in the hospital with heavy security."

Damn! If he talked, Leatrom would not be implicated in the crime. "I take it you have a plan."

"I do. But you should also know, one of our people reported that Jack Desmond didn't die in the attack."

Her mind chewed on the new data as if it were rotting food in her mouth. *If Desmond is alive and Reese is in custody, Leatrom won't be in jail for long.* "This isn't good news, not at all. I thought your people could handle this, Burke."

"Reese is one of our best assets."

Blaine L. Pardoe

"Yet Desmond is alive."

"They haven't made it public yet. The only reason for concealing that information is to allow them to employ assets against us."

She glanced around the arena as she spoke, now looking at it as if searching for a sniper. "That's the most disturbing information. What do you need to resolve this?"

"I want more operatives tasked to the convention."

"Done. What about Reese?"

"Getting in there to kill him is going to be an insurmountable hurdle. I suggest something more dramatic. There will be a great deal of breakage, but it is the only way to be certain. To do it, I will need military assets."

"I don't care if you have to level that place. I want him unable to talk."

"Understood."

"I'll get word to General Judy Woodworth and give you the authorization."

"Thank you, Madam Vice President."

"Burke, we can't afford this level of sloppiness. If this happens again, someone in the leadership of the NSF is going to have to be held accountable. A director-level person, if you understand correctly."

"It will be handled," he replied, then hung up.

Reese is a loose end, one that Burke had better deal with. This also means that Caylee Leatrom may not be framed for Reese's crimes. If I were her, how would I react? The answer to that question had her leaving the arena, surrounded tightly by her Secret Service detail.

Henderson, Nevada

General Reager's Bradley was hit by a machine-gun burst, the bullets dinging and ricocheting off the front armor and echoing loudly inside. The turret banged out three quick rounds as the Bradley swerved hard. Trip didn't flinch at the sounds of battle; his team members, however, were holding on to their seats tightly.

The Bradley lurched to a stop, unleashing another barrage. The sounds outside the vehicle were the familiar staccato of combat: muffled explosions, mortars, and grenades; the purr of machine-gun fire and the bangs and snaps of small-arms fire. He looked over at his air coordinator. "Where is our air support?" he asked between the roaring of the 25mm cannon overhead.

His air-support officer checked his screen. "Inbound in ten."

As if on cue, the rapid *whomping* sound of rotor blades started overhead. At first, they were distant and faint, but grew louder. Trip hit the rear hatch release, flooding the compartment with light as he stepped out, looking skyward.

Captain "Lariat" Paredes's helicopters came in, unleashing missiles in unison. They streaked by overhead, and in the distance, Trip could hear the booming concussions of the explosions. This was augmented by several tanks, pouring high explosives downrange. Edging around the Bradley, he saw a line of black smoke rising across the lines where the Newmericans had tried to make a stand. Most were just green Social Enforcer units, but they were augmented by the 991st Multi-Functional Brigade of the Nevada National Guard. They had thrown themselves across the highway, digging in on either side, hoping to blunt the onslaught of Black Tarantula. As the helicopters peeled off, breaking for the rear to reassess the situation and see what targets they might have missed, Trip stared off in the distance, looking for some sign that the Newmericans would come to their senses.

He had built time into Black Tarantula's timetable for resistance. As much as Nevada as a whole was in support of America, Las Vegas proper was a seething hotbed of

Newmerican loyalists. He had been given assurances that the local businessmen, i.e., the mob, would make sure the enemy would surrender. So far, that hadn't been the case. *Technically, we aren't in Las Vegas yet. Maybe that has something to do with it.*

As more fire was dumped downrange, blowing up a convenience store that was being used for cover, his communications officer called for him. "Sir, I've got a message being sent in the clear asking us to cease fire."

"From who?"

"Unknown, sir."

Trip returned to the interior of the Bradley and pulled on the headset. "This is General Reager. Who is this?"

"This is Lou Bonanno. We just convinced these Newmerican morons to stand down. Stop shooting our direction."

Reager paused, covering the microphone with his hand. "Captain," he called to Harnessy. "Does Lou Bonanno mean anything to you?"

His intel officer nodded. "That's one of our contacts, yes, sir."

Trip turned to his communications officer. "Send the word. Cease fire." He opened his hand over the mic and spoke. "The word's going out. We're holding fire."

Thirty minutes later...

Trip and his small security fire team walked toward the spot where the Newmericans had tried to make their stand. Several Technicals were still ablaze, belching smoke skyward as plastic and metal melted in oozing puddles around them. The debris of battle was everywhere. In the bright sun of the Nevada sky, spent brass glistened.

In front of him was at least two companies' worth of personnel packed into a tight formation, unarmed. Many wore desert uniforms of the National Guard, and the rest were clearly Social Enforcers who had been part of the fighting. They wore a mix of Temu and Wish camouflage and sneakers. Surrounding the Newmericans were personnel wearing urban tactical gear, heavily armed. The white words "Casino Security" were on their plate carriers. Stacks of rifles and weapons were piled neatly away from the *prisoners. Damn, these guys are efficient.*

A man walked out to greet him, beaming with a smile. He wore his own plate carrier, but it strained to cover his girth. He wasn't fat, but he certainly wasn't as fit as the security personnel. As he approached, he stuck out his hand. "Lou Bonanno," he said, shaking Trip's hand hard.

"We appreciate your help," Trip said.

"We've been chafing under these goons for five years. The FedGov has been squeezing us tighter every year. It's just good business to put an end to it. This woke bullshit is a drain on business, and now we don't have to deal with it." There was a lot of satisfaction in his voice.

"Agreed. So, is this all of them?" He gestured to the prisoners.

"All the living ones. A few of the SEs tried to slip out. They ain't slippin' no more, if you catch my drift."

Trip nodded as he walked forward to the prisoners, Bonanno at his side. "Who's the ranking officer here?" he called out.

A female colonel stepped forward. "I am. Colonel Deborah Hines."

"It's traditional to salute a superior officer," Trip reminded her.

Hines' face went crimson, and he could see she was clenching her teeth. "It will be a cold day in hell before I salute any American officer."

"I'm sorry you feel that way," he replied. "I take it you have surrendered appropriately."

"I did. I would rather surrender to him." She glared at Bonanno. "Thank you."

Trip shrugged. "My ego doesn't need your validation. I don't really care who you surrender to as long as you've done it."

"You are working with criminals, General," she spat back. "They will stab you in the back as quickly as they did us—after all we did for them."

"Lady," Bonanno replied, "all you did was try to tax us to death."

"We let you have freedom!" she fired back.

Trip interceded. "That's the problem with your people, Colonel."

"What's that?"

"Freedom is inherent. It's not for the government to give or take away. It simply exists, bestowed by God. Now you don't have yours. With Mr. Bonanno's permission, you and your people will be transported to a POW camp. The SEs in your ranks will be investigated for any crimes they may have committed. Your war is over."

"I demand that—"

Trip cut her off. "Get it through your head, Colonel. You aren't in a position to issue demands." He turned his back to her simply to ensure he wouldn't have to hear any rebuttal she had to offer. "Thank you for your help," he said to Bonanno.

The portly man grinned. "It's good to have the adults back in charge. When this is all over, you come and see me. I will comp you for the weekend of your life, General."

"Would any of your people be interested in coming along with us?"

Bonanno smiled. "Let me see what I can do."

Trip made a mental note that when the war was over, he'd have to take him up on that offer of a comped weekend in Vegas.

Philadelphia, Pennsylvania

Caylee Leatrom had been replaced with a completely new persona—Amanda Treacher. Amanda was older and had graying hair, compliments of a wig she wore. Amanda's nose was shaped differently, and she had wrinkles around her eyes that formed bags, all compliments of silicone prosthetics she had applied. When she walked, it was bent forward slightly, hinting at the onset of osteoarthritis.

Amanda Treacher wore the clothes of a cleaner from the Cleaning Solutions company that had the contract at the Fetterman Center: a dark blue cotton smock. Her gray hair was held up in a kerchief. Getting the job had been easy with her forged documents. Amanda didn't fit the profile of a potential assassin. She was too old, too slow, and almost grandmotherly in how she spoke. Caylee reveled in the part because it allowed her to access parts of the stadium. Also, her cleaning cart was perfect for concealing weapons and other devices she planned to use.

She got to know the stadium well in the days leading up to the Constitutional Convention. There were plenty of avenues of approach for the vice president. She narrowed it down by casually watching the movements of the Secret Service detail scoping out the arena while she worked. Based on what she had observed, the VP would probably enter from the south entrance. That seemed to be the approach security was checking the most.

Caylee didn't interact much with her coworkers. It was best to be a face in the crowd rather than someone everyone knew. When she got away, they would be interviewed, and she wanted them to know nothing about Amanda Treacher. *Some of them are bound to describe me incorrectly. That's how much I have to blend in.*

She spied a fellow operative posing as a member of the lighting crew. She had trained with him years ago: Jesse Berg. *He's good. I almost didn't recognize him.* Caylee didn't show any reaction when she did. That was what he'd be looking for—someone to react, to look away. The presence of Berg suggested that there might be other operatives in play, which simply made her more observant.

During one of her passes, brushing dust off some of the rafter beams where they connected to the outer wall of the arena, she slid two small devices into place. They were smoke dispensers tied to a frequency on a trigger she kept in the fold of her bag that hung from her cleaning cart. These weren't the cheap devices available to civilians, but military grade.

Their purpose was simple: a distraction—something that would disrupt the proceedings and force an evacuation. Jack Desmond had asked for chaos, and the smoke would provide that. It would also serve another purpose. It would force the Secret Service to evacuate the president and vice president immediately. Planned moves of key personnel were highly orchestrated and difficult to penetrate. Unplanned moves, with a hint of panic, presented opportunities. She was counting on that to get her shot.

She had changed her plans for killing the vice president based on the stadium setup. Originally, she had planned to use a handgun for the attack. While she was good with a pistol, and there was little breeze or other intervening factors in the stadium, she knew even her accuracy would be questionable at the range she needed to pull off the shot, given how the seating was arranged and where the security checkpoints and personnel were positioned.

For Caylee, that meant finding a position with concealment, not too far from the target, where she could assemble the weapon and take the shot. The acoustics inside the arena would bounce the noise to confuse matters. Even outdoors, echoes were deceptive, as they had been at Dealey Plaza when JFK had been shot.

Her firing position also needed to have an avenue of escape. As she performed the menial tasks of a cleaning person, she was constantly scouting for the right location. None were perfect. The cleaning cart she used would provide minimal concealment, but the moment she fired, there would be security converging on her.

The best spot was on the ground level, but it would also be the most congested and would have the best security. Behind the stage, she scouted a decent position one level up. She could fall back down a hallway toward the press box area. There was a separate door used by the camera and sound crews to bring in their equipment. Hitting the door would trigger an alarm, though. She was counting on the mayhem from the smoke and shooting to be enough to allow her to get away.

For two days, she smuggled in the parts to her weapon. Breaking the rifle down made it easy to get through security. She was concerned one day when they had a dog on duty at the staff checkpoint. She had packed the bullets in a triple ziplocked bag with coffee and freshly sliced jalapeño peppers. Her training told her that the contents should overpower the dog's scent for the bullets, but until she passed the checkpoint, she didn't feel safe. When it worked, she went about hiding the components in her cleaning cart, using tape to adhere the weapon and ammo parts to indiscreet and unseen parts of the mobile work rack.

She made detailed observations of the security patrols as the delegates came and left, awaiting the formal start of the conference. The NSF staff tended to follow patterns in where they went and what they did. Caylee mentally mapped their routes. While their timing might vary, she had long ago learned that people were creatures of habit and was counting on that in her planning.

Her nights were spent working with a map of the arena, thinking through what she needed to do, attempting to come up with alternate plans should things fall apart. *At best, I'm going to get off three shots. The first one will be the best—it almost always is. Her Secret Service detail will get behind her in their effort to guide her out of the arena, so the shot needs to come from the front or side.* The front was preferable. It gave her the largest target. That also narrowed

Blaine L. Pardoe

the window of time, given the direction she was likely to be moved.

In two days, the convention would be formally starting. Once it did, she would need to be patient and careful. *I should have done this a year ago instead of going after her mother and brother. I underestimated her once, and since then, she's only grown in power and prominence. If she goes down, Newmerica will fall like a house of cards.*

Chapter 11

The Twentieth Amendment: The Privilege of Stable Supply Chain and Commerce

The government has the power and authority to identify critical supply chains and manage them, as needed, to ensure the Newmerican people have the goods they need. Business stability is a privilege that all citizens should expect and will be ensured by the FedGov.

Philadelphia, Pennsylvania

Deja went outside the safe house in the run-down Overbrook Park neighborhood of Philadelphia. An ugly drizzle was falling, casting an ominous mood for what was coming. An operative dropped off the media van they were going to use for cover, tossing her the keys before he walked off without saying a word.

She walked to the covered porch and turned around—the man was gone. Rubbing the keys in her hand, she had the feeling that something was wrong. It had been an emotion that she had been feeling for the last few days, like an itch in the back of her brain. Now it was creeping forward into her thinking.

Everything in this operation had come easy—almost too easy. The hardest part had been convincing Ironsides to undertake the mission, and even that had been easier than she had expected. All it took was to verbally massage his painful memories, persuading him that he was doing something for the good of the nation. She wove in the lie that he would be seen as a hero, and it worked perfectly. Braylon had no hesitation. When the time came, he would pull the trigger, and Daniel Porter would be dead.

The assassin wasn't what bothered her—it was a nagging feeling that she might be being set up. Operatives had scoped out the perfect place for the kill shot, had provided the van, and even the plan. All that was really required was to get Braylon in position and let him do his job. It was too easy.

Beyond that, she began to question, "Why me?" Operatives were all around the convention center. She had walked down there with Braylon to scout the location, and she had seen them, or at least she thought she had. They had a look— quasi-military, somewhat aloof. Why did the vice president want her to lead this? *She has professionals who do this kind of thing for a living. Why me? One of them would be better suited for this operation.*

The VP had offered her a rare chance at redemption. With each passing hour, she felt like that might be a lie. *Is she setting me up, along with Braylon?* At any point in the last few months, the vice president could have reversed her decisions about Deja. *She could have given me my house back, raised my medical care level. She did none of that. Then, out of the blue, she contacts me and gives me this mission.*

The photos of Daniel Porter with the babysitter looked authentic, but the VP had the vast array of the intelligence agencies of the NSF. The photos could be complete fakes, aimed at manipulating her. *She could have checked my file, known about my bad relationship with my father, and used that against me.*

It all came down to trust. Did Deja trust the vice president? There was an implied level of trust there. After all, she had elevated Deja to star level when she had arrested Raul Lopez. Now, though, things felt different. She centered on one realization: the VP benefited the most from the death of

Porter. When the smoke cleared, she would be the president of Newmerica. *Could it be as simple as that?*

The part of her that made her a good SE was that she did her homework. She planned well and did the research. She wished she could point to something tangible that might show deception by the VP, but there wasn't anything—simply a strange feeling of pending betrayal.

Entering the safe house, she saw Braylon reassembling the rifle he would be using. He cast her a smile, and she gave him one back. *He's oblivious to what's coming.* There was guilt in her head as well. Braylon wasn't going to come through this alive. That had always been part of the plan. She had lied to him about escaping and being hailed as a hero. Try as she might to distance herself emotionally from him, she couldn't help but wonder how she was going to live with herself once the deed was done. *He's the enemy—that's what I need to focus on.* It was her only mental backstop.

"Our ride's here," she said, masking her apprehension. As she checked her watch, her level of tension ratcheted up a notch. "We need to hit the road in five."

Braylon finished assembling the rifle and double-checked the action. "No problem. I'm ready."

Deja moved to gather everything they had brought with them from Indiana. She put their clothing into their bags, half folding, half stuffing it in. In Braylon's case, it wouldn't matter. "Don't leave anything here."

"Where are we going after I'm done?"

"Another safe house, this one in New Jersey. Just until things settle down." It was merely another lie heaped on top of the many others she had told him.

She made sure she had her weapon in her hip holster as well, then pulled on an oversized shirt to conceal it. Braylon threw away his cleaning rag and handed her the gun lubricant to pack in the bag. He then put the rifle in a soft case.

They both looked around the small living room. "I guess that's everything," he said.

"Yeah. When you move to the van, do it fast. We don't need the neighbors trying to cash in for reparations points by turning you in for having a gun."

"Right."

"I'll drive us there. Do you have the ID I gave you?"

Braylon pulled it out. It listed him as a tech for the local CBS affiliate, as did hers, all compliments of the NSF. "Remember, if anyone asks, you're just a tech. If they ask any details about yourself, let me field them."

"I know, Tonya," he replied impatiently as she picked up their bags. "Let's rock!"

Fifty minutes later…

Deja angled the van into position so the side door on the passenger side could be opened with a perfect view of the walkway where Daniel Porter would be led. She noticed that her palms were sweaty, as was her brow. Ironsides shifted in the passenger seat. He had been so edgy when they had their IDs checked—she was worried he was going to blow their mission. Somehow he managed to keep it together enough to state his name when asked.

They had checked the interior of the van and found nothing but cables, electrical equipment, and cameras, everything provided by the NSF for their cover. One piece of gear was false. It was a fake front with dials and knobs, but its sole purpose was to smuggle the rifle and bullets. The security team checked under the van with mirrors to make sure there weren't any explosives. There was no way for her to know who, if anyone, in the security detail was aware of what was about to happen. It only served to fan the flames of her tension.

Once they parked, she let out a long sigh and shook her hands to relieve the nervousness she was feeling. "Go in the back and crack open the door. Remember, just a couple of inches."

He tried to get up but had forgotten to unbuckle himself, an indication of *his* nervousness. She got up and moved to the rear of the van as he opened the door. Her plan was simple: Braylon was going to kill Porter, and she was going to kill him. Having lived with him for two weeks, she had started to understand why he felt the way he did. Guilt tore at her for what she was about to do, but there was no way around it. He couldn't live because if he did, he would implicate her, and that might lead back to the vice president. No, Braylon Ironsides had to die, and it would be her hand that did it.

He got the rifle out and loaded it. She leaned forward near the open door at the sound of some commotion outside. Deja knew the signs. The president was in the area. Her eyes scanned the people who were lining up along the sidewalk. One woman looked like a TV commentator, with pristine hair and immaculate clothing. Another handsome man crossed his arms. Her eyes strangely fixed on his short-trimmed black beard and mustache. A camera crew from ABC moved across the sidewalk to set up their shot. "He'll be here in just a minute," she told her partner.

Braylon knelt in the back of the van, steadying the rifle. The suppressor was well inside the van, just as they had planned. He leaned to the left to track his target from a greater distance. They were parked a mere thirty feet from where President Porter would be walking.

Deja reached down and unbuckled her Beretta pistol. It was not going to be easy firing it with her deformed hand, but she had gotten in enough practice to pull it off. Besides, her target was going to be at point-blank range.

"Here he comes…" Braylon said in a low whisper, tightening his grip on the rifle.

The Mojave Freeway, Calada, California

Darius sat in the Humvee, looking down the road at the NSF checkpoint just across the Nevada/California border through his binoculars. Crude white flags were on poles sticking out of the sandbag barricade that crossed the road. A shack stood next to it with a pole arm lowered across the highway. The sandbag wall was about a meter high and crossed both the inbound and outbound lanes.

There was no sign of anyone there. It was as if they had stuck the surrender flags out and fled. To Darius, it looked wrong.

He had served in Iraq, and there was an eerie resemblance to a checkpoint he had seen once. Those memories brought back the recollection of the IEDs that had been placed in and around the checkpoint. As the Humvee idled, he looked around the surrounding flat desert terrain for any sign of someone who might be looking at the stalled convoy.

"What do you have, Red Rover?" Captain Harnessy asked over the secured net.

Darius touched his microphone. "On the surface, it looks like they abandoned the checkpoint."

"So, is it safe?"

"Doubtful. I suspect IEDs."

"Do you really think they would do that?" Harnessy pressed. "We haven't seen much of that kind of response from the enemy yet."

He held back a laugh. "Remember them firing fentanyl back in Texas? Their free ride is coming to an end, and that will push them into desperate acts. We're not just a threat to the government here; we're a threat to their way of life. Desperation makes people get creative and deadly—at least that's my experience. On top of that, there are a lot of veterans living in California. They've seen some of the same shit I have. This has all the hallmarks of an ambush site."

"You're my Cali guy, so tell me what you recommend."

"They've probably got guys hiding in the surrounding area. Once we get in the kill box, they'll set off the IEDs and pop out to mop up the survivors. My recommendation is that we don't play their game. Fire some rounds of HE into that area, blow it to shit—then we drive off to the far-right flank, go through their little sandbag barrier, and be ready to shoot anyone who pops out."

"Let me pass that to the general. Stand by."

Minutes passed, and Darius settled back into the passenger seat. It felt all too familiar. *This stinks to high heaven of an ambush. I hope I'm wrong.* He adjusted his plate carrier as the topside machine gunner turned, sweeping the area.

Four explosions went off almost simultaneously, the roadblock instantly converted to a million bits of debris blasted out onto the highway and into the desert. Sand flew up from the destruction of the barrier wall and from explosive rounds landing around the highway. The concussions were so great that Darius felt the quaking throughout his body. Smoke rolled into the desert wind, dissipating quickly into the charging vehicles. It was a familiar aroma, the smell of burning wood and spent explosives. It conjured more memories from his time overseas. For a few long moments, it was impossible to see anything as more high explosives tore up the area around the now-obliterated outpost.

The driver received orders that he couldn't hear, then the Humvee went off the road, heading to the right. The rest of the column followed, roaring across the sand and scrub brush. It was bumpy, jarring his already aching knee joints. As they were about to hit the sandbag barrier, suddenly the ground not far from them moved, and four men appeared from under the tarp they had used for concealment.

Three started to climb out, preparing to run, no doubt afraid that the vehicles were going to drive right over their concealed position. The fourth man took aim with his M4 carbine, hitting the driver's side of the armored Humvee. It was an ignorant gesture, born of futility and rage. The response was devastating as Darius's Humvee and another returned fire with their machine guns, cutting the shooter in half. Another burst sprayed the trio that was running, hitting them low, kicking up sand with the shots that missed. They fell, face-first, in the desert.

The Humvee hit the sandbags hard, jarring him forward, then back into the seat. More machine-gun fire rang out in the distance. No doubt other ambushers were flushed from their hiding holes. The Humvee swung around the blasted bits of the checkpoint and ran some fifteen feet off the road in case there were other IEDs. Turning around, in the dust swirls, he saw the bulk of Task Force Black Tarantula following on the path they had carved.

"Good call, Red Rover," came Harnessy's voice in his headset.

"Yeah. Chances are there are other spots along the highway. That's what I would do. We should probably go off-road for a few miles just in case."

"Agreed. We all appreciate the assist," the captain replied.

Darius looked out across the shimmering desert in the distance. *We're in California now. This isn't how I planned on coming home. They caused this.*

Philadelphia, Pennsylvania

"Here he comes…" Braylon said in a low whisper, tightening his grip on the rifle. His ears filled with a rush of excitement as he brought the scope's crosshairs onto Daniel Porter.

Tonya had told him to aim for the center mass. That was what he trained for. But his angle was perfect for a headshot. A Secret Service agent flanking the Newmerican president momentarily blocked his line of sight, but he reacquired his target a heartbeat later.

Braylon held his breath, compensated slightly for Porter's stride, and aimed.

He had been nervous that he might jerk the trigger in his excitement, so he concentrated on squeezing it slowly.

The rifle bucked into his shoulder. Even with the suppressor on, the sound inside the van seemed loud. His left ear popped an instant after his shot turned Porter's head into a crimson mist. The impact of the round was enough to cause the president to twist as his body collapsed like a marionette whose strings had been cut.

Braylon couldn't believe it. *I did it!* Two agents dove for Porter's body on the sidewalk while others drew their weapons, aiming them in the direction of the van, desperately searching for the source of the shot. Instinctively, he chambered another round, aiming for one of the agents, and fired again. The bullet caught the man in the shoulder, jerking him back hard as he dropped.

Braylon spun, turning to Tonya, who stood next to where he knelt. There was no hiding the smile on his face. Looking up, he saw the muzzle of her PX4 Storm Compact. *Why is she aiming at me?* Looking past the weapon, he saw Tonya's face. A tear was streaking down her cheek.

The sound of a bullet hitting the van and punching through the metal didn't shake his gaze. *Why?*

There was a flash, then nothing else as Braylon's head erupted.

* * *

Braylon's mouth hung open in that last moment of his life as he looked at the gun aimed at his head. It was a look of confused realization, the unspoken acknowledgment that he had been utterly deceived. She squeezed the trigger with purpose.

The gunfire was loud in the confines of the van, far louder than the rifle he had used. Deja flinched at the devastation her shot had caused. Holding the gun had been hard, not just because of her damaged hand, but because she was an instrument of betrayal. Until the last moment, he never suspected that Deja had set him up. It tore at her. It was one thing to kill an enemy, but another to commit the murder of someone you had lured in. Killing him was a betrayal that only the Bible could explain.

Braylon fell to his side as bullets started thunking through the side of the van around her. "Hold your fire!" she bellowed. "NSF! I've killed him."

Another bullet hit the side of the van as she yelled, this one slamming into her upper right arm. The feeling of being under fire was not new, but the location of the hit, her shoulder, was different. She jerked back into the side of the van, then fell face down onto Braylon's corpse. The blood and gray matter splattered there hit her face as she went flat.

The pain was agonizing. Light flooded in as she struggled to rise up, but she found that her right arm refused to comply with what her brain was telling it. "NSF! Hold your damn fire!" she called, trying to roll over. She felt his blood sticking to her skin but pushed past that.

Agony from where she had been hit made her vision start to tunnel. A twisting dizziness grabbed her brain and held it tight. Bile rose in her mouth, and she feared she might vomit. Her movements were quivering as she collapsed, and the tunnel of darkness closed in around her.

Chapter 12

Thirteenth Amendment: The Privilege of Safe Religious Expression

Citizens have the right to take part in state approved religion as long as the beliefs of that church are not contradictory to the laws and accepted norms of the nation. Those religious entities must support and reinforce the values defined by the government and will be certified by the FedGov. The people will enjoy freedom of a safe, non-offensive, religious expression.

St. Louis, Missouri

It had been just after 0430 hours when the word had reached Major Judy Mercury that the code word, Halo, had been broadcast out of the city. That was Matt McDonald's Sons of Liberty signal that the time had come for the American force to enter the city. While there had been some grumbling given the hour, Mercury assembled her force and started on the route that McDonald had transmitted.

There was no rush. Mercury knew the situation could be fluid. It was better to go slow until she had better intelligence as to what was going on. She rode in a joint light tactical vehicle from the Oklahoma National Guard a few AFVs back from the point. *Let's hope this siege can be brought to a conclusion peacefully.*

The column stopped, and she strained to see what the issue was. That was when she saw the members of the Hole in the

Wall Gang waving them down. Judy got out and walked to the front of the line, where Matt McDonald was waiting.

"What's the situation?" she asked.

McDonald shook his head slightly. "I'm not sure words do it justice."

"Give it a try. Can we secure the city?"

He nodded. "Yes. We need to head to city hall. There's still a lot in motion. I'd recommend holding off on gunfire until we get there. My people can ride in with you."

Judy agreed. McDonald squeezed into her vehicle, and the column started out again. "It started yesterday afternoon. A bunch of locals took matters into their own hands. They ambushed a Missouri National Guard platoon and wiped them out. Then they fired up the rest of the population."

"How bad is it?"

McDonald winced. "I convinced them to keep the mayor alive."

"That bad?"

"They're going to demand that you restart regular food shipments, and I'd highly recommend that you agree to that."

For Judy, there was some satisfaction that her plan had worked, but it also sounded like violence had won the day. While some violence was always expected with Thunderbuns, she had hoped it would be kept to a minimum.

There was a crowd around city hall, thousands of people. All looked angry, though she was unsure where their rage was directed. As the vehicles snaked through them, they cast icy stares at the troops. *It's weird. For a crowd this big, they are relatively quiet.*

The column stopped with a squeal of brakes, and she got out. McDonald pushed his way through the crowd to the front of city hall, with Judy and her people following. When she got there, she was stunned at the sight. *My God...what have they done?*

A tall, crude scaffold had been erected. It was so haphazardly thrown together that she wondered how it remained standing. Swinging under the long horizontal top bar were eleven bodies. The nooses were inconsistent in the materials used, but their dead expressions were testimony to how effective the executions had been. Two were members of the Missouri National Guard—officers, from what she saw of their rank insignia. Others looked like casually dressed civilians, none very old. A few had cuts with dried blood. She recognized several of the faces from the cards she had ordered into the food supply. *Social Enforcers!*

This had been done because she had put out their pictures. It was impossible to escape that thought. A part of her always knew that Thunderbuns would result in targeted violence. To see the end result was disturbing, if only for a few moments. *They deserved this, each one of them. For years, they inflicted social justice on people...mob justice is what it really was.* Seeing them illuminated by the streetlights, it was hard to muster any pity for the dead.

McDonald ushered her up the steps of city hall, where she saw a group of people, their hands tied behind their backs, held by a small mob. One was a military officer. The civilians looked afraid. The officer looked pissed off. A lean young black man stepped forward. "You in charge of the Americans?" he demanded.

"I am. Major Judy Mercury."

"We kept the mayor and the guard commander alive. The SEs —well, you've seen them."

The mayor spoke up. "I demand you let us go."

Judy's eyes looked at her captor. "I don't think so. You answer to the electorate. It looks like they've spoken."

The officer spoke next. "This treatment is unbecoming of military professionals."

Judy only halfway suppressed her laugh. "You were the one holding a city hostage. My choice was simple: level the city to drive you out or let the locals deal with you." He seethed at her answer as his face went bright red.

"We want the food to come in again," one of the captors said.

"Agreed. My people will handle the distribution. We can get the trucks rolling as soon as tomorrow, assuming that the rest of the National Guard surrenders in good order." That created a ripple of relief that washed over the crowd. It was strange that she seemed to be able to sense the mood of the crowd as it changed. *They want this over and behind them.*

"They already did," the skinny leader said, poking a police baton into the ribs of the officer. "Ain't that right, Chuckles?"

The officer winced. "I asked my people to stand down."

"We'll need them to report in, disarm, and be processed."

He glared at Judy. "I don't suppose I can convince you to simply parole my people?"

She shook her head. "No. You certainly wouldn't offer me the same consideration. You fought the legitimate government of the country and lost. There's a price to be paid. I have no intention of you guys signing a document and going home as if this never happened." Her eyes darted for a moment to the dead hanging on the scaffold.

"What about me and my staff?" the major demanded.

Judy looked at him. She hadn't been given guidance as to the disposition of the local government, nor did she feel like asking. *I know Trip Reager. This is my call to make. If I called him, he'd tell me that.* For a few moments, she contemplated her options. Then she settled on the safest course of action. "We are going to restore law and order in the city, starting in just a few hours. No looting, no retribution. Once I have my people deployed, the violence and lawlessness come to an end."

For a few seconds, as Judy paused, the mayor seemed to find relief. "That, however, is in a few hours. Between now and then, I think you need to answer to your constituents." Smiles and devilish grins broke out among those who held the mayor prisoner.

"You have to provide me protection!"

"I don't have to do jack shit. You revolted against America and lost. You must have expected that there would be consequences for that."

"I'm the mayor!"

"I didn't elect you—these people did. Until we have restored order, I suggest that you broker some sort of arrangement with them." She turned her back to City Hall and walked back to her command staff to start handing out orders.

Camp Vindeman, Hinkley, California

Raul Lopez found it hard to believe that Hinkley had ever been a real community. Most of the buildings that remained standing were abandoned. There were some small ranch houses, but they looked more slum-like than a place he would have chosen to raise a family. From what he had been told, there had been major pollution contamination decades earlier. Ted mentioned a movie called *Erin Brockovich*, but Raul had never heard of it.

The camp had been centered in an old industrial building. When his team had liberated it several hours earlier, they had found it almost entirely abandoned. A further search discovered a massive pit filled with the bodies of the prisoners. They had been there for several days, baking and bloating in the hot sun. Most of their skin was blackened, but from what he had been told by the medics, there was no indication as to how they had died.

Three people had been found in the camp alive after an exhaustive search. He came to the makeshift hospital area his doctors had set up. One survivor was a man in his forties, a young pre-teen boy, and a young girl of the same age. The doctors had cleaned them up and had them hooked to IVs. All three looked starved and exhausted as he sat down to talk to them. Introducing himself, he told them he had some questions for them. The two younger ones didn't talk, but the man agreed to answer.

"My name is Raul. Who are you?"

"Mitchell—Mitch Freeman." He spoke as if he were stunned.

"What happened here?" Raul asked.

The man's wide and weary eyes met Raul's. "They ordered us to assemble. I knew something was wrong. They had never done that before. I had heard the rumors about other camps... that they killed all the prisoners, so I hid."

"What happened to the others?" There was a part of him that didn't want to know.

"They said they had drinks for us—that it was a reward for the hard work we had done. They served it out of a big washtub. It was purple. The prisoners—they drank it down like it was champagne. Some got second cups. From where I was hiding, I saw it. I knew not to trust them. The guards never did things like that. You know, reward us."

"Then what?" Raul asked, though he felt deep down that he knew the answer.

"People started to collapse. Some just sat down on the concrete and looked like they went to sleep. A few panicked. They tried to run but only got a few yards before falling down." The man paused and sniffled, fighting back the tears.

"Poison," was all Raul could say.

He nodded, then wiped his nose with his forearm. "I was in the rafters and saw it all. They drove a skip loader in, scooped them up, and drove off with them. No dignity, just scooped them up like they were dirt. A few of them joked about it, like they had accomplished something. One used a shovel to help get the bodies into the scoop."

Raul felt as if someone was squeezing his chest. *How could people be like this?*

"They took them all away. Then they left."

"Which way did they go?" Raul asked.

"North. Out into the desert. I heard them talking. They were afraid to go on the roads because the American Army was in the area."

"How long ago was this?"

The man paused, licking his cracked lips. "They left last night."

"Did they take cars?"

"Two four-wheel-drive trucks, Toyotas—the electric ones. And an old Jeep."

The EVs won't have recharging stations out in the desert. We can still catch them. Raul turned to one of his team members. "Contact General Reager. Tell him I need a plane or a helicopter to go north of here. Tell him the kind of vehicles we're looking for. I just need him to find them. Our people will go in and deal with them."

Looking at the two young children, he couldn't bring himself to ask them how they had survived or what they knew. *Why did the Newmericans bring the children to the camp in the first place? This was never a place for kids. This will scar them for life.* He wondered if their parents were among the dead. Thinking about that only made him angrier. *The guards who ran this place need to face justice.* Looking at the military personnel who had been nearby, listening to the older man's account, he saw the controlled rage on their faces.

Five hours later…

Raul's Humvee driver seemed to enjoy driving off-road. He wasn't having nearly as much fun. Raul was beginning to suspect that the suspension of the Humvee consisted of bricks. Every bump and thump transferred into his lower back. There was no complaining. If the Army personnel weren't commenting about it, he wasn't about to start.

General Reager had sent a helicopter out and had located the stranded vehicles. Raul brought four Humvees with armed troops to apprehend the murderers. They spotted the vehicles stopped in the desert, their occupants gathered around a fire as if they were camping out. It wasn't much of a blaze, but the light traveled far.

The military personnel moved with purpose. "Wilkers, you break right," Sergeant Marks transmitted. "Jonesy, you go left. We're down the middle. None of these fuckers gets away. If they try to drive, shoot out their tires. If they try to run, convince them to stop." Raul wasn't sure what the convincing would look like, but he knew it would be backed up with violence, and he was comfortable with that.

The Humvees executed their drives perfectly. His own vehicle killed the headlights. Raul could see the guards around the fire, looking out at the noises they were hearing. One grabbed a rifle, and a part of him hoped that man would start shooting, if only to justify a response. When they got within thirty yards, the vehicle skidded to a halt, and the headlights went on, blinding the guards.

The troops deployed swiftly, weapons at the ready. Sergeant Marks barked out, "Drop your weapons and raise your hands, or you're dead." His tone was crisp, direct, and left no room for discussion or confusion. The guards attempted to block the bright lights that now bombarded them from three angles. Raul was sure they were thinking of running, but they knew they were surrounded, in the desert, at night.

Slowly, two of the men threw down their weapons. All of them raised their arms. Sergeant Marks ordered his men into action, and they converged on the guards. Raul stepped out of the Humvee and walked toward them, half-tripping on a rock and almost falling. He didn't care. What mattered in that moment was facing the men capable of mass murder.

As he came close to the men, he saw they wore gray uniform shirts. One of the men had peeled off his patch that identified him as a guard. They were stymied, dumbfounded that they had been spotted. The military personnel patted them down and zip-tied their wrists behind them. They were forced down on the desert floor in a kneeling position. Confusion was soon replaced with fear. *Good. You should be afraid.*

"Sergeant, we should shoot these bastards right here, right now," one of the team said. Several of the others voiced the same sentiments. Raul wasn't surprised. They had seen the open mass grave, and some had heard Raul's talk with Mr. Freeman.

"If we shoot them now, we're saving the court system time and the victims' pain," another said.

The strange thing was that he felt the same emotion. He glanced over at Sergeant Marks and saw that the older NCO had an expression of being torn. All it would take was for Raul to say "Do it," and they would be dead within a second.

Closing his eyes, he mentally pictured Ted. *What would he say?* In that instant, Raul had his answer. Opening his eyes, he took a step toward the fire. "No. They go back with us alive. They'll go to trial, and we will all be there. They will face justice."

"Justice sucks," a corporal grumbled. "What if they get off?"

"They won't be tried here in California. We'll have them sent back to Texas for processing," Raul said, then he glared at the prisoners. "And there, they have the death penalty."

Sergeant Marks took his cue. "You heard the man. Grab these assholes and let's get them back. Check their vehicles and secure any evidence you may find."

The soldiers muttered with disapproval but followed orders. Raul went over to Marks. "Good work."

"I would have let them shoot," he said in a low tone.

"I know."

"I wish I had."

"So do I. But we're better than that. If we just murder them, America is the same as Newmerica, regardless of the justification."

Before Marks could reply, Raul turned and headed back to the Humvee.

Cumberland, Maryland

NSF Special Agent Angela Axton got up early the day of the Whitlock funeral. This was a day filled with possibilities. She had long suspected that Hudson was alive. If he was, this would be a time and place he might risk coming out of hiding. Bringing him in would be the culmination of a half-decade manhunt that had left her scarred for life.

It was also a chance at redemption. She had managed to infiltrate the Patriot Liberation Front, baiting them with the idea of trying to kill the president. In her mind, she had only said out loud what they all had to be thinking. They had checked her background and had trusted her, and she had led them all into a trap.

Except Hudson Whitlock. He had shot her and gotten away. Years later, she found him, despite his efforts to live off the grid. Once more, he had escaped. The NSF was convinced he was dead, but his body had never been found. Angela had been the lone voice claiming that he was still out there, alive —dangerous. She had endured being ignored. She had tolerated being demoted to desk duty. There was little doubt that when people saw her, they talked behind her back about obsession. Now she had a once-in-a-lifetime chance to prove them wrong. *He'll show; he won't be able to resist.*

On a sanctioned mission, Angela would have brought in the local NSF to surround the funeral home, staging a perfect ambush. That was out of the question. She had no authorization. Angela was supposed to be relaxing on vacation. *I'm alone on this, and I wouldn't want it any other way.*

The service was supposed to start at seven that evening. She had picked a black pantsuit from her suitcase and hung it up to take out the wrinkles. *Not too loud, yet respectful...I should blend in with the others fairly easily.* If all went as planned, Hudson wouldn't recognize her. It had been years since he had seen her face.

She sat on the bed and started to do her nails. She hadn't painted them in so long it was hard to remember. There had never been an occasion that called for the act. But today... today was going to be different. It wasn't much of a celebratory gesture, but painting her nails bright red appeared to be an appropriate way to commemorate the event. *I don't take enough time for myself. I put all of my focus into redeeming myself.* From now on, things would be better for her.

The television was on, locked onto NCC, the National Connection Channel. It was a hodgepodge of programming—some news, some TRC-approved shows. The sitcom she had on was about an office and the quirky workers there. It was like all TRC content—overamped situations, lopsided diverse casts, weak writing, and humor that was so neutral it didn't elicit laughs. As a child, she had laughed at TV shows. Now she was told that humor always came at the expense of some oppressed group and thus was divisive. Like everyone else in Newmerica, Angela merely absorbed the content with little reaction.

Then the screen went red with a "Special News Bulletin" blazing in white. It cut off the program and hung on the screen. Angela had never seen that before. The screen cut to the NCC news. "NCC has just received a notice from the TRC," the black announcer said. "I've been directed to read it to you as printed."

She leaned in, not wanting to miss a word. "A few minutes ago, in Philadelphia, Pennsylvania, President Daniel Porter was shot." The announcer paused, his voice catching slightly at the end of his first sentence. She could see his lower lip trembling. *My God! How could this have happened?*

The announcer rallied his composure, barely, and continued. "The assassination took place at the Fetterman Center, where the president was planning to do a walkthrough of the facility prior to the start of the Constitutional Convention originally scheduled for tomorrow." He paused and took a sip of water with a trembling hand.

"The perpetrators of this heinous crime have been taken into custody. Early reports have indicated that at least one of the assassins was killed by the NSF. This has not been confirmed at this point in time." *Good! It saves the country the expense of a trial.*

The announcer cleared his throat slightly, then continued. "We have footage of the attack, which we will be playing. The images are graphic and violent in nature and are not recommended for viewing by children."

Angela saw the shooting. Her mind processed it in terms of angles, placement of the security team, and their response. She saw President Porter's head kick backward, then the rear of his head explode. The gore and brains splattered on a short, portly woman in his Secret Service detail. More gunshots were fired, return shots at a white CBS TV van. The puncture holes were clearly visible. Then the footage abruptly stopped.

"According to what we have been handed, the vice president has been informed and has been secured in case this is a larger plot by our nation's enemies. She will be taking the oath of office in a few hours, and we will be covering that live."

The announcer then informed the nation that all businesses were being shut down for the next two days to mark the mourning of President Porter, effective immediately. Angela slumped on the bed. *That means the funeral parlor too. This will delay the service for Hudson's mother. Damn it!* Angela knew that she would have to call there to confirm but was sure they would comply with the orders from the District. No business in Newmerica would dare risk opening their doors in defiance of the government. It just wasn't done.

"To repeat..." and he started to re-read the press release. Grabbing the remote, Angela turned down the volume but watched the video of the shooting again.

A part of her was sad, even though she didn't have a connection to Daniel Porter. For the last five-plus years, he had been a daily part of her life and the lives of all Newmericans. He had led the assault on the White House and seen the end of the Traitor Presidency. He led the Ruling Council and had reshaped the country into what it deserved to be—a progressive slice of heaven. Now he was gone, shot like a wild animal, with no chance to defend himself. It was unfair to her. Angela was angered by what she had seen. *The Americans did this. This is exactly what we can expect from traitors like them!* She went to the bathroom for a tissue and used it to wipe the tears from her face.

The vice president would now be the leader. She was excited by that thought. *Finally, we get a woman in charge!* It wasn't that Angela liked the VP. If anything, her new leader seemed a bit power-hungry. Angela pushed those thoughts down, justifying them with TRC-approved logic. *She had to amass power, given the patriarchy that was working against her. Everyone who has hinted that she was angling for this doesn't understand what it means to be a woman in a man's world. She'll be fine. I bet she brings an end to this war in a matter of days.*

A part of her wanted to call someone back at the NSF and ask them what they knew, but she understood it was too early for such details.

As she watched the silent TV, another banner crossed the screen. *California governor captured by American sneak attack.* She turned it up and caught only half of the announcement—something about fighter jets forcing the governor's plane to land in American territory when he had been flying to Philadelphia for the convention.

Those bastards! This is all part of a bigger scheme to hamstring us. We should have known they would stoop this low, especially after traitors bombed our Capitol. Angela didn't need new reasons to hate the Americans, yet they were giving them to her in heaps today.

She slumped over on the bedspread and hugged a pillow tight to her body. *The best thing I can do is to bring in Whitlock. That will send a message to other fugitives that the NSF will not stop to bring them to justice.* She lay there, listening to the announcer repeat the stories she had just heard over and over again.

Chapter 13

The Thirty-Sixth Amendment: The Commerce Protection Act

The FedGov has the right to monitor, manage, and if necessary take control of any business deemed critical to the proper functioning of the nation. This includes federalizing employees, seizing property and assets, and renegotiating of contracts.

Philadelphia, Pennsylvania

The vice president was beyond excited. Despite that, she masked her joy with a sullen expression of sorrow. She knew the cameras were all on her, and there could be no question that she was deeply saddened by the death of President Daniel Porter. Using a handkerchief, she dabbed at the corners of her eyes, looking to viewers as if she were soaking up tears—tears that didn't exist.

There was concern from her staff to rush her through the swearing-in process out of fear for the continuity of government. She had them hold off. This was a moment in history. The nation was getting its first female leader, and she wanted it staged and set up perfectly. She had ordered the TRC team in the convention center to bring several of the Newmerican flags down so they could be filmed in the background. Black bunting was hastily put up around the stage. A portrait of the dead president stood on an easel just within the camera shot, with a black ribbon diagonally draped across it. No detail was too small.

As to who would swear her in, she summoned the eight female and one trans member of the Supreme Court to perform the ceremony. The VP would not take the oath of office from one justice; she wanted all of them. Since the old Ruling Council had packed the court, there were plenty there to frame this as what it was—a triumph for all women.

She would not be sworn in on a Bible, either. Daniel had been vigorous in reducing the influence of religion in the nation, but even he had been sworn in with a Bible. No more. *We are moving out of the past, and it starts today.* She would place her hand on the new constitution, the one Porter had never seen ratified.

It didn't matter that she hadn't spoken the words yet—she had assumed the mantle of power already. Word had come that American fighter jets had intercepted the governor of California on his way to the convention. He had been such an egomaniac, broadcasting when he'd be taking off on TV, having a film crew cover it, and now he had paid the price. Her response was an airstrike on the Kentucky Capitol building. One bomb found its target, collapsing the dome, while another fell short in a residential neighborhood. The TRC blocked all references to the civilian loss of life. What Newmericans saw was her being decisive and vengeful.

The Canadian prime minister was furious at the Americans for violating his nation's sovereignty, which she found amusing. The governor's flight path had been through Canada, and the Americans had violated their airspace to force him to divert south. She had spoken with the prime minister, expressing her faux outrage at the incident and having him issue warnings to the Pretender President in Nashville.

Secretly, she loved the fact that the Californian Governor was in American hands. He had been a challenger, a rival. One minute, he was a big supporter of the FedGov, and the next, he would be screaming that he needed more federal dollars for...whatever. She referred to him as Slicky Boy because he appeared to be more concerned about how he looked than about what he accomplished. Many saw him as a possible successor to Daniel. Now, in a matter of hours, both men were gone. The void they left was something she wore like a comfortable jacket.

The fall of St. Louis was another matter. She had ordered the TRC not to release news about it and to block any transmissions or posts on the net about it that came from America. It was a daunting task, but one that she had deemed necessary. Another defeat was something that the public didn't need to know about. The rule she was following was one that the government had latched onto from the days of the Ruling Council. If you don't tell the people about some event, it never happened. The VP had learned long ago that the masses would deny something if the government allowed them to. As far as the average citizen was concerned, St. Louis was still in Newmerican hands. Anyone saying differently was, at best, a liar, and was otherwise a traitor, waiting to be turned in for reparation points. It was a perfect system.

She had a speech prepared by the TRC. What they had sent her was horrible. The only part she had kept was, "On this day, our nation mourns." The rest, she wrote. None of them understood the full magnitude of the moment the way she did. As she looked at her handwritten notes, it took a great deal to make sure she didn't smile. *It's perfect. It lays the blame for this, gives us a mandate to move forward, and establishes my place in history.*

Her TRC team told her it was nearly time. Putting the trans justice as the one asking her to raise her hand was sending another clear message about the priorities of the nation. Leaning to a mirror off-camera, she checked her makeup one final time, then stepped forward to take the oath of office.

It took a full minute for her to utter the words of the oath. The words were all a blur to her. *I am finally the president!* When she was finished, she stepped to the podium and waited for a moment for the teleprompter, making it look as if she was speaking impromptu. "I reluctantly assume these duties. Daniel Porter was a brilliant man, a genius who led our people out of the darkness of our past. He was one of the key architects of our nation's Great Reformation. He left huge shoes to fill, and I only hope that I can live up to your expectations." She paused, using the tissue to dab another faux tear and to sniffle.

"In taking this office, I must acknowledge its historical significance. For generations, our people have suffered under the white patriarchy. Today, we have dealt those forces a devastating blow. I am not here to represent men. I am a strong and determined woman. Women can achieve anything in our country, unlike the rebel states where females are forced to accept table scraps from the men in power. The time has come for a woman to rule." Those words brought about applause from the crowd, which she gracefully accepted.

"We are engaged in a great civil war, testing whether a nation forged in the ideals we all hold can survive into the future. The forces that are coming are as dark as Daniel told us they would be. I have been informed by the NSF that the initial reports point to his death being at the hands of a radical alt-right American nationalist. Make no mistake, I intend to hold the rebel leaders accountable for this crime." She liked laying the blame at America's feet. The evidence would back up her claim, even if it was a tiny bit misleading.

"While a murderous assassin stalked my predecessor, the Americans showed the depths of their cowardice. Their jets violated Canadian airspace and intercepted the delegation to this convention from California. Their plane was forced to land in territory held by the rebels. The timing of this act was in conjunction with the murder of President Porter—clearly pointing to their involvement in both crimes." *They did me a favor by arresting the governor of California. This is the kind of stuff that feeds conspiracy theories and solidifies my claim that they were behind Daniel's death.*

"As one of my first acts, I will establish a blue-ribbon investigative committee to determine responsibility in the president's heinous assassination. I want to assure you, the Newmerican people, that those responsible for this crime will be brought to swift justice.

"In one of his last acts, Daniel Porter had a new general placed in command of our armies in the field. Thousands of volunteers from our allies in Mexico and Canada are coming to our aid. I will order our forces into action to take back the territories that the Americans have taken from us. The states that revolted will be brought back into our country, and the people responsible for this civil war will be brought to justice —legal, social, and environmental." The Supreme Court justices she had invited were off camera but applauded. Glancing in their direction, she gave them a slight nod of approval.

"In the last few hours, I have been thinking of the best way for us to memorialize Daniel Porter and his accomplishments. He was a great person: humble and compassionate. At first, I thought that erecting a monument in his name would be the minimum we could do to pay homage to him. But I knew Daniel. We were close friends and patriots. I knew him in ways that few could. He would scorn a marble statue or monument in his name. That wasn't the kind of individual that he was." She paused for a moment, taking a sip from a glass of water at the podium. *I would never have a statue built for him. In a year, he will be relegated to being a footnote in our history. The last thing I want is a place where people can go and try to remember him.*

"No, a statue will not do. The best way for us to remember him is to pass the constitution he worked on with me with such vigor and excitement. I remember in one of our last one-on-one meetings when I told him that the new constitution was a masterpiece, a triumph up there with the Magna Carta or Soros's Open Society. Daniel was so generous. He insisted that I take credit for this crowning achievement in law, but I refused. That was the kind of man he was, willing to step out of the limelight and share with others. We should pass the new constitution swiftly, as written in his own words and thoughts. This is a gift we can give him that honors his efforts and ensures that he will be remembered across the ages.

"Please contact your state delegates and encourage them to do the right thing, to pay their final respect to a great leader and one of the founders of our country." She let that last thought hang in the air for a few moments. *Now I've set the stage with the holdouts at the convention. If they vote against the constitution or try to change it, they will look like they're dishonoring Daniel.*

"For now, however, we need time to mourn our dead. Over the next two days, I encourage all of you to embrace your memories of Daniel. Hold your cries for vengeance until we have properly paid our respects to the man. As always, be vigilant. If you suspect others of being involved in this heinous plot to topple our government, contact the NSF. Thank you all, and bless Newmerica."

Applause came from the delegates who had been carefully seated to make their numbers seem larger from the camera's perspective. There were cheers, probably inappropriate given the death of Daniel, but not enough to bring her wrath. *I have my supporters. They know what this means to our nation.*

With that, the cameras and lights went dark. "Outstanding, Madam President," the producer said. It was the first time anyone had called her president. It felt good...right...and earned. *Mother would be so proud of me. I've accomplished what many thought was impossible.*

And now I need to wield this power like a weapon against my enemies.

Cajon Junction, California

General Reager looked out at the majestic mountains before him. The San Bernardino Mountains loomed to the east. The San Gabriel range merged in from the west. Interstate 15 cut south, through the pass at Cosy Dell, then into the northeastern extremes of Los Angeles. Trip allowed himself a moment not to think about the war, but to absorb the beauty of the mountains flanking Black Tarantula. *I've been all over the world, but there are few places as beautiful as America.*

His scouts were already patrolling the mountain pass to the south. It was a natural funnel point, which made it perfect for an ambush. Since entering California, they'd had a few skirmishes with the National Guard and a handful of SEs who had mustered enough bravery to attempt to take sniper shots at his convoys. Reager's response had been excessive—high-explosive rounds tended to be that way. It was designed to send a message to others who might decide to play hero. The stakes in the game were life and death, and he was more than willing to deliver the latter. He'd allowed the media to film the dead bodies, knowing that when the public saw it, it would erode their resolve.

Taking Los Angeles through siege was not something he looked forward to. If he could intimidate them into surrendering, it was the best option. The city was simply too big for his army...for any army . . . to hold and secure. Darius Thorne, his expert on LA, told him it could go either way. The locals would either fight or cower in fear. Trip hoped—no, prayed for the latter option.

His enemies would want to bog him down; get him caught in a war of attrition. Trip knew it because it was the strategy he would employ if he were them. The key was to not play their game. California's sheer size was staggering, but he didn't need to take it all, only the strategic centers of commerce.

He had an ace up his sleeve, and he expected it to arrive shortly at the tent where he was camped. The desert was hot, but he'd been in hotter and more hostile ones. Stepping back into his tent, he stretched his arms and triceps. Days of riding in the back of a Bradley were taking a toll on his physique. *When this war is over, I'm ordering a big-ass plate of brisket at Pinkerton's back in San Antonio, along with a bowl of their mac and cheese with bacon. To hell with Army food!* Just thinking about the delicacy of Texas beef brisket was enough to make his mouth water.

Judy Mercury's success in St. Louis was something he savored. She reported that there had been some looting, but the population was docile once food trucks started rolling in. He had already given her orders to deploy the bulk of her military assets north into Ohio.

His southern diversionary force had engaged in one pitched battle. The Californian Rainbow Brigade had charged into several of his units, which had led to the brigade's slaughter. Darius had explained it to him simply when it had happened. "They've been told that once America retakes control, they will not be allowed to exist." There was a part of Trip that admired the TRC. *They effectively play off people's fears to the point where they rush to death rather than doing nothing.*

When he had received word of the Newmerican president's death, he ordered it broadcast to all American troops. When the announcement had been read, there had been cheers. For the everyday soldiers, the news came with hope that the war might be nearing the end. Trip shared their enthusiasm but knew that the fighting was going to continue. His thinking was solidified when he saw the swearing-in of the new president. *Things may have actually gotten worse with her in charge.*

"Sir," a voice said from the tent flap. Corporal Darius Thorne stood there, saluting. "I understand you sent for me."

Trip saluted back. "Come on in."

Darius complied.

"Relax, Corporal. We've got scouts out in the pass. So far, there's no sign of any resistance. Pretty much as you thought."

"We're not out of this yet," Darius replied. "Once we get into the city, there are bound to be some SEs who decide to try to kill as many people as they can to hold on to power."

Trip nodded slowly in agreement. "My question to you is simple. If their elected leader were to tell them to surrender, would they?"

Darius seemed to ponder his response for a moment. "Here's the deal. The governor is a far-leftie. No matter how bad things are, the people of California would vote to put him and his crew back in office. I lost my business and ended up in jail for a while. The rioters who destroyed my business—nothing happened to them. It's a crazy-ass system. Citizens will speak against the state government or leaders, they will protest, then they turn around and give him another term."

"Back to my question. Would they stand down if they got the word to do so?"

Darius nodded firmly. "Yeah. When all is said and done, they have been conditioned to do what they are told. It started back with COVID. They told us to do all sorts of stupid stuff, things that we all knew weren't working, but people did them anyway. Most Californians are like the rest of the progressives out there. They would rather have someone tell them what to do than think for themselves. It's just easier to follow orders. Their biggest concern is not upsetting those government stipends from coming in."

"That's what I thought."

Another figure appeared at the tent flap, his security officer. "Sir, they're here."

"Bring them in."

Darius turned to leave, but Trip held out his hand. "Please stay. If nothing else, this might be entertaining."

A pair of officers led in the governor of California. Trip was surprised at how tall he was. His hair was disheveled, his expensive suit coat was wrinkled, and he had sweat stains in his armpits. He gave a dismissive glance at Darius, then turned back to Reager. The governor glared at Trip for a moment, no doubt recognizing him. *That's right, it's me.* "Governor."

"If it isn't the Butcher himself," he smugly replied.

Sticks and stones... "I was hoping we could go through this meeting without name-calling, Mr. New-scum." He slid in his own jab. "I take it your flight was comfortable?"

If he was nervous, the governor wasn't showing it. "You are in a world of trouble now. Your fighters violated Canadian airspace. You have caused an international incident. The word I heard is that Canadian volunteers are on their way to the border right now. You may have sealed your own fate with your illegal arrest of me."

Trip chuckled. "It's a cold day in hell before I worry about the vaunted Canadian military. If they decide to come, they'll be dealt with easily. My biggest concern right now is saving the lives of the people of your state."

"You could withdraw. That would save lives on both sides."

"I don't think so. I don't want to level LA or San Francisco. But I will. If my troops are fired upon, I will drop bombs and bring in artillery strikes."

The governor forced a chuckle in response. "You do that, and you'll be killing innocent people."

"The same people who turned in their neighbors to have them sent to Social Quarantine Death Camps? I've been in the camps. I've seen the dead and dying. If you think you can appeal to my humanity, you need to have some yourself."

"I had no idea what was going on in those camps."

"That's an old line. It got used at Nuremberg, too. Those men ended up hung for using it."

His words hit the governor like a sabot round from a tank. "I don't recognize your authority over me. You're a military commander. Whatever you may think, you don't have the right or authority to charge me with a civil crime."

"That's a question for legal scholars to address. Sadly for you, none are here. I ordered you here for a reason. I wanted to offer you a deal."

The governor shifted on his feet, even smiling. "What kind of deal?"

"As you may or may not know, we've liberated a few camps in your state already. We've captured some of the guards. The paperwork we've found shows that your office was involved in establishing those camps. Some of the guards—well, let's just say that they are willing to talk to try to save their own asses."

The governor's smile was erased instantly. "Go on."

"I don't want to have to kill thousands to take Los Angeles. If you were to issue an unconditional surrender of the state to the American forces, order your people to stand down and cooperate, I could see fit to waive all military charges against you."

"Why would I do that? If Newmerica wins the war, they'll hang me for sure."

"That's a big damn if. I could hold you as a war criminal and deal with you right now. Think of it as a noose now versus a possible noose in the future."

The governor's jaw clenched slowly, clearly not liking the options that were thrown before him. "I'd like to talk to my attorney."

"Denied," Trip replied. "I don't have the time or inclination to play legal games. You either take the deal or not. It's that simple."

The governor shifted back and forth on his feet to the point where it almost looked as if he were dancing. Finally, he stopped, crossing his arms. "All right."

Trip ordered him off to broadcast the surrender. He told the security detail, in full earshot of the governor, "If he says anything other than ordering his people to stand down and recognize American authority, cut him off and bring him to me. I'll hold his trial right here and now in this tent." The officers nodded, and some of the color drained from the governor's face as he was led out.

Trip turned on the radio and waited. Darius looked at him as if to question the bargain he had struck, but Trip only cracked a thin smile. *You need to trust me, Corporal.*

The message was short. The governor identified himself and said that California had surrendered to the American Army. He urged his people not to resist and to cooperate. A few minutes later, he was brought back in front of Reager. "I lived up to my end of the bargain. I take it I'm free to leave now?"

Trip shook his head. "I have no idea why you would think that."

"You dropped the charges against me."

"The *military* charges. I'm now going to remand you over to the American civil authorities."

"That's not what we agreed to!"

"That is exactly what we agreed to. If you refuse to cooperate, I will consider you in breach of our agreement and take whatever actions are available to me. I sincerely hope you understand I'm not fooling around, sir." The "sir" had been as respectful as he could muster, which wasn't much. The governor seemed to understand. With a nod, the governor was angrily led out.

Trip turned to Darius.

"Sir, that was fantastic!"

"I'm glad you approve. If you'll excuse me, I need to declare martial law, then let the folks in Nashville know what happened." As he stepped back out into the heat, Trip found himself grinning broadly at his ploy. *Hopefully, the locals do what Darius said and follow orders. Otherwise, this will be slaughter.*

Philadelphia, Pennsylvania

Caylee, in the disguise of Amanda Treacher, stood at her cart, looking down at the convention floor as the Newmerican vice president was sworn in as president. She hated every moment of it, but there was little she could do. After the assassination of Daniel Porter, security had immediately been tightened. New agents walked new patrols in and around the Fetterman Center. Her plans for killing the VP, now president, had been upended.

As she stood there at her cleaning cart, she contemplated assembling her weapon and taking a shot, despite the immense risks. She had a decent line of sight and was fairly sure she could get a shot off, but escape? That was ruled out. *I didn't come here on a suicide mission.* For such operations, the rules were simple: disengage and find another opportunity, one where she had a greater chance of success. As much as she hated it, her training took over, and she didn't take the shot. It tore at her because she knew she could have killed her target.

Having heard the new president's speech live, she cringed at what this woman would do now that she had all the power of the nation at her fingertips. *She's always been secretly ruthless. The damage she did with the agencies under her control was considerable. Now everything that was Newmerica is in her grasp.* She remembered the Social Quarantine camp conditions, all allowed under the VP's governance. *She's killed thousands already. Now she's in a position to kill more.* If anything, it increased the pressure on Caylee to terminate her life.

Returning to her cleaning duties, she watched her Secret Service detail escort the president out of the hall. Caylee's plans were scrapped now. With her additional security, killing the new president was going to be much more difficult.

There were still ways to do it. A bomb made the most sense. Getting the components would be easy, but the explosives would take some work. Newmerica had banned the sale of bullets, which would have provided good material to work with. Yes, they were available on the black market, but it would be hard to make that connection quickly, let alone get enough to do the job.

Making the explosives would be more time-consuming but would offer the least chance of being caught. Of course, even if she could make the bomb, getting it close enough to the president was going to be a challenge.

As she used her broom to sweep up some spilled popcorn, she saw a camera drone hovering over the stage, filming the delegates conversing with each other. *The drone!* While private drones had been banned in Newmerica, there were a lot of them out there. A heavier one would be capable of carrying an explosive. The best part? A drone was operated remotely, giving her some distance from the site of the attack, and thus, a better chance of getting away.

She had learned how to fly a drone during a class at The Farm, before the Fall. It wasn't something she was a natural at, but she was confident that with some practice, she would be able to pull it off.

In her mind, as she went through the motions of work, she began to assemble everything she was going to need. The drone was at the top of her list. With that, she could determine how heavy of an explosive to make. Then there was getting saltpeter, sulfur, and charcoal to make the bomb. *I'll need a place to test my mixtures, somewhere where no one will see me. The last thing I need is some loyalist turning me in to the NSF.*

Seven hours later...

Breaking into the NBC studios in Philadelphia had been child's play for her. While she had some contacts in Pennsylvania who might help, Caylee opted to take matters into her own hands when it came to securing what she needed. The best place to get a drone was from a media outlet that had several heavy-duty ones used to film news events.

Getting in at 0300 had been easy. She had followed a janitor, claiming that she was a reporter who had left her card at home and needed to pick something up. Once inside the studio, it was a matter of finding the technicians' area. There were large workbenches filled with various electronic components and tools.

They had six drones, each in hard-shell cases with custom foam fitting. Opening each one, she picked the drone and remote control that looked as if it had the least amount of use. She even went to the battery rack and secured extra batteries for the remote.

As she started for the door, a figure emerged from the shadows. It was a security guard in full Rent-a-Cop regalia. This one looked more like he had bought his outfit and belt from Temu—it was that cheap. "Hey, what are you doing back here?"

Holding on to the handle of the hard case that held the drone, she moved in close. "I was just checking out some gear for a morning shoot."

"I've never seen you before," he said, taking a step toward her. "I'm gonna need to see some ID."

He was young, and from his slight paunch, not physically fit. The smart move would be to kill him, but Caylee resisted that. *I just need him unable to call for help.* She took a step, then feigned squatting to put the drone case on the ground. "Sure. Let me get it for you."

She rose like a cobra preparing to strike, swinging the case in a tight arc, landing it on the security guard's jaw. His head snapped hard to the side under the impact. He wobbled a few feet to her left, then tried to stand upright. His legs went wobbly as she coiled back to bring the case around again, this time on the other side of his jaw.

Caylee didn't have to. The guard collapsed, unconscious, on the floor in front of her, just as she had hoped he would. He was alive, but his brain had been sloshed from one side of his inner skull to the other and couldn't compensate for it. Reaching down, she pulled his radio off his belt and stomped on it several times, grinding it under her feet. Glancing down at his body, she smothered any hint of remorse for what she had done. As she left, she knew the security cameras had most likely captured her image, but she wasn't afraid. During the night, she was Caylee Leatrom, but during the daytime hours, she was Amanda Treacher. She doubted that the NSF would even bother to investigate the theft of a drone from a TV station.

As she drove back to the small flat she had rented, Caylee started to think about where she could get the rest of the supplies she needed. In just a few hours, she'd be back at work, and the Newmerican Constitutional Convention was going to be closer to ratifying that massive document they had created.

Chapter 14

Nineteenth Amendment: The Privilege of Fair Housing

Every person in the nation has the right to housing for them and their family free of charge. Home ownership is transferred to the FedGov who will provide guidelines based on equity standards to determine who will live where. Individuals dehomed during this process will be reassigned housing appropriate to the Federal standards and will relocate, at their own expense, to their new dwelling.

Philadelphia, Pennsylvania

Deja Jordan woke up in a hospital bed, and for a few moments, she was confused about where she was. Her last conscious memories were being in the van, pulling the trigger and killing Braylon Ironsides, then getting hit in her arm. The moment that memory came to her, she glanced over and saw the bandages where the bullet had hit her. She felt cold, not freezing, but came to realize that she had been stripped of her shirt and pants and was in a hospital gown. As she tried to flex her crippled hand, the pain from her arm flared to life. It started small but became intense, enough for her to immediately stop her movement.

In a weird way, the pain was good. It meant she was still alive. Between that wound and her hand, she wondered if she would ever be able to hold a gun again, let alone drive a car or write her name. Still, it was better to be injured or crippled than dead.

Sunlight came in from the window, making her wonder how much time had passed. The assassination was still fresh to her, raw and ugly. The splattering of Braylon's brains in the van was an image that was tattooed in her mind...impossible to fully shake.

With it came a sense of guilt. The expression on his face, his lips forming an "oh," he never fully realized her betrayal until that last instant of his life. It wasn't like other times when she had pulled the trigger. Then her foes were armed, a threat. This was starkly different. It was murder. As much as she tried to tell herself it wasn't, she knew that what she had done was cold-blooded homicide.

She could have taken him in alive, but at that moment, it never occurred to her to hold her fire. It had been the plan all along: help Braylon assassinate the president, kill him, and be hailed as a hero once more. The problem was, Deja didn't feel heroic. *I did what they wanted me to do. Now I'm going to have to live with that.*

The door to her room opened, and a nurse came in. "Well, look at who's finally awake," she said, checking the equipment that Deja was hooked up to. Her tone was strangely unfriendly, almost as if she were angry with Deja... or disgusted.

"How long have I been out?" she asked, her throat hurting and feeling dry.

"They brought you in yesterday."

"How bad is my wound?"

The nurse cast her a glare. "You'll have to ask the doctor about that." There was something in her voice, an attitude, one that seemed strangely out of place.

"Is something wrong?"

The nurse said nothing in response. Instead, she walked out of the room. *What the hell is her problem?* Deja shifted in the bed, and her joints ached from the motion. As she moved, she noticed that her left wrist was handcuffed to the bed rail. "Why have they got me cuffed?" She tugged at it and found it quite secure. It confirmed to her that something was indeed amiss.

Her previous concerns that she was being set up started to reemerge. She didn't like this—not at all. A few minutes passed, and the doctor came in. He too seemed to have a dour expression on his face as he checked her chart. "How are you feeling?"

"You tell me. I got shot," she replied. "How bad is it?"

He bent down and looked at the wrapping on her wound. "The bullet clipped your right humerus bone and passed through the underarm. It did some damage to your triceps as it exited. The surgeon had to dig out the bone fragments."

"Am I going to be able to use that arm?" she asked with trepidation.

"Somewhat. The muscle damage was the worst of it. The bullet started to tumble on the way out. It happens when it hits something solid. It will be a while before you can use it like you did." His description of her injuries was cold, lacking even a hint of empathy.

"Can I talk to someone from the NSF?" she asked. "Someone in charge."

"I'm sure that won't be a problem. There are a few of them who want to talk to you." Before she could get any clarity on that, he walked to the door and let himself out.

A few minutes passed, then the door opened. In came a white man, older, with a short-cropped haircut that made his gray-and-black hairs look like they were standing on end. His chiseled jawline and gray eyes made him look like an officer. He approached the side of her bed. "Deja Jordan, correct?"

"Yes. Who are you?"

"I'm Agent Barker with the NSF." He didn't show a badge, nor did he need to. Deja knew he was with the NSF;

definitely old school. "You want to walk me through what happened, as you remember it?"

"I did what I was asked to do," she blurted out.

"Asked? Asked by who? Who were you working for?"

"The vice president."

"The American vice president asked you to undertake this assassination?"

She shook her head. "No, *our* vice president. Cortez."

His light gray eyes went from attentive to disbelieving in a flicker. "That seems a little far-fetched, given what you did. Why don't you tell me this—who else were you working with?"

"I wasn't working with anybody. I was under orders from the VP herself."

"Uh-huh," he replied.

"Seriously!"

"So, you want me to believe that the new president staged a coup and that you facilitated that by killing the president? You, a SE who has already fallen from grace?"

His words tore at her. *I'm telling the truth!* "I didn't kill the president. Brayon Ironsides did."

"But you were in the van with him."

"I killed him!"

"We're still waiting on ballistics from the shot that hit him. With all the bullet holes in the van, I don't know if you shot him or if one of the Secret Service detail did. What I *do* know is that you were with him, and one of our bullets hit you."

"The vice president asked me to do it! All you have to do is ask her."

Agent Barker twisted a grin. "You seriously think I'm going to call the president and accuse her of planning the death of her predecessor? At best, she'd have me locked up in an asylum. At worst, I'd be locked up in a cell next to yours."

"This is insane. I'm a loyal SE. I arrested Raul Lopez, for fuck's sake!"

"Oh, I know who you are. We've reviewed your files. Yeah, you arrested him. Then you oversaw the only escapes ever from the Supermax, including Lopez. You've been given light duty ever since then. You got re-homed, too. Is that why you did it?"

"I didn't do anything other than what I was told to do!" *Why won't he believe me?* "You can check my travel records and see that I flew to the District a few weeks ago to meet with her."

"We checked your travel records and saw that your only recent travel was to Indiana, where we presume you met with your co-conspirator, Braylon Ironsides. You'd be making things easier on yourself if you simply admitted your role in this plot. We already have enough evidence to convict you."

"What evidence?"

"As I said, you snuck out of the country into Indiana just a few weeks ago, didn't you?"

"Well, yes. But that was all authorized."

"You went to Fort Wayne and met with your partner, this Ironsides guy. You provided him with the firearms used, and you planned the assassination with him, didn't you?"

"He wasn't my partner," she snapped back. "I never even knew he existed before now. I was provided a list of people to potentially recruit for this operation."

"So, you admit going to Fort Wayne..."

"Of course I did! It was all approved by the Vice President."

Agent Barker moved alongside her bed and half-sat at the end of it near her feet. "Try to look at this from our point of view. You admit you went into enemy territory and recruited the guy who shot the President of the United States. That doesn't sound like the actions of a patriot to me. It *does* sound like a disgruntled Social Enforcer who was out for revenge against the government. We found you with him and the rifle used for the assassination. From our perspective, this is all in a nice little package. The smart thing is to tell us who you were working with. You know, get all this off your chest. Maybe, just maybe, the courts will look on this favorably when you get to sentencing."

Reality confirmed her worst fears. It *was* a nice package, and she was the party gift. *I was set up from the start. It wasn't enough for me to kill Braylon. I know too much, so they're going to lay the blame for this on me.* She felt angry, then ignorant. *How could I have not seen this coming? I knew what the VP was like. She played me, and I went along with it.* Shame washed over her, and she felt a chill run up her spine.

"You've got this all wrong," she said in a more controlled tone of voice.

"Do you have any evidence that might support what you are saying?" Barker asked.

She shook her head. There was a temptation to rattle off the names of the operatives who had assisted her, but deep down, she knew they would deny everything. *They're trying to lay the blame for this at the Pretender President's feet.*

A darker feeling gripped her. *I will never make it through trial. They want a confession from me. If I give them what they want, I'm no longer useful to them. Worse, I'm a risk to the vice—no, now she's the president. She'll make sure I never live to see the courtroom out of fear of what I might say. And Barker's offer that my cooperation will get me a lighter sentence… there's only one sentence for presidential assassins.* Deja was convinced that Barker was wearing a wire or carrying a recording device on him. *They'll use my voice to record whatever they want me to say. Every time I open my mouth, I'm digging my hole deeper.*

Her betrayal was on levels she had never contemplated. A feeling of utter disgrace consumed Deja as she looked into the agent's eyes. She had viewed the vice president as someone who wanted to help her recover her honor. The VP had used the promise of fame for killing Braylon as another prod to get her to act. There was no one in her corner. *I've never been this alone in my life.* Even as she sat in the bed, she knew her sisters were being interviewed, that fake evidence was being planted against her. Deja's guilt had been preordained. It was part of a narrative written before she had even taken the assignment. *I made it easy for her to manipulate me. I wonder how long she's been planning this.* She had admired the former vice president. Now all she had for her was searing, red-hot hate.

"What do you say, Deja?" Barker pressed. "I'm just trying to make this easy on you."

Resolve. She felt it grow in her chest, and she mentally embraced it. "I've told you the truth. For all I know, you're helping frame me."

"You're making a stupid mistake," he said, getting back on his feet.

"I want a lawyer."

"I'll be sure to let them know that. It might be a while, though. No one is going to be racing to defend the woman who assassinated the president." Agent Barker rose and walked out of the hospital door, leaving Deja alone, angry, and bitter—both at herself and the woman who had betrayed her.

University of California, Riverside, Los Angeles, California

To Darius, the Tomás Rivera Library on the university campus had funky, outdated architecture. The long series of white arches that lined the outside of the structure felt like a remnant of another era, maybe the 1960s. Banners were strung up by the students with sayings like "Fuck America" and "Newmerica Forever." They had toppled the concrete benches from the open area and made barricades out of them, blocking the entrance.

The TRC had called the surrender of California a "false capitulation" and claimed that the governor had done it under duress. The new president of Newmerica had called on all Californians to rise up and drive out the invaders. She claimed they would deport the immigrant population and even said that the Americans would dissolve marriages that they deemed improper.

The problem was that the District was on the East Coast, and the American Army was in Los Angeles. For the vast majority of the population, the smart move was to ignore the Newmerican president. As long as they were fed and taken care of, there was no reason to rise in a revolt that would result in violence.

There were exceptions, and the University of California, Riverside was one of those. The students had rebelled against the occupation, burning two campus buildings and a nearby police station. Several hundred had occupied the library, holding several security guards hostage. It made no more sense to Darius than when he had seen poor people rioting, looting, and burning their own neighborhoods. They were only damaging things they needed. *Who are you really hurting by setting fire to your classrooms?*

General Reager had declared martial law two days earlier. The local news media was so indoctrinated by the TRC that they ran broadcasts about all the things the military could shoot you for. Reager occupied their studios and clarified that it was necessary to restore order. It also sent a message— don't screw around with the American forces. The students ignored that message, opting to play a game of fuck around and find out instead.

Darius understood their thinking. They had enjoyed more than half a decade of wild protests over any little infraction so they could get their way. The college campuses were no longer places of learning—they were indoctrination centers for a new generation of annoying, whining Newmericans. *They're spoiled rotten—first by their weak-kneed parents, and then by the government and the educators.*

He was poised across the grassy commons in Watkins Hall, looking over at the occupied library. Several platoons of troops had been deployed around the library to ensure none of the students escaped. When Reager had asked Darius to go to the campus to convince them to end their seizure, he made it clear that no matter what was negotiated, they were going to be arrested for violating his rule. "Darius, I don't want to level that building, but I will. You do whatever you have to do to get them out of there peacefully. Don't make me do what I'll have to do."

Lifting the megaphone, Darius turned it on and got a light squeal as he adjusted the volume. "This is a representative of the American Army. You are in violation of martial law. Release your hostages and come out immediately, and no one will be hurt." His voice echoed around the campus, and he had little doubt they could hear him.

For a minute, there was no reply. Raising the megaphone again, he prepared to repeat the message, but another voice boomed back from their megaphone. "Go to hell! We are not coming out or letting our hostages go until you leave California!" The voice was that of a young woman. If he had to guess, she was white. He pictured a spoiled nineteen-year-old with a room full of participation trophies.

"I'm afraid you don't understand the situation," he replied. "Your governor has surrendered the state. You've committed acts of violence already. Don't make matters worse by getting yourself killed."

Another voice, this time a male—Middle Eastern, by his accent—came back. "We will only bargain with a Newmerican representative."

Darius shook his head. Glancing over at Captain Harnessy, who stood next to him, he got a shrug in response. "It's like they don't know who they're fucking with," the officer said.

"They don't," Darius replied, lifting the megaphone up again. "You see, that's going to be a problem. There is no Newmerican representative from here all the way to the East Coast. You're going to have to deal with me."

"We ain't coming out," came the female's voice.

Darius rallied his determination. "If you don't come out, we will be forced to destroy the building, and you with it."

"Bullshit!" the female student fired back. "You won't do it! They'll fry you for war crimes!"

Staring across the commons, he eyed the library and its fluttering banners more as targets than anything else. "Martial law has been declared, and you are in violation of it. You can come out peacefully, or we will pull you from the rubble."

The male once more seized the megaphone. "You Nazi bastards! We aren't going to fold like our imperialist governor!"

Darius found it amusing how fast the progressives could turn on their own. Three days ago, they loved their governor. Now he was a pariah. Looking at the building, he came to one simple realization: *This could go on for hours and end up in the same place.* Logic dictated that he demonstrate the error of their ways. Looking over at Harnessy, he outlined his next steps. "They're kids, which means they are essentially stupid. They've gotten whatever they want through a lifetime of temper tantrums. We have to show them that this isn't a bluff." He then provided his commanding officer with the details of his plan. Fortunately, the captain agreed with his approach.

Picking up his communicator, Darius put in his request. "One spotting round," and he rattled off the coordinates.

In the commons between the two buildings, a small explosion went off, followed a few moments later by the sound of the artillery piece that had lobbed it coming in from blocks away. The smoke was almost dead center between the buildings.

Holding up the megaphone, he spoke again. "This is your final warning. Come out now or suffer the consequences."

"Screw you, you fascist!" the female called back.

Turning to Harnessy, he asked, "Sir, can you make sure all our people are away from the windows?" The captain got on the radio and issued the orders as Darius stepped away from the window where he had been standing. Then he picked up his radio and signaled the artillery battery that had fired.

"Adjust twenty meters north. One round. Fire for effect." As he spoke, he kneeled, knowing what was coming next.

The explosion took place about twenty meters in front of the library building, right where he had hoped. The blast blew out all the surrounding windows. He was showered with bits of glass despite taking cover, and he knew the building he was in was a good seventy meters from where the round hit. Darius dusted off the glass and some bits of the Venetian blinds that had been torn away and looked out across the grassy area.

A crater smoked in front of the library. Four of the arches were gone, as were all the banners the students had strung up. The stink of spent explosives hit his nostrils and was far too familiar to him. Every window in the library was gone. Torn drapes hung out of a few of the window frames.

He had positioned the single round not to hit the building but to frighten the students. There was no doubt that many of them were probably cut by shards of glass or even potentially shrapnel. He could have brought the iron rain down on the building itself, but Darius was not the war criminal the students painted him as.

Hoisting up the megaphone, he glared through the thinning smoke. "The next rounds will be brought down on your building. Discard your weapons immediately. Come out now, with your hands up, or you will all be killed. You have twenty seconds." He threw in the time limit so they wouldn't have a chance to get embroiled in a debate among themselves.

His words hung in the air, shattered only by a damaged tree limb cracking free and falling to the ground. "Don't shoot!" came the female voice in a much less threatening tone. "We're coming out."

Darius and Captain Harnessy watched as a line of students emerged, along with their guards. Some were bloody; others looked stunned. The infantry moved out, apprehending them, patting them down for weapons and zip-tying their hands.

"Good job," Harnessy said.

"I did what I could and made the only real recommendation."

"I have to ask," the captain said. "Were you serious about dropping artillery on their asses?"

Darius smiled slightly. "I would have done what General Reager would have done."

"FAFO," Harnessy replied.

"Damn right!"

Chapter 15

The Fortieth Amendment: The National Emergencies Act

The President can declare any kind or form of emergency they deem appropriate. The declaration of an emergency grants the FedGov the right to suspend all other amendments of this Constitution in order to fulfill its obligations to restore the safety of its people. Emergency situations exist for indefinite periods of time.

Butler, Pennsylvania

Major Mercury arrived amidst an exchange of artillery between the American and Newmerican forces. The counter-battery fire had blown up one artillery piece that she had seen as she drove in. The injured and dead were being extracted from the horrific mess. The booming roar of the outgoing artillery made her ears ache. The incoming fire comprised two more rounds, then was followed by silence. *I hope that means we took their tubes out.*

She reached General Rickett's command post in an abandoned Burger King just off the Pennsylvania Turnpike. Some hastily filled sandbags surrounded the building. Judy waited for several minutes as a staff officer went over to talk to the general. Then she was ushered in.

"Reporting for duty," she said, saluting.

He returned a quick salute. "The infamous Major Mercury," he replied, then gestured to a booth that he was using as his desk. "I have to tell you, I'm glad to see you."

"Thank you, sir," she replied, taking a seat across from him.

"How are your people?"

"They're on the road about a half day behind me. Aside from some road wear, they are good to go."

Ricketts grinned. "You taking St. Louis without a fight was a feat of brilliance."

"I can't take all the credit, sir. My planning team proposed the idea."

"My hat's off to them, too. I think I can use your help here."

She nodded and leaned in. "We're ready to get into a fight."

"Blind Weasel is a few days behind schedule. A number of militia units were thrown together out of Pittsburgh and merged with the National Guard. You probably heard the fire as you came in."

"Yes, sir. Are you thinking you want to deploy my people against them?"

Ricketts shook his head. "Right now, they are slowing us. I have a force coming around the south of Pittsburgh, and it's not encountering any resistance. Once they see that, they're going to realize that the city is surrounded. I'm hoping to take a page out of your playbook and get them to surrender without having to fight them."

"Pittsburgh wasn't on the list of targets, as I recall."

"True, but I can't leave a major city like that sitting in my rear area where it can cause mischief."

"Where are you thinking my units can help?"

The general pulled out a paper map showing Ohio and Michigan. "I'm not sure you heard, but the Canadians got their undies in a wad over us sending jets into their country. They asked for volunteers to fight us, calling themselves the Redblack Brigade."

"I heard something about them."

"The Sons of Liberty tell us they crossed over from Windsor and are encamped in the downriver area just south of Detroit. I've got a few units poised on the border between Ohio and Michigan, but if Michigan's witch of a governor commits her National Guard units to join these Redblacks, they could punch through into Ohio and cause some major havoc." He dragged his finger along the map to show the most obvious axis of attack, down I-75 at Toledo.

"You thinking of sending me there to hold the border?"

Ricketts winced. "Not quite. Look. Your people have, shall I say, a knack for operating behind enemy lines. I don't want to park and wait for them to attack. I want a spoiler attack, aimed mostly at these uppity Canadians. Scatter and bleed them good so we don't have to worry about their involvement."

"Won't that trigger the Michigan governor to send in her National Guard?"

"She's at the Constitutional Convention and the funeral for that traitor, Porter. She's far from her military commander. That, and we've learned that a lot of Michiganders outside of Detroit and Ann Arbor are fed up with Newmerica. The SOL has been operating in the state too. If they do try to make a run for your force, they have some plans for sabotage that will slow them down."

Judy eyed the map, following every north and south road along Michigan's southern border. "What's the ground like?"

"Not so much hilly as it is tree-covered—pines, mostly. Lots of little ponds and lakes, too. The clear areas are farmland. The roads are there, but from what our SOL contacts tell us, some are in pretty rough shape."

Judy surveyed the map. "I've got a few regiments of National Guard and some Sons of Liberty troops. If that is indeed a brigade of Canadians, we might be outnumbered."

Ricketts gave her a half-cocked grin. "I've got some 82nd Airborne troops that jumped to our side, about a company's worth. I can also give you some troops from the 76th Infantry, one brigade's worth. We had them in our reserves for unexpected contingencies, and this seems to fit the bill."

Judy said nothing as she surveyed the map. "That should be enough to do the job." *Assuming no surprises.*

"I don't need you to conquer Michigan. I just need them unable to cause me trouble in my rear," Ricketts replied.

"How soon?"

"ASAP, of course. This is the Army! You should be able to divert your force heading this way to Toledo, if that's where you plan on jumping off. I can get you the other units in two days."

"What about air support?" She felt like she knew the answer but had to ask.

"We've got damned little, but so does the enemy. Michigan's Air National Guard could prove pesky. However, they have a lot of aircraft. We can give you several crates of *insurance* to help make sure they aren't too annoying."

Stingers...anti-aircraft missiles. Perfect. "Fair enough," Judy said. "Where are their biggest ANG bases?"

"Selfridge, north of Detroit, and the 110th Wing is operating out of Kellogg ANG Base in Battle Creek."

Leaning forward, her eyes found both of them on the map. Her mind was already cranking through the logistics and possible plans. Their topography gave the advantage to the defender. *I'd like to avoid giving the enemy any edge. They know these highways are the best routes in and will make it hard for us to catch the Redblack Brigade off guard.*

Her eyes fell on Toledo. "Sir, do we have any ships?" she asked, pointing to Toledo, then tracing her finger north up to southern Detroit.

Ricketts broke out a big smile. "As a matter of fact, there's a lot of shipping on the Great Lakes. Yes, we can scrounge up ships for you—more than enough."

"Very well. Is there anything else?"

"I will get you the contact information for the SOL operating in Michigan. I'll order the 76th and 82nd to report to you when they get to Toledo. Orders will go out immediately."

Judy rose to her feet. "Thank you, General."

"Major, grab their Canadian balls hard and twist 'em good and tight."

Judy smiled back. "It would be my honor."

Rosamond, California

Raul's vehicle stopped at the edge of the desert, kicking up dust as it came to a halt. His opinion of California was mixed. Los Angeles had been the biggest city he had ever imagined. Neighborhood on top of neighborhood, so many people in so little space. It stank, too, especially in the areas where the homeless were, which was almost everywhere. Bags and dumpsters of garbage were scattered everywhere. It was as if the city's most basic services weren't doing their jobs.

Flanking LA to the west was the desert. At first, he thought it was beautiful, the vast openness. As he looked out from the community of Rosamond, he saw a few hills, but otherwise a hot, rippling, tan emptiness. The plants that grew there were weeds. There were no trees, no shade, just a blankness that never ended. Somewhere out there was Camp CA 46, Camp Tlaib.

Since the surrender of California, Raul had been forced to divide his unit to relieve the staggering number of camps. With the Army making its way north, they kept close to the military in case they needed support. Most of the camps were abandoned, the guards fleeing to avoid justice. Other California camps ordered the mass execution of the prisoners. It was an idiot's choice, thinking that more murders might somehow erase their crimes. Some simply surrendered, hoping for mercy.

Camp CA 03 in downtown LA had been the most disgusting in terms of living conditions. There were three unfinished skyscrapers in Los Angeles, the Oceanwide Plaza project. Plagued with money issues, the buildings were erected but never fully finished, never even occupied. They had turned one of the buildings into an urban Social Quarantine camp.

When they entered the building, the guards had already fled. The people had been forced to live in a structure that had only a little running water, no bathrooms, and no elevators. There were over three thousand people living in their own filth. There were no beds, no furniture, no comforts of normal living.

The prisoners had been used for "urban renewal" projects in the city. They performed manual trash pickup and tended parks, only to be returned at night to their high-rise hell, as many referred to the skyscraper. Glass from the windows had been broken out so people could get fresh air at night. It was a disaster. There were victims with cholera, typhoid, and a host of other diseases, none being treated. Raul had commandeered an entire wing of Los Angeles General Hospital for their treatment. When the staff complained, Raul had his team enforce his orders at gunpoint.

"I don't see the camp from here," he said to his driver as he squinted across the desert.

"Distances out here are deceiving. Things close to the ground get distorted with the heat. It's off beside the hill to the right," the driver pointed out. Focusing his gaze, Raul did see a few shacks. *Maybe there are more on the other side of that hill.*

The driver continued, "The access road to the camp is about a half-mile up. There's only one way in or out."

"Did our scouts see any signs of the guards?"

"No. Nor are there any vehicles there. Our teams think they boogied."

Raul drank in the information. If the guards weren't there, it would be easier. "And the prisoners?"

"They saw some movement. Someone is alive in there. The front gate is wide open."

They probably didn't leave because they have no idea where they are. He had seen it with some of the other camps. Some prisoners were too weak to leave, and some were fearful that it was a trap of some sort, that they'd be shot "escaping."

"All right," he said with a sigh. "Send the word. We go in hard and fast this time. Have the medical teams in the middle of the column." His people knew the drill by now, but he still gave the orders regardless.

The Humvee roared up the road and turned right sharply, jostling the riders. The "road" they were on was little more than a dirt trail of tire tracks that jutted into the desert. They drove around the far side of the hill out in the flat wastes, and Raul was surprised by the sight. The camp consisted of eight massive metal buildings, surrounded by smaller barracks, ringed with a fence. It looked more professionally constructed than the other camps he had been in. This one utilized better materials, almost looking professionally constructed. *Why is this place different?*

He saw several prisoners walking about the camp, some clinging to the fence, looking out. They were sunburned, skinny, and sullen-eyed. They reached the open main gate, and his vehicle stopped, once more kicking up dust in the desert wind.

"All right, everyone, you know the routine. Let's make sure this place is secure, then let's get the medical teams a place to work. Go ahead and call in the ambulances. There are bound to be some people needing transfer."

Three hours later...

"Right this way, sir," Sergeant Marks said, leading Raul into one of the large metal buildings. He was greeted with air conditioning, which was a pleasant surprise. There were stainless-steel vats in the room, the kind used for storing chemicals or liquids of some sort. There were bags of a substance stacked in racks along the walls. Piping and plumbing ran between tanks. There was hardware on the floor, machines that did, as best as Raul could tell, processing, though he couldn't be entirely sure. *What were they up to here?* he thought as he looked around the structure.

"We interviewed some of the survivors to piece it together."

"What is this?"

"This is a methamphetamine plant. It's the same inside the other big buildings. They're cranking out meth in vast quantities here."

Raul went to the bags that were stacked. All bore Chinese lettering, along with stamps indicating they had passed customs in Mexico. "They were making drugs here?" He remembered his sister telling him such stories, but he hadn't thought he'd find such a place.

"On an industrial scale. The Californians had a policy to cut drug-related crimes by giving users state-made drugs. This is one of their production facilities."

It made sense, in a bizarre way. "So that's why this place is nicer than the other camps."

"Yes. They still kept the prisoners on starvation-level rations, but the facilities here had to be clean and well cared for. Their filtration system must have cost millions of dollars all on its own."

"They used the prisoners to make drugs to keep their people hooked," Raul said, more to himself than to the sergeant.

"For the most part. Most of the material used in the process came in from the cartels throughout Mexico."

Raul turned to the bags. "There are Chinese markings on those."

"The cartels were middlemen, from the looks of it. China was using them to get the stuff up here."

"Why? It makes no sense."

"Sure it does. They were selling the raw materials, allowing the state of California to be a distributor for them. They knew California would never be able to produce enough meth to take care of everyone's needs. People have no brand loyalty —they don't care where they get their next fix from, so the cartels would continue to sell their meth here too. From their perspective, they profited at every step of the process."

"I take it that the guards were skimming off the top, taking some of this to sell on their own," Raul growled.

Sergeant Marks crossed his arms. "I didn't ask, but I can. I don't have to, though. Chances are they were. I wouldn't be surprised if the truck drivers took some of the cargo as well. There wasn't a lot of security around this process. It looks like they spent all of their money on production."

It angered Raul, shaking him to his soul. He tried not to think of the government as a criminal enterprise, but the evidence was all around him. *I wonder if all governments are the same way. Are they all run by criminals? Are the government employees all lining their own pockets?*

Raul fumed, and Marks shattered his silent rage. "Sir, what do you want me to do about this?" He waved his hand around the building.

A part of Raul wanted to give the order to have it blown up. Drugs were a horrible curse in the nation, and this was the government actually acting as drug dealers. As much as he wanted it destroyed, his mind came upon another solution, one that would be better. *The whole world needs to know what is happening in these camps, and how corrupt the state of California and Newmerica really are.*

"Post guards around this building. Send word back to General Reager. Tell him we need television news teams out here. Tell him what we've found and that we want to show it to everyone."

Marks let a half-smile rise to his face. "I'm on it." He spun and left.

Raul surveyed the vast room and shook his head. *This is what you get when there's no one to check what the government is doing. Corruption on a scale where it's industrial.*

Cumberland, Maryland

Angela Axton arrived just after the start of the funeral service for Jolene Whitlock. As she entered the grieving room of the Upchurch Funeral Home, she noted that it was a closed-casket ceremony. There were only two small floral arrangements placed on the bier in front.

It was a small group of no more than twenty people. She was thankful that no one was openly weeping. She slid into the back row, trying hard not to look as if she were surveying the audience. She was sure that if Hudson were alive, he would be there. Her heart was racing at the prospect of finally catching her prey.

There had been a hitch—the assassination of President Porter. That had delayed the service by two days. She had been forced to call the office and extend her vacation, something her supervisor had been happy to grant her.

Her eyes darted to various people in the room, but from the rear, it was hard to make out faces or features. She had come to grips with another possibility, which was that Hudson might actually be dead. If that was the case, he obviously wouldn't be there. One way or another, Angela was going to get confirmation of whether he was alive or not.

Angela wasn't going in unprepared. She had her sidearm in her purse. In the privacy of her hotel room, she had practiced pulling it out to make sure she could do it quickly and effectively. If she did spy Hudson, her plan was to engage him away from a group of his family members lest they decide to intervene on his behalf. If all went as planned, she would confront him as he left, guiding him out of the building with her pistol shoved in his back.

The minister got up and began with a prayer. He spoke about Jolene Whitlock in glowing terms. "A loving mother and grandmother." Angela didn't see small children in the room, so she assumed they must be older. He talked about her making apple pies for the church bake sale. Angela felt it was disingenuous. *Why not tell them that she was the mother of a domestic terrorist?* That was a part of her life that no one talked about.

No doubt her family doesn't see it that way. To them, Hudson was a patriot. *A veteran who did what he did for the betterment of the country...that's how they probably think about it.* These were simple people. She could see that by the off-the-rack clothing they wore. Only two of the men even wore suits. *No one here is loyal to Newmerica. I'll bet a few of them had beers to toast the death of President Porter.*

As she waited, playing the role of mourner, she saw someone enter the room. The man walked past her row to the front line of chairs. When she saw his face, she recognized it. *It's him!* He wore a beard, long and scraggly, with streaks of gray hair trailing down his face, but it was Hudson Whitlock. When he got to his row, a woman there hugged him.

Years of searching, of being ridiculed by her colleagues, were finally over. There was a momentary flash of aggression that hit her. In an instant, Angela wanted to pull her gun, walk up behind him, and pull the trigger. Bringing him in alive was more of a bonus. She knew there were no ramifications for such a killing. The NSF and the government had a lenient policy when it came to killing escaped felons.

No, I want him alive. There was a part of her that was still an FBI agent, still holding on to a fragment of some sort of moral obligation that she couldn't quite shake. She gathered her thoughts and composure, deliberately slowing her breathing. *Don't deviate from the plan. When they leave, I'll come up behind him and walk him right out of here.*

The ceremony ended with the minister quoting several passages from the Bible. The last quote struck her as strange for a funeral, but she glossed over it. Proverbs 17:13. "Evil will never leave the house of one who pays back evil for good." Angela assumed it had something to do with Jolene Whitlock's life, which she couldn't care less about.

Her eyes bored into the back of her target. The crowd filtered out of the room, moving in silence, shuffling past her. She was sure that to them, she was just a mourner, not a threat. When Hudson started to turn around, she turned and made her way to the door, limping slightly from the old injury he had given her. Each footfall reminded her of just how much he owed her. *Be calm and deliberate. Don't let him make this a confrontation. Get him outdoors and deal with him there.*

As she slid around several of the mourners, she stood next to a tall man who gave her a high degree of cover. Angela saw Hudson move out of the room. He wore a suit that had been purchased at Walmart, she was sure of it. His shoes were not dress shoes, but a battered pair of loafers that showed their age with cracks and worn heels. He didn't see her. Pausing for a few moments, he spoke with another man there, who nodded in response, then hugged him.

Hudson turned to talk to someone else, leaving his back to her. It was perfect. She took four steps toward her prey, discreetly pulling out her handgun. She snugged in close behind Hudson and pressed the gun into the center of his back. Leaning forward, she whispered in his ear, "You are going to walk to the door, and we're going out to the parking lot. If you say anything or try to run, you're a dead man." To accentuate her point, she poked the gun harder into his back.

Hudson seemed frozen, and she wondered for a moment if he had heard her. *Surely he feels the gun.* "I said move."

Then she heard a metallic click next to her right ear, followed by another near her left. Two guns... *shit!* Cold steel pressed against the base of her skull. "All right there, Little Miss NSF. You hand over that gun or your head is going to ruin that wallpaper and my nephew's jacket."

It was her turn to freeze in place. *How did they know?* She turned her head slightly and saw two women with guns aimed at her, and the form of the tall man she had been hiding behind with his gun pressed to where her neck and head connected.

No! This can't be happening! Her brain tried to process what was happening, trying to come up with some way that she might salvage her moment, if not her life. There was no solution other than to do what she was told. Angela felt shame consume her as she pulled her gun out of Hudson's back. A hand from her left reached out and jerked it from her hand while someone else pulled her purse from her shoulder.

The man in front of her—the dead man, according to the NSF —slowly turned to face her. His eyes were full of fire. His smile told her he was savoring the situation almost as much as she had been a few seconds earlier. *How could this happen?*

"There hasn't been a day gone by that I haven't thought about this. What was your name that night? Backdraft? Angela Axton, the person who set up my entire cell to be killed or captured. Well, how's that playing out for you now?" His Southern drawl felt even more insulting. *I should have been smarter than this!*

The gathered members of the Whitlock family chuckled, cementing her humiliation and cranking up her fear.

Chapter 16

First Amendment: The Right to Safe Speech

Individuals are permitted to express them themselves safely, with respect and consideration of others. People have the right to be protected from words or phrases that are hurtful. A list of banned assault speech will be maintained by The People's House.

Philadelphia, Pennsylvania

"Madam President," the chairman of the Joint Chiefs of Staff exclaimed. "What you are asking for is against treaties that have stood for decades." His anger and concern were apparent on the live video feed. Going to the Pentagon was far beneath her now. *They should consider themselves honored that I'm doing this live stream, rather than just as a phone call.*

"You have the weapons in storage. What I am asking you to do is deploy them. What good are they if you don't use them?"

"Chemical weapons are dangerous for both sides. Militia units in the field don't even have gas masks or gear. With a change of wind direction, we might kill as many of our troops as the enemy," the chairman stated.

"The use of these weapons will panic the enemy," the president countered. *Why are they so afraid of using the weapons they have?*

"If we use them, there's a chance they will respond in kind," he retorted. "It's a slippery slope."

"Do they even *have* chemical weapons?" she asked.

"With the number of bases that have defected to their side, I would say so, yes."

"Why are you so hesitant?"

"The use of these weapons violates treaties. All of us will have this blood on our hands."

The president shook her head. "Putin used chemical weapons on his own people, and the world didn't come apart. They barely used harsh language against him. We're not using them on another country. This is a civil war. There may be momentary cries against us, but in the end, as long as we win, there will be no long-term risks to you or me."

"As I said before, it's a slippery slope. If they fire back with the same weapons, none of your SE units have the proper gear."

"Then get it to them."

"That takes time. Doing that is also going to tip off the enemy. If they see us handing out gas masks and MOPP gear, they're going to know what we are planning and may strike first."

She balled her fists as she looked at the camera. "Let's try this from a different angle, General. I'm ordering you to deploy chemical weapons to the field. If you refuse, I will have you fired and brought up on charges in a People's Tribunal. Then your successor will do it. One way or another, those weapons are going to be deployed. You can either be part of that solution or strung up after you're found guilty... your choice."

He was angry and doing a good job of holding it in, to his credit. "This is going to take some time, Madam President," he said through gritted teeth.

"Make it happen, or I will put someone in your chair who can." Then she cut off the video link.

Her first few days as president had been a string of frustrations. The surrender of California was something she had tried to keep quiet, but word had gotten out. While the Americans held Los Angeles and all points south, the northern half of the state was still not occupied by military forces. General Woodworth, her new commanding general, was assembling resistance in the San Francisco Bay Area, hoping to bloody the Americans as they headed north. She'd convinced the Oregon National Guard to deploy to San Francisco for the defense there.

Washington State refused to commit its troops to California. It claimed that military forces from Idaho and Montana were on their eastern border, threatening invasion. As much as General Woodworth wanted those troops sent south, she wasn't prepared to cede Washington State to the enemy.

Then came the reports that skirted the Big Tech barriers and her own TRC about the Social Quarantine camps. The TRC had run regular news pieces, labeling the footage coming out of the camps as deepfakes, doctored images designed to undermine morale. At first, it was working fine. No one wanted to believe that the government they supported was capable of such horrors. That made them guilty. People were quick to dismiss the images. Years of doing what they were told paid off in the short run.

But as more footage seeped in, the harder it was becoming. Everyone in Newmerica knew someone who had gone to a camp. Some came back, but others never did. Hundreds of thousands were turned in by their neighbors and friends for reparation points. From what internal polls were saying, her own people were starting to realize that they may have had a part in crimes against humanity.

She channeled that fear. A new public campaign encouraged volunteering, giving the collective guilty a chance to go down fighting. It was working—not as much as she had hoped, but some of the citizens were enlisting. For the time being, the war on the home front was at bay.

She still had military challenges and opportunities. Michigan, along with the Canadians, was preparing to attack south to force the Americans closing in on Philadelphia from the west to pull back. The governor had made a number of demands in exchange for her action, some of which the president agreed to simply to get her moving. *She's jockeying for a bigger role in my administration. Well, she's wasting her time. I've never trusted her, even before the Liberation.*

From New Hampshire, an enemy force had skirted New York and was on I-95 north of Philly. Woodworth had created a series of defensive lines to slow them down, and for the time being, it seemed to be working. No one knew for how long.

To the new president, it felt like everyone was converging on her in Philadelphia. She had used it to prompt the members of the Constitutional Convention to hurry up their voting. Several times she had appealed to them, evoking Daniel's name and memory to keep the pressure up on them. The holdup was that the members all wanted to add amendments to the document. As it stood, it was almost unreadable now at almost two thousand pages. *Later today, after the funeral, I will give them the proper motivation. Anyone holding up this process will face a tribunal. Let them contemplate their votes in light of that.*

"Ma'am," came the voice of her admin over the speaker. "I have the Chinese leader on line one. The translators are online as well."

"Good," she replied, picking up the handset. "Good day, General Secretary," she said, hearing the translator convey her greeting.

He replied, "Allow me to extend my condolences for your loss, Madam President—as well as to congratulate you on your new position."

She loathed the theatrics of diplomacy, the fake formalities and faux respect. *He's about to learn that I'm not Daniel.*

"Thank you, sir. It is a difficult time. I wanted to reach out to you to ask a favor."

"A favor?"

"Yes. I know from our internal investigation that your lab in Wuhan was responsible for the release of COVID-19, which led to the pandemic." She paused, letting him drink in her words.

"I assure you, as I have assured the media, that our lab had nothing to do with that."

Of course you deny it. To admit it would make your nation liable for all those deaths and trillions of damage around the globe. "Sir, I know that our NIH funded that virus's gain-of-function research. I'm not calling about assigning blame. As I said, I need a favor."

There was a pause as the translators did their job. "Proceed with your request."

"I need a new variant of some sort, either COVID or the flu. My intelligence people indicate that your researchers have created new virus types that are even more lethal than COVID-19. I would like a sample of one of those."

Her request clearly caught him off guard, and he muttered to other people who might be in the room with him. "What do you need this for, if it did indeed exist?"

"I seek to save lives by bringing this ugly civil war to an end. A pandemic would help with that."

"Madam President, to release such a virus, if it existed, would not be containable. Your own people would be infected, as well as the rest of the globe. We are talking about millions dead—with links to my government."

"To be clear, you were responsible for the last pandemic. All I am asking for is a technology share. You would have plausible deniability should anyone make a connection to your people."

"While I refuse to admit responsibility for COVID-19, I recognize your request. I assume you understand that this is no small ask on your part. I need to talk to my advisors and my scientists before I can provide you a response to this most unusual ask on your part."

He's stalling, buying himself time. That was expected. "Of course. I look forward to your response to this private request."

"Thank you. And again, please accept our condolences."

"I appreciate it, sir." She hung up the phone.

I need a fallback if the Pentagon doesn't deliver. I would hate to unleash another pandemic, but the Americans are closing in. Desperate times call for desperate measures. No one would expect Newmerica to be responsible for another global pandemic. She knew that once a virus took hold, the other countries would be inwardly focused and wouldn't see how she would be exploiting the disease to defeat her enemies. With any luck, General Reager and the Pretender President would die from the virus. That alone would be enough to cripple the war being waged against her.

Her watch beeped, and she read the tiny notice. Daniel's funeral. It made sense to have him buried in Arlington National Cemetery, but that meant leaving the convention, so she had the TRC plant a story that he had always wanted to be buried in Philadelphia. His wife had objected, but she was overruled with a curt phone call. That saved her some travel time and got the ugly task over with. *No one is going to care where he's buried once the war is over. I'm going to slowly erase him from our history of the Great Reformation regardless.*

Rising, she brushed off her dress. *I suppose I'll have to whip up some tears for his wife and kids and, of course, for the camera.* As she started for the door, she felt confident that she had set several initiatives in motion that would preserve Newmerica forever.

I-5, West of Los Banos, California

Oily smoke rolled skyward north of where General Reager's Bradley had pulled off the highway. *Another IED, damn it!* He knew that the surrender of California was not a foregone conclusion, even after the governor called for it. Martial law had helped considerably, enabling his people to use lethal force to protect themselves. There had been pockets of resistance in Los Angeles, but he had overcome them with brute force and the assurance that there would be no immediate repercussions for the local population.

Once his resupply ships had been unloaded and his equipment fully prepped, the drive north to San Francisco had been slow. The Newmerican resistors had planted bombs, staged ambushes, and even blown up a few bridges to prevent him from moving as quickly as he wanted. Trip had expected some of it, but they were proving more dogged than even he had anticipated. *It's almost as if they don't want us liberating them.*

One positive aspect of taking Los Angeles was that a number of California National Guard vehicles were captured. The fresh hardware replaced some of the damaged equipment or vehicles that needed extensive maintenance. No one was walking to San Francisco, that was for sure.

Other aspects of the conquest had been going better than he could have hoped. The humanitarian nightmare of the Social Quarantine camps was being addressed. Raul Lopez had done a remarkable job of getting the survivors the medical care they needed and rounding up the guards when possible. The camps were really more of a network of slave labor and extermination. They had their own infrastructure of transportation and supply, which was alarmingly efficient.

His other military operations were proving effective as well. General Ricketts had sent a message at sunrise that Pittsburgh had asked to send a negotiation team to discuss terms for the city. Colorado had become a Wild West sideshow, with the

267

Newmericans falling back to Denver and Boulder while the Sons of Liberty mopped up the surrounding counties, rooting out pockets of resistance. The situation in Denver had suddenly become fluid. Denver's mayor had been caught trying to sneak out of the city with a considerable amount of money presumably withdrawn from the city's accounts. The SOL unit, the Liberty Bells, apprehended him, but an angry mob, furious at the mayor trying to flee, got there first. The mayor was hospitalized after the mob beat him, and when word got to the deputy mayor, he started surrender talks.

Trip's day had been going well up to this point. Word from the southern border was that a caravan from the cartels was ambushed by the Twenty-Fifth South Carolina Tortilla Militia, and the handful of survivors were fleeing on foot back to Mexico. The Texas Rangers had a similar encounter in New Mexico, fighting a pitched two-hour battle that left the cartel in full retreat. *If we're lucky, they'll stay on their side of the line for the rest of the war.*

With the fall of St. Louis, the country was split in half from Chicago to the Gulf of Mexico. Minnesota still held out, as did Michigan, but from what word he had received from General Ricketts, Judy Mercury was about to be turned loose on Michigan in the form of a spoiler attack. *It's a perfect mission for Judy.*

His forces were methodically working to surround Philadelphia and ultimately make their drive to the District.

Trip knew that the fighting for the District was likely to be the endgame for the war. It was a bastion of liberal bureaucracy. As the nation's capital, it was the last place that the rats of government were likely to surrender.

He had been counting on the Constitutional Convention lasting longer, but his intel reports indicated that the delegates were about to finish their work. The new president had done what LBJ had done with the Civil Rights Amendment, evoking the name of a dead president to get it passed. *She's a crafty one...that's for sure.*

While on paper the war was going well for the Americans, Trip wanted it over. Too many people had died already. Even though most were "the enemy," he also knew that in a civil war, everyone killed was really from the same country, and that ate at him. *Last night I went through half a bottle of Pepto getting my stomach to settle down.*

Captain Harnessy came out of the Bradley where he was standing. "IED," he reported.

"I figured as much," Trip replied. "How far are we from San Francisco?"

"One hundred and twenty-three miles."

Trip cocked his head. "That's an awfully specific number off the top of your head."

"I've gotten to know you, sir. It pays to come prepared."

Trip grinned just enough for the captain to know he approved of his efficiency. "We're likely to have more of these little surprises along the way, aren't we?"

"One of our drones spotted what looks like a series of entrenchments at Patterson, where we had planned on cutting west toward the city. They seem to know where we are heading and are making preparations."

"How's the ground there?"

"Hilly, no trees to speak of, but good defensive ground."

"Can we bypass it?"

"Yes, sir. We could head west just up the road a ways, but that means crossing the hills and hitting San Francisco via San Jose from the south."

Trip had made his plans to avoid the direct route. Coming in from the west to San Francisco had been his preference, but the enemy was prepared for just such a maneuver. *Maybe they wanted us to see their fortifications, to force us to drive to San Jose. That's what I would do—try to force us to make decisions that go to the defender's advantage. I bet they have some nasty surprises in San Jose waiting for us if we come from the south. Coming in from the east—that would be something they wouldn't expect.*

There was always the option of going cross-country into the lush, grass-covered hills, but Reager didn't want to take that up. Road travel was difficult enough on his hardware. Going cross-country was going to lead to a few breakdowns. Worse, the hills were unknown territory. It wasn't going to be fast enough for his liking.

He'd been in ambushes before, and his experience said the best way out was to plow right over the ambushers, getting out of the kill box as quickly as possible. It wasn't pretty, but it was effective. "I don't like the thought of someone playing me. We're going to continue north on this road. When we're five miles out, I want the columns to stop. We will deploy for battle."

"Understood. I'll relay the orders."

"In the meantime, have our forces drive on the shoulders and any flat ground they can find along the road. No point in making it easy for them to set off more IEDs."

West of Patterson, California

One hour later…

Trip crawled up on the grassy knoll and peered off into the distance. The intersection he was hoping to use was surrounded by barricades of what appeared to be crushed cars. The blocks of metal were stacked like Hesco barriers to form a fortification that covered I-5 and prevented the use of the road west that snaked into the hills. Around the entire firebase was an unmanned trench—not deep enough to stop a tank, but enough to significantly slow other vehicles. *If no one is manning it, it's because something's in it.* The barriers had razor wire strung on top of them. Someone had erected a watchtower with machine guns in it. There was little doubt that they had mortars tucked away deeper in the base, and probably more IEDs ringing their defenses.

His own forces were concealed by the hills flanking the interstate. As he studied the enemy position, he spotted the barrel of a tank and at least a dozen Technicals armed with machine guns, and at least one with an old recoilless rifle that he doubted had been fired in twenty years, if not longer. Several flags fluttered in the wind—the California state flag, three different Newmerican flags, and one for the California Volunteer Corps, no doubt one of the defenders. There was no sign of panic or preparation, no rushing of troops to defensive positions, an indication that his force hadn't been spotted yet.

Lowering his binoculars, Reager made his way down the hill and over to his Bradley. Several of his officers were present, huddled near the lowered rear ramp. "So far they haven't spotted us," Trip said. "I intend to change that shortly."

"Your orders, sir?" Captain DeYoung asked.

"Charge," Trip replied in an almost flippant tone.

"You're serious?" Captain Earhart asked.

"I am. We're going to go at them full throttle. There's at least one tank there, and we should assume a few more. Whatever is left of the Veteran Volunteer Corps is there too, and they are all veterans. They're there to clog us up. I refuse to play their game. We come in eight abreast, pouring firepower into that base at full charge. They will fight, and then they'll panic."

"What about their IEDs?"

"We just keep going. Let their fear work to our advantage. That trench they have around the place is probably just something to slow us down so they can tear us apart like sitting ducks. Don't give them what they want; it's that simple. We'll end up with a few damaged vehicles, but I'm done messing around with this harassment bullshit." That comment brought nods from his officers.

"Trigger," he said to Captain DeYoung, "you get the honor of the middle. Captain Earhart, you have the right flank. Captain Russou, you have the left. Go right into their barriers. Our artillery will lay a rolling barrage in front of you. Plow into that firebase."

"What about our infantry support?" It was a legitimate question. Tanks were always fearful of infantry with anti-tank weapons.

"They'll come in right behind your assault wave. If all goes right, they'll be rounding up prisoners by the time they get up there. It is my intent that you will go through them like shit through a goose."

"When do we roll?" Russou asked.

Trip checked his watch. "Five minutes. The artillery barrage will be your kickoff." Looking into the eyes of his officers, he saw a mix of tense excitement and determination. "We didn't get much of a fight for Los Angeles. This one is going to be a lot different. If there are no other questions, get your people positioned and ready to roll."

Five minutes later, from the rear of his Bradley, he gave an order he rarely uttered. "Black Tarantulas—charge!"

Philadelphia, Pennsylvania

Caylee carefully adjusted the flight of the drone she had stolen for her bombing mission. She had learned quickly just how sensitive the controls were for the Beast, as she referred to it. It had a great camera on it, but she ended up replacing the TV camera with something she could monitor and that was lighter.

She had spray-painted over the media logo, replacing it with stenciled NSF-DHS lettering. If the Secret Service spotted her drone, it would force them to hesitate. They might assume it was a different department of the NSF operating the drone.

Her test flights had been done far from prying eyes. They had gone well, far better than she had expected. Through them, she learned she could handle the drone well enough for the mission. She had concluded that it was far easier to cut the power to the drone and let it fall than to try to rig a remote release for the bomb. It also simplified getting the bomb on target. Her flights also taught her that she needed to be at least a hundred feet up, or the sound of the drone might tip off the Secret Service detail that would be protecting the president.

It grated on her nerves that the VP had now been elevated to the presidency. *I'll bet she was behind his assassination in the first place. She always has been power-hungry...willing to do whatever it takes to get ahead.* The president has been gathering control of the machinery of the Newmerican government for years. *She was behind that false flag attack on the Capitol just to gain control of the TRC. That's how low she'll go.*

The stakes for Caylee's mission had gone up. When Jack Desmond had sent her, it was to be a disruptor for the convention, preferably by killing the VP. Now the VP was the president. When Jack had enlisted her, Caylee thought she would be cutting the head off the snake. Now that was more evident than ever.

Newmerica would probably continue, but it would be in chaos for days, if not weeks. One thing she had seen while working in the convention center was that the delegates were rarely on the same page. They bickered with each other constantly. There were so many flavors of progressivism, and each one had to have top representation, which led to a never-ending sea of arguments. The supporters of women's rights struggled with the trans community, who insisted that men who had transitioned should compete in sports with women. It was just one example of the bizarre dichotomy of their political spectrum. *Everyone needs to be recognized, or be a victim, or both. It's like a kindergarten class with no teacher to set the boundaries and rules...a mini Lord of the Flies.*

Some of their factions are prejudiced against other factions, all of whom believe they're being marginalized.

She made several bombs to test the detonators, their weights, etc. Making homemade gunpowder was more tedious than dangerous. For shrapnel packed in around the charge, she used small nails, carpentry tacks, BBs, and bits of broken glass bottles. Caylee tested one of the bombs for its effectiveness out in the country and was impressed with the damage it caused.

As for where the attack should take place, she decided that the best target was the hotel where the president was staying. When they pulled the presidential limo to the curb, the president would have to walk thirty feet to reach it. Caylee would have to drop the bomb before the president made it into the armored limo. Otherwise, it would do damage, but not kill her. *I should be able to take her out if I can get this within fifteen to twenty feet of her.* There were countless other factors in play, though, that made Caylee nervous. An armored Secret Service agent between the president and the exploding bomb could render all of her work moot.

The target hotel was the DoubleTree, three miles away near the airport. Caylee scouted the site carefully, determining that her best vantage point was on the sloped roof of an abandoned hangar. The slope blocked her direct line of sight to the hotel, which would protect her from the Secret Service on the ground spotting her.

She knew from experience that the Secret Service would have drones in the air as well, so she opted for a spot near a roof access hatch. The plastic half-open hatch would provide some cover from above, hopefully enough for her to pull off her mission.

When she went to check out the location for the third time, the security detail was in the area, patrolling, forcing her to abort. It was frustrating, but she had trained for four weeks at the Service's facility and had a working knowledge of their protocols. *They're just making it difficult for anyone to plan something out. By constantly changing and patrolling different areas, seemingly at random, they make an assassin's job even harder.*

When she returned to her flat, she settled back on her couch and watched the TRC news, since news from outside of Newmerica was carefully screened and even AI-edited by the regime's allies in Big Tech. As she saw the replay of the assassination of President Porter, her eyes viewed it with renewed scrutiny. *Where were the teams moving in advance of their charge? How was it that they didn't search that van before bringing the president down that sidewalk? All of those personnel in the area should have been checked and cleared by the Service.* The more she thought about it, the more she realized there were too many mistakes that were made. Even the news report was incomplete. It listed the assassin as Braylon Ironsides and made mention of a possible co-conspirator. *Why not release that person's name? It would generate tips and leads for the authorities.* Keeping the public in the dark about something as important as the assassination of a president practically screamed for conspiracies and conspiracy theories.

Slowly, the focus of her thinking changed. *What if this was a conspiracy—by the vice president?* It made sense to Caylee. America would benefit from the death of Daniel Porter, and it was easy for the new president to lay the blame on Nashville. But who *really* benefited from the assassin's bullet? That answer was easy: her own target, the new president.

It wasn't hard for Caylee to picture her doing something like this to seize power. If anything, it was in her very essence; core to her personality. *My God, of course she did it! While she's calling out all of the conspiracy theories, she's glossing over the most obvious one: that she did it!* In that moment of realization, Caylee wanted to kill her even more.

Her thoughts about the president and the assassination kept her up at night. It was the nature of her business. Most of the time, she could shut off her thinking and get some shut-eye, but on this night, her mind kept going over the shooting. It was there, right in front of everyone, but no one could see it. *No, they saw it. They've been conditioned by the government not to speak up about what they saw.* Eventually, she managed to get to sleep, though it was a restless night. *Tomorrow is the big day.*

There were estimates that the convention would take another two days before their final vote on the new constitution. That limited her window of opportunity. The heavy rains that were coming down in the morning meant that she couldn't risk trying the attack as she had hoped. The storms would be blowing out by midday, meaning that Caylee could possibly try the attack when the president drove back to the hotel that night.

Amanda Treacher wasn't going to report to work. That ruse had served her well. No, now was the time for Caylee to be the only persona she had. She packed her bomb and checked the power levels on the drone, then put fresh batteries in the control system. Then she checked her personal sidearm and made sure she had extra magazines tucked away where she could get to them quickly.

This journey began a year ago. I'm going to end it this evening.

Chapter 17

Sixteenth Amendment: The Government Unification Act

The individual states exist to support the FedGov and its mission. The state authority is subject to federal oversight, rules, governance, and regulation. Furthermore, state legislators cannot pass laws that interfere, override, or supersede the laws of the FedGov.

Philadelphia, Pennsylvania

Deja watched the news from her hospital bed, and her worst fears were confirmed. "The assassin, Braylon Ironsides, was working with an unnamed accomplice." The only person Braylon had been working with was her. *I'm not being made into a hero for killing him. I'm being set up.*

It all made sense. This was a state-sponsored assassination. The new president needed to tie up all the loose ends, and Deja was one of those. *She played me perfectly. I'm the ultimate patsy in this whole affair. They will run with a well-crafted narrative that I'm a disgruntled SE out for revenge. I'm nothing more than her Lee Harvey Oswald or, even worse, her Jack Ruby.*

Her mind ran through the scenarios that the NSF might use to silence her. Certainly, a trial was not an option. There was too much risk of her revealing the role of the new president in the killing. No, they would have to kill her. She tugged on the handcuff that held her to the bed. *They'll never let me have a chance to reveal what I know. That means they'll do it here, in the hospital.*

Grim resolve came over her as she shut off the news report. *Now it was sickeningly clear to her. No one has come in to interview me. They should be all over me, but instead, I'm sitting here alone. I probably wasn't supposed to survive the assassination in the first place.*

Her injury was better, though still quite painful when she moved. They came in every few hours to uncuff her and allow her to go to the bathroom. No one was willing to engage in conversation with her. No doubt the hospital staff thought she had a role in Daniel Porter's death. That mental acknowledgment weighed heavily on Deja.

It was tempting to let them do what they were inevitably going to do. Her own sisters already hated her. If they were told about her involvement in the assassination, they would only bolster the case against her. Her mother was dead. Thankfully, she would not be dragged through this nightmare by the media or the NSF. The seduction of simply letting them kill her was hard to shake, but she managed to do so.

Lying in bed, fuming, she drove the grim thoughts of assisted suicide out of her mind. *I haven't done a thing wrong. I was badly wounded when Raul Lopez escaped. He had help, including a former operative. She had sent two operatives there to prevent it—why am I to blame for his escape?* Deja dug deep within herself and decided that she wanted to live despite the odds. *The world needs to know what a bitch the president is—that she conspired to kill Porter to grab power.* Those thoughts alone gave her strength and purpose.

Why did she pick me? The answer was right in front of her. The new president couldn't say her operatives failed because they reported to her. *If they failed, then she failed.Of course, it was orchestrated, preordained!She needs a fall guy, someone to heap her own failures on. That's me.* As logical as it all was, it didn't help her current situation.

Eyeing the handcuff on her left arm, her only good arm, she was frustrated. Picking locks was always simple in a movie, but in the real world, it was difficult, and with handcuffs, even more so. She didn't have tools to work with, either. She looked around the room, trying to find any camera that might be hidden there. No doubt someone was monitoring her around the clock.

She was still hooked up to monitors and an IV. That also didn't make sense, other than it allowed them to control her even further. *I bet if I disconnect those lines, there'll be someone in here in a matter of seconds.*

The only time she was freed was when she was allowed into the bathroom, and even then, she took the rolling stainless-steel "tree" that held her IV with her. Still, it was her only real opportunity to be disconnected and out of sight. *I doubt even they would set up a camera in the bathroom.*

Even if she did overpower someone after being unlocked to go to the bathroom, attempting to run out into the hallway was not likely to work. If the NSF was there, which was highly likely, she'd be apprehended in a matter of feet. Looking out her window, she saw that she was on the second floor. The windows weren't the kind that opened, which meant breaking them, but she was willing to take that chance.

She didn't see her clothes, which also posed a problem. If she did get out, she'd be easy to identify, wearing a hospital gown. *I need to work this problem one step at a time.* Before she could come up with a solution, a knock sounded on her door, and it opened.

The man was tall, wearing light blue hospital scrubs. He looked more like an athlete than a nurse. What struck her was his dark beard and mustache. *I've seen him before...where?* Then it hit her. She had seen him just prior to the shooting. *He was right there, along the sidewalk!* As he moved beside her bed, she saw that he carried something in his hands.

"How are we doing this morning?" he asked.

"Fine."

He pulled out a syringe. "The doctors have asked me to give you a steroid booster to help with the antibiotics." His intent was clear. He was going to inject it into the IV tube hooked to her arm.

That's no steroid! That's how they're going to kill me. Nice and clean...She died of complications from her injuries. That's what they'll say.

"I need to pee," she said, sitting up.

"Let me just take care of this."

"No. I gotta piss. If you don't let me, you'd better get some clean sheets 'cause I have to go now!"

He set the syringe down on the rolling table, took out keys to undo her handcuffs, and pulled off her heartbeat monitor. "Thank you," she said, grabbing the IV tree and pulling it alongside her as she made her way to the bathroom.

It's now or never, girl! Locking the door, Deja jerked out her IV, wincing at the pain of having to use her right arm to do it. Looking around the bathroom, she saw nothing that could be used as a weapon. Then she realized that she could use the stainless-steel stand. She untwisted the pole from the base. The top of it had several crossbars for hanging up IVs. Tossing her own bag on the floor, she gripped the stand, using her left hand much more than her injured arm.

"Hey, you okay in there?" came the man's voice from the other side of the door.

As if you care... "Yeah, I'll be out in a minute."

She gathered her resolve. *This guy is probably an operative. He's trained to fight. My only hope is surprise.* She moved beside the door, clutching the metal pole tightly. Then she turned off the lights.

He banged on the door after another few minutes. "What's taking so long? Do you need help?"

Deja didn't reply.

She heard him working the lock, attempting to jimmy it. She curled the pole back like a baseball bat and waited in the dark.

The door flew open, and the operative stepped in as she swung. She hit him in the throat with so much force that he staggered back. The pole vibrated and even bent from the hit. His eyes were wide as he reached for his throat, then his face went crimson, almost to a shade of purple. Panic tore at his face as he fell backward to the floor. She stepped through the doorway, pulling back to deliver another blow, but his eyes rolled back, and he went limp.

I must have crushed his fucking windpipe! She set the pole down and bent to remove his scrubs. They were going to be big on her, but that didn't matter. Pulling them off made her gunshot wound throb with pain, but Deja pushed through it. Time was not on her side. Sooner or later, someone would check the camera and see that something was amiss.

His shoes were too big, but she laced the sneakers tightly to hold them on. Then she dragged his body to block the door to slow down anyone coming in.

Her attention went back to the pole. Picking it up, she advanced to the window. Rather than swinging it, she jabbed the pole hard, shattering the glass in the center of the pane. She worked the rod hard to clear the jagged bits along the lower sill out of the way.

She heard someone pounding on the door. The ground looked a long way off, but Deja didn't care. Drawing a deep breath, she climbed up and jumped to the ground, hopefully into freedom.

West of Patterson, California

Darius heard the outbound artillery cutting through the air above him as his Humvee lurched forward. Explosives landed in the middle of the Newmerican firebase, sending debris flying into the air. Mortars landed next, smaller blasts but still devastating. His Humvee's machine gun fired short bursts at indiscriminate targets situated to hold their ground.

The tanks unleashed volleys of high explosives a second later, engulfing the base in explosions and carnage. A tank fired from within the defenders' perimeter, and Darius winced as he saw a Bradley in the line explode, spraying the grass with hot melted metal and chunks of armor. From within the barriers came a salvo of artillery and mortar fire as the Newmericans tried to counterattack. One of the Humvees off to his right lost a tire in an explosion, grinding into the sod, furrowing deep and throwing the crew out as it rolled with an ugly thud.

These were not young college punks who could be intimidated. These were seasoned veterans. More artillery poured into the enemy positions. A series of secondary explosions went off, no doubt small ammo dumps being hit. Flames lapped skyward, and glowing bits of debris rained down throughout the area.

His driver swerved as machine-gun fire, tracers, and bullets sliced through the air. Some hit another Bradley, throwing up sparks as they glanced off the armor. The Bradleys all let loose with their 25mm cannons as if on cue, banging shots as they roared toward the Newmericans. There were so many explosions hitting the firebase that it was hard to see what the impact was on the defenders. Darius could only imagine the terror and panic they were experiencing on top of the concussions and shrapnel.

An explosion went off to his left, blasting an M1 Abrams tank's tread, skidding the vehicle to an abrupt halt. That didn't stop it from unleashing its devastating 120mm smoothbore. As Darius's Humvee passed the tank, it fired. The front wall of crushed metal blocks that formed part of the defensive barrier exploded, throwing the cubes, equipment, and a human leg into the air.

They were rapidly closing in on a trench that surrounded the enemy. It was going to be a bumpy ride, one he hoped was possible. The topside machine gunner reloaded as the Humvee got closer.

Without warning, the trench lit up, turning it from a long hole into a wall of fire. *Those fuckers filled it with oil or something flammable.* For a millisecond, he felt the Humvee slow as the driver tried to figure out if he could drive through it. Then the vehicle lurched, pushing Darius against the back of the passenger seat.

A pair of bullets hit the armored glass windshield, chiseling out divots as Darius looked over at the younger man behind the wheel. "You're going to drive through that?" he asked.

The kid didn't look at him but nodded a response. "Those are my orders." He then raised his voice so the troops in the passenger compartment could hear him. "Hang on. This is going to be bumpy and hot."

It was an understatement.

The vehicle roared over the dirt embankment and dropped hard into the flaming trench. The flames were all around them in that instant, the black smoke obscuring their view. Darius was afraid they would be stuck there, slowly burning to death, but the Humvee came up the other side of the trench, bringing with it burning fuel in its wheel wells as it aimed straight at the enemy.

The machine gun purred, this time not in short bursts but in longer spurts. Darius saw the bullets riddle the tall tower that was dumping a stream of fire down on several other targets. It was as if all the machine guns locked onto the tower at once. Tracers filled the air as the guns chewed away at the wooden structure. A Bradley's cannon joined in, and the tower crumbled at the base, dropping to the ground with a thud. Darius wasn't concerned about survivors. There was no way anyone could have lived with all the bullets that were being fired.

More explosions tore at the defenders' position, blasting huge holes in the process. His driver turned sharply, aiming for a fresh gap in the defensive barrier. "All right, guys. I'm going to get us inside. I'll stop there, and you are going to have to deploy fast."

Darius grabbed his weapon, holding it tight. The Humvee swerved again as more bullets thunked and dinged against its armored hide. The driver punched right into the hole, clipping a block of metal—a crushed automobile. The driver hit the brakes, and the vehicle skidded to a stop right in front of a tent that was a smoldering ruin.

He opened his door, and bullets smacked into it, forcing him to dive to the ground. The smell of burning rubber hit him hard as he lay flat, bullets flying over him. Another explosion near the rear of the target position threw debris into the air.

Darius rolled to his side, bringing his weapon to bear, looking for a target. He saw a flitter of movement, really nothing more than a shadow in the distance. He aimed and fired. So did the machine gunner. The woman reeled as the machine gun tore her nearly in half. She fell, and the grenade she was holding exploded.

Not seeing any other targets, Darius rose and darted for cover behind a crushed car block. Just as he got behind it, a bullet tore into it. He curled up tighter than a person should have been able to, if only for a second. Small arms fire cracked all around him, and he edged around the block, lying flat and looking for the source. Darius was both relieved and disappointed that he never found it.

Grenades went off to his far left, four in rapid succession, as the Bradleys continued their rapid fire. Then, almost eerily, the gunfire dwindled and stopped, except for an occasional pop. Slowly, he rose, still wary that there might be enemies nearby. Then he saw them—six uniformed troops emerging from a hole only twenty feet away. They were filthy, but their hands were in the air. The looks on their faces ran the gamut from shocked to furious.

Darius walked toward them, holding his rifle on the center of the group. The American forces seemed stunned to see them. No one was acting, so he did. "Get over there, pat them down, and make sure they don't have any weapons." Several members of his squad sprang into motion, following his orders.

As he got closer, he recognized two of the defeated troops. They were from his former unit, the Veteran Volunteer Corps. One of them saw his face and had a similar reaction. "You're fighting for *them* now?" the captured soldier asked, the contempt in his voice clear.

Before Darius could respond, someone screamed. He wheeled and saw a person rushing toward them holding two grenades in their hands. It was impossible to tell if it was a man or a woman. One of his troops fired two shots, hitting the person, not realizing the danger that now posed. "Grenade!" Darius said, diving for the ground.

The dead berserker's two grenades went off in one conjoined explosion. Smoke, shock, and a spray of blood filled the air. As Darius stood, he saw that two of the prisoners were dead, including the man who had identified him. The bomber had only caused a few minor wounds in the American troops but had injured all of his own people with the suicide attack. *Was that the intent? Or did they just fail at getting to their real targets?* Like all things with Newmerica, it was an unknown, mixed with confusion and idiocy.

Medics were called for, and Darius tasked one fire team to make sure there were no more holes where attackers might be hiding. He used the moment of calm to brush the dirt from his uniform. Patting his breast pocket, he discovered that the medal he carried there was missing. *Damn!* He started looking on the ground for it, retracing his steps back to where he had hidden behind the scrap metal block. There, in the green grass, was the medal.

A sense of relief came to him as he picked it up, put it in his pocket, and fastened the button. The medal wasn't a good luck charm. It was a reminder of where he had come from. More than that, he carried it to honor the woman who had received it. It was hard for him to put into words why it was so important to him. It simply was.

Looking around at the firebase, he saw other small pockets of survivors who were being rounded up. A medic arrived and started treating the surviving prisoners first since their injuries were the worst. Elsewhere, the other survivors were being checked for weapons and grenades. The smell of burning oil still hung in the air, along with the stink of opened human bowels from the grenade attack. It was a horrible smell, one that even a good shower wouldn't wash away.

"What was this place?" Darius asked one of the prisoners. "What did you call it?"

"Firebase Schiff," the man responded, rubbing the gauze that was wrapped around his arm. "Why?"

Darius locked his gaze with the man. "A fight like this needs a name, so when I'm telling folks where I fought, I can tell them what the battle was called."

"We didn't expect you to rush us the way you did."

"I suppose that's why we did it."

"What happens to us now?"

"Your war is over. They'll send you to a POW camp."

The man nodded once, understanding what he was being told. "You may have beaten us, but your reward is San Francisco."

Before Darius could get clarity on what the prisoner meant, the man was led away. *What's waiting for us in San Francisco?*

Chapter 18

Seventh Amendment: The Retirement Act

The nation has the obligation to ensure that retired individuals are financially sustained. The government will establish a just retirement age. Individuals that reach that age will be provided state sponsored subsistence, medical care, and housing based on race, gender(s), and contributions to the nation.

Erie, Michigan

Major Mercury's force had avoided taking I-75 north into Michigan, opting for State Highway 24, which ran parallel to it. It was a slower rate of travel but gave her force a greater sense of secrecy and avoided the route that the enemy would have easily anticipated.

Her force, dubbed Task Force Pontiac, was only half an hour away from Flat Rock, where the Canadian Redblacks were encamped. She had taken the precaution of sending infiltrators to sneak across the border and head for the Air National Guard bases in Michigan. Each carried armfuls of Stinger anti-aircraft missiles. Their role was simple—to position themselves somewhere at the end of the runways. When the Michigan Air National Guard scrambled fighters, they would shoot them down. Once the enemy lost a few jets, they would be forced to halt takeoffs out of fear of losing more crews and equipment. Her teams would flee, then return if the ANG decided to try more flights. A small number of well-armed patriots could effectively cripple local air superiority. It had always been that way. Creative, determined people could always overcome technology, given the right resources.

The mosquitoes were thick. One person joked that they must be the state bird, and Judy found herself agreeing. There were deer flies too, slow-moving but capable of delivering a nasty bite. She had slapped one on her arm only to watch it fly away. *I never thought I'd look forward to getting back to Ohio, but here I am.*

There had been a lot of concern that the Redblacks would drive south and take Toledo. From what she had seen of Toledo, she thought it might be good to let them have it. But the Jeep plant there was cranking out vehicles the American Army needed, and the steel mills were deemed strategic. That meant sticking with the plan and making a spoiler attack into Michigan.

Despite taking a side road, she was fairly sure the locals they passed had informed the authorities that she was on her way into the state. She was counting on panic to paralyze them for a few precious minutes. There wasn't a lot they could do before she pounced on the Canadian volunteers.

Mercury didn't have a lot of love for Canadians, nor did she have a lot of hate. Their government was one of the first to ban free speech. Their prime minister jailed his political opposition, too. In many respects, there was little difference between Canada and Newmerica, though the Newmericans were far more brutal. To Judy, it was almost as if Canada was a state of the U.S., with a misplaced passion for independence. One of her officers referred to them as Gay North Dakota, and she thought it wasn't too far off as a description.

As her attack force rolled forward, her radio blared. "Alpha, foxtrot, one. We have an enemy force coming from the west. At least two companies of irregulars."

Damn. I knew things were going too well. "Pontiac forces, we have incoming. Get off this highway and deploy to the west and north. I want the rear of our column to curl back to the south in case they try to get around us. Get our mortar teams to the east and have them grab whatever cover they can find."

Her people moved without question or hesitation. Many shifted to the thick pines that lined the roadway, relying on them for concealment. Her mortar teams went to the east, picking cover behind a small knoll. Machine guns were quickly set up with good overlapping fields of fire. To the west, the terrain was irregular. There was a swampy patch, black and ugly, that would stop any assault to the northern end of her forces. Not far off the highway, the ground became a wide open stretch up to farmland, open and flat, recently plowed and seeded for corn that poked out of the ground a few inches in height. She couldn't foresee anyone attempting to cross such ground. It would be slaughter. She got out of her vehicle and looked at the ground again. Maybe her scouts got it wrong…

Then she saw a dozen or so technicals burst through the tree line in the distance. The trucks were filled with people, some armed with machine guns on crudely welded tripods. The vehicles tore into the open field at full throttle, heading toward her force. The vehicles were followed by small clusters of troops on the ground, running straight at her. It was hard to think of them as squads. They weren't moving like trained infantry.

Flags fluttered from a few of the technicals. Pulling out her binoculars, she saw the University of Michigan blue-and-gold flag on two vehicles and another with the Michigan flag. *My God, they're college students.*

Her radio crackled. "Sir, do we open fire?" came Lieutenant Fuller's voice.

She felt her stomach knot. *Stupid fucking college students. They'll be massacred if I give the word.* The students opened fire first, a few sporadic shots, followed by streams of machine-gun fire.

This is murder.

She heard them scream, the sound echoing in the distance. "Wolverines!" She knew the reference from the government-banned movie *Red Dawn*. It was also the mascot of the University of Michigan. From what she could see, the students didn't even wear uniforms. They had rushed off to fight in a war with no sense of tactics, no fear—only their hate of America.

I have no choice, she thought as they loomed closer. "Pontiac, open fire," she transmitted, then repeated the order.

The students rushed into the wall of fire. Two Technicals were hit and immediately stopped. Another tried to swerve but was going too fast, and the dark soil was too soft, rolling the vehicle and throwing out the occupants in the back. Mortar fire rained down on the students near the rear, throwing dark clods of soil into the air along with bits of the attackers.

One remaining Technical stopped and sprayed her line with bullets, only to be turned into metallic Swiss cheese from small arms fire in response. Fire burst from the battery compartment on the EV truck, burning bright yellow and sending a rolling gray smoke cloud upward to mark the death of the vehicle. The flames turned into a forge, a column of smoke and crimson rising skyward.

The students who had been bravely charging across the field suddenly realized the insane folly of their rush. Some broke and ran, while others stopped, falling flat, a few on their knees. Judy watched as their assault withered under a hail of bullets. They had no flags with which to surrender, and even if they did, they didn't possess the rational thought to do so.

"Cease fire," she broadcast. "All units, cease fire."

The noise level dropped to almost nothing. Now she could hear the crackle of the flames from the one dead Technical as the inferno slowly started to dwindle. Another's engine roared, but with two flat tires, it simply turned the cornfield into gray smoke as it spun out, not moving. There were cries of pain, anger, and almost mindless weeping from those in the field who were still alive.

"Major," came the voice of one of her officers, Lieutenant Cobb. "I can organize a force to go after the ones who fled."

Judy shook her head. "Let 'em go. Taking them prisoner is just a burden to us. Besides, they'll tell their friends what it was like to mess with the American Army. Instead, let's get some ambulances for the survivors and get them off to the hospital."

The battle had lasted only a few minutes, but it took an hour to round up the survivors and get them off the field. One student who proclaimed himself the commander of the enemy was brought before her as she prepared to have Task Force Pontiac roll out. He was splattered with mud, wearing Wrangler camouflage cargo pants and a green T-shirt.

"You the one in charge?" he asked with a hint of entitlement in his voice.

"Yes, I am."

"I'm Todd Kramer." He spoke his name as if it would register with Judy. It didn't.

"We're sending you and the non-wounded back to Toledo. Your wounded are on their way to the hospital in Monroe."

Her words meant nothing to him—she could see that on his face. "You have a lot to answer for," he said. "What you did here was a crime against humanity. I know what I'm talking about. I'm a second-year law student."

"I hope you're a better lawyer than you are a fighter," she retorted.

"You didn't fight fair. You led us into a trap. When this war is over, you'll be brought to justice for what you did." His arrogant defiance was stunning given what he had just been through.

"First off, I didn't lure you in. You stupidly charged us. Second, your thoughts about me are based on a false presumption."

"Which is?"

"That we're going to lose." With a jerk of her head, Todd Kramer was led off with the other prisoners. Judy turned and watched him, amazed that he never fully understood what he had done wrong. *They never should have tried to attack us. Whoever encouraged them to lead that assault has their blood on their hands.*

Turning her gaze north up State Highway 24, she knew they had to get moving. *First the Wolverines, next the Canucks...* "All right, Pontiac forces, let's roll!" she broadcast over her radio.

Woodside, California

General Reager had summoned Raul, which made him nervous. The general had given him free rein with the liberation of the camps in California and had committed resources to him. So far, he had never called him in for anything. *The fact that he wants to see me means something has changed.* That alone made Raul nervous.

Trip arrived in Woodside, a community that butted up to a hilly area off to the west just outside of San Francisco. From what Raul had learned of the Army's advance to the city, they had caught the defenders in San Jose off guard and out of position, as Caylee would say. There had not been resistance after San Jose, but for some reason, the advance was slow. Raul suspected that he was about to learn why.

The driver who had brought him pulled up by a Bradley fighting vehicle that was surrounded by officers. Raul got out and saw General Reager. The general had lost weight since the last time they'd talked. He saw Raul and motioned for him to come over. "It's good to see you again, Mr. Lopez."

"Please, I go by Raul."

"Fine by me. Thank you for coming on such short notice."

Raul caught an aroma in the breeze, a mix of garbage, sewage, and other smells he didn't want to try to identify. In a weird way, it reminded him of the Social Quarantine camps, but he didn't see a sign of one. The thick trees flanking the road blocked his vision. *Maybe he's found another camp.* "What can I help with?"

"Just through these trees is a big wildlife area, the Jasper Ridge Biological Preserve. My scouts came across it, and... well, it's not like anything I've ever seen before."

"What do you mean?"

"It's easier to show you," Reager said, and started walking on a trail that led up the hills. Raul followed, as did two security personnel with weapons. As they walked, he saw trash. Not bags of garbage, just loose trash—food containers, wrappers, plastic bags, etc. The stench he smelled when he had arrived grew stronger as they marched.

After fifteen minutes, they came to a small hilltop. There was a larger hill looming in the distance. Looking down, Raul was stunned by what he saw.

It wasn't a camp. There was no organization, no fence surrounding it. Shacks and sheds were thrown together with random construction materials. Everything from road signs to cheap plastic tarps was used. There were a few cars not being used for transportation but for shelter. Smoke from a few small fires drifted up to be caught by the wind.

People were milling about, almost like zombies. A few looked up at where Raul and General Reager stood but seemed to look right through them. Raul turned and saw that the entire region was filled with an endless sea of sheds, tents, and humanity.

"They're the homeless," Reager explained. "Thousands of them, maybe more."

"I thought they were sending them to tiny towns to house them," Raul said.

"Another Newmerican lie. Or maybe a Californian lie. It's hard to tell at this point. Does it really matter?"

"How do they survive?"

"Until a few days ago, they received food shipments from the government. From what I've been told, a lot of it was spoiled —the stuff that the grocery stores were going to toss. I saw one woman with a green loaf of bread. She just peeled the moldy parts off and ate what was left."

Reager shifted on his feet. "A lot of these folks are hooked on drugs. Per your own findings, the state was giving them meth, coke, pot, heroin…whatever they needed. Those shipments stopped four days ago. A lot of these people are hip-deep in withdrawal. It's led to some violence."

"I—I don't know what to say." Raul was more shocked than angry. Liberating the camps had numbed him a little to sights of humanity in shambles, but the scale of this was astounding. *The people who did this need to face justice. It's as bad as many of the camps—worse.* "We have to help them."

"Agreed. It's the reason we are talking now."

Raul was stunned. "I—I—this is beyond me. I've never seen anything like this."

"Yes, you have," the general assured him, putting his hand on Raul's shoulder. "So have I. I wouldn't trust these people's lives to anyone else."

"Me?"

"I got reports of what you've been doing, Raul. You are compassionate. Word is that you could have killed the guards you've captured, but you showed restraint. You took command of hospitals to tend to the prisoners who needed medical care. My officers look up to you. That's why I sent for you. I need you to help with these people."

"The size of this...I just never..."

"I have declared martial law. That allows me to assign the locals to assist you. I'm increasing your team, obviously, to help. Things cannot be left like this. These people need their dignity restored—they need to regain some semblance of a normal life. You'll have the authority to house them in the surrounding homes if need be."

What Reager was telling him was overwhelming, but he was also committing resources to the effort. "What about the Social Quarantine camps?"

"The people who worked with you know what to do. That task will continue. This is a massive humanitarian crisis. I need my best man on this, and that's you."

Raul heard the words and nodded in response. This wasn't what he signed up for, but his country needed him. *This war has cost so many people their lives. This is a place where I can save some of them.* "All right. I'll do it."

"Good," the general replied. "Let's get you back to HQ so you can get started."

"We'll need the media here too. This needs to be filmed—documented," Raul said. "People need to see what they did to their countrymen."

"Agreed. Whatever you want. This is your show."

Raul shook his head. *That people would do this to other people...it's sickening.* It made hating the Newmericans easier. He wanted to give in to that hate, but he wouldn't allow himself to. *I will never be as evil as them.* "I won't let you down, sir."

"I know," Reager said, turning around and starting back down the hill.

Cumberland, Maryland

Special Agent Angela Axton couldn't see anything with the burlap bag over her head. It stunk of old oats, and wearing it made her feel claustrophobic. Since the Whitlock family had taken her prisoner, they had driven her for approximately fifteen minutes on winding and twisting roads. Her hands were zip-tied so tight that her fingers were numb. She had considered complaining but realized that her hands were the least of her problems.

They had forced her into a chair, hard. Her feet were tied to the legs. The chair didn't feel particularly sturdy, but she knew that even if she did manage to tip over and break it, she'd never get away. It was best to conserve her strength.

She could hear footsteps around her, and through tiny gaps in the burlap, she could make out at least three people in the room. They conversed just out of her earshot, which was frustrating. The fact that they hadn't just killed her outright offered some degree of hope. *Maybe they want to negotiate something.* It took some effort, but she managed to maintain her composure.

Someone from behind her pulled the bag off. Angela knew she was in a barn, an older one from the looks of it. The smell of hay hit her, and she knew it would play hell with her sinuses, but that was the least of her problems. Sitting backward on a chair in front of her was Hudson Whitlock. In his hands was a Ruger.

"You know my favorite part of this?" he asked with a slight drawl in his voice. "I didn't have to do much other than put in an obit for a fake funeral."

Fake! Damn. This was a set-up from the start! Her calm was shaken with that bit of news. "How'd you know I'd come?" she finally asked.

"You think you're the only one with cyber people? A buddy of mine noticed how an NSF account kept searching through my past IDs on a regular basis. I knew it had to be you."

"Listen, Hudson—"

He cut her off. "Don't even think about telling me what to do, Angela. That ship sailed years ago. It took some digging, but I figured out it was you who led that raid back in Kentucky to try to get me. It looks to me like you're downright obsessed with me."

He was right, but Angela had no intention of giving him the satisfaction. "You think a lot of yourself, don't you?"

"My mother always says that about me," he replied proudly. "But this isn't about me, Agent Axton. It's about you. You know something? I knew you were a traitor even before the night you captured and killed all my buddies. You were there, working for the FBI, dropping little hints and ideas in our heads, getting us all riled up to try to kill that traitorous bastard Porter."

"Those weren't my ideas. You and your little cell of terrorists were going to commit violence one way or another."

He cocked a grin. "It's funny that you've been able to sell yourself on that lie. I actually think you believe it."

"It's true."

"Really, Miss FBI Agent? Who came up with the idea? None of us ever talked about killing Porter. Who suggested that as a course of action?"

Her jaw clenched. "You would have sooner or later," she said in a deeper tone of voice.

"It must be fun living in your little fantasy world…the one where I'm the bad guy and you're the good cop. I still remember when the FBI didn't create crimes to arrest people, like you did. They just arrested criminals."

"You are distorting the truth."

"Am I?" Hudson asked. "Did I have a criminal record until I met you?"

"You haven't been convicted, but that doesn't mean you didn't do anything. I knew you back then, Hudson. You were one of the most militant members of the PFL. You hated what the Ruling Council did the night of the Liberation."

"The Fall," he corrected her.

"Whatever. You were going to do something. You may want to tell yourself that wasn't the case, but deep down, you were more than prepared for violence. If I helped you arrive at a target, it was only so we could finish the mission and have all the PFL arrested."

"You led us into an ambush. Except I saw it coming. The others didn't listen to me. You had them won over. I told them that our background check on you was too perfect, but they didn't think you'd ever betray them. I knew better. It was too easy, and when something is too easy, generally it's wrong."

Hudson leaned in close enough for her to smell his breath as he spoke. "In the last few years, I thought about everything that went down. Until you came along and corrupted my thinking, all I wanted to do was kill some minor officials, be a fly in their ointment. You persuaded us all to think bigger, to take out the chairman of the Ruling Council. Has it ever occurred to you that you *made* me the domestic terrorist you claimed I was?"

"Don't try to lay that on me, Hudson. I didn't make you. You made me. For the last five years, you've been my obsession. There isn't a day that goes by that I don't think of bringing you in."

He grinned in response. "I could feel you out there, poking around for me. It made me smarter, more cautious."

"Really? What good has it done you? Look at you. You've been living off the grid somewhere. You knew you were a wanted man. You had to be looking over your shoulder constantly."

Hudson nodded. "That's mostly true. It was a damn miracle that I didn't drown in the river the day you and your Feddies tried to bring me in. I got shot in the shoulder, too."

"I knew you survived. We never found your body."

"Yup. But I know for a fact that your friends in the NSF had written me off. You were the only one who was sure I was still out there."

"How did you know that?"

Hudson paused, savoring the moment. "You made the mistake of thinking that every one of your comrades at the NSF was loyal to Newmerica. I had a source there, someone to give me some intel on you. That was how I found out about your obsession and constant attempts to try to find me."

A traitor! Of course. It makes sense. The realization stung. She bit her lower lip, if only for a second.

"What?" Hudson pressed. "No witty response? Yeah, that's right. The NSF is full of people loyal to the real president. Despite all of your witch hunts to find them, a lot remained right under your noses."

"Who was it?" she asked.

He laughed. "As if I would tell you something like that."

She looked down. "I seriously doubt you are going to let me go. Otherwise, why go through all of this?" She twisted in the chair to demonstrate that she was restrained.

"True. But my momma didn't raise a fool. I know enough never to trust you, regardless of how short your life is going to be."

His words dug deep. Hudson was going to kill her. She'd told herself that was the case, but there was always a chance, however slim, that she was wrong. He had played the death card now, and there was no way that she could see her way out of this predicament. Logic and procedures said to keep the suspect talking, to drag things out as long as possible. Perhaps an opportunity to escape would present itself. For the first time in a while, Angela turned away from the NSF/FBI handbook. This was beyond the rules. This was deeply

Blaine L. Pardoe

personal. "If you're planning on killing me, why not just do it right now? Why all the drama?"

Hudson stood up. "You ruined my life. I was forced to live under a half-dozen aliases. I knew you were monitoring all my family and friends. Because of you, I missed Christmases, birthdays, real funerals, graduations—all the little events that make up life. I didn't want to put the people I cared about at risk. You did that to me. You made me a non-person, a fugitive. I doubt I've had more than a dozen good nights' sleep since that evening we spent on the rooftop in DC."

"What you got, you deserved."

"For a while, I used to think that. But one thing kept me going. You. You stabbed me and my friends in the back. Hell, you even tried to kill me twice. You showed up here with the intent of arresting me or killing me."

"I wanted to bring you in. I wanted them to see that I wasn't crazy."

Hudson seemed to understand. "Well, that didn't work out quite the way you planned."

"No, it didn't."

"You hounded me like a good coon dog. I just used your determination against you. Obsessions are like that. They eat you from the inside out. But while you were fixed on me, I got fixed on you. I learned that you didn't have much of a social life. Your career got stalled."

"Because you shot me."

"Well, you killed all of my buddies. The ones who were captured, you made sure they got the death penalty. Yeah, I shot you. It hardly seems like a fair exchange. You're trying to blame me for how your career went—well, that seems like a cop-out. You aren't owning up to how much of that falls on your shoulders."

His words hit her like a spray of birdshot—nothing fatal, but painful nevertheless. *How much of where I ended up was my own fault?* It was easy to blame Whitlock for everything that had or hadn't happened in her life. *Was it me all along?* "Maybe you're right. Maybe not. Does it really matter?"

"It doesn't. My initial thought was to kill you as soon as we got here. My brother-in-law said that talking to you was a mistake. I wanted to see you one more time, face-to-face. I wanted you to understand what you had done to me. To be frank, I wanted to see your eyes when you realized that everything you'd done for the last five years was a waste. It didn't lead you to me. It just led you here."

"Why? Was it important to you?"

"Because, in your last few moments of life, I wanted you to see that from that night in DC on, I owned you. I was everything in your life that mattered. And then, in the end, it was all a pathetic waste of time and effort. All those years of me living rent-free in your head got you nothing—" He pulled out his gun. "But a bullet."

Her last moment of life was the impact, jerking her head back. Then came the eternal darkness of death.

Chapter 19

The Forty-Sixth Amendment: The Privilege of Protection by the State

Anyone in Newmerica is entitled to protection. This includes national defense by the military and protection from those that do not follow the law from the National Security Force. Both of these entities are controlled, managed, and administered by the Central Authority.

Philadelphia, Pennsylvania

The Newmerican president listened intently to the roll call vote for passing the new constitution. Delaware and New Jersey delegates had been hesitant. Their fear stemmed from the renewed American military offenses. They were worried they would end up on the wrong side of the conflict. *That made them cowards. The worst kind, the kind of people who turned their backs on their values.*

She met with them with a two-pronged approach. First, she assured them that America was about to suffer a military setback. Second, she threatened them with retribution that they couldn't fathom. She didn't mask the second point. "Remember, the NSF and SEs are already in your states. If you stab me in the back, we will destroy you and your state." Her threats were not idle, and they understood. As they were called, Delaware and New Jersey joined their brothers and sisters in their votes for the new constitution.

She stood at the podium and applauded the delegates. To her, they were a necessary burden. Now there was no executive branch of the government—only the Central Authority. Congress would be morphed into the People's House. There was no need for the Senate, no juggling of bills between houses. *We streamlined everything going forward.*

The biggest sticking point was the reduction of power to the states. It was the nature of bureaucrats to coddle their power. It was a warm blanket for them. Now that the constitution had been passed, they were reduced to glorified administrators. She had assured them all during the debates that they would still have great sway over their states, but the reality was far simpler in her mind. *They will bow to the Central Authority, or perish.*

If only the Pentagon was as easy to deal with as the delegates. She had ordered them to provide chemical weapons to deal with the American attacks. So far, they were dragging their heels. They gave her a lot of technical responses as to why the weapons hadn't reached her troops, clear examples of mansplaining. She sensed fear on the Joint Chiefs' parts. *They're worried that when we use the weapons, they'll somehow be held accountable. They fear defeat. If we win, their worries are gone. If they don't respond soon, I'll order the chairman replaced. If that doesn't work, I'll send in the NSF and take the weapons by force.*

In the distance, outside the arena, there was a rumble. It sounded like thunder, but she knew differently. It was American artillery. She had gotten word that the enemy was slowly closing in on Philadelphia. *They want to disrupt or prevent us from ratifying the new constitution. Well, they're too late.*

At the podium, she banged the oversized gavel several times. "Attention. I will have your attention." A wave of silence washed over the delegates. "The votes have been cast, and I thank you for your participation in this historic event. I declare this constitution passed." She slammed the gavel down again. Applause erupted, as she had expected.

"Now, will the delegates line up and sign the document?" she said, gesturing to where the massive cover sheet for the constitution had been placed. There were dozens of pens, souvenirs for their signers. No doubt many would compete to see who could have the largest or most flamboyant signature. *Everyone knows of John Hancock, and they will all be hoping for the same recognition this time around.*

She was the final signer, in a special space that was large and blocked out for her. *In a strange way, Daniel's death is what got this done. If he had been alive, this might have dragged on for months. Daniel, wherever you are, you should be thanking me.* Taking a gold pen out of her coat pocket, she completed the deed.

Moving back to the podium, she banged the gavel again. "Thank you for your service," her voice boomed throughout the arena. "We have now officially put the ugly, slave-infested past behind us. The patriarchy that exploited us, used our citizens to hold onto power and line their pockets is now little more than a fading memory," she said as her eyes darted to the teleprompter. "Our people will no longer be crushed under the weight of our past. We are now unburdened by what has been!" She savored the cheers and applause that momentarily drowned out the rumble in the distance.

"I now declare this ceremony concluded." She banged the gavel, turning to the delegates and enjoying every moment of the glory they were heaping on her. Some of them moved forward and shook her hand. Others congratulated her as balloons dropped from the ceiling, every color of the rainbow showering the stage.

After half an hour of sycophants paying homage to her, she was led to the limo by her Secret Service detail. They would stop at the DoubleTree, where she had several other private meetings planned, then they would be departing for the District. The trip to the hotel was slower than usual. There were more cars packed on the road. As she glanced over, she saw that each vehicle was loaded down with personal effects and even pieces of furniture. They were refugees, fleeing the approaching American Army.

Seeing them gave her a moment of anger. *Cowards! Why won't you stay and fight? We just worked hard to ensure that you would have a glorious government, and you run rather than defend what I've given you.* The president saw them as weak. *What they need is the proper motivation. When I get back to the District, I'm going to sign an order: no retreat. I'll order the civilians to stand their ground and defend their nation. Anyone who doesn't will face a tribunal and execution.*

As they pulled up to the DoubleTree, the Secret Service got out and made sure the walkway was clear of bystanders. One of them opened the door to lead her in while another moved alongside her.

She moved toward the doors. Suddenly, she heard gunfire. Whipping her head around, she felt the hands of the agents grab her, lifting her right out of her shoes and turning her around to get her back into the limo.

There was a boom, an ear-shattering explosion that threw her and her agents off their feet and onto the walkway. Her ears had popped. Everything was muffled as people shouted orders all around her. Touching her cheek, her hand came back with blood. *I've been hit!* The moment she saw the blood, she felt the pain. "I'm hit!" she called out, but her voice sounded weak, smothered by the chaos around her.

At her side, she saw the male Secret Service agent. He was face down, and from under him, blood pooled on the concrete. Smoke stung her nostrils, a smell that she was unfamiliar with. A bomb? Or was it the Americans shelling her? Her mind was a jumble of confusing thoughts and fear about how badly she had been hit.

Hands grappled with her, dragging her to the armored limousine. They tossed her in as one of her ears painfully popped back to normal. A female agent lay across her, keeping her pinned to the seat. The door slammed shut, and someone called out, "Drive, drive, drive!" The limo lurched into action, almost spilling the agent on top of her onto the floor. As they whipped out of the DoubleTree, the agent twisted off her. "The hospital, now! Scramble Bravo Team and have them clear the ER. The president has been hit!" she barked.

The president saw that her hands were quaking, the right one still covered with blood. "I'm bleeding," she mumbled, adrenaline rushing through her body. For the first time since the chaos started, she noticed that her breathing was rapid bursts, and her heart was pounding in her head like bongo drums.

"Hold still, ma'am," the agent in the back with her said, her own fear clearly worn on her face. "We're going to get you to the hospital. Just stay with me, okay?"

Somehow, she managed to give the agent a nod of acknowledgment. *I could have been killed! Everything I've worked for would have been lost! Whoever is responsible for this is going to pay.*

Berkley, California

Trip looked over at the line of protesters that crossed I-580. Kids. None looked a day over twenty-one. The college had organized the protest, no doubt designed to hold the task force at bay. From the banners and professionally printed signs they carried, he surmised that they wanted the American Army to leave California. *That shit isn't going to happen.* They were six people deep and blocking all the lanes of the highway. *We're in fighting vehicles and have guns. Do they really think we're going to sit here forever or leave?*

As he stood on the hot freeway, he heard the chant ringing in the air. "Hey, hey, ho, ho, the racist Army's got to go!" Hearing it, he shook his head. Racist was a word that the Newmericans dropped almost as much as Nazi. Long ago, he had reached the point where the words no longer had meaning. They had been misused and abused so often that the definitions no longer mattered. *If these snot-nosed college pukes ever actually met a real Nazi, they'd probably shit themselves.*

Shooting them was an option, but Trip wasn't that kind of general. No doubt, his counterpart in Newmerica would do it without hesitation. These students were a nuisance, like a pebble in a boot. *Newmerica allowed them to gum up traffic whenever their little feelings got bent out of shape. They encouraged this brand of BS. They're about to find that there's a new sheriff in town.*

He walked in front of his Bradley and saw the line some fifty yards ahead. "What do you want to do, sir?" Captain Harnessy asked.

"I will try to reason with them."

"Then what?"

"I haven't gotten that far yet," he said, stepping forward. His two-person security detail moved up alongside him as he boldly walked a few yards in front of the students. The chanting died off, and a young girl stepped forward. She clocked in at three hundred pounds. Her hair was both pink and yellow to the point where she looked like an anime character. The nose ring wasn't attractive; it made her look more like an animal than a woman. "Y'all need to turn your tanks around and leave."

"That's not happening. In just a few minutes, we are going to drive right up this road."

"We ain't movin'!"

"That's a choice on your part. Not a bright one, but a choice. I'd recommend you reconsider."

"You ain't going to drive through us. You have to play by the rules."

The entitlement is strong with this one. "These 'rules' you refer to don't exist anymore. I declared martial law. You are in violation of that. Technically, I can arrest you, detain you, drive over you, or shoot you. While I have plenty of ammo, I'd rather use it on the enemy. For the moment, we aren't enemies. If you don't move, that changes. You become enemies, and as far as I'm concerned, targets."

"You wouldn't dare." It was clear to Trip that she had never been spoken to like this. *Her parents, teachers, and the government never taught her common sense. I guess that's going to fall on me.*

"Do you know what they call me?"

"The Butcher."

"That's right. Do you think I earned that nickname by letting a bunch of kids tell me what to do? Do you even know what that name means?"

"There are a lot of us."

Her comrades were all saying things like, "Yeah!" Their bravado was woefully misplaced.

"Look, I'm done with this debate. You move, or there will be consequences." He turned and headed back to DeYoung's M1 Abrams. When he got there, he turned and saw that the students were still defiantly blocking the highway.

Trigger was standing out of the hatch. "No luck?"

"Fire a machine-gun burst over their heads, a nice long one. Something to make them shit themselves."

DeYoung grinned and barked out the orders. The turret gun purred a few seconds later. Many of the students panicked, diving for the highway. While he didn't see excrement, he noticed some had wet themselves as they fled, the stains showing on their pants. Others ran for cover. The fear the machine gun instilled in them was thick in the air as Trip made his way back to his Bradley. As the firing stopped, more students used the sudden silence as their chance to flee.

"Detail a company to go out and round up the ones who didn't run," he said to Harnessy.

Blaine L. Pardoe

"Yes, sir. You want me to have them hauled to jail?"

Trip looked at the defiant few who remained. "No. Load them on a truck and haul them to Raul Lopez. Tell them they are ordered to perform community service for forty hours. Leave a fire team behind to guard them. If any of them try to sneak off, shoot to kill."

"With pleasure, sir."

The orders went out, and soon the few who remained were being moved to a truck for transport to the homeless encampment. As Trip watched them go by, he saw the chunky girl who had engaged with him. It was impossible for him not to notice the wet spot in her crotch where she had urinated in fear when the gunfire started. She glared at him, then called out, "You can't do this to us. We have rights!"

"Kid," he said calmly, "you don't have jack shit. Your rights ended the moment you decided to block us. You're lucky I didn't drive over you out there. The days of you clogging up traffic every time you get your panties in a wad are over. The adults are back in charge."

It was clear to him that she had more she wanted to say, but she didn't get the chance as she was manhandled into the back of the truck. *Let her see what her perfect progressive state is all about. A few days of scooping human waste or picking up garbage will hopefully teach her a thing or two. If not, at least we will get some work out of her and her buddies.*

Trip's mind shifted as the column of vehicles started out once again, driving over the banners and picket signs. *Next stop, Sacramento.*

Philadelphia, Pennsylvania

Caylee climbed up the internal ladder to the roof access point. It was now or never in terms of taking her shot at the Newmerican president. She had heard over the radio in her car that the new constitution had been ratified. *If she gets back to the District, surrounded by an entire city of loyalists, it will be next to impossible to take her out.*

After she popped open the plastic roof hatch, she pulled out the drone case and locked the armatures into place. Carefully, she attached the bomb, pulling the safety device she had made to arm it, then turned on the remote control. The smaller camera on the drone was working fine, though all it showed was the pea gravel of the rooftop. She remained half on the ladder, with only her upper torso poking up.

In the distance was the DoubleTree. On the flagpole was the latest Newmerican flag, a rainbow fist grappling with a black fist on a field of yellow. An occasional breeze hit the cloth, giving her a sense of wind speed and direction.

Five minutes later, she spotted the flashing lights of the police escort for the president's motorcade. Drawing a deep breath, she turned on the drone. The blades purred as they came to life. Her takeoff was jolting, making her heart pound as she worried she might blow herself up. Her forced calm was what allowed her to take control of the drone, eventually getting it to the desired altitude.

As the limo slid to the front of the DoubleTree, she angled the drone overhead, bringing it over the limo, then the sidewalk. Her eyes checked the flag again and saw it start to flutter as a light gust of wind caught it. Caylee's eyes were fixed on the tiny monitor as she adjusted the flight path to try to take the breeze into account.

Suddenly, a spray of pea gravel from the roof hit her face, followed a moment later by the crack of a rifle shot. *Damn, I've been spotted!* She lowered herself slightly on the ladder as the president came into the camera view of the drone. Another pair of shots came at her. One cut her hair and hit the hatch behind her, shattering the plastic.

She saw her target and killed the power to the drone.

Caylee was off the roof when the sound of the bomb going off hit the building. There was no time to process everything.

The Secret Service would be converging in a matter of seconds. She threw away the now-worthless controller and pulled her sidearm, moving fast for the rear door.

As she opened the door that led to her car, gunfire hit it, punching through the metal and foam, forcing her to dodge to the side. *Shit.*

There was another door she had scoped out, and it became her objective. Caylee broke into a full sprint across the back of the hangar as two more shots burst through the door. Her mind was already processing that she would not be able to get to her car, so she'd have to flee cross-country. *I can make it, I know I can.*

She hit the door at a sprint, and it burst open. She saw a figure ten yards away to her left wearing dark tactical gear. She fired mid-stride, two shots. The first missed, and the second hit the upper part of his chest on his body armor, sending the Secret Service agent toppling backward.

More shots fired at her from the right. One was close enough to feel it cutting through the air next to her. She juked to the right, then the left, making targeting her harder. The gunfire behind her was sporadic as she headed for the perimeter fence. She had cut a hole there on one of her earlier surveillances of the hangar just in case this very scenario played out.

She reached the line of ugly scrub trees and made a dive for the hole, landing mostly on the other side. Something held her left foot. *No!* Twisting, she saw a Secret Service agent pulling her back.

Her trio of shots hit the agent mid-body, sending him reeling back. Scrambling, she got her legs through the fence and turned to run through the brush, hopefully toward freedom.

Something hit her in the rear shoulder. It felt like a bee sting for a moment, then much hotter. *Damn!* Another shot slapped into the ground right next to her. There were at least three agents, all dropping into prone positions, their rifles aimed right at her.

Getting up wasn't easy. The pain in her shoulder fought her at every moment, but she got back up and ran diagonally to make herself a smaller target.

Then something hit her—a full tackle from her left by another agent. The officer was big, and he plowed into her at a sprint. As she hit the ground, the wind was knocked out of her lungs, and she struggled for a moment to get air as he grappled with her gun. As she got a burst of air, she twisted the gun in his grip, firing and taking off his ring finger in the process. Both of them were sprayed with blood, and he groaned as he sat astride her.

Aiming the gun at his head, she squeezed the trigger just as someone kicked her weapon. Caylee lost her grip on the gun as it went flying. With a twisting squirm, she thought she might actually get free from the officer on top of her. Raising one knee, she was about to rearrange his groin with her knee when another kick hit the side of her head.

The blow was strong, knocking her head violently to one side, sloshing her brain. Her vision fluttered for a moment, then she passed out.

Chapter 20

Fifteenth Amendment: The Privilege of Clean Air and Water

The population has a right to air and water that meet the cleanliness standards maintained by the government.

Chester, Pennsylvania

Deja Jordan was wet from both sweat and the grass she had been moving through. The scrubs she wore were stained from when she had ducked under a car as a police helicopter flew overhead. Deja wasn't sure they were looking for her, but she also wasn't taking any chances.

She was constantly checking to ensure that she didn't have pursuers. She had killed an operative and knew they would be relentless in hunting her down. Deja didn't have a destination in mind; all she wanted was as much distance from the hospital as practical.

It had been a miracle that she had gotten as far as she did. She had drifted through several neighborhoods, trying to look as innocent as possible. When she found unlocked cars, she slid in and stole whatever change she could find, as long as no one could see her robbing them. She had around eight dollars' worth of coins—not a lot, but enough to perhaps buy a meal if she ever dared to stop.

When she found a plaza with several restaurants, she went behind them to check the trash for edible food. In one, she found a half-loaf of stale bread that some patron had tossed, and a cold hamburger that had several bites taken out of it. Stuffing the bread in her scrubs, she nibbled around the edges of the burger. She hated mustard but didn't flinch as she ate the cold meat and soggy bun.

Night was falling, which made her somewhat nervous. The neighborhoods she was wandering through were not the best. To some, she might look like easy prey. Every so often, she reached into the pocket of her scrubs and pulled out a piece of bread to eat just to give herself some sense of security.

She had no phone and no map, just a general sense of the direction she was walking. With no place to sleep, Deja trudged through an endless sea of neighborhoods. She saw people and avoided them. The fear of pursuit by operatives bent on killing her made her shy away from contact.

That is, until she saw a man sitting on a bench in the front yard of a clearly abandoned house. A small fire was burning, and he was roasting something on a spit. It was meat. She could smell it, and the moment she recognized it, her mouth watered from the aroma.

Slowing her gait, she started to walk past him, her eyes fixated on the meat. "You're welcome to have some," the bearded man said in a friendly tone. "It isn't much, but it's hot."

Deja hesitated. Instinct told her to move on, to ignore the man. Her stomach overrode that. "Are you sure?"

He nodded and gestured to the bench. Deja slowly sat down as he pulled out a big hunting knife and cut off a piece. He wrapped it in a paper towel and handed it to her. "I seasoned it with fire sauce packets from Taco Bell."

It was warm in her hands, but she still couldn't identify it. "What is it?"

"Squirrel. He got hit by a car. If you get something crunchy, just pick it out. Sometimes their bones shatter."

Squirrel. In her entire life, she had never imagined eating squirrel, but the intoxicating aroma drew her in. She nibbled off a small piece to test it and was shocked at how tender and good it tasted. Her next bite was much larger.

She pulled out the bread she had left and offered it to the man. He broke off a piece and thanked her as he ate. The food felt good in her stomach, despite how it looked. It was the first time since she had fled that she felt any hint of being calm. Deja thanked him at least three times.

"You're new at this," he said as he finished.

"New at what?"

"Living on the streets. I can see it in your eyes. Don't worry, I'm not a serial killer or anything. My name is Bob. My mom called me Robert, but she's the only one who ever did."

"I'm . . . Tonya," she said, defaulting to her fake ID.

"Nice to meet you, Tonya," he said.

She nodded to the house. "Is this your place?"

"Hell no," he replied. "I'm from Newark. I had a real nice house there. Almost had it paid off back in the day."

"What happened?" she said as she savored her last bite.

"Government-mandated diversity. I was a fireman. Great career. After the so-called Liberation, we got a new chief. She demanded that we diversify the department. Some crap about people wanting to be rescued by people they could identify with, or some such bullshit." He paused, a silent acknowledgment that he was white and she was black. It was as if he was waiting for her reaction but got nothing. Deja's days of judging others had passed.

"Then what?" she asked. Deep down, she already knew the answer. What she was asking for was the details.

"In one of the classes, I did a stupid thing. I spoke up. I told the chief that when someone's house is on fire, they just want the fire out—that they don't give a hoot in hell what color or sexual preference the rescuer has."

Deja dipped her head, somewhat in shame. *I was a part of that whole system.* "You got fired."

The man nodded. "That was the start of it. Lost my job, my pension, everything. I went before a tribunal and was sent off for a year to Social Quarantine. When I got back, someone else was living in my house. They had redistributed my wealth."

In the distance, Deja heard the rumble of thunder. Glancing skyward, she saw no sign of a coming storm, though. "I'm sorry to hear that" was all she could bring herself to say. As a Social Enforcer, she had been a tool for implementing such policies. She had always seen it as just cause, but now, sitting on a bench in some rundown Pennsylvania city, it suddenly seemed wrong. And if it was wrong, then everything she had done in her life since the start of the Great Reformation had been wrong as well. *I was set up for the presidential assassination, and now this.*

"I've been on the streets since then, though there is some hope. With the Americans closing in, maybe they will unfuck all of this and set things right."

In a strange way, the man reminded her of Raul Lopez. *He's not a criminal. He's a victim of circumstance.* He looked at her. "So, what's your story?"

Deja wanted to tell him everything but knew she couldn't. In her mind, she crafted a short version of events. "Someone in the FedGov tricked me into doing something pretty bad. They set me up. Their plan was to kill me, but I escaped."

He wiped his mouth with his own paper towel. "I'd ask what you did, but it's pretty clear you don't want to say."

"I wouldn't tell you. Just knowing would put your life in danger."

He chuckled. "Lady, I was a fireman. Being in danger was something I dealt with every day."

Looking at him in his tattered hoodie and dirty jeans, she saw what Newmerica did to good people. Just a few years ago, she would have been one of the people to send someone like him to Social Quarantine. *How many people did I send off?*

Who was I to judge them? The guilt she felt was sitting on the small bench next to her. Deja sniffled, then wiped a tear from her eye.

"You okay?" he asked.

"Yeah. It's been a hell of a week."

"Where are you going?"

Deja hesitated. "I don't know. I was just so focused on getting away; I never thought about the next step. I don't even know where I am."

"This here is Chester, south of Philly."

Nodding, she wiped another tear from her cheek. "I guess I could go home."

The man shook his head. "You say the baddies are after you? Your home is the first place they'll look, along with all the parts in between here and there."

In her weariness, that had never dawned on her. "You're right."

"Of course I am."

"Where would you go?"

He pondered that question for a few seconds. "I'd go to the last place they'd expect me to."

His words made sense, but that was a place she feared. "In my case, that would be like Psalm 23, walking through the valley of the shadow of death."

"You said you were being pursued by the FedGov. One thing I've learned—they aren't very smart. I'll grant you, they are brutal and vicious, but brilliance is a rarity in their ranks. If you do something unexpected, that will throw them off, mark my words. It might be risky, but I'll bet you can pick a place they would never look."

Deja nodded. There was one place that fit that bill. *I'm going to the District. They would never expect me to go right into their seat of power.* "You've been a big help, Bob," she said, standing up. Her knees protested, but she ignored the cracking sound and jabs of pain.

"You take care, Tonya," he said, breaking off a piece of the bread she had shared with him and tucking it in his mouth.

Deja knew where she had to go. Now all she had to do was beat the US Army there.

San Francisco, California

Corporal Darius Thorne walked through the Hayes Valley neighborhood slowly, soaking in the details and noticing the changes. It had been a long time since he had been there, some of which was beyond his control. A big part of him didn't want to go back. He had come to see the coffee shop he had operated with two of his brother veterans one last time.

Darius had been busy in the last week. The biggest event had been the surrender of Twitter's headquarters. Their original headquarters had been bombed at the start of the war. The survivors had relocated to a data center outside Silicon Valley. For years, Twitter, Facebook, and Reddit had been extensions of the Truth Reconciliation Committee. They censored the internet and ratted out anyone who might post something that was contrary to the Newmerican philosophies.

The employees had threatened to blow up their servers, as if holding social media hostage was going to deter General Reager. "Go for it" had been his response as he sent in the troops. Darius had been with the troops when they went in. One young woman threw a cup of hot coffee at him, and he responded by breaking her jaw with the butt of his rifle. Deep down, he knew he should feel guilty about what he had done, but he didn't. *They're acting just like those college students— cocky little shits.*

America sent in a small army of technicians to take over the Big Tech companies as they were cleared of their staff. Darius had heard that they restored free speech, severing the links to the TRC permanently. He wasn't sure what free speech was anymore. Years of censorship and organized online bullying that spilled into the real world—he wasn't sure how he felt about it. A lot of personnel he served with seemed happy about it, so he took it for what it was, a good thing. Some of the former employees were asked to stay on and assist, which they did. Many of the arrogant little pricks defied the military personnel. A few tried sabotage. They got beaten for their actions. It wasn't right, but it had the desired effect. The remaining employees suddenly became enthusiastic about helping.

At Facebook, the executive staff barricaded themselves in their suite of offices and broadcasted live to try to show the Army's oppression. Their spurts of defiance didn't last long. They got what they wanted, handcuffed on a live feed for the whole world to see. It didn't change the results other than delaying it for ten minutes. Facebook's feed to the Newmerican FedGov was severed, and a message was posted for the entire world. The age of censorship was over. The TRC's grip on controlling the web was over. *Now the truth will go out to a lot of people who have hidden from it for years.*

Darius had asked for one day's leave and had been granted it. San Francisco was where he and his partners, veterans all, had built and run All Jacked Up. The coffee shop had been his pride and joy. For him and his buddies, it had been a place where they could support each other and do something positive in their lives. Years in the Middle East had soured, scarred, and traumatized each of them in a different way. The coffee shop was a bastion of hope for them.

Then came the riots, the shooting, and a chain of events that had cost him everything.

As he looked down the street where the shop had been, there were no open businesses. The exteriors of the buildings were covered with spray-painted gang symbols or outright profanities. None of it offended him. He had been in the Army, where profanity was considered a second language. It did hurt him to see that all the little shops that had been there, flourishing, were now boarded up.

Litter was heaped in small piles, probably carried by the winds. As he approached the coffee shop, he found that it too was boarded up. Common sense told him to turn and walk away. It wasn't his property anymore. All he was going to find inside were memories, good and bad. Standing in front of the faded plywood at the door, he wondered who had put it up. *Probably the landlord. Back then, they probably thought businesses would come back. They had no idea what Newmerica would do to the economy.*

Grabbing the top corner of the plywood, he pulled it off easily. The inside was dark as he stepped in. Glass crunched under his feet as his eyes adjusted to the dim lighting coming in from the doorway he had just opened. Darius looked around and saw that everything was covered in a thick film of dust. He remembered the customers sitting at tables, talking, laughing, enjoying life. Now all the furniture was in a heap along one wall. Spiderwebs stretched between upturned chair legs.

The walls had graffiti sprayed on them as well. The word "Racist!" caught his eye, and he found himself shaking his head at the sight of it. As a Black man, he felt doubly insulted. First out of the ignorance of the vandal who put the word up, and second at the misplaced hatred it was intended to deliver. *Stupid-ass kids.* If they hadn't broken in, threatening them, his whole life would be different.

The counter was still intact, though many of the tiles on it had been smashed. Walking around the end of the counter, he saw that someone had been living there, probably years ago. Food wrappers, trash, and dried feces marked the space where he and his buddies had worked, joked, and served the public.

All Jacked Up existed more in his mind than it did all around him. As he looked at what was left of his business, his mind tried to replay the memories he had there. It had been a happy place. Their customers had loved them. He knew a lot of them by name, and they knew him. It had been taken from him, as had his battle buddy partners.

Darius found himself hating Newmerica more than ever. *All the far-leftists ever did was destroy. They lied to people and said they made things better, that their ideas were somehow superior. None of that was true. They erased the things they didn't like...the things that didn't fit their twisted version of reality. To them, people are commodities. Businesses are things from which they can take cash to fund their pet political projects.*

Darius had seen the results of indoctrination in the college students he had confronted. He had witnessed the massive homeless camp. Twice he had been in Social Quarantine death camps and had seen an enemy darker and more vicious than anything he had experienced in Iraq. *We are the liberators, but so many of these people have been brainwashed into screaming that we are still the enemy.*

In the dank space, Darius resolved that when the war was over, he would come back. *It's the best way for me to honor William and John. I will reopen this place. It won't be easy, not at first, but I owe it to them and everyone else who has suffered under these bastards.* As he turned to leave, he saw a green sheet of paper in a frame on the wall. The frame was askew and dusty. Moving in front of it, he saw that it was his business license. Unhooking it from the small nail, he tucked it under his arm. It was proof of what had been there and a reminder of the silent commitment he had just made to come back.

Chapter 21

Fifth Amendment: The Clean Air and Water Act

Those that reside in the country have a right to clean air and water as determined by standards set by the President and approved by The People's House. Those that violate these standards will be considered environmental criminals and are subject to prosecution.

Flat Rock, Michigan

Major Mercury looked through her binoculars at the abandoned Ford Motor Company plant and the tents that had been erected in the parking lot. The tents weren't military but a rainbow of colors, all civilian in origin. Cars and trucks were parked throughout their base. A Canadian flag, crudely stuck in the bed of a truck in the middle of the encampment, fluttered in the breeze. *Canadians. How dare they intervene on the part of the Newmericans?* She could make out figures milling about, seemingly unaware of what was about to happen to them.

The battle against the Wolverines the day before had practically broadcast their presence in the area, but the Canadians didn't seem at all concerned. They hadn't even put up scouts or pickets. The Newmerican news broadcasts said that an American raiding force had ambushed several busloads of unarmed students from the University of Michigan and had killed them all. Judy had gotten used to the distortions and mistruths that Newmerica was known for.

Flat Rock was a dull community, from the looks of it. I-75 snaked through the middle of the city, slicing it in half. The auto factories and the businesses that supported them were the only real commerce there. Many of them were shut down, clearly for some time. Adding to the worn industrial vibe that the town threw off, the skies were purple, blotting out the sun. It didn't look like rain, nor did it look like it would clear.

Mercury tried to avoid unnecessary deaths, with the emphasis being on her own troops. The Canadians needed to be knocked out of the fight before they could put one up. She had her artillery deployed in an abandoned plaza. Her tanks and fighting vehicles were set up to jump onto I-75 and drive straight at the Canadian forces.

Judy had toyed with dropping the artillery around the Canadians' base simply to frighten them, but she worried they might counterattack. That meant dropping the barrage in the camp. It didn't have to be much of a barrage to cause damage and destroy their camp. The survivors, as soon as they could rally, would find themselves facing off against a column of her armor. If they were smart, they'd stand down. *They're Canadians...I have no idea how they'll respond. Hopefully, they aren't enthusiastic to die for the Newmerican cause.*

"All right, Captain Cartwright, bring the rain," she said into her shoulder mic.

Two blocks away, the artillery opened up. Judy, perched on the roof of the three-story building, saw the explosions land in the Canadian camp. A truck was thrown into the air, exploding as it landed. Tents were shredded. It was hard to see the troops, but tents of nylon were no match for artillery shells.

Swinging her gaze, she saw her armored force come into line of sight with the Canadians. Machine guns added their staccato to the booms of explosions. The irregular row of tents on the perimeter was riddled and then collapsed. The artillery stopped as planned as the armor joined in. Rapid booms from the Bradley's main armament and their smaller explosions devastated the easiest targets: the vehicles. Fires erupted from destroyed EVs whose batteries had been ruptured.

Then she saw survivors rushing out, their hands in the air. Several held white sheets, one of which was on fire behind the man running with it. *They folded faster than the French Army.*

"Hold your fire. I'm on my way."

Four minutes later, Judy arrived at the lead tank. The stream of survivors snaked from that tank all the way back to the inferno that now filled the old parking lot. Mercury eyed them with scrutiny. *This was far too easy.* On her way over, she made sure her fire teams on the perimeter stayed sharp.

The Canadians were a mix of young college-aged students, none of whom had probably ever fired a gun. They were intermingled with older men, most of whom had consumed a lot of Canadian pork over the years, from the looks of it. They were hunters, maybe a few veterans in the mix. *Does being a vet in the Canadian Army count for anything?* She doubted it.

"Who's in command?" she demanded of the group.

"We were still working that out," one of the men at the front of the group said. "Them kids wanted us to be an autonomous collective, whatever that is, eh?"

"All right," she said, avoiding the opportunity to laugh. "Surrender your weapons. You'll be coming back with us."

Another man, much younger, jumped into the conversation. "You can't take us prisoner. We're Canadian citizens. You don't have the authority."

"I'm in no mood to argue," Judy replied. "Your citizenship doesn't mean shit to me. When you declared you were here to fight America, that made you the enemy. You tossed aside any protections you thought you had. You are enemy combatants and will be treated according to the laws that are in place."

Another young man spoke up. "Our prime minister doesn't recognize America."

Judy no longer held back her laughter. "Your prime minister can't recognize what a woman is. If he has a problem, he's invited to track me down and make his case. Hell, I look forward to the conversation. In the meantime, you're with us."

The larger man leaned in as the others grumbled about their new fate. "My buddies and I, we brought our own guns. The Michigan National Guard promised us weapons and ammo, but never delivered." As he finished, another car in the camp exploded. The Canadians all flinched, but not Mercury.

"I'm sorry to say that I won't be taking time to catalog who owns what weapon. You came here for a fight, and we obliged. Maybe next time, you'll decide to sit at home and let us work through this ourselves."

"You violated our sovereignty," he said defiantly.

"And what did it get you? You should have stayed in that frozen hell you call home. Instead, you came here and got the shit kicked out of you."

Her words were as effective as a kick to his gut. The dejected man bowed his head and was led off by her infantry forces. Judy looked off in the distance at the smoke rising from the factories in the north. *We're right on the doorstep of Detroit. All I have to do is give the word, and we can cause a lot of havoc and do a lot of damage.* The temptation was great, but she managed to hold it at bay. *We've been lucky so far. Pushing it might undo everything we've accomplished. We made the Wolverine howl and the Redblack bleed. That's enough for anyone.*

"Let's move with purpose. The longer I'm in this state, the less I like it," she ordered, glancing up at the rolling purple skies. "Round up these Canucks and let's get back to the homeland." Her people immediately picked up the pace of their activities.

Suddenly, a tech sergeant rushed up to her. "Major, we just got word. There's a National Guard unit heading this way from the northwest."

"Size?"

"Unknown."

Judy contemplated the news. *Damn it! I came to negate the Canadians, not fight it out with the National Guard.* "Show me on a map," she ordered. The tech sergeant complied. Flat Rock wasn't the kind of place she wanted to fight and die in. "We're going to need to move fast! Get the word out—we have enemy forces heading this way. We'll go south to Monroe. We'll use the town for defense. If they want to fight, we'll make them bleed for it."

The tech sergeant adjusted his headset. "Sir, their lead vehicle…it's got a white flag on it."

Judy paused for a moment. This was a circumstance she hadn't planned on. "Get my Humvee. Let's go see what they have to say."

Willow, Michigan

Judy sat down across from Brigadier General Mike Bennet of the Michigan National Guard. He had the looks of a man who had fought in battle before: the leathery skin, the stocky build, and the ribbons to support his history. Her seat was a collapsible chair that someone had provided for the meeting. Bennet seemed uncomfortable in his chair but never broke his gaze.

"Would you mind repeating that?" she asked, still dumbfounded by what he said.

"As commander of the 177th Military Police Brigade, I would ask your permission to change sides in this conflict and offer my unit, as well as the 63rd Troop Command, our service in the American Army."

It's got to be a trap. "General, if I seem skeptical, it's because I am."

"It's pretty simple, Major. Our governor is a few fries short of a Happy Meal. She's been using us as a glorified police force since the start of this conflict. She had us deploy to Ann Arbor and gave us orders to come at you and invade Ohio. Having met with my staff, we have come to the conclusion that this war is ending soon, and there's a damn good chance that we will end up on the losing side. None of us like that or support her. As such, we are prepared to switch sides to avoid the humiliation and justice that would come if we fought you Americans."

"What about the Wolverines who tried to hit us?"

"We advised against that attack. She insisted that they do it. Damn fool kids, and damn her for encouraging them. I tried to reason with them, but they just weren't thinking straight."

Judy paused, leaning back for a moment against her Humvee. "General, you have to understand. I didn't come here to take ground, just to make sure the Canadians weren't a threat."

He nodded in response. "I wasn't entirely sure of your intentions, but I rolled the dice on what you were coming north for. That's why we held off on arming them. The governor was sure you were going to try to capture her in Lansing. That's why she had us deployed in Ann Arbor—to block you."

In a strange way, it made sense. The Newmericans were hurting, and no one wanted to be on the losing side of the conflict once the shooting stopped. *What is the real harm of accepting? As long as I don't put my people at risk—there is none.* "All right, General, I'll pass the word on to my command."

General Bennet looked genuinely relieved. "Where do you want us to deploy?"

"Stay right where you are. Until we get you baked into the chain of command, hold on to Ann Arbor."

Bennet saluted her, and Judy saluted back. *This is the weirdest war I've ever fought.*

Woodside, California

Raul Lopez watched as the cement-mixing truck dumped its load into the foundation forms. He had raided a uniform company in San Francisco to get gray working clothes for the homeless he was directing. At first, they were like the walking dead. Once he had organized feeding and cleaning stations for them, he gave them something far more important—a purpose.

Easily half of them were drug addicts who had been cut off from their free state drugs. There had been fights and four murders in the camp since he had arrived. Raul had hauled off the drug addicts to hospitals where he had them quarantined until they made it through their withdrawals. Only then were they brought back to the hills over Woodside.

Raul gave the homeless something they lacked—a new reason to get up every day. Their purpose was to build a community, their own community. Raul had asked the Army to round up construction crews and bring them in. One company built cookie-cutter hotels and suggested that such buildings would be perfect for the homeless to live in. Raul told the encampment that those who worked on the building of the structures would be the first to live in them. To his amazement, the majority of the people showed up to help. Raul used one construction company just to train them on how to handle the tools safely. *When they walk out of here, they will have new skills, hopefully something that will lead to work.*

He had sent teams to forage daily at the grocery store warehouses to keep people fed. Field kitchens staffed by the

Blaine L. Pardoe

Army and volunteers from the camp made sure everyone had food in their bellies.

As Raul watched the concrete foundation being poured, he was surprised to see General Reager standing behind him, surveying his work. "That's a lot for one week's time," the general said.

"We will be occupying the building in a week," Raul assured him. "Some of the city officials came here and told me that this was public land and that I didn't have the right permits."

"What did you tell them?"

Raul smiled. "I told them I didn't care. Then I asked them for their addresses so we could move some of the homeless into their houses."

Reager chuckled. "I love it."

"I thought you were in Sacramento, sir."

The general nodded. "I was, but there wasn't much of a fight there. The military forces fled north rather than slugging it out with us. I get the feeling they're heading to Washington State to make their last stand." He paused for a moment to watch a crane in motion overhead.

"When we got there, we found conditions similar to these. I'm beginning to think I got hoodwinked when the governor surrendered the state to us. While they were slaughtering conservatives in Social Quarantine, they did nothing to help their homeless community except drug them up and let them live in their own filth."

"Fixing this problem isn't easy, but I've seen what can change things for these people."

"What's that?"

"Hope and purpose. Some of these people are lost causes. They have mental problems and such and need to be institutionalized, but they are the minority. The majority just want a fair chance and a leg up. I have people teaching them construction skills. They are building their own futures right here. Getting them uniforms makes them feel like they are part of something. Even if it is just manual work, it makes them feel like they're doing something important."

"Pretty profound for someone your age. Damned brilliant. Where did you learn that?"

"The Youth Corps. I was in it at the start of everything. In a strange way, it led me here."

The general chuckled. "I love the irony of turning a Newmerica program into a solution for a problem they couldn't figure out."

Raul's journey had been long and hard, but it had been necessary to get there. "You didn't come all this way just to watch us pour concrete, did you?"

"No, I didn't." General Reager pulled out a small white box and held it between them. "I need you to take on a bigger role. Like I said, we are finding these kinds of camps everywhere. On top of that, the locals are all uppity about some young civilian commandeering their stuff. I needed a solution that doesn't involve having to deal with them, and it turns out it was pretty easy."

"What's that?"

"You."

"Me? I'm the one they are upset with."

"I don't give a flying fuck at a rolling donut if the locals are upset, Raul. I've got bigger challenges up north that need my attention. In the meantime, the country needs a man to do what you are doing here, only all over the state. I called Nashville, and they agreed. Your buddy Ted made sure the president was on board. We all agree—you're the best person for this job."

Opening the box, Raul saw a golden eagle pin holding arrows and some sort of branch.

"With martial law in place, we all thought it better that you be in the Army, with a rank commensurate to your authority. I'm having the Corps of Engineers report to you as well."

Raul felt his face go red. "What rank is that?" he said, looking at the box.

"Colonel. You'll report to me. We need you to help these people, Raul."

The use of his new rank felt strange, but he plowed through it. "What about the relief of the Social Quarantine camps?"

"That's under you as well. You'll be getting a lot more in the way of resources. You're going to have to learn to delegate your responsibilities to others. I need you to be a leader, the kind of leader these people deserve."

Raul took the eagle insignia and held it in his fingers, twisting it around. "I don't know what to say."

"Say yes," Reager replied.

"Yes," he said.

Reager took the pin from his fingertips and put it on his collar. "This will do for now. The uniform is on its way. You'll need a team put together and on the road north pretty soon. The camps up around Sacramento are at least as bad as this one." Once he pinned the insignia on, Reager saluted him.

Raul was stunned by the gesture. For a moment, he didn't know what to do. He did his best to duplicate the salute back to Reager. "I won't let you down, sir."

"I know you won't, Colonel Lopez," the general said, turning and walking away.

As Raul stood there, he wished he could get ahold of Caylee to tell her the news. *She will be surprised... so will Maria!*

Epilogue

The Fiftieth Amendment: The Climate Denial Act

Climate change is irrefutable both scientifically and sociologically. Anyone who denies or contradicts climate change will be immediately referred to a People's Tribunal and Social Quarantine.

Monroe, Michigan

Major Mercury adjusted her headset as General Ricketts' voice boomed in her right ear. "Major, I'm glad you accepted their surrender, but this is a damned bizarre set of circumstances."

"Yes, sir," she replied.

"You were supposed to cripple the Redblacks."

"Which we did."

"Yes. Now you've got two brigades holding a major city in Michigan. Ann Arbor, of all places. What a liberal shithole."

"It's bound to make the Ohio State fans happy," she said, and instantly regretted it.

"Not funny, Major. I've never been a Buckeye fan."

"Sorry, sir."

"We didn't go there to take and hold ground. This was supposed to be a damn raid!" The channel went silent for a moment as the general regained his composure. "I'm going to have to relay this to General Reager."

"Sir," Judy said, gaining her composure. "Don't just tell him I took Ann Arbor. Ask him if he wants me to give it back."

The District

Caylee Leatrom's hands were handcuffed behind her back. Her legs were shackled and tied to the legs of the steel chair. The prison interrogation room had an obnoxious LED light that flickered every few moments, casting shadows for an instant on the dull gray walls. They had brought her in wearing a hood, but she saw a sign when they had taken it off that told her she was in the District Jail.

The old jail had a stink to it. Some of it was ancient body odor, an unhealthy dose of mold and mildew, a hint of grease, and a touch of filth. It had been a dump in the days before the Fall and had gone downhill since. With the old District of Columbia being intertwined with the FedGov, it was the most likely place she would be brought if captured.

She knew there were three armed operatives in the next room. The fact that there were three of them was a compliment. *The odds are about equal.* They had been her escorts since her capture in Philadelphia.

Caylee remembered the drone dropping and the bomb going off. Her captors all seemed pissed off at her, so she knew she had killed someone, hopefully the president. For a full hour or so, she sat in the chair. At one point, she had called out to go to the bathroom, but no one had responded. Finally, she just wet the rag of a uniform they had put on her. The smell of her own urine was actually more desirable than the stink of the jail.

The door opened in front of her, and she lifted her head. Four armed Secret Service agents in suits entered, their weapons at the ready. *Here we go. The joys of interrogation.* Then, in the doorway, she saw something that made her heart sink.

The Newmerican president.

The woman had one cheek bandaged, no doubt an injury from her attack, but she was very much alive. *Damn!* Caylee wasn't used to failure, not on this scale.

"Caylee Leatrom," the president stated almost gleefully, as if she were having to hold back her joy.

"Imagine my surprise, Madam President."

"I can't tell you how much I've looked forward to seeing you again, especially like this."

"Let me guess. You're pissed about me killing your mother and brother."

The president curled her fist and planted a blow on Caylee's face. It was a decent punch, not bad for a soft politician, but still far from crippling. Caylee returned her gaze to the Newmerican president. "Not bad. I don't suppose I could convince you to undo these cuffs so I could teach you the right way to do it?"

"You know, Caylee, if I were you, I would hold off on the witty comments. I'm the last person you want to piss off."

"I beg to differ. You are my favorite person to upset. God knows I've done it a few times."

The president threw another punch, this one higher on her cheek. It stung but was still weak by her standards. *I've been hit by better people.* "So, you came down here to have me killed?"

"No," the president replied. "I wanted you to see that your attempt to kill me failed."

"I don't know. It looks like I left you a nice scar on your cheek."

The president wasn't amused—she was angry. It was written all over her face. Her brow wrinkled, and her jaw moved forward as she clenched her facial muscles. "You killed two Secret Service agents and wounded two more. And, of course, me. It was a bold move, I'll give you that, but it was a failure. I went on the air before coming here to tell the world that the Pretender's plot to kill me was foiled and that you, the infamous Caylee Leatrom, are in custody."

"I never thought of myself as infamous."

"You may think this is all fun and games, Caylee, but I'm here to tell you it's not. You will face a People's Tribunal for what you've done. You'll be found guilty, then slowly put to death for the entire world to see."

She didn't respond to what the president said. Instead, she stared back. The president continued, "What? No cocky response? Good. I came here to let you know that I have beaten you. You have failed, and in a short time, you'll be dead. I won."

Using her toes and leaning hard, Caylee suddenly jerked, moving the chair two inches on the floor. The metal legs on the concrete squealed as she did it. The president jumped back, and the Secret Service agents leveled their guns at Caylee.

That was all she had intended to do. She wasn't looking to escape at that moment, only to send a ripple of fear into the soul of the president. Looking up at her, Caylee smiled broadly. "Afraid? You should be," she said.

The president managed to regain her composure far faster than Caylee thought possible. She returned the big smile. "You can struggle and strain all you want. You're in my country, my city, totally under my control. I can have you killed simply by giving the word. The only reason you're still alive is that I want to rub the nose of that bastard in Nashville in the mess he's started."

Caylee sat straight up again. "The war is almost over," she said. "How long do you think you can hold off when the District gets surrounded?"

A glint of arrogance twinkled in the president's eyes. "You may think we're on the ropes, but that would be a mistake."

Before Caylee could respond, the president spun in place and walked out of the room.

Appendix

Newmerica's Constitution, The Bill of Privileges (The First Fifty Amendments)

First Amendment: The Right to Safe Speech

Individuals are permitted to express them themselves safely, with respect and consideration of others. People have the right to be protected from words or phrases that are hurtful. A list of banned assault speech words and phrases will be maintained by The People's House.

Second Amendment: The Right to Have Free Government-Sanctioned Education

It is the responsibility of the state to set learning standards and provide approved education to the population.

Third Amendment: The Right to Control Your Own Body

People residing in the country have control over all aspects of their person with the exception of mandated vaccines or treatments. Birthing people control the life of their bodies and anything coming from their bodies up to one hour after birth.

Fourth Amendment: The Empowerment of the Electorate

Anyone in the nation may cast a vote from the age of sixteen on. Individuals who reside in multiple locations may vote in each jurisdiction where they reside. The right to fair and safe elections is recognized at approved government voting centers and websites. The FedGov will maintain the approved voter roll for the nation. Those individuals who do not vote will have their votes allotted as seen fit by the National Board of Elections.

Fifth Amendment: The Clean Air and Water Act

Those who reside in the country have a right to clean air and water as determined by standards set by the president and approved by The People's House. Those who violate these standards will be considered environmental criminals and are subject to prosecution.

Sixth Amendment: The Right of Justice—Legal, Social, and Environmental

Individuals in the nation have a right to equitable justice weighted to their protected classification. This applies to legal, social, and environmental justice. Only suspected guilty parties will be charged with crimes and will be provided ample opportunity to prove their innocence. Trials will be fair and free of bias, with balanced juries of varying social and economic status, sexual preference, and race as defined by the government.

Seventh Amendment: The Retirement Act

The nation has the obligation to ensure that retired individuals are financially sustained. The government will establish a fair retirement age. Individuals who reach that age will be provided state-sponsored sustenance, medical care, and housing based on race, gender(s), and contributions to the nation.

Eighth Amendment: The Right of Meaningful Employment

Individuals have a right to work in a job equal to their skills, education, and the needs of the nation. They will be provided wages and benefits according to standards outlined by The People's House. Those who are unable to find meaningful employment will be provided an appropriate job within the FedGov.

Ninth Amendment: The Privilege to Free Medical Care and Treatment

Anyone living in the nation has a right to free medical care, treatment, and drugs. The government will establish appropriate tiers for medical care based on criteria they will publish annually. No one will be deprived of the treatment they deserve.

Tenth Amendment: The Right of Equitable Government.

The powers and authorities granted in this Bill of Privileges shall be applied to guidelines established by The People's House. These privileges will be applied according to an aggregate social credit ranking, weighted appropriately.

Eleventh Amendment: The Privilege of Internet Access

It is the responsibility of the government to provide free access to an internet that is unfettered from lies, misinformation, propaganda, and deliberate disinformation.

Twelfth Amendment: The Privilege of Public Safety

Citizens have the right to feel safe in public. Only sanctioned government agents may possess guns or ammunition in order to preserve public safety. The right to feel safe in public shall not be denied to the people.

Thirteenth Amendment: The Privilege of Safe Religious Expression

Citizens have the right to take part in religious expression as long as the beliefs of that church are not contradictory to the laws and accepted norms of the nation. Those religious entities must support and reinforce the values defined by the government and will be certified by the FedGov. The people will enjoy freedom of safe, non-offensive religious expression.

Fourteenth Amendment: The Right to Ethical and Balanced Information

News outlets and those who post on the internet must have their stories approved by the Truth Reconciliation Committee to ensure they are free from disinformation.

Fifteenth Amendment: The Privilege of Clean Air and Water

The population has a right to air and water that meet the cleanliness standards maintained by the government.

Sixteenth Amendment: The Government Unification Act

The individual states exist to support the FedGov and its mission. The state authority is subject to federal oversight, rules, governance, and regulation. Furthermore, state legislators cannot pass laws that interfere, override, or supersede the laws of the FedGov.

Seventeenth Amendment: The Right to Clean Energy

The population has a right to energy that is clean and produced by the government for consumption. Energy will be allocated according to the needs of the state and guidelines that the FedGov will publish.

Eighteenth Amendment: The Right to Live Free of Negative Influences

The government has the obligation to protect the population from negative influences—those who speak out against the nation. Anyone who does not support the actions of the FedGov is to be considered a domestic terrorist and will be dealt with accordingly.

Nineteenth Amendment: The Privilege of Fair Housing

Every person in the nation has the right to housing for themselves and their families free of charge. Home ownership is transferred to the FedGov, who will provide guidelines based on equity standards to determine who will live where. Individuals dehomed during this process will be reassigned housing appropriate to the federal standards and will relocate, at their own expense, to their new dwelling.

The Twentieth Amendment: The Privilege of a Stable Supply Chain and Commerce

The government has the power and authority to identify critical supply chains and manage them, as needed, to ensure the Newmerican people have the goods they require. Business stability is a privilege that all citizens should expect and will be ensured by the FedGov.

The Twenty-First Amendment: The Privilege of Protest

Members of the population are free to protest, boycott, or express their opinion to any non-government entity.

The Twenty-Second Amendment: The Privilege of Travel

The population of Newmerica is free to travel. Traveling over three hundred miles requires a travel permit and prior authorization. Travelers are required to carry their FedGov identification ID at all times in order to ensure security. Traveling over three hundred miles must be on approved green modes of travel.

The Twenty-Third Amendment: The Privilege of Work

Everyone in Newmerica has a role to play in the success of our great nation. The state has the obligation to make sure that everyone contributes to the country for the betterment of all. The government will establish a consistent job hierarchy and make assignments for all workers, including voluntary work. In return, the state will grant an appropriate number of days off, a share of the profits from employers, and transparency in business operations.

The Twenty-Fourth Amendment: The Privilege of Nutritional Health and Meals

People in the nation are entitled to food that meets the standards of the government. Furthermore, children under the age of eighteen are entitled to a free breakfast and lunch. A strong body leads to a productive member of our society.

The Twenty-Fifth Amendment: The Online Safety Clause

The internet is to be a free space, accessible at no charge by everyone in the nation. It is to be free of misinformation and offensive images or words. The government will ensure that the net is safe for everyone and is cleansed of anything that might lead to incorrect thinking.

The Twenty-Sixth Amendment: The Crimes of the Past or Reparations Act

Newmerica was forged out of the ashes of a corrupt, repressive, bigoted, racist, and misogynistic past. The taint of that past requires a new equitable balance in society, and it is the role of the government to provide that balance. Further, where past injustices have been established, reparations are to be made to those impacted.

The Twenty-Seventh Amendment: The Limitations of Powers Act

No official in the FedGov can serve more than twenty-five years in elected or appointed positions, with the exception being the president and vice president. This ensures that long-term programs will reach successful conclusions. Further, any official deemed no longer productive in their role can be removed at the discretion of the president.

The Twenty-Eighth Amendment: The Freedom from Harmful Influences Act

Individuals residing in the nation have a right to be free from the influences of those who might harm them physically or emotionally. This pertains to online experiences as well as those that are not online. The government will maintain a list of those individuals who are members of groups or organizations deemed to be a threat, as well as online identities of known domestic terrorists.

The Twenty-Ninth Amendment: The Privilege of Citizenship Act

The requirements of citizenship in Newmerica are that you were born of someone who was a previous citizen, or if you have been granted a waiver by an approved Border Enlightenment judge or agent. Citizenship entitles individuals and their families to the full breadth of benefits outlined in this constitution.

The Thirtieth Amendment: Newmerican Alliances Act

The relationship between Mexico, Canada, and Newmerica is hereby codified as permanent. The Newmerican nation will levy no taxes, tariffs, quotas, or other trade restrictions on these eternal partners and friends.

The Thirty-First Amendment: The Carbon Footprint Control Act

In an effort to reduce individual carbon footprints, the president of Newmerica has the authority to govern the energy use, output, and form of all appliances, heating and cooling systems, and devices that utilize electricity. Furthermore, the president can set production by gas and oil companies as well as set rations for consumption by consumers.

The Thirty-Second Amendment: The Privilege of Farmland Protection

The People's House will set allocations by state for the amount of farmland that will be utilized for production and determine what crops, if any, are to be grown.

The Thirty-Third Amendment: The Privilege of Legal Representation

Individuals residing in the nation have the right to free representation should they be charged with a legal or environmental offense. Social justice does not require representation, and none shall be provided.

The Thirty-Fourth Amendment: The Privilege of Habitable Equity

Residents in Newmerica have a right to live in equitably balanced neighborhoods. The states will establish the appropriate ratios of occupation by city and neighborhood and will allocate housing according to equitable guidelines determined by The People's House. Any costs of resettlement are the responsibility of those individuals who are appropriately redistributed.

The Thirty-Fifth Amendment: The Gender Fluidity Act

The right of an individual to identify themselves by whatever gender they desire is a right within the nation. There can be no discrimination based on genders. The FedGov will maintain a list of the known and approved genders. Individuals creating new genders will have an annual period in the month of November to submit their new identities for consideration.

The Thirty-Sixth Amendment: The Commerce Protection Act

The FedGov has the right to monitor, manage, and if necessary, take control of any business deemed critical to the proper functioning of the nation. This includes federalizing employees, seizing property and assets, and renegotiating contracts.

The Thirty-Seventh Amendment: The Rights of Unionization

All working-age individuals residing in the nation shall have the right and obligation to be part of a union to represent their interests. Those who do not have an existing union that addresses their work will be part of the National Union, hereby established by this amendment.

The Thirty-Eighth Amendment: The Roles of State Government

States have those rights granted to them by the FedGov. No rights or authorities are presumed at the state level. The state governments exist to provide administrative and legal support at the local level under the unified direction of the central government.

The Thirty-Ninth Amendment: The Marriage and Children Act

Individuals have a right to engage in marriage with who or whatever they deem appropriate as long as the parties involved consent to the union. Anyone can be deemed a birthing individual regardless of gender, sex, or religious disposition.

The Fortieth Amendment: The National Emergencies Act

The president can declare any kind or form of emergency they deem appropriate. The declaration of an emergency grants the FedGov the right to suspend all other amendments of this constitution in order to fulfill its obligations to restore the safety of its people. Emergency situations exist for indefinite periods of time.

The Forty-First Amendment: The Privilege of Supporting Law Enforcement

Individuals charged with a crime must answer questions posed by authorized law enforcement officers. Innocent people have nothing to hide, and no one is to be sheltered by the silence of the guilty. Failure to respond to law enforcement's inquiries is a felony.

The Forty-Second Amendment: The Privilege of Pronouns

Individuals may mandate that others address them by their desired pronoun at that point in time. Misusing, mistaking, or not using the appropriate pronoun is considered a civil rights criminal violation (felony).

The Forty-Third Amendment: The Environmental Production Standards Act

All business entities must meet their FedGov-determined standards for carbon emissions. Those companies or organizations that fail to meet these standards will be transferred to the control of the government until such a time that they do.

The Forty-Fourth Amendment: The Separation of Powers Amendment

There are two branches of government in the nation—the Central Authority and the People's House. Members of the People's House are determined by the population of the states they represent and are elected to twelve-year terms. They possess the authority to appropriate funds and establish a budget.

The responsibility for executing plans and administering the nation falls to the president of the Central Authority. The former judicial branch now resides in the Central Authority. The president is elected by popular vote for ten-year terms.

The Forty-Fifth Amendment: The Privilege of Service

Every voting-age individual residing in Newmerica is expected to donate four weeks of public service per year. The approved services will be maintained by the Central Authority. While this is mandatory volunteer work, everyone taking part will be provided a stipend to cover expenses, as determined by the People's House.

The Forty-Sixth Amendment: The Privilege of Protection by the State

Anyone in Newmerica is entitled to protection. This includes national defense by the military and protection provided by the National Security Force. Both of these entities are controlled, managed, and administered by the Central Authority.

The Forty-Seventh Amendment: The Right to Representation

Individuals in the nation are represented by three entities. The first is their elected representative in the People's House. The second is their union affiliation. The third is the lobby. Each state will establish a People's Lobby that is empowered to represent the people of the state, contribute to political campaigns to the benefit of their constituents, and speak on their behalf.

The Forty-Eighth Amendment: Debt Erasure Act

All prior and previous debts and economic commitments made by the former government are hereby waived. This includes all student loans, federal housing loans, the prior national debt, etc. The right to start with a clean economic slate is the right of every Newmerican.

The Forty-Ninth Amendment: The Border Alignment Act

Newmerica is best when it is diverse. As such, the nation will not maintain any barriers or personnel aimed at prohibiting immigration. No law shall restrict migration into and out of the nation. Anyone crossing the border is entitled to the rights of citizenship.

The Fiftieth Amendment: The Climate Denial Act

Climate change is irrefutable both scientifically and sociologically. Anyone who denies or contradicts climate change will be immediately referred to a People's Tribunal and Social Quarantine.

The Blue Dawn Series concludes with the next book,

The Despot's Heel

www.ingramcontent.com/pod-product-compliance
Lightning Source LLC
Chambersburg PA
CBHW051059030726
47504CB00006B/1703